Exodus:

Empires at War:

Book 7

Counter Strike

by

Doug Dandridge

"Missile impact in three minutes," called out the voice of the Tactical Officer of the *Manila*. Klaxons were going off all over the ship, including the control room where the Emperor stood.

The tactical plot showed the incoming missiles, spread out in formations that would distribute their attack over several minutes. Not the best of formations for an attack, but they had the advantage of having closed before detection, making counter missile engagement short and indecisive. The plot also showed all of *Manila's* escorts moving at best emergency speed to get between the missiles and the heavy cruiser. A moment later all of the escort ships for the carriers started to move away from their charges, frantically trying to join the other light cruisers and destroyers in the screen. And leaving their hyper VII fleet carriers unprotected, except for their own defensive fire.

"We need to get you out of here, your Majesty," said Senior Agent Catherine Mays, the head of his protection detail, putting an armored hand on Sean's shoulder. "Please. We have to move."

Sean looked at her for a moment, wanting to protest, to demand that he be allowed to stay at his post. *But my post is nothing in this battle. Everything has run fine without me.* Sean nodded and let her lead him away, the other men and women of the detail forming up around them in the corridor. There were some Marines in the corridor as well, looking all directions to ward off any threat to their Emperor. The corridor was otherwise empty, everyone else on the ship at their battle stations.

"We need to hurry, your Majesty," said the woman, keeping him moving until they got to the sealed hatch near his quarters. At least it had been sealed, up until this moment. Now it was wide open, as was the hatch inside the three meters of open space. And inside of that was his special ejection capsule, with three acceleration couches waiting.

"In you go, Sir," said the woman. "And hurry."

"Missile impact in two minutes," called out the voice over the intercom.

Sean patted the woman on the arm. "Thank you, Catherine. And get your people to their own pods."

Sean walked into the capsule and fell into one of the couches, letting it strap his suit in. Two of the Marines, a Sergeant and a Corporal, followed him in and fell into their couches, slapping their particle beam rifles into the racks provided. The hatch sealed closed, leaving Sean and the two Marines alone.

Kind of silly sending a pair of Marines to guard me, he thought, linking into the ship through the pod's interface. *If we get picked up by an enemy, there isn't a whole lot they can do, except die beside me.* He slapped the pistol holstered by his side, imagining using it if he was picked up by the Cacas, making them kill him so he didn't become some kind of hostage.

The missiles were on the way in, on final approach. Every escort was jamming for all it was worth, doing all they could to mask the heavy cruiser. The *Manila* herself was oriented to put him into space on a path that would hopefully avoid all the debris if multiple ships were shattered.

Twenty light cruisers and fifty destroyers, most of them specialized anti-missile ships, were firing for all they were worth at the incoming missiles. Forty of those ships were interposed between the enemy weapons and the flagship, while the other thirty were further to spinward. They were still targeted by the enemy missiles, but most of the counter fire was directed toward the missiles that could end up targeting the flag. Only the weapons they couldn't bring to bear for the protection of *Manila* were firing in their own defense. Even the carriers were firing everything they had at the missiles coming at the flag squadron, ignoring their own defense.

Sean took a moment to look around the pod, which was much more advanced than the standard model, with three meters of armor and its own electromag field. When he had been told about it, he had insisted that in the future all pods be improved, if not to this standard, then at least enough to significantly improve the chances of his spacers. Then his attention was again taken elsewhere.

Dedication

This novel is dedicated to Larry Southard, a true fan and friend who had helped me immeasurably. You got your wish, Larry. A death of cosmic proportions.

Contact me at BrotherofCats@gmail.com
Follow my Blog at http://dougdandridge.com
Follow me at @BrotherofCats

For more information on the Exodus Universe, visit http://dougdandridge.net for maps, sketches and other details of this work.

Acknowledgements: I would like to thank all of my fans, especially those who sent emails or commented on blogs about how much they enjoyed the first four books of this series. Your kind words gave me the impetus to continue through the not so kind words left in some reviews. And special thanks to Ruth de Jauregui, who helped with the covers on all of the Exodus series. Her changes improved all of the covers.

Books by Doug Dandridge

Doug Dandridge's Author Page at Amazon

Science Fiction

The Exodus Series

Exodus: Empires at War: Book 1

Exodus: Empires at War: Book 2

Exodus: Empires at War: Book 3: The Rising Storm.

Exodus: Empires at War: Book 4: the Long Fall.

Exodus: Empires at War: Book 5: Ranger

Exodus: Empires at War: Book 6: The Day of Battle

The Deep Dark Well Series

The Deep Dark Well

To Well and Back

Deeper and Darker

Others

The Shadows of the Multiverse

Diamonds in the Sand

The Scorpion

Afterlife

We Are Death, Come for You

Fantasy

The Refuge Series

Refuge: The Arrival: Book 1

Refuge: The Arrival: Book 2

Refuge: Book 3: The Legions

Doppelganger: A Novel of Refuge

Others

The Hunger

Daemon

Aura

Sign up for my Newsletter at Mailchimp to receive news about upcoming projects, releases and promotions.

Cast of Characters

The Capital

Emperor Sean Ogden Lee Romanov: Born Year 971 (29 years old). Fifth child and the third son of the late Emperor Augustine Romanov.

Doctor Jennifer Conway: Physician and Fiance' of Emperor Sean.

Grand High Admiral Sondra McCullom: Chief of Naval Operations.

Field Marshal Betty Parker: Commandant of the Imperial Marine Corps

Grand Marshal Mishori Yamakuri: Army Chief of Staff.

Prime Minister Countess Haruko Kawasaki.

Lord Garis: Minister of State.

Lord T'lisha: Phlistaran Minister of Security.

Lord Halbrook: Minister of the Exchequer.

Laura Goolsby: Speaker of Commons.

Mohamed Ishner: Chief of Scholars.

Ekaterina Sergiov: Chief of Imperial Intelligence Agency.

Samantha Ogden Lee. Sean's cousin and Regent.

Countess Esmeralda Zhee: Member of the Lords' Opposition Party.

Count Cornwell: Member of Lord's Opposition Party.

H'rressitor: Gryphon Minister of Commerce and Industry.

Baron Emile von Hausser Schmidt: Leader of the House of Lords.

Archduke Percival Marconi: Leader of the Lords' Opposition Party.

Capital Police Lieutenant Ishuhi Rykio: former Naval Commando.

The Fleet

Commodore Duchess Mei Lei: Hyper VII battle cruiser

squadron commander.

Captain the Duke Maurice von Rittersdorf: Squadron Commander hyper VII destroyer squadron.

Ensign Lasardo: Rittersdorf's tactical officer.

Commodore Bryce Suttler: Commander HIMS *Seastag* (Stealth Attack 421).

Lieutenant SG Walter Ngovic. Tactical, HIMS *Seastag.*

Grand Fleet Admiral Duke Taelis Mgonda: Admiral in command of Hyper VII battle force.

Grand Fleet Admiral Gabriel Len Lenkowski: Commander: Battle Fleet.

Vice Admiral Mara Montgomery. Commander, Hyper VII Scout Force, Battle Fleet.

Admiral Chuntao Chan: Director of Fleet R & D.

Commodore Natasha Romanov. Commander of NTR Light Cruiser *Orleans.*

Captain Stella English: Commander light cruiser HIMS *Lancanshire.*

Chief Petty Officer First Jana Gorbachev: Former Prisoner of the Ca'cadasans.

Captain Mary Innocent: Sean's Intelligence Officer.

Captain Javier Montoya: Captain, *Augustine I.*

John Jacobs: Sean's Steward.

Fleet Admiral Benjamin O'Hara: Naval Commander of the *Donut.*

Commodore Natasha Sung: Commanding Officer, exploration mission to the far side of Ca'cadasan Space.

Commander Marc Dawson: Engineering Officer, *Augustine I.*

Rear Admiral Kelso: Sean's Flag *Captain* and Chief of Staff.

Captain Vincent Oldenburg: commander of the *King Edward II.*

Captain Hyori Gae: Admiral Kelvin's Flag Captain.

Captain Lauren Hoyt: commander, Hyper VII BB *Genghis Kahn*.

Petty Officer First Satrusalya: Naval Commando.

Captain Svetlana Komorov: Wing Commander, Inertialess fighter wing.

The Donut

Doctor Lucille Yu, PhD: Assistant Chief Scientist and Engineer of the *Donut* Project. Born Year 928 (72 years old).

Jimmy Chung: IIA Agent in Charge, Donut.

Imperial Army

Cornelius Walborski: Cadet Lieutenant and two time holder of the Imperial Medal of Heroism.

Major General Samuel Baggett: Division/Corps Commander,

Major General Walther Jodel, The Preacher: Army Ranger Brigade Commander.

Brigadier General Dagni Thorwaldsdottir: Assistant Division Commander.

Lieutenant Jay Cummings: Platoon Commander: Main Battle Tanks.

Colonel General Mich Satapatra: Ground force commander, Massadara.

Lt. General Jonah Nowitski: Commander XXXXI Heavy Corps.

Major General Lanbardran: Phlistaran commander of the One Ninety-fifth Heavy Infantry Division.

Sergeant First Class SanJames: Ranger Platoon Sergeant.

Ca'cadasans

Great Admiral Miierrowanasa M'tinisasitow: Ca'cadasan conquest fleet commander. Born 2843 AD (1,418 years old).

High Admiral Kellissaran Jarkastarin: Third Cousin to the Emperor and rival of the Great Admiral.

Elysium

Archduke Horatio Alexanderopolis: His Imperial Majesty's Ambassador to the Court of the Elysium Empire. Born Year 821 (179 years old).
High Lord Grarakakak, Brakakak: High Lord of Elysium Empire.

Others

Sonia Rupert: IIA Agent, former member of Imperial Protection Detail.
Citizen Prestor Johnson: Trillionaire and developer of *Congreve* System.
Devera Walborski: Warrant Officer Medic and the wife of Cornelius.
Rebecca Walborski: Sean and Devera's adopted daughter.
Dr. Larry Southard: Mathematician and Astrophysicist, expert on Supernovas.

The Story So Far

In 2254 the human species had spread to eight star systems after the discovery of the Subspace drive, allowing humankind to achieve pseudospeeds of over eleven times the speed of light. That was the year the human species first encountered the long lived Ca'cadasans, three meter tall horned carnivores whose empire had been expanding for thousands of years. That was the year the aliens attacked the Epsilon Iridani V *colony. When the heir to their imperial throne was killed after the colony had surrendered, the Emperor ordered the complete extermination of the human species. After a short, sharp war, humanity had no other option than to try and flee the killer aliens. The six Exodus ships were built, each capable of moving fifty thousand humans in cryostasis, along with all the knowledge of the human species. One ship is known to have gotten away through subspace, a dimension through which the more advanced hyperspace faring Ca'cadasans are not prepared to follow. Four generations of crew navigated the Exodus III over ten thousand light years in a thousand years, reestablishing humanity in a system of eight stars in orbit around a black hole, the Supersystem. Once the home of an extinct species that had helped raise most of the intelligent races of the area to technical civilizations, it was also the perfect region for the newcomers. Over the next thousand years the New Terran Empire fights, wins and expands in a number of wars, improving their technology at breakneck speed, becoming the dominant military power of the region. Humanity also improves its genome, becoming stronger, faster and smarter, and seemed destined to rule the Perseus Arm, given time.*

On the thousand year anniversary of the empire, Emperor Augustine I is having prophetic dreams, the gift and curse of his line. He has seen the ancient enemy returning, finding the human species disunited in its three governments, and utterly destroying them. Augustine has fought to expand the military, running into obstructionism from the Lords House of Parliament. It is an uphill battle in the Constitutional Monarchy the Empire has become. Meanwhile, the Donut, a century long engineering project, is nearing completion. The enormous station, built as a ring around a black hole, and using the swirling gravitational energy to generate wormholes, has begun to make the many portals that will be used to eventually link the Empire. And spies have infested the Empire, a race of shape shifters who make most security measures moot, adding sabotage and espionage to the problems facing the Emperor.

Sean Ogden Lee Romanov, the third son of the Emperor, is a serving naval officer on a battleship in a relatively quiet sector, with no thoughts of ever assuming the throne. He was a mediocre officer, despite his superior intelligence. With two brothers ahead of him in the succession, and a still young father, the throne seems like the least his worries. By this time the Ca'cadasans have made contact with some of the enemies of the Empire, and sent the information back to their leaders. The ancient enemy has been found, and can now be eliminated. Ships begin to disappear in Sector IV, and sightings are made of vessels that fit no known description. Many people refuse to believe these are the Ca'cadasans, and some think that Empire must have fallen in the near past. The Emperor continues to try to rally support for increasing the size of the human military, while Parliament fights him on the economic effects of such a move, and alien powers protest that the humans are planning territorial expansion.

There is an attempted assassination attempt on Sean, and a successful attempt on the Emperor and his two older sons during a tour of the Donut. The assassin is an officer of the Imperial Protection Detail, causing distrust to grow among the agencies charged with the security of the Empire. The same day as the assassination, the Leader of the House of Lords is killed in his home. Sean is now the heir to the Empire, and the man who must be seated as soon as possible on the throne, but he is almost a week's one way com range from the capital.

The Ca'cadasans now attack, sending large fleets into several industrial or base systems, and smaller forces to many other stars. The Massadara system, a major Imperial base, is one of the systems attacked. Sean is serving on one of the battleships that happens to be in that system, and is aboard the vessel as it heads into combat with the enemy. Word comes to the system that Sean is the uncrowned Emperor, and his ship, against his protests, is ordered out of combat. His ship, the Sergiov, *heads out of the system before the main battle begins, a small Ca'cadasan force on its heels. The main battle is joined, and, though it inflicts casualties on the Ca'cadasan fleet that is only about a decade ahead in technology, it is defeated, and the system falls.*

The Sergiov *is battered by the enemy, and Sean is rescued from the ship by Captain Mei Lei and her hyper VII battle cruiser. The battle cruiser fights its way out of the system with the help of Commander Bryce Suttler's stealth/attack ship, and, along with Commander Maurice von Rittersdorf and his destroyer, starts on the voyage to get Sean back to the capital and the throne. The Ca'cadasans track the two vessels, and Sean escapes on the destroyer while Mei sacrifices her ship in a battle with the Ca'cadasan supercruisers. The battle cruiser* Jean de Arc *falls out of hyperspace in a catastrophic translation, a low survivability event, but nonetheless manages to survive and starts the long journey home.*

Rear Admiral Mara Montgomery is dispatched with her scout force to locate Sean and get him back to the capital, while von Rittersdorf plays hide and seek against the Ca'cadasans, trying to get the unseated Emperor to safety. Von Rittersdorf catches one of the much larger Ca'cadasan ships in a brilliant ambush which destroys the enemy ship, while causing severe damage to his own. Montgomery's task force enters the system, and she dispatches the other two supercruisers, then takes the

Emperor aboard her flagship. Von Rittersdorf begins the long journey home in his crippled ship with escorts. Sean learns that one of the nearby systems is under siege and, against the protests of the Admiral, orders her to take her ships to break that siege and evacuate the colonists on the frontier world. Meanwhile, the Leader of the House of Lords advances plans to put an Imperial Cousin on the throne while the true heir's whereabouts are unknown. The Ca'cadasans invade and take the kingdom of New Moscow, and make serious inroads into the New Terran Republic, the sister governments to the Empire.

On Sestius IV Brevet Brigadier General Samuel Baggett fights the landing of the Ca'cadasans with his mixed command. Farmer and ex-hunter Cornelius Walborski deserts the militia to get his pregnant wife to safety. Though bleeding the enemy, Baggett is forced to fall back into the wilderness before the enemy ground warriors. Walborski's son is born, but his wife is killed while they are running from the aliens. The farmer goes mad, and stalks the jungle with the skills he had learned as an assistant hunt master, killing many aliens in the jungle. He meets the legendary Preacher of special ops fame, now a retired Ranger and current minister on the planet.

Montgomery's task force takes the system and the planet, and evacuates all those that want to leave, just before a larger enemy force enters the system and forces it to flee. Sean meets Dr. Jennifer Conway, who has lost her own fiancé' in the invasion, and falls in love with her. The scout force fights a running battle back to Conundrum base, rescued at the last moment by the fleet of Duke Taelis Mgonda. Von Rittersdorf makes it to safety, while Mei Lei and her crew are rescued from hyper by another battle cruiser. The XO of the Jean de Arc, *Xavier Jackson, falls out of hyper while trying to rescue some crew who could not get off the ship. Surviving the translation, he is rescued by beings from legend, the Ancients that everyone assumes are extinct.*

On the Donut it is discovered that an ancient race known as the Yugalyth, another creature from legend, capable of changing its very body form over a period of days and duplicating any creature, is at large. A Yugalyth agent imitates Dr. Lucille Yu, the station Director, and attempts to destroy the huge construct. Dr. Yu uses quantum teleportation, an experimental technique that only succeeds in moving about half the material being teleported to its target, to teleport negative matter to destroy the bomb the creature put on the station attitude control board. The new enemy is discovered, one which originates in the realm of the Empire's close ally, Elysium.

The Knockermen, a reptilian race in the Elysium Empire, revolt against the dominant Brakakak. The Brakakak eventually curb the revolt, but are forced to commit their entire fleet to searching out the rebels and breaking the rebellion. The leader of Elysium and his family are forced to take refuge with the Terrans during the battle of the capital.

Sean comes back to the Supersystem by the wormhole gates that are now being deployed through Imperial space. Chief of Naval Operations Gabriel Lenkowski gathers a fleet that transports Sean to the capital planet, where, with a large force of Marines, he lands during the coronation ceremony and stops the Lords from crowning his cousin. Sean is now Emperor, Commander and Chief of the Imperial Military, and, given his wartime powers, the most powerful Monarch in a century. His companions go off to other commands; Mei Lei to a battle cruiser squadron, one equipped with new wormhole launched weapons; von Rittersdorf to lead a new destroyer squadron; and Baggett to command of a heavy infantry brigade. Cornelius Walborski, on the recommendation of Preacher, joins the Imperial Army with hopes of being augmented and becoming a Ranger.

The Ca'cadasans hit Conundrum, the HQ of Sector IV, hours after Sean jumps through the wormhole from there. They take the system, and land troops to complete the conquest of the planet. Sean is forced to engage in a hit and run war against an enemy that is still more advanced, and more powerful, than his own fleet. He orders his units to refuse combat when possible, and only to fight when they can inflict maximum damage on the enemy. Q-ships, militarized merchant vessels with quantum teleporters capable of sending antimatter into the interior of an enemy ship, bait and destroy Ca'cadasan raiders. The Lords go on the warpath against Sean, demanding that he commit his fleet to a major battle. His prophetic dreams indicate that one of the core worlds, the heavily populated industrial planets at the heart of the Empire, is a target. But the dream does not tell him when.

Wormhole gates are dropped in occupied systems, then maneuvered to planetfall, allowing ground forces to insert. This is done on most of the occupied worlds, allowing the units to engage the aliens in Guerilla warfare. Preacher leads a Ranger brigade against the Ca'cadasans on the surface of Conundrum, and the campaign forces the enemy off the planet. The Lasharans, religious fanatics, are again attacking the frontiers of the Empire, and Baggett's unit, as part of a heavy infantry corps, is sent to take their home planet and occupy their primary temple, breaking their will.

The Ca'cadasans strike at the Cimmeria system, utterly obliterating the two inhabited industrial worlds located there. Sean retaliates by sending forces through wormholes to strike behind the main enemy fleet and destroy their bases. The Fenri Empire, old enemies of the humans, sign an alliance with the Ca'cadasans, and the New Terran Empire launches a spoiling attack on those aliens. The logical beings of the Crakista Empire, seeing the Ca'cadasans as the greater threat, join the human cause, ordering their military to offer all possible aid to the humans. Things are beginning to look up until the Ca'cadasans launch yet another assault, almost overrunning all of Sector IV.

Sean and Jennifer become lovers, a fact taken advantage of by the Yugalyth agents, who kidnap her and threaten to kill her if Sean does not place himself in their hands. Sean agrees, and has himself equipped with a pair of small wormholes that allow him to kill the kidnappers when they think they have him in their power.

Cornelius completes Ranger school, finds a new love himself, and is assigned to the planet Azure, one of the deadliest in the Empire. He and his men stalk the Ca'cadasans through a jungle that is enemy to both, and encounters a new client race of the Ca'cadasans, the supremely competent hunters called Maurids. Cornelius saves and is saved by a young girl, Rebecca, and completes the mission his company couldn't, destroying a Ca'cadasan headquarters. He returns to the capital system again a hero, one of the few to win the Imperial Medal of Heroism twice. He marries, and gains a new mom for his baby son, and his adopted daughter, Rebecca.

Sean, in need of a victory, plans an ambush for the Ca'cadasan fleet in the Congreve system, a frontier world made up to look like an industrial developing planet. The Cacas, using the Knockermen, send in a strike force to take out the Donut. And the Empire sends in a strike against the Fenri Empire, the new ally of the Ca'cadasans. Cornelius attends Officer Candidate School and is well on his way to becoming an officer, while the Opposition Party of the Lords continues to cause trouble for the Emperor, threatening a No Confidence Vote in Parliament.

The strike into Fenri space is a success, taking the heart out of their fleet and capturing several of their industrial planets, sending the small mammalians into a frenzy. The Fenri still have some power in their fleet, and organize an offensive that kicks the NTE naval force out of their space, stranding Baggett and his soldiers on the surface of one of the planets.

The Ca'cadasan strike force makes it to Elysium space, commandeers a Brakakak light cruiser, and takes the station in orbit around that Empire's capital world. The Cacas jump through the wormhole to the Donut, bringing thousands of troops *and four Quarkium devices, intending to destroy the station. The Knockermen destroy the Brakakak station with the device that they were given by the huge aliens. And Walborski, heading through the* Donut *on a short leave to see his wife and children, finds himself involved in another battle.*

Sean lures the Ca'cadasan main fleet into battle, springing his ambush, and ravaging the enemy fleet. They turn into a tougher opponent that he planned on, and some of the enemy fleet escapes to head back to their base, leaving the Imperial fleet with a lesser victory than wanted, and higher casualties than expected.

Prologue

SECTOR VII SPACE. NOVEMBER 20TH,1001.

The pirates must have thought they were undetectable, their base built on one of the moons of a Saturnesk gas giant in orbit around an ember of a red star. The small star was twenty light years from the nearest inhabited system, off the travelled space lanes, while giving the pirates a base close enough to some of the major transit lanes of Sector VII. Yes, they felt secure, their small fleet faring out from the base to strike shipping, taking vessels and slaves, and much wealth in materials and machinery, then returning to their undetectable base. Selling the slaves and wealth to merchants of a shady nature. But though the system was undetectable, its activity hidden by distance, the corsairs that fared out were not, and eventually something was bound to happen.

Captain Stella English looked at the viewer that showed the small system ahead, hoping that the information that had been extracted from the captured pirates was accurate. But then, a score of them had given the same information, every one of the crew that had known the exact coordinates of the system. *Amazing what chemicals and nanoprobes can gather*, she thought, a slight smile on her lips. She had no sympathy for the scum who preyed on the weak and innocent. Whatever pain or suffering they had to endure was just fine with the commander of Task Force 481, her current command.

Her flagship, HIMS *Lancanshire*, was lurking in normal space, moving toward the system at point five light. She and the rest of the force had translated into normal space outside of the detection range of most vessels, it being hoped that the ramshackle fleet of the pirates would not be equipped with the most advanced of sensors. None of her eight vessels were equipped with a wormhole, and it had been decided to run in with communications locked, even the new sublight com system.

The eight hundred thousand ton light cruiser was the most combat capable vessel in the force. Three of her other ships were two hundred thousand ton destroyers, while the remaining four were one hundred thousand ton frigates. She had asked for another cruiser, or at least a couple more destroyers, but this had been all that was available. And besides, they were just pirates, no matter what the captives said about the corsair force.

"We'll be entering planned firing range in ten minutes, ma'am," said her Tactical Officer.

"Thank you, Mr. Banks," she told the officer, nodding her head his direction. *I wish we could capture them, and bring them to trial*, she thought. There was something much more satisfying about seeing them sentenced to life imprisonment, or possible death, in a court of law. Something that could be publicized, and maybe act as a deterrent to other potential scum. *Sure, Stella, and maybe we'll get the Easter Bunny to start making the rounds again*, she thought with a snort.

Basically, there were too many of them to try for any kind of closing and capturing strategy. She counted eleven frigate and destroyer class vessels in orbit around the moon, as well as several intact freighters that had to be recent prizes. And one ship that had truly surprised her. *Just how in the holy hells did they get an old battle cruiser. I wouldn't think they would have the manpower to take such a thing on a combat patrol.*

But that was the one reason she was not going to risk her command trying to capture the pirates. At close range a ship like that, an ancient *Majestic* class BC of about five million tons, could take out her whole command in a close in beam fight. Beam weapon technology hadn't changed that much in the past hundred years, though targeting and defensive tech had, as had the power of said beams. Still, a five million ton platform was capable of truly impressive close in fire. While missile tech had increased by leaps and bounds, and she had a clear advantage in that area.

"We have an approaching ship in hyper," called out Banks, looking back from his board. "In the ten million ton range."

"What in the hell do we have calling now?" asked the Helmsmen.

"Hold up on the fire plan for a moment," ordered the Captain, visions of an old battleship entering her mind. "Let's see what we have first off."

A half an hour later the ship appeared from out of hyper, less than a light minute away from the human task force.

"That looks like a Vergasa freighter," said Banks, and Stella grunted in acknowledgement.

What in the hell would they be doing here? she thought. Vergasa was a minor power in the region, a kingdom of no more than a hundred inhabited systems. They engaged in legitimate trade with the Empire, as well as some more shady operations. *Like trading with pirates*, she thought, studying the ship in the viewer. *They have to have a buyer for their ill-gotten gains. Why not Vergasa?*

"Signal the other ships that we will open fire on

the pirates in one minute," she ordered her Com Officer. All of the vessels were within twenty light seconds of each other, less than two seconds by subspace com. She thought it was unlikely that the Vergasa ship would have a subspace com, and couldn't alert the pirates anyway.

"Fire," she ordered, and *Lancanshire* bucked slightly as her tubes accelerated a spread of missiles at the target. She started swinging from side to side, bringing her port tubes, then her forward accelerators, then her starboard tubes, to bear. In half a minute she had sent a spread of a hundred missiles toward the pirate base, accelerating at five thousand gravities. The other ships released half of their own magazines, adding over two hundred more missiles to the swarm. It would take three hours for the missiles, already traveling at point two five light from the velocity of the launching vessels, to reach the enemy base. They would reach their maximum safe velocity of point nine five light an hour and a half into flight, and would strike the enemy it the most advantageous attack profile.

"Order *Maes* and *Grimm* to take that freighter and board her," ordered the Captain, looking at the side holo that showed the commercial vessel, which as yet hadn't reacted to the presence of the human ships nearby.

"Captain of the *Grimm* is asking the rules of engagement," said the Com Officer.

"He can't destroy her," said English. "But he is ordered to disable her if she resists."

"We have graviton emissions from the pirate base," said Banks. "Three ships are starting to boost."

The roaches reacting to the light, thought the Captain with a slight smile.

Over the next hour the rest of the pirate vessels got under way, as their crews transferred from the moon to them. She hoped the enemy ships would come for her, hastening the missile attack. She should have known better. They scattered, trying to escape. But there was no escape, as the missiles had been targeted on their individual vessels in case they tried such a tactic.

"They would have done better if they had stayed together," said Banks, as the vector arrows on the plot showed the enemy ships all on separate courses.

"They aren't military vessels," said English, watching as her missiles started tracking the individual ships.

A little over three hours later the missiles started to make contact with ships that were still trying to build up their velocity. There was no way they could outrun the missiles. The pirate vessels started to fall off the plot as their primitive missile defense systems tried to deal with modern weapons, and failed. They got some of them, but never enough. The only exception was the battle cruiser, which, though battered by near misses, was a survivor.

"We're receiving a transmission from *Grimm,* ma'am," said the Com Officer, and Stella motioned for her to put it on the screen.

"We've boarded the freighter, ma'am," said the Captain of the DD *Grimm*, looking out of the com holo. "My Marine commander is reporting that it's, sickening aboard. Lots of human equipment. And, they tried to get rid of the human prisoners they had, with, particle beams."

English felt her stomach turn as she thought of

the terror that must have been the last feelings of those people as the Vergasa started vaporizing them with beam weapons. Unfortunately for them, that was not the way to get rid of all evidence. There was almost always a residue.

"Clap the bastards in irons, Captain," she told the other officer. "We'll let a Naval Magistrate decide their fate. Were there any survivors?"

"No, ma'am," said the Commander who was the captain of that destroyer. "Not a one."

"What do you want us to do about the big bastard?" asked Banks, pointing to the icon of the battle cruiser that was coasting in space with no acceleration. "Capture him?"

"No," said Stella, her nausea over the death of prisoners turning into rage. "I'm not risking any of my ships getting close to that thing. Light him up with another spread."

She looked over at her Helmsman. "Put us on a course toward that base. We'll let our Marines search it, and I hope to God for their sake that the bastards haven't committed more atrocities on the base."

Hours later she knew that was a forlorn hope. All of the pirates had evacuated, and so were dead aboard the remains of their ships. While the dead slaves lay all over the base, where the pirates had left them, not even bothering to try and dispose of the bodies.

Chapter One

There is no avoiding war; it can only be postponed to the advantage of others.   Niccolo Machiavelli

THE *DONUT.* NOVEMBER 21ST, 1001.

"Did we really have to bring along so much of this shit?" asked Petty Officer First Satrusalya, holding one end of the large container by a handle. "This stuff gives me the shakes."

Cornelius looked at the man, who was larger that he was. Being an augmented Naval Commando, using the same process the Ranger had undergone, that meant he was stronger, and just a bit slower due to his mass.

"I don't really like it either," said the Cadet Lieutenant, eying the tube that was a magnetic containment device filled with one of the deadliest known substances, negative matter. Only antimatter was more feared. Negative matter canceled out itself and normal matter on contact. Once out of its containment there was nothing that was proof against it. The only positive thing about the negative matter was that it could only cancel out the same mass. "But I like the idea of a hundred gigaton or larger bomb going off near me even less, and this stuff may be the only thing that will cancel it out before it kills us."

They were moving quietly along the wall that separated the corridor from the kilometer thick supercable that was one of the supports the aliens had to sever to destroy the station. Five Rangers and the other Naval Commando were in the lead, crouched low, weapons ready. Cornelius walked just ahead of the two men carrying the container, while the last Ranger took up the rear, thirty meters behind and his watch covering that direction.

All of the men were veterans, and Cornelius trusted them to do their jobs competently. Cornelius had been in special ops for a far shorter time than most of the men, and was not yet a commissioned officer. The double award of the Imperial Medal of Heroism made him a trusted leader, however, someone these tough warriors were in awe of.

The Commando in the front, Petty Officer First Khrushchev, the leader of that element due to his experience operating aboard spaceships, held his hand up and knelt down, waving the officer trainee forward. Cornelius ran to him, making no sound, and came to a kneel beside him. He didn't even have to ask the man what was going on. His hypersensitive ears picked up the sound of fighting, both directly ahead and to the left down another corridor. *The Marines must be to the front, and Chung and his people to the left*, he thought. The Marines, in heavy combat armor, would be trying to blast their way through the Cacas arrayed to protect the bomb. The IIA Agents were a decoy force, hitting the Cacas down another angle of approach, trying to draw the enemy away from this one.

"We're getting close," he whispered to the Commando, who nodded back. They were avoiding com link for the moment, thinking that the enemy might pick it up so close to their lines. Rangers and Commandos were trained to operate without electronics. At this time they were carrying more powerful weapons than they usually did, and two of the men had the backpacks of laser cutters on their backs, just in case.

"I hope they don't set the damned thing off before we get to it," said Sergeant Pasco, one of the Rangers.

"I wonder why they haven't already?" asked Specialist Owusu, his eyes scanning the corridor ahead.

"They want to set them all off at the same time," said Cornelius. "Not give us a chance to make repairs before they sever another cable."

He listened for a second more, then waved his hand to get everyone moving. They hadn't gone more than fifty meters before Khrushchev was again raising his hand and stopping the formation.

"They're right ahead," said the Petty Officer, gesturing with his rifle down the corridor.

Cornelius listened carefully, the movement of the armored Cacas sounding from ahead. *We need to get through them quickly. Then hit the Cacas that are facing the Marines from behind.* He was starting to wave the other men forward when a particle beam came ripping down the corridor and struck Khrushchev in the chest.

*   *   *

The General was in communication with both of his forces that had gone after the lower side cables of the station. The com was going in and out, even though he had men stationed along the way to relay the signal. The enemy jamming was getting more powerful, and he was afraid they might also be listening in.

And what in the hell is keeping those dolts from getting to their target? he thought, following one of his groups on a tactical holo. The other battalion, almost four hundred males, was already in position, their weapon ready to take out that support. But the battalion he was watching had run into opposition, and were having to fight their way through. They were still over ten kilometers from their target. That might be close enough to take out the cable, but probably not.

The other bombs were set four kilometers to either side of the central cable, close enough for the dual explosion to take it out, and also destroy much of the lower hull of the station, weakening it further.

They only have another hour and a half to get to the target, he thought, feeling the stress of the situation, almost overwhelming anxiety that his mission might fail. *We can't allow it to fail*, he thought, linking into the com and sending reinforcements to the bogged down unit. That meant weakening the defense of the port central side bomb, but it was more important to get that peripheral weapon to its target. *If only I had those other males*, he thought. But the Knockermen had set off their bomb on the Elysium station before he had gotten all his troops off. Those males would have died anyway if they had gotten to the human station. But they would have died for a purpose.

"The humans are increasing their pressure," said the commander of the troubled battalion. "They are attacking with increased ferocity, no matter the loss."

Of course they are. Because they know if we destroy this station, they have lost their war. "I am sending you reinforcements, Battalion Commander. Keep pushing forward. You must get that weapon to its target."

I wonder if we could have sent the warriors through space to the target, thought the General, second guessing his own orders. Then he thought about what would have happened if he had sent hundreds of males and the weapon through space, where the enemy would have been able to attack them with ship borne weapons. He would have lost the attack force, and the weapon.

"We're pushing ahead," said the officer. "But I can't guarantee we'll get there before the weapon goes off."

The General growled, recognizing a plea to stop the countdown.   He wouldn't respond.   The Commander had his orders, and would follow them to his death.   Stopping the countdown meant that the other weapons were at greater risk.   And he wasn't about to take that risk.

He followed the progress on the com, sweating out the lack of progress as the armored males fought armored humans.   The humans were skilled warriors with powerful weapons, and the progress started to bog down, while the reinforcements also ran into an enemy that was determined to keep them from linking up with their comrades.

Minutes ticked by, and the icons of his troops continued to fall off the plot, while the humans icons, representing the soldiers that were engaged with his males, continued to increase.   It was looking like a losing battle on that front.   *It could still work*, he thought, his denial that this mission was a failure kicking in.   *It has to work.*

"We're starting to lose our perimeter," came the call of the Regimental Commander who was holding one of the bombs.   *The one I took the warriors away from*, he thought.   He had robbed the successful force to reinforce one that was already a failure.

The General looked at the manual detonator, determined that all the bombs would go off before the humans got to them.   He reached for the arming switch, then pulled his hand back.   *The bombs are fused so they will go off if they are tampered with.   There is nothing they can do to them.*   He pushed the cover back over the remote detonation switch, and left it in the hands of the Gods.

*   *   *

"We've got one of the bombs, Dr. Yu," said the Marine Colonel that was leading the force that had stopped the port side Caca battalion from getting their bomb to the support cable that was their target.

Yu looked over the holo at the bomb behind the Colonel, taking in the structure of the device. Superficially, it looked much like the devices she had seen in Admiral Chrone's presentation. She pulled up the schematic of those devices, and compared them to the bomb that was now in the center of the holo.

"You need to spray the center of the device, Colonel, making sure to hit the control box on top and through to the center, where the quarkium device is actually located."

"What about the ends of the device?"

"Do not allow any of the negative matter to come in contact with anything past thirty centimeters of the centerline. The ends are antimatter weapons used to set off the quarkium reaction, which sets off the subquark detonation."

"How much antimatter?"

"Up to a kilogram at each end. About eighty megatons if it breaches containment."

"I guess I need to evacuate everyone but the engineers and myself."

"You don't have time for that, Colonel," said Lucille, concerned about her station and its safety more than a battalion's worth of men. *Which is awful,* she thought. *But if that bomb goes off as a subquarkian device, it will kill many more.* "Take the tank and spray that device, in the manner I told you."

The officer stared back at her for a moment, and she afraid he was going to order an evacuation anyway, wasting precious time. "Colonel, if I were there I would spray the device, without hesitation. Unfortunately, I am not there, because they needed someone who could talk to several attack groups at one time. But believe me, we don't have the time."

"Right," said the Colonel, turning to his engineers and grasping one of the spray devices himself. He spoke to the engineering sergeant who was holding the other device, and they both aimed at the center part of the device. "On the count of three. One. Two. Three."

Both men pulled the triggers on the sprayers and sent streams from the nozzles that funneled the negative matter through magnetic fields to the outside world. The streams shot out, under high pressure as the magnetic field in the tank squeezed. It only took a couple of seconds to send out kilograms of negative matter. It hit the normal matter of the device and cancelled both out. The center of the bomb disappeared up to twenty centimeters into the case, including the entire control mechanism. The men sprayed again, destroying more of the bomb. A third spray ate over halfway through the bomb, negating much of the material and sending metal vapor into the air as much of the rest of the matter broke up under the assault.

"I think that should do it, Colonel," said Yu.

"I'm on the spot, Ma'am, and I would prefer to be safe," said the officer. He and the other man sprayed again, and once again, until there was no more negative matter in the tank.

That was a waste, thought the Director, looking at the bomb that was more or less gone through its center. *We could have used that material for wormholes. But I can't say*

I blame the men on the spot. Now we just need to get those other three bombs, and we're good.

*   *   *

The force that hit the bomb where the troops had been pulled from the perimeter struck on five axes, from three sides on the level of the bomb, as well as from above and below. It would have taken a division to hold all the approaches, and the above and below routes were covered by mere platoons, not enough to seal off all avenues, especially when the assault was launched in force down all avenues at once.

The outer perimeters of the Cacas were still fighting the Marines coming at them on their level, while the assault force of Naval Commandos came from above and took the bomb in seconds of intense fighting. They duplicated the techniques of the Marines who had disposed of the first bomb, and then there were two.

*   *   *

The beam converted the torso of Khrushchev to red tinted vapor, while his head and shoulders, arms still attached, fell to the floor. The legs tottered for a second before they joined his staring head on the floor. The beam continued on in a sweep that the other men ducked under, then flew down the hall to hit the canister of negative matter being carried up the corridor. The beam sliced into the tank and released the compressed gas.

The trailing man yelled out and ran back as the gas dissolved everything it touched.   Petty Officer First Satrusalya moved as soon as the gas started billowing out of the rent in the tank, bits of the skin on his hands and parts of the sleeves on his uniform disappearing, disintegrated by the negative matter. He still moved fast enough to jump forward and away from the disaster, which caught the other man who had been carrying the canister full in the body. The Ranger disappeared, taking almost the same amount of mass of negative protons with him. The rest ate at the walls, ceiling and floor, as well as the air around the tank, until it had all cancelled out.

Cornelius stared in horror at the place where a man had ceased to exist, not even an apparent atom of his body left. It was horrible what had happened to Khrushchev, but there were still identifiable remains there. And even worse, the means of disposing of the bomb were gone. *That's why we brought along the laser cutters*, he thought, trying to drive the images of the death of two men from his mind, especially the total elimination of one. *If that damned bomb goes off, we'll all be just as gone, even if it does leave some of our atoms to fall into the black hole.*

The Cacas continued to put fire into a position that was untenable from its lack of cover. The beam flew overhead, forcing Cornelius to attempt to push the atoms of his body into the floor, unsuccessfully of course. He fired his own weapon, sweeping it at chest level a hundred meters down the straight corridor. "We need to get out of here," he yelled to his men. The negative matter and its heavy container were the reason they had taken a corridor in the first place, that and the need for speed. "Put something on them that will take their attention off us, and someone find us an alternate route."

"Fire in the hole," called out Specialist Owusu, just after a beam forced Sergeant Pasco to roll into the wall to avoid it. What looked like a streak of light came through the center of the corridor. Something exploded about two hundred meters up the corridor, followed by a cloud of smoke and the shimmering of a falling invisibility field.

"Good job," said Cornelius, glancing at the other Ranger. He looked back in time to pick up a target through the billowing smoke, the horned head of the crouching Caca unmistakable. He automatically developed a sight picture through his scope and squeezed the trigger, sending a bright beam that split the smoke just before it covered the target again. The body that fell forward from the smoke to hit the floor hard, hole through the faceplate, showed that his aim had been true.

"I've got us a way out of here, sir," called out Satrusalya over the com.

"Show me," ordered the Lt, relieved that the Commando was still functional. The map of the local station came up on his visual centers through his implants, and he started to crawl back, firing a beam every couple of seconds down the corridor, as he looked at the route the Commando was proposing.

That could work, he thought, flinching in mid thought as another beam came out of the now clearing smoke and was within ten centimeters of getting a hit on him. The other men were also backing up, though they were concentrating more on putting fire on the enemy. They were still very exposed, and if not for all the preventive jamming going on through this part of the station, electronic warfare that really didn't affect their systems as they were able to adjust for what was coming, they would all have already been dead meat many times over.

"Let's do this, people," he said over their implant coms, now willing to risk them since the enemy already knew they were here. "Hit them with another one, Owusu," he told the Specialist who was carrying the small hyperv launcher. "Then you and Falstaff keep up the particle beam fire. I want them to think we're still coming from here."

Cornelius linked into the com to contact Senior Agent Jimmy Chung, the leader of the other, larger element that was to be the decoy for his force. "How's it going, Agent Chung?" he asked, knowing part of the answer as he heard the angry buzzing of particle beams in the background through the ears of the augmented Imperial Secret Service Agent.

"We're getting slaughtered here," yelled the Agent into the com. "I hope you're making some progress with your part of the mission."

"Nothing good to report here either," said Cornelius as he slid around the corner of a cross corridor and got back to his feet. "We've lost the negative matter, along with two of the men carrying it."

"Shit. Well, isn't that just the best news I've heard all day. I've lost twelve agents here, and I'm not even sure we're causing them slight anxiety. We just don't have the weapons and equipment to go up against heavily armed soldiers. And now we don't have the stuff we need to disarm the bomb."

"This Ranger isn't about to give up on the mission, Agent Chung," growled Walborski into the com. "We die from those things taking out the station, or we go forward, with a chance of achieving something, even if we still die. And I'm going forward. I'd appreciate it if you would support us."

"What do you want us to do, Lieutenant?"

"Leave enough people there to keep up some fire on the Cacas, while keeping to the best cover that they can. Then send the rest of them around to this position."

"You think this is going to work, Walborski?"

I sure hope so. Because if it doesn't, there won't be enough left of us to make a nanite. "I can't guarantee that it will work, but if you have a better plan, tell me about it now."

"We'll follow your lead, Ranger," said the Agent after a moment's hesitation. "I'll be bringing my people around as fast as we can."

The link cut off, and Walborski ran around to the door that Satrusalya had opened, following the rest of his men into the chamber. The Commando had opened the hatch in the far corner that led into a ventilation duct. The station had an enormously extensive ventilation system, with state of the art security systems that were in place to prevent just what they were attempting. But, since they weren't the enemy, those systems would not be engaged to stop them.

"I'll lead the way, if that's OK, sir," said Satrusalya, nodding toward the opening.

"Go ahead, PO," agreed Walborski. "You know this shipboard stuff much better than I do. Just get us behind them, and I'll be happy."

*   *   *

"We've gotten two of them, Doctor," said Marine General in charge of trying to boot the Cacas off the station.

"What about the other two?" asked Lucille Yu, sitting on the edge of her seat as she stared at the holo schematic that showed one of the outer lower cables cleared, as well as the bomb set to the other side of the lower central cable. Unfortunately, the bomb set up at the other outer lower cable was armed and ready, as was the other central cable bomb. *Theoretically, we should be able to survive those two bombs, if they are in the predicted range. If they're much more powerful, or our theories of how much stress this thing can take are wrong, then we're still screwed.*

"We have Marines and other troops trying to get to that outer bomb, but they're running into stiff resistance. As far as the other central bomb goes, I really don't think we're going to be able to get it before they set it off."

And Jimmy's with the group trying to get to the outer one he's talking about, she thought, her anxiety spiking at the thought of her lover in danger. *And if that bomb isn't disarmed, there's no way he's going to survive if it goes off, no matter what happens to the station.* "Try your best, General," was all she could think to say, as inane as it sounded. *Of course they're going to try their best, up to giving their lives.*

* * *

Damn, but this place is cold, thought Cornelius as he crawled on his hands and knees through the duct. There was a reason for the frigid temperatures, one that he approved of, as the very cold outer skin of the duct was helping to mask their own body heat from any sensors that might try to locate them through multiple walls. He was tempted to contact Satrusalya on the com, and ask how much further they had to crawl along this hard surface. A little taller and they could have walked, but as it was they had the choice of crawling or crouching. *And we'll get there when we do. No use bothering the PO with useless questions.*

"We're here," whispered the PO into the com, and the group of men came to a stop behind the Fleet NCO. The Commando opened the hatch to the maintenance room just a bit and sent a small swarm of microbots out of the duct.

The Lieutenant watched the take on the bots, relieved to see that the room was empty. Not that it was unexpected. The enemy had limited manpower, and could only cover so much. More of the bots moved up and down the duct, then into side ducts that were too small for a human to navigate, much less anything but the small repair robots that worked the ventilation system. There was one in each side duct, and the microbots landed and linked with the machines, bringing them under the control of Cornelius' implants. The repairbots moved to the end of the ducts and inserted groups of thin fiber optics into the grills. Soon the Ranger was looking at several hundred meters of corridor, and the enemy that was set up in multiple defensive positions along that hall.

"It's your plan, PO," said Cornelius, coming to the floor and walking soft footed to the side of the Commando. "Execute, and we'll follow your lead."

Satrusalya nodded. Cornelius noted that the man had patches of skin missing on hands and neck, as well as holes in his clothing, the effects of the spreading cloud of negative matter he had barely outrun. He realized, seeing one hole that extended into the bicep muscle, that the man had to be in pain, but was fully engaged with the mission, just like the rest of them.

The Commando took a grenade out of his side bag, one marked with the dragon head's symbol for antimatter, a warning that this was not ordinary explosive. Only a small amount, less than a gram, it would still do a job on the Cacas in the hall. He handed the weapon to a Ranger, then pulled out another one. Both men armed the weapons, then looked at each other for a moment.

Satrusalya hit the door switch, and the heavy alloy portal slid into its recess without a sound. There was no one in the hall, something they had been sure of based on the feeds from the repairbots, but still a great relief to see with their own eyes. Satrusalya leaned out, looking to the left and throwing his grenade with all of his considerable strength, while the Ranger did the same to the right. They leaned back into the room just before shouts sounded out. Satrusalya hit the door close button, and the door slid closed as the men all backed away to the far wall of the room.

The twin explosions came less than a second later, within a hundredth of a second of each other. The augmented men depended on the ear protection of the tactical helmets all were wearing to protect their hearing. It was barely enough, as the walls of the chamber shook from the fury of the blasts. Cornelius's link with the repairbots was instantly severed as the blasts spread into the vents. The door shook in its frame, and a large dent appeared in the wall as something was slammed into it, hard.

The Lieutenant counted to five, then nodded to the Commando. Satrusalya hit the door commit again, frowning as nothing happened for a moment. He hit the commit two more times, and the door finally slid open, not as smoothly as it had before.

That was a hellofa blast to warp a door like that at that distance, even a little bit, thought Cornelius, setting his rifle to fire and moving through the door behind the first two men. As usual, his testicles wanted to crawl into his body as he went into what could be the line of fire. His adrenaline kept him on his feet, and he was sure he was addicted to that feeling, the only thing that kept him going into what seemed like certain death.

He looked left, saw nothing moving save smoke, then right, in time to see one of his men take out what looked like the only Caca who had survived that blast. *Luck is a relative term,* he thought as he ran that way, Satrusalya on his heels. *Lucky enough to survive a hundred ton equivalent grenade, only to die a moment later as you try to gather your senses.*

The position they had taken out, one set to sweep this corridor with fire for a kilometer of its length, was an abattoir. A dozen Caca bodies, two heavy particle beams and a trio of rocket launchers, they would have slaughtered anything coming down the hall. Most had been killed instantly, parts of their armor crushed, blood flowing from helmets that had not been strong enough to protect them from the overpressure of the blast. A pair were missing limbs, probably catching the full brunt of the blast. There was a hole through one wall that looked large enough to have been made by a Caca arm, blood smeared on the edges.

"Fire in the hole," yelled Satrusalya, prepping another of the grenades. All of the men got low, using the bodies and equipment of the Cacas as cover. The Commando threw the grenade down the hall like a football, the weapon swishing through the air from the strength of his arm. He ducked down just before a particle beam burned through the air where he had been standing, then more beams pierced the air, from their angles aimed at the grenade.

Another thunderous explosion, flames reaching up the corridor and almost getting to the men.

"Move out," yelled Cornelius, jumping to his feet and starting up the corridor, his rifle at the ready.

"We have movement behind," called out Sergeant

Pasco, waving them down.

"It's Owusu, sir," yelled out the big Specialist, jogging down the hall with his rocket launcher, a dozen figures in police style tac op clothing running with him. "I've got company."

"Follow us," said Cornelius, turning back and sprinting down the corridor, depending on the augmented troops and agents to keep up with him.

Because of his speed of action he caught the next layer of Cacas off guard, just setting up to cover the corridor after losing contact with the males further down that the humans had wiped out. There were only six of them, and thirty beam and high speed projectile weapons took them out before they could react.

"Follow me," yelled Cornelius, continuing on, jumping the bodies, knowing that the speed of their assault could take the objective, as long as they didn't let caution slow them down. *We're going to do this*, he thought, his running speed up to fifty kilometers per hour, faster than the best unaugmented athlete. *We're going to do this.*

A particle beam speared out, hitting Sergeant Pasco dead center, while another flew past Cornelius and struck someone further back.

"Open fire," yelled the Lieutenant, firing his particle beam from the hip. "Give them hell." At the end of the last word he went into a warbling call he had heard in a movie, something called a rebel yell.

Everyone with him fired as fast as they could, sending particle beams and grenades down the hall. Hypersonic rounds cracked by Cornelius' head, making him flinch a bit, forcing him to run straight so the firing lanes would stay open.

Another flare of particle beam fire came down the

hall, cutting down two of the Secret Service Agents. That was the last fire the enemy got off as they were overwhelmed by a charge from another era of warfare, that only worked because of its shock value.

Cornelius hurdled the last of the Cacas who had deployed before the room. As he sailed over their bodies, he became the focus of a half dozen aliens in a fair sized storage room. They were standing around a large mechanism that could only be a bomb, and three of them were turning his direction with rifles coming to shoulders.

"Die, you fucking assholes," yelled Cornelius at the top of his lungs as he swung his particle beam into one of the aliens, exulting in the kill as the proton stream ate a hole through its faceplate. He was sure it would be his last kill, as two more weapons were tracking his way, and even with his advanced reflexes, he couldn't take out both of them before a proton beam tore through him.

Angry red lines swung by, and it took him a moment to realize that they weren't coming from the enemy weapons, but were actually hitting the Cacas, who fell backwards as multiple beams tore through both of them.

Cornelius landed lightly on his feet, breathing hard, still not sure that he was alive. The other people streamed into the room and fanned out, making sure the space was clear of Cacas, then securing every entrance in.

"Good job, Lieutenant," said a wide eyed Agent Chung, walking up and patting Cornelius on the back. "And just let me say, you are one crazy son of a bitch. I'm glad you're on our side."

Cornelius nodded his head, still trying to catch his

breath, the fear from what he had done finally catching up with him. His arms were shaking, and he felt like his legs were going to give out under him any moment.

"I'd follow you into hell any day, sir," said PO Satrusalya, walking up, a smile of relief on his own face.

"You just did," said Cornelius, swaying a moment.

The Petty Officer was at his side in a moment, giving him a supporting shoulder and a look of understanding.

"Is he going to be alright?" asked Chung.

"He's going to be fine," said the Commando. "Just a bit of adrenaline rebound."

Cornelius took a couple of clearing breaths and straightened up, looking at the weapon.

"So, sir," said Satrusalya, following the officer's gaze. "What are we going to do about that thing."

"I don't have a clue," said Walborski with a grimace. "Unless someone can come up with an idea, I guess we get to see what the center of a hundred gig explosions looks like."

Chapter Two

Once we have a war there is only one thing to do. It must be won. For defeat brings worse things than any that can ever happen in war. Ernest Hemingway

CONGREEVE SPACE. NOVEMBER 21, 1001.

"We've received word from the *Donut*, your Majesty," came the voice of Rear Admiral Kelso, the Emperor's *Flag Captain*. "They've disarmed two of the devices the Cacas have brought aboard.   The other two…."

"Thank you, Admiral," said Sean Ogden Lee Romanov, Sean the First, Emperor of the New Terran Empire. *And those other two could still possibly destroy the station, and our hopes of winning this war.*

The Emperor paced the deck of his flag bridge, no longer needing to be ensconced in the holo control room that had been developed for his use as battle commander. Most of the stations on this bridge were unmanned, the crew having been dismissed for relaxation, food and sleep, recovery after the rigors of battle. Many aboard the *Augustine I,* the twenty-seven million ton vessel that was the first of her class, had not survived the battle. This deep into the mass of the ship there had been few casualties. Unfortunately, many of the battle stations were close to the surface of the ship, where the weapons, defensive screen projectors and the engine components responsible for normal and hyperspace travel were housed. Where the crew that manned and repaired them were needed. And that area of the ship, the outer skin, the armor, laser rings and particle beams, was a mess. Over a thousand men and women had died in the battle, to add to the numbers of over a thousand other ships that had either been destroyed or sustained major damage.

My battle, he thought, shaking his head. It had been a good battle plan, luring the enemy fleet here for an engagement on his terms. But, like most plans, it had not survived contact with the enemy. They had still ravaged the enemy fleet. Less than one in five of the Caca ships that had entered the system had left it. But he had also lost almost half of the fleet he had brought into the battle. His Admirals were all telling him what a great victory it had been. But in his gut, his emotions, it didn't feel like any kind of victory at all.

Snap out of it, Sean, he told himself, walking up to the tactical holo and ordering it by link to switch to an expanded view of the half of the Empire that was involved in the war, some of it up close and personal, some more peripherally, or engaged with another enemy. *We don't have time for me to second guess everything that goes wrong. We hammered the bastards here, and, by God, we're going to do it again in the very near future.*

He looked at the holo, studying what it showed him about his dispositions. One spot that stood out like a festering sore was the incursion into Fenri Space. That incursion had gone well at first, and they had really hurt that enemy, taking away some of their most important border worlds and causing severe damage to the Fenri fleet. But that had changed, as the Fenri had reacted with unexpected force, the Fleet had retreated, and now he had six Imperial Army divisions trapped in their space.

"I want a staff meeting called, immediately," he told Kelso over the link. "We need to discuss strategy, and issue orders, now."

"How about twenty minutes, in the flag conference room, your Majesty," said the head of his staff.

"Do it. I'll expect everyone involved to have some general idea of the strategic situation, so we can hit the ground running." Sean severed the link and went back to studying the plot, bringing up his military dispositions and committing them to his implant memory. *We might just be able to do this,* he thought, juggling the pros and cons in his mind. *We just might be able to knock those little assholes out of this war, or at least make them wish they had never gotten involved.*

*   *   *

"You sure you want to do that, your Majesty?" asked Grand Fleet Admiral Gabriel *Len* Lenkowski, sitting in on the conference by holo projection through the wormhole com. "With another operation coming up in the near future?"

"Hell," said Grand Fleet Admiral Duke Taelis Mgonda, also sitting in by com holo. "We've got the tech to pull it off. Might as well use it while we can."

The unspoken statement in there was that they might not be able to count on the *Donut* in the future, with that future still up in the air. They might only have the wormholes they now possessed into the foreseeable future.

"And your opinion on the matter, Sondra?" asked the Emperor of Grand High Admiral McCollum, the Chief of Naval Operations.

"I say hit those sorry shits with everything we have, your Majesty," said the woman, sitting in a chair almost a thousand light years away, on the capital planet of Jewel. "From what I understand, the window for the supernova really doesn't start for another month, so if we give them two weeks of hell, we can still be ready for the kickoff of *Bagration*.   It will be tight, but it would be nice to secure that flank. In the long run, I think it will help with our concentration of forces."

"Mary?"

Captain Mary Innocent, Sean's Staff Intelligence Officer, looked up from her flat screen with a look of concentration on her face. "I concur, your Majesty," said the woman with a slight strained smile. "With a few reservations. We can't really be sure when the supernova event is going to kick off. We have research vessels near to the star, but something like this has never before happened in the Empire."

"And by that, you mean two supergiants spiraling into one?" asked McCollum.

"Exactly, ma'am. I think we need a real expert on scene to observe the star. A theoretical astrophysicist who specializes in supernova events. And I think I have just the man."

The holo came up over the table, showing a middle aged man with a pleasant expression on his face. Intelligent eyes looked out of the holo as it rotated to show everyone at the table his face.

"Dr. Larry Southard, of the University of New Detroit, on the planet of that name. Specializing in Mathematical models of stellar decay, including novas, supernovas, and even hypernovas. Over a hundred and forty peer reviewed papers in the field, a stint in Exploration Command, and considered the foremost expert on the phenomenon. I think we need a man like this eyeballing the star as it goes through its final stages, so we have the best possible judgment on when it's going to blow."

"Get him," said Sean, nodding. "No matter what it takes. If he won't be reasonable, call up his reserve commission. But get him on a research ship orbiting that star. I want to know to the second when it is going off, as soon as he can figure it out."

Bagration depended on that star going supernova. When a large object like a blue supergiant blew up, it not only sent huge waves of photons from across the electromagnetic spectrum out at the speed of light, photons of gamma rays, xrays, visible light and the searing heat that accompanied those masses of photons. They also sent most of the star's mass as superhot particles, at high speed, though not at anywhere near the speed of light. And, of course, the gravitons that had been coming out of the mass of the star, telling the Universe that it was there, continued to move at light speed into the space surrounding the expanding mass. They changed in quality and quantity as the mass expanded from a high gravity source to a much more dispersed source of matter.

Gravitons also travelled through hyperspace, moving at light speed across the more compact expanse of the other dimensions. In hyper VIII they were moving at a pseudospeed of over one hundred and sixty times the speed of light. And there would be millions of times more of them released by the explosion than was normal for the extant stellar body. They reverberated through all levels of hyper, transmitting the thunderous roar of the explosion, as it were, through hyper, for hundreds of light years in each direction, and swamping the *sounds* given off by the graviton emissions of smaller objects, such as star ships. For weeks at a time ships would be very hard to detect, if not simply impossible. And the star in question was the combination of two very large supergiants that had spiraled together, leading to an unprecedented explosion.

And hopefully, we'll be around long enough to shield the planets within killing range of that monster, thought the Emperor. Because any supernova was deadly to the planetary systems around them, and a monster even more so. Everything fifty light years and out was at risk from deadly particle radiation. Fortunately, the closest inhabited system was about eight light years away, giving the Empire over ten years to put up the particle shielding the one habitable planet needed to keep its life in the state of living.

"OK, people. Let's get those hulls rolling. I want the Fenri to feel our wrath, then switch back in time to hit the Cacas."

"I hope we have enough to accomplish both missions," said Len, his eyes narrowing. "If we get bogged down in the Fenri Empire, we might have problems with disengagement."

"Then I want to minimize those problems, Len. That's why you're going to command that operation. Anyone got a good name for it?"

"How about *Surigoa*," suggested Duke Mgonda, referring to a naval battle in old Earth's World War 2, in which the United States defeated the Japanese last gasp in the Philippines in one of four separate actions.

Sean took a second to check his link to look over the reference, then nodded his head. "*Surigoa* it is, your Grace. And I think we can commit some of our newest tech to hitting the bastards, though we'll still be light on wormholes." The problem being, as all present knew, that they still couldn't reliably move a wormhole equipped ship through another wormhole. Meaning that they still lost over sixty percent of the unmanned test ships in trials, and no one wanted to suggest sending a manned warship, even a destroyer, much less a battleship, through such a high risk transit.

"So we're a go on Operation Surigoa," said Sean, looking at the nodding heads of all gathered. "And Bagration as soon as we have the window. So now all we have to is finalize our dispositions for the operation, and get them where they need to be." *As if that will be easy*, he thought with a smile.

*   *   *

"It was a pleasure having you aboard, your Grace," said Rear Admiral Kelso, taking the Archduke's hand in his own.

His Grace Percival Marconi, leader of the Opposition Party of Parliament, smiled. "I wish I could say that it was enjoyable, Admiral. But it was most informative. Especially seeing that young man in action during the heat of battle. I have a much better appreciation of the hardships we face, and the potentials for success."

"Glad to hear it, your Grace," said the Admiral, returning the smile.

And I've got some butt to kick in my own party when I get home, thought Marconi, looking at the mirrored surface of the wormhole that would take him to the Central Docks, the *Donut* still not a safe destination. *Especially Countess Zhee, if she tries to pull some kind of power play.* Marconi was a power to be reckoned with in the Lords, and he had many friends in all of the triple houses of the Parliament. At the moment he was feeling slightly ashamed at his efforts to obstruct Sean, and Augustine before him. *But I acted in good faith*, he thought, looking at the wormhole, waiting for the green light to proceed. *Good faith, and mistaken beliefs. Now it's up to me to make amends for my actions, and swing the full support of the Lords to this Emperor's side.*

The light turned green, and the naval rating who was the watchdog for transport waved him on. The wormhole system could absorb quite a bit of the difference in velocity of the sending and transmitting stations. Quite a bit didn't mean anything above point two c. With missiles and particle beams that was fine. The military wanted them to come out at high velocity. With people, not so much, as slamming into a wall at point zero one c was still enough to completely pulp the body into a thin aerial mist.

"You just fight the war, Admiral," said the Archduke, turning before he walked through the mirror. "And we'll get you what you need." With that, he stepped through the wormhole, and into the disorienting stretching of time that its travel entailed.

*   *   *

FENRI SPACE. NOVEMBER 22ND, 1001.

"There goes the last of our orbital defenses," said Lt. General Jonah Nowitski, the commander of XXXXI Heavy Corps, of which Brigadier General Samuel Baggett's Three Eighty Fourth Heavy Infantry Division was part.

Baggett looked at the holo above the tactical table of his HQ bunker, seeing the last of the defense satellites the Fleet had left in orbit blinking for a moment before fading. The icons approaching the planet were still there, though the orbital satellites had scored some hits while that Fenri fleet was on final approach.

"Seems like such a waste to have put them there in the first place," came the deep voice of Major General

Lanbardran, the Phlistaran commander of the One Ninety-fifth Heavy Infantry Division, which, along with the Forty-third Armored Division, made up the Corps that had attacked this planet. "They are so fragile, and fleeting. Just targets for the enemy to knock down."

Baggett agreed. The satellites lacked even the defenses of the larger forts, while their only real striking power was in the missiles that they carried. Even a near miss by a powerful warhead would take them out. But they had been all the Fleet had been willing to leave behind when they bugged out. *With the promise that they would return*, he thought, wondering how much truth there was in that oath.

"The enemy is six hours from orbital insertion," said the Corps Commander, whose command was only at half strength as it was. "I intend to hit them hard as soon as they start landing operations."

That was the standard tactic to oppose an invasion. Shore batteries, missiles, lasers, particle beams, even projectile cannons, waiting, powered down and in hiding, until the enemy ships started to pump out their assault shuttles. That was when the enemy would be at their most vulnerable, with openings in cold plasma fields. Still, those planetary guns could only count on getting in a couple of shots before they were taken out by kinetics. Really, the only defense against an enemy fleet was another fleet, and theirs was nowhere in evidence.

Baggett shook his head as he looked at the display of ground assets they had. Enough to sting that enemy, if not stop them. And he wondered how heavy the enemy response would be. *Probably heavy as hell*, he thought, looking at his secondary and tertiary command positions, his out if they discovered this position. *And if they knock out the Corps and other division commanders, I get to move up rank again*, he thought. *Not that I really want corps command. Hell, I really didn't want division command, not at the price the Major General had to pay.*

"When can we expect fleet support?" asked Major General Natasha Romanov, a distant cousin of the Emperor, but, from what Baggett could tell, a woman who had gained her rank honestly. It was a stupid question, of course, since Nowitski had no answer, and everyone knew as much. But it was the same question that Baggett wanted to ask, and he was sure Lanbardran as well.

"From the number of troop transports the enemy has in their force, my intelligence staff estimates we will be facing at least six heavy divisions, or as many as fourteen lighter formations, replied the Corps Commander, ignoring the question."

So at best we'll be outnumbered four to one, thought Baggett. *About proper odds to take a planetary surface, especially when they have the high ground of orbit. And there's no telling what Marines the warships carry, and how many they might be willing to deploy. Probably all of them, if it allows them to take the planet.*

"I think we have done as much planning as we can, since our next step will depend on the enemy's," said the Lt. General. "I have looked over all of your contingency plans, and approved them."

Baggett nodded again. He had tried to come up with every response he could think of to every action the enemy might pursue. That was staff work that he did not have a lot of experience with, being as he had been a battalion commander a year before. It had been on the job training to try and master the most basic of general staff training, and he was thankful that the corps commander had looked over and approved his dispositions and responses to enemy action.

"I will let you people get back to making your last minute plans," said Nowitski, looking out of the holo at each of the division commanders. "It has been an honor serving with you. From this moment on, we will go to landline and short range transmission only. So I will only contact you if it is vital to the battle plan."

The holo died after the CO said those words, and Baggett made a mental note to make sure that his division was also on tight com discipline, at least until the battle was joined and the jammers came online. It wouldn't do for the still distant enemy to get a fix on his division's transmissions, and hit them with kinetics as they were inserting into orbit.

Chapter Three

Thus it is that in war the victorious strategist only seeks battle after the victory has been won, whereas he who is destined to defeat first fights and afterwards looks for victory. Sun Tzu

THE *DONUT*. NOVEMBER 22ND, 1001.

"So what in the hell do we do with this thing?" asked Cornelius, looking at the large container that held an explosive device of a magnitude he really couldn't comprehend.

"We sure as hell can't disarm it, can we?" said Jimmy Chung, standing beside him.

There was the Naval Commando, Petty Officer Satrusalya, standing with them, as well as another Secret Service Agent and a civilian who had been dragooned for his expertise on this part of the station.

"If we had negative matter," said Cornelius, shaking his head.

"But we don't," yelled Satrusalya, glaring at the bomb. "And it's no use talking about what we don't have."

Chung's eyes unfocused for a moment, the sign of a link. "We can get some more negative matter here. But it will take a while."

"How long?" asked Cornelius, who had seemed to have taken command of the group by dint of leading the assault that had gotten them here.

"Fifteen minutes. A half an hour. Maybe more."

"We aren't going to have more than five minutes, Government Man," growled Satrusalya, glancing over at Chung.

Ten at the most, thought Cornelius.

We need to get this thing off the station," said the PO, pointing to a hatch in the floor. "Where does that lead to?"

"There's a storage room underneath here," said the civilian, a Doctor Boudreaux. "It fronts the bottom part of the station."

"Then that's what we need to do," said the Naval Commando. "Drop this bitch into the bottomless pit, and let the hole take care of it."

"Sounds like a plan," said Cornelius, looking around. "Anyone got any idea of how to move this damned thing."

"I think I can come up with something," said Boudreaux, moving to the hatch, which was more than large enough to accommodate the bomb. He started working the controls to the hatch while looking up at the other men. "I might need some cover, if the room under here has Cacas in it."

Fortunately it didn't, and the scientist moved down the ladder that connected the edge of the hatch to the floor, a Ranger leading the way, two Agents following. Cornelius stood by the bomb and waited, afraid to leave it, lest something come along and take it from him. He tapped into the com link and found that his fear was not unwarranted. There were still Cacas in the area, though busy with the Imperial Marines they were trying to contain. *Which doesn't mean some of them won't think of the bomb and come to check on it. Especially when no one answers their com calls from this area.*

The scientist came running back after climbing the stairs, a stout device held in his hands that he didn't seem to be having any difficulty moving. Following him were the other three men, each with a similar device in hand.

"What are those?" asked Cornelius, as the scientist attached his near the front side of the container.

"Antigravs," said the man, supervising the installation of the second unit near the front, while Satrusalya made sure the other two were secured to the rear. "They make it much easier to move objects in the cargo areas. Activating, now," he said, pushing a button on the first one he had attached.

The heavy bomb rose slightly into the air, now a couple of centimeters above the floor.

"Help me get it to the hatch," said Boudreaux, grabbing the handle on the unit and lifting.

Cornelius grabbed another handle, and four men pushed the bomb toward the hatch. The antigravs took all the weight, but the massive device still had all of its mass, and they had to maneuver it carefully, not allowing it to build up too much momentum as they got it near the opening. It still overshot some, their combined strength unable to slow it in time, and with some grunts they pushed it back till it was over the opening. The Lieutenant breathed a sigh of relief as he saw that the hatch was just big enough to accept the bomb. They could have always turned it on its end, but that would have been a trial and error proposition, and one he really didn't think they had time for.

Four men went down and accepted the bulk of the bomb handed to them. They lowered it to the floor of the lower chamber, and Cornelius jumped the five meters from hatch to floor, his augmented bones and muscles easily absorbing the shock. "What now?" he asked.

"There's an access hatch over there," said Boudreaux, pointing up the chamber. "We'll have to put the bomb through lengthwise. Otherwise, it won't fit."

"And is that hatch an airlock, Doc?" asked Satrusalya, frowning.

"I don't think so," said the scientist, his eyes widening. "Oh, crap. What the hell am I thinking?"

"What's the problem?" asked Cornelius, looking from face to face.

"If we open that hatch, we expose this compartment to space. And none of us have suits."

"Well, shit. Is there another place we can push this bitch out of?"

"There's a hangar for maintenance craft about a kilometer up the ring," said Boudreaux.

"We don't have time for that," blurted Cornelius. "We've got to get it out of here, now."

"If I can have one volunteer, I think I can wrestle it out," said the PO.

"Without a suit?" asked the incredulous scientist.

"I've done it in training," said the large man, nodding his head. "Not really pleasant, but doable. And if we don't do it now, we won't have the chance later."

"I guess it's my job," said Cornelius with a sigh, not really looking forward to doing what the man was talking about. "Everyone else out of the room. Now."

"Good luck, Ranger," said Chung, just before he jumped out the hatch and closed it behind him.

"What do you want me to do, PO?" he asked Satrusalya, wanting to get this over with before his nerve broke.

"Help me wrestle this thing over to that hatch," said the man. "We'll need to turn it on end to fit it out. I think it'll fit, but if not, we'll have to widen it with the laser cutters we brought along. How are your nanobubbles? Have you had a refill lately?"

"About a month ago," said Cornelius, thinking of the small diamonoid spheres that contained pressurized oxygen, floating through his bloodstream. They were standard equipment for all Imperial military personnel, allowing them to supply their muscles and nervous systems with oxygen in a hostile environment. At full charge they could supply a human with an hour of breathing gas. And a month after charge they would still be at ninety five percent capacity. "The last time I used the system was in training. And we were under water."

"Well, this is going to be very different from water, Lieutenant," said Satrusalya with a frown. "In fact, the one thing you don't need to do is hold your breath. With our augmented bones and muscles, there's not really much chance that you'll rupture a lung. But, just to be safe, blow out everything in your lungs as soon as the air starts getting sucked out."

"Can we lower the pressure to a vacuum before we open the hatch."

"Probably," said the PO. "But it could take some time. This kind of room was never intended to act as an emergency airlock. It was intended to be opened to space in a more sedate manner, and only when necessary."

"We don't have time for that," agreed Cornelius, grabbing hold of the antigrav handle. "Order the system to start cycling the air anyway. Any reduction of pressure differential has to help."

The other man grunted in surprised agreement as he grabbed the handle of another antigrav. "You aren't so dumb, for a grunt," said the man with a laugh as they moved the massive container toward the hatch.

"I'm not sure about that," said Sean, returning the laugh as they moved the bomb along slowly, not wanting to let its inertia get out of hand. "After all, here I am on a suicide mission with a stupid Spacehead."

Both men laughed, the camaraderie of facing death together drawing them closer. As they neared the hatch, they started to swing the bomb casing until its cylindrical shape pointed down. And now it was obvious that the bomb was not going to fit. Not by much, only a few centimeters on each side of the slightly oblong weapon, trying to fit it through the circular hatch.

"We'll have to open the hatch and cut," said the Commando, setting the antigravs to station keeping, a setting would keep it in place no matter the forces pulling on it, as long as they weren't too severe. *Can you hear me on your link?*

Because we aren't going to be able to talk to each other when this chamber evacuates, he thought. *Loud and clear,* he sent to the other man.

Then bond a handhold to the deck and hold on, said Satrusalya, doing the same himself, putting a handle shaped object that had been made for just this purpose and setting the nanites on its ends to bond to the hull metal.

Opening hatch now, said the Commando, reaching over and keying in the safety code that overrid the system that was set to keep the hatch closed with unsuited people in the chamber. The hatch slid open swiftly and air started rushing out.

Sean opened his mouth, letting the air in his lungs rush out as well, sliding his body along to the hole, the head of the laser cutter in his right hand while his left kept a death grip on the handhold. He looked through the hatch for a moment, down at the distortion in space that was the black hole. The light of the stars behind it were bent around, forming a ring of light circling the dead stellar mass. It was the most frightening thing he had ever seen, a mass that could swallow a planet, even a star.

Most black holes were surrounded by deadly radiation, the result of their accretion discs and the matter that constantly fell into them. This black hole had been swept clean of any and all debris larger than molecular dust, and had very little in the way of radiation, other than that produced by the natural virtual particles of Hawking radiation. The station itself was protected by electromag fields.

We could have erected a cold plasma field here, he sent to the Commando as he shifted back a little and fired up his cutter.

Not enough time, sent back the other man, his own laser cutting into the hard alloy of the hatch frame.

Fortunately, they did not have much cutting to do, as the hard alloy of frame and hatch were very difficult to cut. In a moment it was done, and Cornelius got to his feet without the pressure of flowing air to push him out. Nor was there any air in his lungs, which hurt like a bitch. His vision was slightly blurred from the pressure of the fluid inside pushing against the tissues. His joints ached, a symptom of the bends, the nitrogen in his blood bubbling out due to the lack of pressure around him.

Let's get it out, sent the Commando over the link. *Here, help me.*

Cornelius nodded and grabbed hold of an antigrav,

pulling the weapon down, breathing a mental sigh, the only one he was capable of at the moment, as the cylinder slid through. There was a bit of resistance, while both men pulled with straining muscles until it pushed through the obstruction.

The bomb fell through, dropping away. Satrusalya had set the antigravs to then go to the opposite setting once they were through, pulling them toward the greatest gravity source in the region, the black hole. In an instant the bomb was speeding toward the black hole, where it would either be swallowed up with a blip of radiation, or explode too far from the station to do any damage.

He was admiring his work when the Cacas blasted through one of the doors and atmosphere came screaming back into the chamber. Enough to propel him through the hatch and into space, to start the long fall toward the hole that would crush him out of existence.

*   *   *

"That's the third one, Doctor Yu," said the Marine General commanding station security.

The Director of the *Donut* Project looked at the schematic that showed the device falling from her station toward the black hole, an object a hundred gigaton explosive device would not even affect.

"Are, are the people who pushed it off the station OK?" she asked, feeling rising anxiety at the fate of Jimmy Chung, whom she had not been able contact for the last ten minutes. Not that such was surprising, since the station com links were overloaded with vital traffic.

"They took severe casualties, ma'am," said the General in a low voice. "Both my Marines, and the ad hoc force we sent in from the other side."

Ad hoc meaning the on leave special ops troops, and Jimmy's people. "Thank you, General," she said, looking at the man's grim face.

"We're still hoping we can get to the last one before it goes off," said the General, the expression on his face showing he really didn't believe that would happen. "We...."

The holo went blank for a moment, while warning klaxons started sounding across the control room that fronted Yu's office. She jumped up from her desk and ran into the room, her eyes darting around the chamber at the multitude of stations with screens up, their operators staring intently at the scenes being presented there. Some of those scenes were from sensors along the curve of the station, looking toward the area the Ca'cadasans had taken. A bright point had appeared there, toward the center of the width. Large pieces of hull flew from the area, heading toward the black hole.

They detonated the last bomb, thought the Scientist, staring at the large trivee scene that had appeared over the high wall of the chamber. The bright area expanded, moving kilometers to all sides of the blast. It kept growing, until it had encompassed a circle ten kilometers on the underbelly of the station. And another schematic showed the internal damage, reaching out five more kilometers. The schematic showed that the central cable, a kilometer thick of hard but flexible carbon strands, had been severed, over a kilometer if its length simply gone.

The station shuddered, the shock wave finally reaching their area, and more warnings went off. "We're being pushed off our optimal orbit," called out one of the control room crew.

"Take control of the grabbers," ordered the supervisor, the best man they had for this job, called up as soon as the emergency struck. "We need to get this girl under control."

Lucille looked up at another schematic, this one against the wall over the entrance to her office. It showed the circular form of the station, and the black hole in the center, and two other circles. One was the optimal orbit of the station, the other the point of no return, the point at which the station could no longer recover from a destabilization. And due to the push of the massive explosion, they were drifting that way.

*   *   *

Cornelius really had no hope of making it back to the station. He was drifting toward the hole, not at the acceleration of the bomb, which had the efforts of its antigrav units pulling it toward the gravity well. But he was picking up speed.

The big objects coming out of space, silhouetted against the bulk of the *Donut*, looked like angels in his eyes. The two Marines grabbed him, one on each arm, and started to boost back to the station. A couple of seconds into the boost the heavy battle armor suits closed in around him, cutting off his view of the station.

What the hell, he thought, as a bright light shone around the edges of the suits. *The one we didn't get,* he thought, thankful for the protection of the heavy armor and their electromag fields. A couple of objects flew by at high velocity, really just streaks, and one of the suits jerked as something slammed into it. Nothing too bad, as both suits kept boosting back to the station. *And if it had hit me, I would definitely be dead by now.*

It took several minutes, well within Walborski's

time frame for continued oxygenation from his nanobubbles. Still, he was feeling the effects of the vacuum on the rest of his body. *But I'm going to make it, Devera, honey*, he thought, seeing the approaching station as the suited Marines turned until they were again beside him.

The airlock door closed behind him as he and the Marines settled to the floor, and air hissed into the small chamber. Cornelius pulled in a deep breath, and almost vomited as the pain shot through his lungs.

"Take is slow, Ranger," said one of the Marines over his suit speaker. "The alveoli of your lungs have been damaged some by the exposure to vacuum. You'll need to replenish the liquid layer in your lungs in order to exchange gases again."

Cornelius simply nodded, unable to speak, while the inner door opened. The Marines helped him in, while a Naval Medic ran up and started to inject him with meds, nanites and nutrients. They helped him to a seated position on the floor, and the Medic handed him a vaporizer bottle and told him to start inhaling the vaporized water.

"I thought we had lost you, LT," said Satrusalya, coming up and sitting next to him, a vaporizer in his hand as well.

"I have a confession to make," said Cornelius in a hacking voice. "I'm still a cadet lieutenant at the Academy."

"Well, you're an officer to this Spacehead, Ranger," said Satrusalya, giving Cornelius his hand. "I would serve with you any day."

"And the Emperor will sure be glad to see you made it as well, Walborski," said Jimmy Chung, walking up to the pair.

"You know the Emperor?" asked the now wide eyed Commando.

"The Emperor pinned two Imperial Medals of Heroism on this man himself," said Chung. "He may just get a third one for this one. As might you, Satrusalya."

"I'll put in the word myself," said Cornelius. "What you did in that room took balls."

"Says mister big testicles to me," said Satrusalya, with a laugh. "But I'll take it."

*　　*　　*

The blast of the one device, bigger than anything ever seen in Imperial space not of natural origin, vaporized the cable along a one kilometer length, as well as the outer hull for five kilometers in each direction. Five kilometers further on large pieces of that hull flew off into space, to fall into the black hole within minutes. Internal divisions, floors, walls, bulkheads, were also vaporized for several kilometers into the station, along with everything that was contained within those chambers. Ten kilometers further everything was smashed, machinery ripped apart, people pulped. Some of the blast moved through openings, tram tunnels, lift shafts, spreading the fury in seemingly random directions. In some sections, thirty kilometers from the blast, all organic forms were vaporized, while across a bulkhead there was no effect. In several places the top of the station blew out.

The region affected was more than the area of ten thousand battleships, an area almost beyond comprehension, though only a tiny portion of the enormous station. On the outer areas of the devastation robots and emergency personnel went to work containing the damage. In the area of total devastation there was nothing to be done, and over ten thousand sentient beings were gone, mostly Ca'cadasan commandos and human Marines. And, of course, the station had been pushed off kilter by a blast that none of the designers had ever envisioned.

*   *   *

"I think I'm going to lose her," yelled out the Tech that was supervising the grabber array on the *Donut*. The station was moving toward the point of no return, the section opposite the blast shifting closer to the black hole, as the section nearest the explosion drifted out under the impulse of the force of the weapon.

"How much power are you giving the grabbers," said Lucille, running over to the man's station.

"One hundred percent," said the Tech. "All they'll handle."

Lucille looked up at the schematic, cursing under her breath. She looked back at the sweating Tech. "Give them one hundred and ten percent."

"That could burn them out," argued the Tech.

"And if we hit the hole, it doesn't matter if the grabbers are intact or not. Now give them everything you've got." *There's supposed to be some extra capacity built into the units*, she thought, praying that it was true.

"Giving them one hundred and ten percent," said the Tech, his fingers striking the panels and overriding the system. The power meters on the system climbed past the blue columns that indicated normal power, moving into the red zone that was the warning that too much was being asked of the millions of units.

The station continued to move on its path to disaster, everyone in the control chamber staring at the schematic. There was a shudder through the floor, not as sudden or strong as the one the explosion had caused, but in some ways more powerful. The fabric of the station stressing and straining under the multiple forces pulling on her.

"I'm losing some of the grabbers," yelled the Tech.

"How many?" yelled Lucille, glancing at the control panel.

"About point one percent," said the man. "With more going every second."

"Keep the power feed going," said Lucille, thinking of ordering another increase, weighing the odds in her mind. "One hundred and twenty percent," she ordered.

"We're going to lose more," blurted out the Tech, his fingers inputting the new orders.

We could lose several percent and still have an increase in power, she thought, *but is it enough?*

"I think it's working," yelled the Supervisor.

The column showing the percent of failed grabbers was climbing, passing one percent, then to two, then speeding up and hitting four. The remaining grabbers were still pulling at space harder than all of them would have at one hundred percent power.

And then the station barely moved away from the point of no return. Slowly at first, barely noticeable, then speeding up.

"Ease off a little of the grabber power when she crosses the fifty percent line," said Lucille, putting a hand on the Tech's shoulder.

More were overheating, but they would have to pass ten percent before that was a problem. They reached eight percent overheated when the station hit the halfway line, and the Tech pulled the power back to one hundred and ten percent, then to one hundred a few moments later.

"She's going to make it," shouted the Supervisor in glee. The station was speeding up, getting closer to the mark.

"Back them off to fifty percent," said Lucille. "I don't want her to rebound past optimal.

It took several more minutes for the station to slide into that optimal orbit, and only then did Lucille allow herself to feel the relief that they had saved the situation from falling into disaster.

"Setting grabbers for automatic station keeping," said the Tech, pushing several control panels, as the klaxons and flashing lights died.

"How many of these do I have to go through?" whispered Lucille. She turned to the Supervisor. "Get repair crews to work on the damaged cable and hull sections. I want us at one hundred percent integrity as soon as possible." *Which will probably take a couple of months, but we can be operational again in twenty-four.*

"Lucille," said a voice over her internal com link. "Are you alright?"

"God, but it's good to hear your voice, Jimmy Chung," she said over the link, a smile stretching her face. "I thought maybe I had lost you. Was getting rid of that bomb your doing?"

"I wish I could claim that it was me," said the Agent, his voice sounding as weary as she had ever heard it. "No, it was our legendary warrior. The man's a machine."

"Walborski, again," said Lucille, not really surprised at the answer. "Did, did he make it?"

"I don't know how," said Jimmy after a short chuckle. "I don't think he knows how to die. If he doesn't get another medal out of this, I don't know if anyone would ever deserve one again."

"Director Yu," said a voice interrupting on the com. "Priority call for you. It's the Emperor."

"I've got to take that call, Jimmy. But I can't wait to hear your tale." She cut the link and picked up the other call, anxious to give the man who ruled the Empire the good news.

Chapter Four

War involves in its progress such a train of unforeseen circumstances that no human wisdom can calculate the end; it has but one thing certain, and that is to increase taxes. Thomas Paine

CONGREEVE SPACE. NOVEMBER 22ND, 1001

Thank god, thought Sean, after he had gotten off the com with Director Yu. *If we had lost that station, I don't know what we would have done. We have to increase security on that thing, and fast.*

Sean got up from his chair, where he had been sitting, waiting anxiously for the news to come, good or bad. *What the hell am I going to do with that boy?* was his next thought, a smile on his face. *I've already given him two of our highest award for bravery, and I have a feeling that he will be earning more. The day the Cacas killed his wife was the day they birthed one of their worst nightmares.*

He thought for a moment, a difficult thing to do with his fatigue. *A knighthood in his immediate future. He can't refuse that. And at least a Golden Sun.* That was the second ranked medal in the Empire, and Sean thought Cornelius would probably gather several of them as well before he was through.

"I'm turning in," Sean spoke into the chamber's com system. "Do not disturb, unless it's something vital." *I have to delegate some of this stuff. Like Jennifer said, I have the best people possible in their positions, so it's about time I used them. And Len should be on his way in the next couple of hours. If anyone can handle the situation with the Fenri Empire, it's him.*

With that last thought the exhausted monarch left

the room, ignoring the bodyguards that fell in around him, and made his way to the nearest lift, looking forward to being able to close his eyes. And hoping he didn't have another dream to disrupt his serenity.

*   *   *

Jennifer had been exhausted after the battle, even though she had done nothing physical, other than staying awake and supporting Sean. But emotionally she had been overtaxed. Not that she was not used to stress, just a different kind. She had fought for people's lives in the rare situations where medicine actually had trouble preserving life, which didn't happen all that much in civilian life. The child she had saved from the ravenous fungus that had attacked him on Sestius, for example. Most often even a catastrophic mistake by a surgeon could be rectified by putting the patient into cryo, and later fixing the damage. And that was when nanites couldn't just be injected into the damaged area and put to work.

Military decisions were completely different, as she had learned. Ships that had been converted to plasma and small pieces, along with their crews, could not be placed in cryo. They could not be rebuilt. She had watched as those ships had been destroyed following the orders of her fiancé, and she had been able to tell from his expression that he felt every one of those deaths, knowing that they could not be avoided, and still feeling responsible for them.

She was having a nightmare about that battle, seeing Sean calling out orders to his people, trying to avert the disaster heading his way. That disaster was in the form of hundreds of Ca'cadasan ships, driving through their fire, accelerating, launching swarms of missiles as they closed into beam weapon's range. And

Sean was trying to come up with a solution, something to save his ship, and his love, his eyes looking over at her as he grimaced at the fate that awaited them both.

A hand on her back woke her from the nightmare, her breath hissing in at the start that the touch evoked. She started to turn, ready to fight whatever it was that was coming at her out of the night.

"Easy," said a gentle voice in her ear. "It's just me. You're having a bad dream."

Sean climbed into the bed and pressed his body against hers. She dismissed the dream from her mind as she concentrated on the warmth and scent of the man now next to her. With a shifting of her body she turned around to face her lover, her arms going around his body, feeling the hard muscle of his chest against hers, and corded strength of his back.

"How can you go through that?" she asked, looking into his eyes and seeing the pain that still resided there. "How can any of your people hold up to that."

"Because someone has to," said Sean with a head shake. "If we don't, then who will."

"You could stay in the capital, and let your senior officers handle the battles for you," she said, tightening her grip around him, feeling that if she didn't hold tight he would simply fade away. "You know, like most Emperors."

"I can't do that," he said, shaking his head. "I know, I have the wormhole coms to stay in touch. I could give orders from complete safety, but I won't. That would be unfair to the men and women I order into danger."

"I can't go through that again," said Jennifer, tears spilling from her eyes. "I'm not strong enough to watch so many die, and not be able to do anything about it."

"You're stronger than you think," said Sean after kissing the tears from her cheeks. "But you really have nothing to do but observe, and that's cruelty, plain and simple." Sean took in a deep breath, releasing it as if trying to clear tension from his body. "I don't want you to come on the next operation," he said, almost blurting out the words. "I know you want to be with me. But as you said," Sean said hurriedly, "this is pure torture to you. And it would make me feel better if you were safe."

Jennifer lay there for a moment, her hands caressing the back of her lover, while his own fingers gently played across her upper arms and shoulders. *I don't want to be away from your side. But I'm really accomplishing nothing by being aboard ship. Except to satisfy my own urges. And is that fair to all the other serving men and women in this fleet, who are separated from their own loved ones?.*

"I will agree to stay on Jewel with two conditions," she finally said, putting a finger to Sean's lips. "And by stay on Jewel, I mean most of the time. You will still need me to be your ambassador across the core worlds. Which, with the wormhole gates, shouldn't be too much of a hardship." Especially with her predilection for extreme nausea during hyper translation. Not that wormhole travel was pleasant, with its stretching of subjective time during transit. Just less unpleasant than ship travel.

"And what are your two conditions?"

"One," she said, tapping him on the lips with her right index finger. "You stay on board the biggest, baddest ship in the fleet, and surround yourself with bunches of other ships. After all, you wouldn't expect

Len or Taelis to lead from the front during a battle."

"I wouldn't," he started to say.

"Oh yes, you would," she stopped him in mid-sentence. "You have the mindset of a Medieval king, wanting to lead from the front so you can hit your opponent over the head with your mace, or sword, or some other silly ancient weapon. And they stopped doing that crap when firearms made the battlefield too dangerous for royalty. I've read my history, mister, so don't tell me that doesn't go through that anachronistic mind of yours."

"But, *Augustine* is a heavy warship. I need her firepower at the decision point of the battle."

"Then take another ship for your flag, you idiot," she said in exasperation. "Maybe a battle cruiser that could flee if necessary, though I'd feel better if you chose a standard battleship. And don't tell me that sets a bad precedent. Most fleet commanders through history have stayed away from enemy fire, when possible. At least those who grew up with any kind of tech. So, promise me you'll make the smart play, and stay out of close in combat."

Sean thought for a moment, then nodded his head. "OK, I can do that."

"And don't think you can just lie to me and do what you want," she said, a pouting expression on her face. "I have my sources. And with wormhole com, I can find out where you are."

"OK, I give up. I was thinking that, but I won't try to fool you."

"Good. Play games with me, and you will lose."

"Yes, ma'am," Sean said with a laugh. "And what's the second condition?"

"I want to get married. Not sometime in the

indefinite future, but now. Well, not on this ship, but as soon as we can get back to Jewel. And then I want to get pregnant, with your child. You have a succession to think of, you know, and the sooner you have an heir, the better, especially with your insisting on putting your Imperial ass into the hot zones."

Sean was silent for a moment, and Jennifer worried for a moment that she might have pushed him too far.

"We can be married in a week," he said with a smile. "That's kind of rushing things, but since we have the wormholes in place through most of the Core Worlds, I think we can get our guests to and from the ceremony on time."

"That would be wonderful," said Jennifer, with a thought through her implants disabling the sterilization protocols on the nanites in her ovaries. *But I'm not fertile, yet*, she thought, monitoring the state of her reproductive system in disappointment. *Of course they will make alterations to my child*, she thought, something that had caused her some trepidation in the past. But, since talking with the geneticists, she was now of the opinion that most of her genetic contribution would remain. It would be her child.

"Now," she said, kissing him on the lips and maintaining the connection till she was almost out of breath in her passion. "I know we can't conceive a child until we're home, so the geneticists can have a go at the zygote. But that doesn't mean we can't practice. If you're up to it." From the feeling of him against her, she was sure he was.

*   *   *

SECTOR III PACE, OUTSIDE OF FENRI SPACE.
NOVEMBER 24TH, 1001.

Len Lenkowski still didn't like traveling by wormhole, though he had to admit that it had a lot of advantages. The *Donut* was over a week's travel time from his ship by hyper VII, and *Anastasia Romanov* was only a hyper VI ship, which would have taken a month to make the same trip. That didn't include the sixty light hours of normal space they would have had to traverse within the gravity well of the hole, a trip of at least ninety hours travel time. Instead, he had been able to take one step and cover those multiple hundreds of light years. But the disorientation was unnerving, to say the least.

"Welcome aboard, Admiral," said the full Captain that had been sent to greet him, saluting the six star flag officer who had once had another star on his collar before his demotion to a combat command. She was a petite woman with Asian features, red hair, and green eyes.

"Thank you, Captain?"

"Hyori Gae, sir. I'm a native of New Seoul."

"And you are?"

"Admiral Kelvin's Flag Captain, sir. I was sent to escort you to the Admiral's flagship, *King Edward II*."

Lenkowski nodded, remembering the man that he had recommended himself to command the expeditionary force into Fenri space. *And what a joy it must be for a Fleet Admiral to have to greet the man who is there to take away his operational command. At least he will still retain a task group command within the fleet.*

"What kind of ship is *King Ed?*" he asked the pretty woman on the way out of the wormhole chamber to a tram. The Admiral stopped for a moment, and looked around at the station.

"She's a superbattleship," said the Captain. "Hyper VI. And no sir, none of the action occurred near here, from what I heard. The bombs were set about five thousand kilometers to spinward."

This thing has twenty-five million kilometers of circumference, and we have barely begun to use it, he thought as a tram decelerated into the station and its doors slid open. He followed the Captain into the tram and took a seat. Another man started to get on, and Gae held up a hand to keep the Marine from entering.

"I thought you might want to ask me questions about our dispositions, sir," explained the Captain after the door closed and the tram started on its way.

"I already have a pretty good idea what you have," he told the Captain. "There will, of course, be more coming once you get your end of the ship gate erected. But we will need to move the wormholes around, at least some of them. The ships coming through the gates won't have any, and some of them will be designated flagships of new task forces."

The Captain nodded her head and activated a flat comp she pulled from her belt pouch. As the Admiral talked, she made notations, then repeated his orders back to him to make sure she had gotten him correct.

She's a very efficient officer, he thought as the tram accelerated for some minutes, then coasted for ten before it decelerated into another station. *Maybe I should preempt her for my own staff.* He thought that over for a minute before dismissing the idea. His own staff would be following along in a couple of hours, and it wasn't fair to take away Admiral Kelvin's command, flagship and flag captain.

"We will have some army brigades coming through in their transports," said Lenkowski as they disembarqued and walked quickly to the next gate room.   "We'll want them assigned to the proper convoys, ready to offload when they reach the planet."

They approached the door to the gate chamber they wanted, this one guarded by a squad of Marines in full battle armor. All of the gates in this room led to ships or military installations, not to be accessed by the common traveler who might wander in. Len thought that there would soon be more guards on chambers like this, as well as upgraded security on all gate rooms. *We almost lost this thing due to not having sufficient security*, he thought as the guards scanned his DNA, then poked him with a needle for a deep scan, making sure he wasn't one of the shifters.

And I hope to God they catch that damned shape shifter that was impersonating Admiral O'Hara. He had been classmates with the real Fleet Admiral Benjamin O'Hara on Peal Island. He had never really liked the man, but he had been a competent officer, who had risen to his rank through merit and ability. And now he was most probably dead, since the damn shifters tended to kill those who they would imitate.

"This way, sir," said the Captain, leading the way to one of the gates, this one with a pair of Marines guarding it as well, as were about a dozen more portals that must have led to other flagships.

Len hesitated a moment after the Captain preceded him. *God, but I hate this. But I'll hate it whether I go through now or wait, so might as well do it.* He stepped through the portal, and once again experienced the stretching of time and space, feeling disoriented as he stepped onto the deck of the superbattleship at the other end.

"Admiral on the deck," yelled out a voice, and Len turned to see a line of officers waiting, hands raised to berets in salute. One wore the red beret of a ship's captain, and beyond them were a line of red coated Marines holding ceremonial rifles at the ready.

"Permission to come aboard, Captain?" asked Len, returning the salute.

"Permission granted, sir," said the Captain, dropping the salute as soon as Len had, then extending his hand. "Captain Vincent Oldenburg, commander of the *King Edward II.*"

"Named after an Earther,?" asked Lenkowski, trying to remember where he had heard that name before.

"Yes, sir. One of the Kings of old England," the man said with pride in the name of his ship. "Not the nicest man in the world, but a true warrior king."

"Is Admiral Kelvin aboard?"

"No, sir," said the Captain. "The Admiral moved his flag to the *Pharaoh Ramses I*, since he figured you would want *Edward* for your flag."

Len grunted a reply as he pulled up the ship on his link that the Captain had just designated. *Ramses* was also a superbattleship, twenty million tons of warship, same as *Edward*, and the largest class of ship he would have in this command. He would have liked to have a couple of the new dreadnaughts, a name he knew the Emperor despised. *Maybe we could call these ships heavy battleship, and redesignate the new vessels superbattleships.*

"Let me see your flag bridge. I want to have a look at the tactical holo." That was something he could do on his link, now that he was aboard the ship and officially in command of the fleet designated as Battlefleet Sector III. He stilled like to look at the full sized holo in its tank, though he scanned the dispositions on his link on the way to the flag bridge and its huge holographic tank.

"Your bridge, Admiral," said Captain Oldenburg, leading him into the large chamber, which had scores of stations, half of them manned at the time.

Lenkowski waved the men and women back into their seats as soon as they jumped to their feet. He would take the time to meet with them later, once they started on their way. Now, he wanted to see what he had and what he needed to do.

The holo showed the G4 star that was at the center of this system, as well as the eight planets that orbited around it. The fourth world was the system prize, one which had until recently been a border outpost of the Fenri. That world was green and blue, and with a thought the Admiral expanded it on the holo, looking at the shape of large continents sitting amidst deep oceans. A world they had freed from the Fenri, all of its slaves now free citizens of the New Terran Empire.

It would be so easy to just fortify this system and let them come at us, thought the Admiral. That the territorial xenophobe carnivores that were the Fenri would try to take this system back was a given. Such a plan would have the greatest chance of success. They could totally crush the bulk of the enemy fleet, with minefields, orbital fortifications, and well hidden fleet units that could engage when they wanted to.

The only problem was they had troops trapped behind enemy lines, a lot of soldiers. And the Empire was not about to leave them in that position. *So we have to fight our way there, relieve the Army, and defeat the enemy so totally that they are out of this war.*

He continued to look at the holo, moving his view out to beyond the hyper barrier, where the warships were gathered, almost a thousand of them, the remains of the original expeditionary force, with some reinforcements. And a couple of hundred ships that were recognizably not those of the Empire.

"Do my eyes deceive me, or are those Magravi ships?" asked the Admiral, looking at a battleship that, while built along general human lines, was still subtly different. The Empire supplied them with the tech they had needed to build up their own fleet, after their liberation from the Lasharan Autocracy.

"That they are, Admiral," said the Captain, nodding toward the ship the senior officer was studying. "They arrived seven hours ago, and we are expecting some Klashak as well."

Both were really unexpected additions to his order of battle. The plan had been for both alien forces to contain the Lasharans, but many in the Admiralty were sure that the religious fanatics were well and truly contained, after the total defeat of their fleet, and the merchant ships they had tried to use to smuggle guerilla fighters across the borders. Obviously, the two alien governments had thought they had more ships than needed for that task.

The Klashak were an interesting species, one of live bearing amphibians who required a humid environment to survive, whether that was on their planets, ships or suits. Klashak were physically strong and mentally agile, and had been valued slave labor to the Lasharans. Until the Empire had interfered, and taken all of the amphibians' systems away from the Autocracy.

The Margravi were even more interesting. A ten limbed insectoid race, their exoskeletons only allowed them movement on light gravity worlds. Their muscular systems required a higher level of oxygen than most species, and the number of worlds that suited their forms were limited.   Instead, they used other species as allies to farm their worlds, while they mostly inhabited great space habitats and asteroids, low gravity environments that allowed them freedom of movement.

The most unusual attribute of the insectoids was that they were a true group mind.   An individual Magrav was about as intelligent as a Terran cat, the old, unimproved variety. With their minds linked together with the radio emitting organs of their brains, they were frightfully intelligent.   The only weaknesses of the group mind was the limited range of their transmissions, and the susceptibility of their linkage to jamming.   On ships that was not a problem.   Their strength was that each military unit fought as a whole, with little regard to the fate of any single member of the swarm, as long as the mission was accomplished. The weakness to their organization was that the makeup of the mind changed according to its number of living members, and that makeup could change with illnesses and death. It was like a huge brained organism going into battle, and losing some of its mind, memory and processing power with every death.

Because of that difference from other species, Len knew he would have to think carefully about how he deployed the aliens.   That he would use them was a given. The insectoids were totally fearless, incapable of feeling any kind of individual sense of self-preservation. Only the species was important, and only the mission of the group was vital to its existence, as it affected the survival of the race.

About a light minute in from the flagship was the most important construct going up.   The frame was almost completed, three kilometers on a side, able to handle even the huge superfreighters that would be bringing materials to this area. Lenkowski looked at the information below the still uncompleted gate, seeing that the estimated time of completion was a little under three hours. *And then we can start bringing in ships from the Supersystem*, thought the Admiral. Many of those ships would come from the same force that had just won the battle against the Ca'cadasans, those with little to no damage. None would have wormholes on board, since it was considered much too risky to send ships through a wormhole gate with other holes aboard. Other ships could bring more wormholes out to this region, in about three weeks to a month, long after the operation had started, and hopefully finished, successfully. But the technology of wormhole gates would be primary to this battle, allowing communication between task forces, and in bringing major fleet forces to bear that could be sent back to the Supersystem after the battle to be redeployed for the next operation against the Cacas.

We'll be doing most of our planning on the way, thought Lenkowski, trying to will the gate to get finished faster, and of course failing to have any effect on its construction time.

"Show me to my office," he told one of the bridge officers, then followed the man to his day cabin just off the main corridor leading to the flag control room. The office was spacious enough for several admirals to work in, with holographic windows on the walls looking out over the local space, beyond the hull that was five hundred meters away from this most protected area of the ship. It had the feel of an observation room, without any of the drawbacks.

Len sat at the huge desk and opened the holographic control panel, getting to work on setting his dispositions and strategies for the attack. He already knew what was coming through the gate, and what he had in hand, and now his task was to come up with the best allotment of forces to get the job done with maximum damage to the enemy, and the least possible harm to his own fleet.

The time passed by quickly with the mental effort of work. So quickly that the Admiral was not aware of how much had gone by, until the com signal brought him back to the here and now.

"They're coming through, Admiral," said the voice from the flag bridge.

Lenkwoski didn't need to ask who they were. He got up from his desk after shutting down the holographic control panel, then headed up the corridor to the flag bridge. More of the stations were manned now, people monitoring the new arrivals and transmitting their gathering points to them. The central holo tank showed a couple of new icons moving from the gate to the outer system, identification text under each. A viewer on the forward wall was centered on the gate, and the next ship coming through.

It was a standard battleship, fifteen million tons, with the ID *Prince Walter Konev* underneath. It came through almost sedately, since there was no emergency on this end, and no one wanted a massive warship slamming into the frame of the gate. As soon as it was completely through, moving at a half kilometer a second, it accelerated away at a hundred gravities, clearing the vicinity of the gate at almost a kilometer per second per second. Moments later the nose of the next ship poked through, repeating the procedure as it headed off on the tail of the last vessel. The third battleship in that squadron came through soon after, then the first unit of the next group.

A couple of minutes later the first of the ships that Len had been waiting for with anticipation. A twelve million ton hyper VII fleet carrier that was not intended to engage other ships in close combat. No, each carried over a hundred inertialess fighters, just like the ones that had caused so much damage to the Cacas at the Battle of Congreeve. None of these ships had been blooded in that battle, but they were four more ships and attack wings that would gain their experience against the Fenri, before being later unleashed against the Cacas.

Two hours into the transfer the scout force started off, over a hundred battle cruisers, two hundred light cruisers and four hundred destroyers, the eyes of the fleet. They would sweep space in four task groups, each with one wormhole equipped flagship, giving Len near real time intelligence. Hopefully they would be able to blast through anything the Fenri tried to put in front of them. If not, they would at least fix the enemy forces so the main fleet could come up and destroy them in detail.

After four hours all of the warships that were going to come through had exited the hole, one every ten seconds on average, with a few longer breaks as new units maneuvered into place. Over fourteen hundred ships, predominantly heavier units. And Len looked over his new order of battle, over four thousand ships, besides the scout force. He figured the Fenri would still outnumber him in total units, but not in tonnage and firepower. And even if they did outnumber the humans in the last two categories, Len was still sure the New Terran Empire's tradition and tactical flexibility would carry the day.

The next half an hour was spent with the Fleet train coming through.   Freighters, superfreighters, antimatter tankers, missile colliers.   And ten assault ships, carrying three more heavy divisions, the relief force for the troops still trapped in the Fenri Empire. More ships would come later, troop transports, more freighters, and the ships that would escort them from here to Len's battle force.

"Fleet reports ready," said the Fleet Com Officer, looking back at Lenkowski.

"Is my staff aboard?" asked the Grand Fleet Admiral.

"Their shuttle is on final approach," said the officer. "They should be docking in three minutes."

"Order the first task groups to jump to hyper, then," said Lenkowski. "Let's go ahead and raise the curtain on this thing."

Moments after the order was transmitted the first task forces jumped to hyper. Minutes later the next TFs jumped, and after them others.

"Jumping now," came the voice of the ship's Captain over the com, moments after Len had been informed that his staff was on board. The hole in space opened up in front of *King Edward II*, and the twenty million ton ship left normal space, heading into harm's way.

Chapter Five

I am extraordinarily patient, provided I get my own way in the end.   Margaret Thatcher

CAPITULUM, JEWEL. NOVEMBER 25TH, 1001.

Samantha Ogden Lee sat at her desk and shook her head. *What next?*, she thought. *Isn't it enough to have to fight a war with the Lords, as well as with several enemies from without the Empire. Now they want me to put together an Imperial wedding. Just the security on that thing will be a nightmare.*

The wedding of an Emperor, or, in a few cases in the past, Empress, was just about the biggest deal there was in Imperial Society. The only thing that was bigger was a coronation, and they had just gone through one of those. Not only would Sean be legally bonding himself with Jennifer, making her the vessel of any heirs he would be bringing into the Galaxy, but she would be considered the Empress. Of course, if Sean died, she would not assume the throne. She would be the Empress Mother if there was an heir, or a Dowager Empress if there wasn't. Sean's closest living relative would be the next in line if there wasn't an heir.

The problem with an Imperial Wedding, at this time, was the people who would have to miss the ceremony due to wartime duties. Everyone and anyone would want a seat at that wedding, and some who would otherwise be automatic attendees would leave empty seats, which many would be fighting for. Security would also be a nightmare, especially with the shape shifters, the Yugalyth, added to the equation. Everyone would have to be checked out, and there would be more guards than were the norm, making the space even more dear.

The ceremony would normally be held in the Reformed Catholic Basilica in Capitulum, which could seat several hundred thousand people, while several million more waited outside to see the couple when they left the church. They could seat more people if they held the ceremony outside, perhaps on the palace grounds, or in a major stadium, of which the city had many. That would lead to even greater security problems, with the Emperor and his bride exposed to long distance fire. Technology could provide some protection, but would it be enough?

And the Lords will raise hell that the Emperor is marrying a commoner, she thought with a frown. *It doesn't matter that she has been given the title of duchess. They will still see her as a commoner, and the Emperor's choosing of her, and not someone from an old family line, as a collective slap in the face.*

Samantha sighed again, wishing she was still a serving Fleet officer. At least then she only had to worry about dying.

"You have a call from the Prime Minister, ma'am," said the voice of her assistant over the com.

"Haruko," said Samantha as the holo of the Prime Minister, Countess Haruko Kawasaki, appeared. "How goes Parliament?"

"Like herding especially obnoxious cats," said the small woman on the other end of the com. "Though I do have report a major triumph."

"The Archduke?"

""That's the one," said Haruko, nodding. "It seems he underwent a religious conversion while he was with the Fleet. He came back a full convert, and immediately attacked Countess Zhee and her clique in the Opposition Party."

"And Zhee? What was her response?"

"She was livid. The good Countess threatened to throw Marconi out of their party. Then she stormed out of the chamber after she called for a walkout."

"Shit. That doesn't sound good." Samantha was already having a lot of problems with the Opposition Party. With an angry Zhee stirring up trouble the problem might be rising to the proportions of a true crisis. *And I would sure hate to have to throw that clique into jail. Well, that's a lie. I would love to throw them all into a cell. But the problems would outweigh my pleasure.*

"Actually," said the other woman, her smile growing, "it was very good. Only about a third of the party followed her from the chamber. The rest stayed, in a show of solidarity with Marconi."

"So we broke her power base?" asked Samantha after a short laugh.

"Or we added to his," said Kawasaki, nodding. "She will never be able to muster more than forty percent of the vote for her platform, even if she can convince all the other parties who are her group's historical allies. It's more likely that she'll carry less than twenty five percent of any vote."

"So she won't be able to swing a No Confidence against Sean?"

"Not after what Marconi did after she walked out," said Kawasaki, smiling once again. The woman shut her mouth and continued to smile.

"Don't keep me in the dark, my dear," said Samantha finally, her anxious wish to know overcoming her desire to not play the Prime Minister's game.

"He asked to speak before the Lords. And he gave a speech that made him sound like Sean's greatest fan.

And a staunch supporter of the Fleet and Army. Marconi is a dynamic speaker, one of the reasons he was such a pain in the ass to us up to this point."

"Maybe we should ship some more of the Lords to the front lines," said Samantha, after a moment's thought. "If it doesn't convert them, it might at least get rid of a couple of the fools."

"And maybe Marconi should be the Prime Minister," said Haruko in a quiet voice.

"Why do you say that?"

"He's much more effective speaker," said the Prime Minister. "He has a much easier time rallying the troops."

"I'm not sure I'm ready to trust him that far, Haruko," said Samantha, choosing her words carefully. "You are someone I can trust. That Sean can trust. Plus, you aren't that bad at swaying a chamber yourself. So, no. I'm not letting you out of your job."

"I would prefer to serve where I am," said the Countess, a look of relief on her face. "And what about the *Donut*? I heard that the attack was foiled through official channels, but nothing about how much damage the Cacas caused."

"It was close. Too damn close, as far as I'm concerned. It will take months to repair all the damage. Maybe as long as a couple of years. But she'll be making wormholes again this time tomorrow, after they check out all the generating systems."

"That is good," said the Prime Minister, nodding. "I don't know what we would do without it."

"We lost communications with the Elysium Empire at the time of the attack," said Samantha, something she also was worried about. "The earliest we can expect a message through the hypercom link is late tomorrow," she continued, referring to the line of stations that sent com lasers through hyper VIII, moving the signals at one hundred and sixty thousand times the speed of light through that higher dimension as compared to normal space. Elysium was just over two thousand light years from Jewel, and the relay could send a message from one capital to the other in one point seven days. That had been considered blazing fast, until the wormhole system came along. *And we won't have that in place until we send another one by hyper VII ship to the Elysium capital, which will take weeks.*

"What do you think happened at the other end?" asked the Prime Minister, her eyes wide.

"I don't know, but it can't be good. Their end of the wormhole was on a heavily guarded station, so it would have taken a major assault force to take it. And estimates are that at least two thousand of the damned things came through from Elysium space. Add to that a blast of considerable proportions that came through the gate, and the fact that the Cacas were dealing in hundred gig warheads, and I have a bad feeling that something horrible has happened there."

"I hope they are OK," said the Prime Minister. "I have liked all of the Brakakak I have met."

"I hope they are too," said Samantha. *And not just for their sakes, though there is some of that sentiment as well. But they are powerful allies, and if the Cacas took them out, the fight becomes that much more difficult.* "I'll send you the news as soon as we get it."

"Please," said Haruko, looking at something off the holo for a moment. "I have to run, Regent. Another of those infernal meetings I'm expected to preside at. But we must schedule a lunch, just the two of us."

"I would love that, Countess," said Samantha, meaning every word. The woman was one of the few true friends she had. "If we ever get the time to do anything for ourselves."

The holo faded, and Samantha found herself once again going over the reports of her subordinates, the only way she could keep up with all the information that was flowing toward her from the lower levels of the government. *I wish I could read the original reports myself*, she thought, looking at a document on the progress of the Bolthole Project. *Instead of something filtered through others. But that is the price of assuming a position of high power in an organization like an Empire.*

*   *   *

ELYSIUM SPACE.

What a flippin mess, thought Ambassador the Archduke Horatio Alexanderopolis, looking at the crater on the outskirts of the Brakakak city that lay a hundred kilometers north of the capital. The large piece of station, at least a couple of hundred thousand tons, had come through the atmosphere, propelled by the explosion of the enormously powerful warhead, and slammed into the ground. *At least it didn't hit the center of the city*, thought the human, who had been the Ambassador to this Empire for over four decades, learning the language and customs of the majority avians like few other non-Brakakak.

The damage was still horrific. Buildings into the city for more than two kilometers had collapsed, parks and open areas incinerated many kilometers further in. The strength of modern building materials underscored the fury of the strike. The buildings could have withstood a close blast by a megaton device with only surface scarring. To completely collapse them took quite the ground strike, on par with the most powerful of ship launched kinetic weapons.

"How many?" he asked the Brakakak who sat beside him in the transport.

"Three hundred thousand here," answered High Lord Grarakakak, the leader of the Elysium Empire. "We estimate about a hundred thousand of them were children."

The Ambassador winced at that figure, knowing that the birdlike creatures loved their children more than anything. And were willing to go to any lengths to protect them.

"The total across the world, including the station, is just under ten million," continued the leader of the Empire, now sole ruler since they were at war. The soulful brown eyes of the avian looked into those of the human for some moments, before looking back out over the city. "We have evidence that the Knockermen were involved in getting the foul creatures onto our station. Somehow, they captured one of our light cruisers and used it to get the assault force onto the station. And while the Cacas were taking the wormhole gate and getting their force to your station, the Knockermen moved a device that must have been provided them by the big aliens to take out our space dock, and the ships in it."

"What are you going to do about the Knockermen now?" asked Horatio, almost afraid of the answer. He was hoping that this attack, much as he regretted it happening at all, would galvanize the Brakakak to fully commit to the war against the Ca'cadasans. Now it looked like they might be forced to concentrate on their internal problems once again.

"Oh, they will pay for this," said the grim faced High Lord. "You can count on that. They can count on that. But we must find the ones who are responsible. We are not barbarians, to simply go in and kill sentient beings indiscriminately. We will teach them a lesson, and punish the guilty, while protecting the innocent."

I was afraid of this, thought the human, looking away, back out of the transport at the devastation outside. Not even planned devastation, more of an accident than anything else. And now the angry Brakakak would put most of their effort into finding and punishing the rebels in their own Empire. "And what will you do with your fleet? Recall it?"

"No," hissed the angry avian, surprising the Ambassador. "These creatures who brought these weapons into our home system must also be punished. The fleet we have dispatched to aid your Empire will continue to their destination, and will continue on to whatever deployments your Admiralty decide upon. We will, in fact, send more ships to you, since whatever actions we will take against our internal rebels will involve mostly lighter vessels, cruisers on down, and ground forces. So we will send you more battleships."

"That, would be most welcome, Lord Brakakak."

"And what of your station?"

"With the wormhole down, we won't know until a message comes over the hyperwave link," said the Ambassador, his anxiety level spiking as he thought about what might happen to their war effort without the wormhole generators.

"Pray the Gods it is still intact," said the High Lord, giving a very human head shake, such as he had learned from his time with the Ambassador. "But even if it is not, we are sure that you will find a way. Your people are most innovative, and they will come up with something."

Horatio looked over at his old friend. *I hope you are right, High Lord. But I think we need that station, and if they brought some warheads onto the* Donut *like the one that destroyed your dock, I fear that it may be gone.*

* * *

CAPITULUM, JEWEL.

Countess Esmeralda Zhee slammed her fist against the arm of her chair once again, causing all the people in the room to flinch. She was the smallest person in the room, barely a meter and a half tall. With a different skin tone and finer features she could have been mistaken for a Malticoran. As a countess, she was not of the highest social rank in the chamber either. But she held political power well beyond that of anyone else in the gathering, due to over a century sitting in the Lords' chamber, dealing and making connections. *And now that damned Archduke has pulled half of my political following away from me. I will not stand for that.*

"There really is not a whole lot we can do," said Duke Walther Konig, frowning. "I know none of us want to admit it, but there it is."

Zhee looked from face to face, seeing no hope in any of them. *It's not that we're not patriots*, thought the Countess, who had dueled politically with three Emperors, including this new upstart. *We are the greatest of patriots, working for the good of the Empire, trying to bring the most competent leadership to the rule of the realm. Our own.*

"I am not willing to accept that there is nothing we

can do," said Zhee, scowling at her last supporters. "This Emperor is going to lose this war, and none of us, the entire species, can afford that loss."

"He just won a great victory," said Konig, glaring at Zhee. "I've studied what I have been able to gather from the reports coming back from that battle. Sean did not always make the best of decisions, but his generalship was competent. And, seeing as how he is so young, I am sure he will only improve."

"If we are still around by that time," screamed Zhee, pointing her finger at the Duke. "Now, are you on my side, or theirs."

Konig smiled and stood up, looking around the table. His gaze fell last on Zhee. "And you think you would make a better leader than Sean?" he said with a laugh. "You, who have no military experience. Who have no claim to the loyalty of the military, who you treat as idiotic servants who need to kiss your ass. I'm through with you, Zhee."

"I'll break you, your Grace," said Zhee, standing up to her full height, something which was not intimidating in the least. "I'll make sure that you are thrown out of the Lords."

"I have a hereditary seat, Countess," said the Duke with a barking laugh. "It will remain in my family for life. Now, have fun sitting around playing your power games. I will be talking with the people who actually have the best interests of the Empire at heart. And not a bunch of elitist fools who only care about themselves." The Duke gave the room a nasty gesture with his hand and walked from the chamber.

Zhee stared after the man, realizing that she had lost yet another powerful supporter. She was stunned for a moment, before her personality asserted itself, and she only felt hatred toward everything and everyone who stood in her way. *I will get back at them. At all of them, no matter what it takes, or how long.*

Chapter Six

Every soldier thinks something of the moral aspects of what he is doing. But all war is immoral and if you let that bother you, you're not a good soldier. Curtis LeMay

FENRI SPACE. NOVEMBER 26TH, 1001.

Brigadier General Samuel Baggett winced as he watched another kinetic warhead come down, this one a strike to one of the refugee camps they had established to protect the former slaves of the Fenri. Some of those slaves had told him that such would happen, that the Fenri, having their property taken from them, would now want to destroy that property. But the humans and their allies hadn't really believed it. And now millions of those slaves had died, with over a billion more at risk.

And we really don't have any way to protect them, thought the soldier, looking at a feed from the area. It was heartbreaking, to see so many sentient beings of all ages lying dead on the ground, not counting the thousands who must have been vaporized by the strike. *We didn't have bunkers to put them in, and the few remaining Fenri underground shelters had filled up too fast. Dammit, we needed our own bunkers for our people.*

He felt responsible for what was happening to these people. They had not asked for the New Terran Empire to come in and make them the targets of their former masters. They had freed the slaves as more of an afterthought of taking the planet. But in freeing them, they had become responsible for them.

"Assault shuttles are on approach," came a call

over the com net.

Baggett closed his eyes for a moment, dismissing all concerns for collateral damage. *I've got a job to do.*

The enemy had come into orbit several hours before, fighting the few shore batteries the Lt. Gerneral Nowitski had allocated to challenge them. It had not been enough. The humans hadn't really expected it to make much of a difference. The enemy had taken out the orbital defense satellites at range, what few had been left, in an uneven exchange of fire, then closed to far orbit to start pounding the planet with kinetics. Fifteen laser batteries and a dozen missile platforms had fired on them, getting a couple of hits that did some damage, before being taken out from space. The problem was, even though the planet was now covered with electronic warfare jamming that made it almost impossible for space based sensors to look through, and holographic projections to spoof visual, once a weapon fired on orbital platforms, it could be targeted and hit.

The refugee camps had just been too damned big to hide, and the holographic projectors had been in too short supply to cover all of them completely. It may have seemed cruel to not cover them, but the mission came first, and the cover and concealment of the soldiers was a mission priority.

Now hundreds of shuttles were flying from the Fenri ships, carrying loads of troops. Accompanying them were hundreds more craft, orbital to atmosphere fighters and ground attack ships that would try to protect the shuttles, then try to gain air superiority and support the troops.

Baggett looked at the scene on his HUD, then assigned the ground batteries he wanted to engage them with.   The order went out, weapons were given missions, and the guns and missiles opened fire.

High in the atmosphere, dozens of craft exploded, spilling armored troopers into the sky. Not all the hits were to troop carriers, and more than a dozen fighters and attack ships were destroyed as well, raining down their pieces from the sky in fiery trails. The human weapons got off another shot, or sometimes two, before lasers and particle beam strikes came down from above, taking most of them out. The shore guns had all been set on remote control, their crews not on board, so there were few human casualties. Not all of the guns were targeted and destroyed, and several survived to get off more shots. The first wave of the enemy suffered over ten percent casualties, but the survivors came on, and more came in a second wave.

Baggett tasked the next battalion of guns, tank like lasers, particle beams and projectile weapon projectors, and even more mobile missile batteries. They also took out two and a half times their number in enemy craft before being targeted and destroyed.

And that's it, thought the Brigadier, looking at the casualty figures for his antiair assets scroll across his HUD, and seeing no functional weapons. *Now all we have left are suit fired weapons, and they aren't going to do anything to aircraft at altitude.*

"All soldiers, prepare for close assault," he ordered as the shuttles came lower. His suit comp, much more advanced than those of most of his subordinates, started tracking the paths of the shuttles in his area, with the help of data being sent down by Corps. The comp crunched the data and assigned probabilities to landing zones. Baggett examined the probabilities and made his guesses depending on them, then sent the information to his brigade and battalion commanders.

The shuttles dropped lower to the ground and streaked at less than a thousand meters altitude toward the flat areas where they would disgorge their troops. Vehicle and suit mounted antiaircraft weapons opened fire, taking one shot and moving, shoot and scoot. Most of the shots were misses, but several craft in each attack formation went down trailing smoke.

Baggett grunted in satisfaction as twelve of the fifteen assault zones that his comp had suggested, and that he had approved, turned out to be accurate sites, while three others that had been considered low probability turned out to be targets.

"They're coming in," he called into the com. "All units are weapons hot. Give them hell."

The shuttles dropped their troops over the landing zones, the small forms of armored Fenri falling on grabbers out of the aircraft and lowering themselves to the ground. Particle beams and hyper velocity rockets reached into the air to swat many of the enemy down. The Fenri fired back, engaging the humans at a major disadvantage, out in the open, while the Terran troops shot from cover. Hundreds of Fenri dropped heavily from the sky in smashed and broken suits, while more were released, including the first mecha of the invasion, five meter tall suits piloted by Fenri, their version of light attack vehicles.

Fenri reached the ground, as they had been bound to given their numbers. The ones on the ground started to assault the human positions around them, not making much headway, but at least distracting the humans from firing on the dropping infantry, allowing more of them to make it to the ground and feed the assault.

"Tank battalion," yelled Baggett into the com, as his infantry closed with the enemy to engage in very close combat. "Prepare to assault with task groups on these axes, at points alpha, delta, gamma, omega and epsilon." He looked at the areas he had specified, wishing he had enough tanks to hit all the landing zones, and realizing that he did not. *We'll just crush the ones we can, and work from there*, he thought.

    *   *   *

Lt. Jay Cummings checked out the terrain on the holographic plotting system of his Mark IV King Tyrannosaur. The one thousand ton monster was at one hundred percent operating capacity, and was thus the most dangerous war machine on the surface of the planet. With over a meter of the toughest carbon alloy known to the human race, and destroyer class electromag projectors, it was almost impossible to kill by anything not specifically made to do so. Unfortunately, there were things on and above the battlefield that were made to destroy vehicles such as this.

"All weapons go," said the gunner, in his own turret compartment to the right of the officer's.

Cummings looked at the schematic, satisfied that the main magrail cannon and its two coaxial particle beams were all goes. A quick look showed that the laser crosses on both sides of the turret, primarily defensive weapons, were also charged and ready.

"We ready, Moesta?" he asked the Staff Sergeant who was his second in command, and the one who would fight the tank if he were killed.

"Ready as we'll ever be, LT," said the woman from her compartment at the back of the turret. "Cold plasma is fully injected into the electromag field."

"Tank Charlie Two," said Cummings into the com. "Ready to rock?"

"You've got that right, LT," said the commander of the only other tank in the reduced platoon, which was missing its third unit, destroyed in an earlier battle. "Let's hit these bastards."

"Wait for the signal from company," cautioned the Lieutenant, looking at the tactical plot and seeing the other four tanks of the reduced company on the holo. They had started out with ten of the monsters, and Cummings was pretty sure that they would have even fewer after this action, no matter the outcome.

"All units, let's roll," came the call of the Captain over the com.

"That's it," yelled Cummings, feeling the combined rush of fear and excitement raise his adrenaline levels through the roof.   "You heard the man, second platoon. Let's roll."

Acknowledgements came from the other six crew members, then the commander of the second tank. The driver started them forward, using the company commander's vehicle as his guide. The Tyrannosaur accelerated ahead, reaching a hundred kilometers an hour within seconds. That was only half speed, but it was all they needed for this mission.

"We're being targeted," called out Moesta.   "I think we can expect some KE rounds."

"Evasive maneuvers," called out the CO.

At that command all of the vehicles went into seemingly random paths.   Adjusting their velocity, slowing down, speeding up, turning from side to side. Their jamming systems went to full out, adding to the interference that was already spoofing enemy sensors. Smoke ejectors added their mix to the atmosphere, meshing with the holographic projections that hid everything underneath from visual.

The ground shook underfoot, while a cloud of dirt and dust rose up into the sky, adding to the obscuration of the company. Another weapon struck, while a particle beam ripped through the cloud cover to rip a trench in the ground ahead. Cumming's tank lifted over the trench on grabbers, coming down on the other side and juking to the left just in time to avoid another kinetic weapon.

"Targets ahead," shouted out the CO. "All units. Take enemy under fire as they present. Fire at will."

"Target acquired," called out the gunner. "Round up. Firing."

The tank bucked as the main gun, telescoped to its maximum length, sent a penetrator down range at three hundred kilometers a second. It looked like a beam of light, fixing and smashing a large mecha six kilometers ahead. The twin particle beams fired a moment later, sending streaks of red fury into the enemy positions.

The hit mecha was still turning through the air in several pieces when the gun spoke again, hitting another mecha. Two more fired back, sending hypervelocity rockets at the tank. One hit straight on the frontal armor of the turret, bouncing away with an enormous clang. The other was hit by one of the defensive lasers and pushed off course, a clean miss.

The gun spoke again five more times while the tank closed the distance. Three killed mechas, including one massive machine that had to mass half that of the tank. The others flew through groups of enemy troopers, slicing through a dozen suits and killing more Fenri with the concussive effect of a hundred kilogram shell tearing them apart within their armor.

One of the tanks was knocked out by mecha fire, enough of the machines concentrating their heaviest weapons on the vehicle to stop it in its tracks, heavy turret spinning through the air above it. Another was caught by a near miss of a kinetic warhead that stopped its progress, just before a particle beam came down from orbit to shear through its tough armor as if it were paper.

Tanks rolled through the landing zone, all of their secondary weapons, laser crosses, defensive turrets, targeting anything that moved that was not of Imperial origin. Cummings' tank shuddered from the hits of weapons that would have killed a lesser machine. Even some hits from weapons that had an outside chance of killing a Tyrannosaur. They might have gotten bogged down in that close in fight, overwhelmed by an enemy that was able to surround them. But the company of heavy infantry took that moment to hit the distracted Fenri from the flanks, destroying all resistance. The carnivores were brave, to a point, but lacked the altruism that allowed humans to continue fighting, no matter the odds. They broke and ran, to be picked off by humans who destroyed their smaller groups.

The last vehicle killed belonged to the Company Commander, and after the four remaining tanks overran the enemy positions, Cummings found himself the sole remaining officer in a company that was more of a reinforced platoon. His second tank made it through as well. Good fortune?

We took out this landing zone, thought Cummings as he directed his company back to their assembly area, his drivers taking advantage of all the cover and concealment that was the obscured surface of the planet. Their prepared positions were waiting, and the massive vehicles slid under cover in the caves that were made up of the rubble of the city, powering down and preparing for the next mission.

*   *   *

Phlistarans were a mighty warrior people, while also paradoxically being a relatively peaceful species. They had fought wars before the humans had discovered their race, mostly in their more primitive stages. The eras of armored warriors charging the lines of their enemies to the glory of kings. They really didn't have cavalry and infantry. As dracocentaurs, each being was his own mount, they were a little of both, and their ancient art showed many scenes of charges that carried the day.

As they advanced in technology and moved into space, they were able to restrain their more primitive emotions, though they always lurked just below the surface. They had barely left their own star system when human ships came calling. They saw the writing on the wall, and assimilated themselves into the human Empire posthaste. Their loyalty to the humans had allowed them to gain advanced tech well before most alien species, and their service in the Imperial military had earned them trust beyond most others as well. And for five centuries they had treated the human Empire as an integral part of their own society.

"Prepare to charge," ordered the Phlistaran battalion commander as his unit lined up on the high ground overlooking the landing zone.

Each of his troopers was clad in a heavy armor suit, actually better armored than their human counterparts, with much heavier weaponry. All had been worked up to almost a frenzy, a battle madness that their ancestors would have recognized. There was an enemy ahead who had threatened fellow members of *their* Empire, and they would make that foe pay for such temerity.

The commander looked on his HUD, prioritized his targets, and made his last second adjustments. *That's a lot of open ground to cover*, was his initial thought. Unfortunately, his people weren't good at sneaking around. Their basic builds kind of worked against stealth. As did their inability to get low to the ground or climb. But they could run. And with the augmentation of their suits, they could run like the wind.

"Charge," yelled out the commander, starting forward at the trot himself. A roar came across the com net, over four hundred voices resonating from the enormous chests of the sentients.

The enemy saw them coming in an instant, and fire was soon to follow. Several Phlistarans fell off the HUD, among almost a hundred that had taken hits. Their tough armor proved its worth, bouncing shots off while their moving forms made it difficult to keep the beams in contact with beings that had gotten up to a hundred kilometers an hour, while dodging and swerving to make themselves the most difficult targets possible.

"Fire," yelled the Lt. Colonel, aiming his own heavy rifle toward the enemy, while the heavy weapons packs on his back swiveled into place.

Particle beams reached out from four hundred rifles the size of the heavy squad weapons that humans used, slashing into the enemy positions. Three hundred back mounted cannons sent fifty millimeter rounds downrange, while a hundred mortars opened fire, looping sixty millimeter rounds into the enemy positions. Missiles left two hundred launchers, seeking the opponent's heavy weapons and mecha. And lasers swept out, seeking every incoming object that might endanger the being carrying the weapon.

Of course, there were collisions between weapons and munitions going out. With so much in the air, it would have a miracle if there hadn't been. Missiles and shells intersected beams and exploded in midair, most far enough away to cause little problem to the launching soldiers.

What the fire did to the enemy was terrifying. Beams ripping through the ranks of soldiers who had just landed and hadn't found positions yet. Mortars exploding within what positions there were, their sensors seeking out the hollows that troops could hide in. Cannon shells popped explosively as they hit suits, or detonated at closest approach and sent out sprays of shrapnel.

Explosions lit the formation through the dust and holographic projections that surrounded them. Large Phlistaran forms flew into the air, head over heels, as the Fenri answered with their own heavy weapons. Beams converged on centauroid targets that came clear for moments before plunging back into obscurity. Some entered cover intact, others as smoking meat in ruptured suits. Phlistarans had tough hides underneath the armor, able to withstand hits from low velocity projectiles. Particle beams ate through that hide into organs like the matter of any other organic beings.

The Fenri formed a firing line, trying to beat off the attack, and suffering even more casualties under the firepower of the larger beings.   And then the Phlistarans were among them, many of the large aliens dropping their rifles to hang on slings, pulling pairs of heavy pistols from holsters. Now they were in their element, ancient cavalry equipped with modern weapons, running rampant among smaller infantry that was just trying to get away.

Here a Phlistaran trooper ran into a clutch of Fenri, pistols spitting proton beams, forefeet, cased in armor, molecular edged blades protruding forward, disemboweling another Fenri. There a large alien knocked Fenri to the ground with a spin of its three meter long body, swinging a sword made of the same material as its foot claws, slicing limbs and heads from armored forms. And further on a Phlistaran stopped in his tracks, while his backpack unit spat a missile at a large mecha that was trying to stop the charge with its fearsome weapons. The mecha took a direct hit, blowing to pieces across the area, its last act the particle beam that killed its killer.

Of the four hundred centauroids who had started the charge, less than two hundred came through the other side. Of the nine hundred Fenri they had attacked, only a handful ran from the fury of a species they recognized as their physical superiors.

*   *   *

"Attack," yelled Baggett into the com, running out of his bunker, rifle in his hands. *I know this is not something I'm supposed to engage in*, thought the Division Commander, his headquarters staff at his heels. But at heart he was still a battalion commander, and his men needed to see him sharing in the danger of a close assault. The danger he was asking them to face.

And besides, they needed every suit they had, and he just happened to be occupying a twenty million imperial command suit, even more expensive than the larger heavy support suits. They were already heavily outnumbered, and every suit was an asset they needed at this moment. The Corps Commander might dress him down later for putting his hide on the line, battle capable suit or not. *But I'd rather ask forgiveness*, he thought.

This assault was a landing zone that hadn't received the attention of tank units. It was a straight on infantry assault. And the battalion conducting the assault was the weakest of those in the division, less than three hundred effectives. The addition of his hundred man headquarters section, all in heavy armor, was a major reinforcement.

The landing zone was only five kilometers away, almost on top of the bunker. As Baggett came out of his shelter his HUD picked up the hundreds of troopers who were coming out of hiding to congregate for the assault. The other battalions had already started their assaults, some had finished. The enemy knew something was up, but most of the attention from above was elsewhere. Or at least he hoped so.

Artillery started lofting shells at the enemy under the screen of jamming. A hundred shells were in the air before the first hit, its crumping sound coming across the kilometers. Enemy countermeasures started taking out some of them, but not enough. And anything firing at the shells was not being aimed at the infantry that was closing on them.

Baggett got his suit up to eighty kilometers an hour, their maximum over rough ground. If they took to the air, they could also go faster, but would become much easier to target. Instead, they stayed low, taking advantage of the obscuring smoke and dust, as well as the holographic projectors on their suits, which were sending false images in random directions around their real physical matter.

Artillery switched to a rolling barrage, augmented by the heavy support suits throwing mortars and rockets into the mix. Shells started coming down a hundred meters from the enemy lines, throwing up dirt and smoke. The next came in twenty meters closer to the enemy, then twenty meters closer. Half the tubes fired, while the other half moved, shoot and scoot, trying to avoid counter battery fire from the enemy. That worked, somewhat, though some tubes were lost to each change over when their crews didn't move them fast enough. Still, the barrage worked as planned, and the human infantry came rushing out of the cloud of dirt and dust as the artillery moved on.

The humans opened fire as soon as they acquired targets, moments before the enemy could react. The shocked Fenri reeled in confusion as many went down to particle beam blasts, and others to the back mounted auto cannon. They fell back, trying to find a rally point, when the human suits closed the distance and hit them hard.

The human suits were stronger due to their size, and also carried thicker armor. Being larger, they could afford to pack thicker armor per their size according to the square function of surface area. They carried greater mass, and the collisions between Fenri and human resulted in Fenri thrown onto their backs.

Baggett shot a Fenri who looked to be some kind of leader, then vaulted the body to slam into one that looked like a higher level commander. His right arm came back, the razor claws extended, and he slammed the molecular blades into the armor of the Fenri. The creature's faceplate raised to reveal a face that snarled for a moment, before its expression changed to one of pure agony.

The General threw the alien from him, and raised his rifle with his left hand, firing a grenade at a concentration of enemy that looked like it was getting its act together. The thirty-five millimeter shell exploded in the center of the group, not powerful enough to get a kill, but causing damage to the sensors of a pair of suits. He swapped the rifle back to a right handed grip and fired, downing a Fenri, then swinging the beam into another.

They never gave the Fenri time to regroup. Less than five minutes from the time the first humans had made contact with the first Fenri, the fight was over. There were few survivors, and those were too demoralized to do anything but surrender. The humans ran from the scene of the battle, twenty-six Fenri in powered down suits carried along for the ride. The human battalion had lost a total of eighteen killed, twice that many wounded, in return for over a thousand Fenri.

Baggett ran for seven minutes and some odd seconds to his next position, jacking into the Corps command net on the way. The news was good, if not totally positive. The Fenri had only succeeded in taking two landing zones. That was the good news. The bad was that the enemy was quickly reinforcing those zones, bringing down all their shuttles to drop off troops and munitions, and heavier weapons such as tanks. There looked to be no hope of taking back those zones, and the enemy had an entire planet to choose from for more. But the humans had bloodied their noses, and from now on the Fenri would operate with caution against the hated humans who had invaded their property.

Chapter Seven

We hang the petty thieves and appoint the great ones to public office.   Aesop

THE *DONUT* AND SECTOR IV SPACE. NOVEMBER 27TH, 1001.

Dr. Larry Southard really hadn't expected to see much adventure at his age.   Not that he was an old man, but, hitting one hundred and seventy, he was not what anyone would call young. He had spent his youth in Exploration Command, while working on his Doctorate and Post Doc in Nuclear and Stellar Physics. That had been an exciting twenty years, charting new systems, seeing new worlds for the first time. But that time had come to an end, and he had thought he had earned a life of academic ease, teaching others the theories of stellar evolution, including his own. Somewhere in between had come another PhD, this time in advanced Mathematics.

Ease did not come for quite some time. Instead, he had ended up on a number of University sponsored expeditions, including a study of the only star in local space ever observed prior to and during its collapse and explosion into a supernova.   After that had come papers that had cemented his reputation as the foremost expert in supernovas in the Empire.

And then had come the ease he had expected, the life of a well-respected academic at the University of New Detroit, on the Core World of the same name. There he expected to live and work until he retired, after which he would spend his last thirty or forty years of life again travelling the space ways, this time as a tourist.

Unfortunately, thought the normally cheerful man who now had a perpetual scowl on his face, *I should have read the fine print on my Naval Reserve contract. Always subject to recall in time of war*, he thought, wanting to spit on the floor of the corridor that led to one of the wormhole gate rooms. *For life.*

"Captain Southard," said a naval Commander, saluting the professor who was dressed in his civilian travel clothes.

"That's Doctor, please," he said, refusing to return the salute. "I may have to play some of your games, but I refuse to play that one."

The look of surprise on the Commander's face almost caused the Professor to smile. Almost. "Very well. Doctor Southard," said the man, shaking his head.

And he thinks he honors me by giving me a rank two above what I had in the Navy. Bah.

"You have priority through to your destination, Doctor," said the Commander, looking at a flat comp. "Someone really wants you there."

Southard nodded and followed the man to the gate room, this one boasting a squad of heavily armed Marines at the entrance. All of the Marines had their visors up at the moment, and from the expressions on their faces, Southard could tell that these people were tense. This would not be a good place to cause a scene, not that he had been planning one in the first place.

The Commander led him through the room, past the watchful eyes of a number of Naval Shore Patrol, all armed with holstered particle beam pistols. The Commander led him to one of the portals, this one with even more armed guards, again Marines.

"This one leads to a ship near to your final destination," explained the naval officer. "From there you can catch transport to the research ship. And good luck, Doctor."

Southard nodded, looking at the portal like it was a dangerous carnivore. The memory of the first translation through a wormhole was still fresh in his mind, since he had just walked out of one less than ten minutes before. It hadn't been a pleasant experience, one he would have compared to having died and found out that one had gone to exactly the afterlife one had been dreading. *No use delaying*, thought the scientist, realizing that it would just make things worse in the waiting. With a firm grip on his bag he stepped through, across the light years.

* * *

SECTOR IV SPACE.

"All I wanted to do was to kill the bastards," screamed Master Chief Jana Gorbachev, glaring into the eyes of the psychiatrist who had been tasked with treating her. "I was just doing my duty. Surely the Emperor realizes that. So why can't I talk with him? He would clear this mess up in a moment."

And the Emperor is the reason you are here in a military hospital, thought Commander Sheila Blackmoore, the psychiatrist assigned to the enlisted woman's treatment. *If the brass had anything to do with it, you would be in prison, awaiting a trial on charges of cowardice in the face of the enemy. Or dereliction of duty, at least.*

"The Emperor wanted you here," said the Commander in her best calming voice. "He wanted you to get the treatment you needed."

"But I don't need any damned treatment," screamed the woman, her voice rising high. "Can't you see that I'm fit for duty."

"I see anything but," said the Commander, crossing her legs and giving her patient a frank gaze. "Right now, your anger is out of control. You are out of control."

"I just want to be on a weapon's station, on board one of his Imperial Majesty's ships."

"Until I certify you as fit for duty, you're not getting near a weapon's control board on a fast attack craft, much less a capital ship. And right now, there is no way I can certify you as fit. You have a lot of work ahead of you before that will happen." The Commander reached for her cup of coffee and took a sip. "So, tell me more about how the Cacas treated you aboard their ship."

"I don't want to tell you about how those damned bastards treated me," yelled Gorbachev, putting her head in her hands. "I don't want to think about what they did to me. The only thing I want to think about is what I'm going to do to them."

"We need to get past your anger," said Blackmoore, shaking her head. "And concentrate on your pain."

"You want to know about my pain," shouted Gorbachev, jumping to her, feet, fists clenched, a look of complete madness on her face. "I'll show you pain."

The Master Chief took a step forward, then froze in place. *Good thing we put a neural bypass program on her implant*, thought the Commander. The program was highly illegal in the freedom loving Empire, allowing control of the subject's physical movements as it did. It was only legal under the orders of a Medical Doctor, and only as a last ditch restraint for violent patients. And Gorbachev could definitely be called one of those.

"Back into your chair," said Blackmoore to the woman, her voice one of the dozen or so that the program was keyed to obey. Gorbachev took a step backward and sat down, her eyes points of raging fury. "Catablast," said the Commander, the free word that released the patient from total restraint. She had come up with the word herself, something she remembered from her days of playing virtual role playing games. A Catablast had been a terrible beast to fight, as this patient looked like she would be a terrible patient to treat. *The hurt just runs too deep*, thought the Commander. *We may have to try something a little more, drastic.*

There were programs she could put the Master Chief through, virtual reality that would allow the woman to live through her traumatizing memories, and deal with them in a more useful manner than simply going into a rage and wanting to kill something. *That's the only way we're going to get anywhere, I'm afraid*, thought the Commander, calling up her link and sending the medical orders into Gorbachev's file.

The only problem with virtual therapy was that it could backfire, putting the patient into a catatonic state. The odds were low as to that happening, but they were there. And if that happened, the only other treatment would be to purge her brain, completely wipe it, and reprogram her with the stored memories that all military personnel were required to record each and every year they were in service. Unfortunately, in the Master Chief's case, the only memories she had recorded before the trauma were over eighteen months old. And depriving her of that much of her existence would take a court order, by an Imperial Judge, since it was akin to the mind wipe used for some major crimes. It was something a mere physician couldn't order. And something she would be loath to do even if she could.

*   *   *

SAURON SYSTEM. NOVEMBER 29TH, 1001.

"Welcome aboard the *Genghis Khan*, Commander Collier," said Captain Lauren Hoyt, returning the salute of the lower ranking man, then offering her hand.

"Thank you, ma'am," said Scott Collier, feeling a flush of anxiety on meeting his new commanding officer. This was a plumb assignment, the flagship of a Grand Fleet Admiral like Duke Taelis Mgonda. And one of the new hyper VII battleships.

Khan had just finished her builder's trials and shakedown. She had missed the battle of Congreeve, but, as the most advanced ship of her type, and due to the damage to the Duke's previous flagship, had been chosen as his battle headquarters.

And I'm the new chief engineer, thought the beaming Commander. *Khan* had her own chief engineer through the trials, but he had been reassigned to Admiral Chan and the Research and Development Board. The only reason Scott could see for his getting the command was prior service as the assistant engineer on a hyper VII battle cruiser.

"I understand that you have never been on a VII battleship before," said the Captain with a frown.

She wonders if I'm capable of handling this assignment, he thought, nodding his head. "I studied all the specs on the ship while on the way here," said the Commander. "And I am very familiar with VII hyperdrives."

"Yes," said the Captain, in a tone that said she

wondered if that were enough. "Well, I assume you will want to check out your department. Ensign Takeo here will show you to your quarters, then to the engineering control section. Your effects will be transferred to your quarters within the hour, and we will be having a get together tonight in the Captain's mess."

Right, thought Collier, hoping he could remember all of that amid everything else that was going on. "And how long until we actually deploy?"

"Your guess is as good as mine, Commander," said the Captain. "I guess it depends on when the supernova blows its top. But you should have at least a couple of weeks to get your department organized to your liking. Now, I have duties to see to. So, we will see you tonight at the dinner."

The young Asian woman led him to his quarters, which were in the rear central capsule, only fifty meters from the antimatter reactor control room that was also the central control of engineering. He had his own living room, kitchen, and a larger bedroom than he was used to even on a space station. Warships were large, and even after all the mission critical equipment was installed, there was plenty of room for crew comforts. Senior officers had their own quarters. Junior officers shared, two to a central living area, with their own private bedrooms. Senior NCOs had the same arrangement, with the exception of the Chief of the Ship. Junior NCOs shared four to a living area, though that area was larger than that given to junior officers. And on a ship like *Khan,* even the junior enlisted had a small personal room, eight of them on the central living area.

And that didn't even consider all the recreational spaces, gyms, bowling alleys and game courts, virtual reality chambers. Many mess halls serving the standard chow of the Fleet, which was considered very good indeed. Ships had been known to stay on deployment for years at a time, and the Fleet didn't want the crews going stir crazy.

For the moment the quarters were completely bare of any personal touches. He had several chests full of mementoes to liven the place up, knick knacks, pictures, a couple of models. And a very lively little dog that had been his companion for the last decade.

"Let me see engineering, if you please, Ensign," he told the young officer, who led him out of the room to the nearest lift station.

The Ensign tried to make small talk on the way, but Collier was too anxious to see his new domain. *The lass probably thinks I'm a stuck up ass*, he thought as they left the lift at the station right outside the door to the control room.

A pair of Marines in medium armor stood outside the door, and Scott found himself being scanned before he was allowed in the room.

"Can't be too careful these days, sir," said the Corporal in charge of the team, doing a deep scan of Collier with a needle probe.

"It was a good idea even before these shape shifters," agreed Scott. After all, the chamber beyond this door had control of the matter antimatter reactors of the ship. The wrong hands on the controls, with the proper codes, could blow the sixteen million ton ship out of space.

"You check out, sir," said the Corporal, looking at the screen on the probe. "Please key in a code word on this pad," said the Marine, offering another device to the Commander.

Collier thought for a moment, then keyed in a word he thought would be easy for him to remember, and difficult for anyone else to guess. The thick door opened, and the Commander walked into his new domain.

"Chief Engineer on deck," yelled out Ensign Takeo after they walked through the entry corridor and into the outer control room.

"At ease," said Collier, gratified to see that everyone had jumped to attention quickly, but wanting to end the silliness as soon as possible. "We will have a department meeting in fifteen minutes," he told the assembled crew. "I want to get to meet all of you people, if that won't be a problem."

There was some stifled laughter at that pronouncement, then a question. "Do you want us to bring the off duty shifts here?" asked the Senior Chief on duty.

"I think we can let them get their rest," said Collier, anxious to see what would be his baby.

The next corridor was only twenty meters long, but ten of those meters were through the thick armor that was the last protection for the matter antimatter reactors, both from within and without. And, past another meter thick door, was the engineering control room.

Collier walked over to the master control panel, looking at the seat that would be his station most of his time aboard. He ran a hand over the board, being careful to not push any of the lit panels. He pushed one that he recognized, and was delighted to see the power meters to the twin reactors come up as a holographic projection. At the moment the graph showed a mere hundred megawatts being generated, enough for a ship sitting at station. The gradations on the graph went up to a hundred pentawatts, a marvelous number, almost unlimited power that would be under his control. Or at least under his control depending on the orders of the Captain.

It looks like an enormous amount of energy, thought the Engineer, pulling up a holographic schematic of the ship that showed the power couplings heading off to all the major systems. The laser rings, particle beam accelerators, electromagnetic field projectors, the grabbers, all energy hogs which would need to be fed during an action. And, of course, the hyperdrive projectors, the biggest energy hog of them all, and what made the massive ship the speed demon that she was.

Dismissing one holo, the Engineer called up another, a view of the twin reactors sitting in their cradles, each over three hundred meters tall by two hundred wide. They both had twenty meter thick shells, wrapped in a tight weave of superconducting cables that siphoned off the excess heat. Collier switched the view to the inside of the dormant reactor. *Yep*, he thought. *They're pretty much all the same.* The inside was a mass of magnetic field projectors, heat exchangers, and electrothermodynamic converters.

And I need to get up to snuff on everything in here, he thought, pulling up more schematics. *The Captain may wonder if I'm able to handle the job, and it's up to me to prove her wrong.*

Chapter Eight

We make war that we may live in peace.   Aristotle

CONUNDRUM SPACE. NOVEMBER 30TH, 1001.

Commodore the Duchess Mei Lei called off her attacks while still a day away from the Conundrum System. At first the attacks had resulted in a more than favorable exchange between her forces and those of the enemy, as the disorganized Cacas basically fled the Congreeve system. Then the enemy had become more organized, and she had started losing almost the same tonnage as the foe.   The last couple of days, the exchange had started favoring an enemy who had organized and congregated, and had a battle plan of their own to deal with the hit and run hyper VII forces.

I just can't send people to their deaths for no good reason, thought the Commodore, looking at the tactical plot that showed the enemy force closing on the hyper VII limit of the Conundrum system. She had no intention of following them into that system. She had a good idea that such would result in the destruction of her force. *No*, she thought, looking at the forces she still had under her command. *The best thing I can do now is form a ring around this system, a light year or two out in normal space, and use my wormhole equipped ships to keep tabs on their comings and goings.*

She knew the Empire still had stealth/attack ships in the system, keeping watch on anything that came and went there. But once the enemy ships were more than a couple of light months away from the hyper barrier, the spy ships couldn't track them. *Maybe some of the ships should be picketed out two light years, and some more at five*, she thought. That way they would be able to keep tabs of any movements that went around the system as well.

"Send those orders through the wormhole com," she told her Flag Com Officer once she had finished putting them into the record. "I'll be in my cabin if any coms come through that I need to respond to."

The Com Officer acknowledged, then went to work on her board, while the Commodore walked out of the flag bridge. It was a short walk to her cabin, only twenty meters of hallway. The Marine guards saluted her as she approached the door. She still thought it ridiculous to have Marines guarding her quarters, but regulations called for such, and, after the incident on the *Donut*, orders had come down that regulations were to be obeyed to the letter as far as security was concerned.

Satin waited for her, sitting up within a meter of the door, as if he had known she was coming. "My good boy," said Mei, leaning over and petting the cat, eliciting a deep purr. "Miss me."

The cat meowed, a sweet sound to the ears of the woman. Mei smiled at the beast that had shared so much of her shipboard life, then walked into her kitchen to grab a snack. The cat ate first, of course, fresh gourmet fish that she had stored in her cabinets. Like most good pet owners the care of her animal came before her own hunger. The cat attacked the fish while she made herself a sandwich.

I have a steward for this, she thought as she put roast beef, turkey and Swiss cheese on the multigrain bread, then spread some hot mustard on it. But she liked taking care of small details like this herself. It calmed her, and after the stress of over a week of action, she needed the calming.

Sitting on her couch with her sandwich and a cup of tea before her, she turned to the holo to see what the news feeds were saying about the war. Not that she expected any more accuracy than was usual, but she wanted to get a handle on the opinions of the crowd. The latest report came up, the talking heads discussing the battle of Congreeve, and what it would mean to the Empire.

And as usual, they are making guesses that have no basis I reality. But at least they are giving Sean the credit he deserves.

Satin jumped up on the couch beside her, rubbing against her leg as he eyed the sandwich. "No you don't, you little shit," said Mei, grabbing the sandwich from its plate before the feline could get any ideas. She took a bite, savoring the mix of flavors, which to her commoner palate was as tasty as any of the meals her cook made for her.

"I have an incoming com for you, ma'am," came a call over her link. "It's Admiral Mgonda."

Christ. You would think they would give me a moment to eat. "Put him through," she said, placing the remains of her sandwich on the table. The cat started heading for it, and she put a hand out to shoo him away.

"I hope I'm not interrupting on your special moment," said Grand Fleet Admiral Duke Taelis Mgonda with a smile.

"Your Grace," stuttered Mei. "Admiral. I was just taking a break to get some food."

"And getting a little down time," said the smiling man. "Quite alright, Admiral. After all, your force has been continually engaged for almost a week after the battle ended for the rest of us. I think all of your crews could do with a break. Unfortunately, we still have need of you and your ships to be our front line."

"Yes, sir. And we will do our best to keep tabs on the enemy for you. Can I expect any relief?"

"No, Admiral. You cannot. You will remain on picket until such time as the offensive commences. I'm sorry, but there it is."

Admiral, thought Mei, her eyes widening as what the other man had called her finally penetrated her consciousness. "You called me Admiral?"

"You, Duchess, are from this moment forward promoted to the rank of rear admiral," said the man who wore six stars on his collar. "Based on your performance in the last operation, and the needs of the Empire for someone of higher rank to command the scout force."

"And Admiral Montgomery?"

"She is being bumped up to full Admiral," said the Duke, referring to the four star rank. "We're moving her to command of a battle group and turning her loose behind enemy lines. So battle fleet needs a new scout force commander, and you are it."

"I thought that was a three star rank," said Mei, frowning, not because she wanted an additional promotion, but because that was normally the way things were.

"Soon enough, Admiral. We have to get you through some temporal hoops before you can get that rank. But I see it in your future."

"Sir. I did not mean to ask..."

"I know you didn't. But the fact is, you are an exceptional leader, and one we can't afford to waste commanding a small scouting force. But for now it will have to be two stars, though you will command the authority of a vice admiral."

"Thank you, Admiral," said Mei, bowing her head.

"I will try to live up to your expectations."

"That is not all I am calling you about," said the Admiral, looking out of the holo at the cat that had jumped back on the couch. "That's just like the one the Emperor has."

"I know, sir," said Mei, her smile growing. "I gave his Majesty his own as a gift, since he seemed to like mine so much."

"That is the other thing, Admiral," said Mgonda. "The Emperor will be announcing his wedding to Duchess Coventry as soon as he gets back to the capital. The wedding will occur a week after his arrival, and he has requested your presence."

"I don't see how I could, Admiral. My command…."

"Can probably do without you for a day or two. Which is all the time it will take for you to come in by gate, attend the wedding, and take a portal back to your command. Not like the old days, Admiral, when you would have been away for two or three weeks. So pick the commodore you want in charge while you're gone, and make your preparations to come to Jewel. That's an order from on high, and not one I want to try to disobey."

"Yes, sir," said Mei, laughing.

"Keep up the good work, Admiral. And someday you might be in my position. Or even CNO. Mgonda out."

The holo went blank, and Mei shooed the cat away from her sandwich. Not that she felt very hungry after hearing all of the news Mgonda had given her. But she had to fuel her body, so she took another bite of sandwich.

Sean and the Doctor, she thought as she ate. *They were*

already engaged, but we all thought the actual marriage would be at least another year in the future. I guess the idea of an heir has come up, and it would be a good idea for Sean to get one into the world, if he plans to keep leading from the front.

"I would like to talk with Commodore Lacy," she told her com officer over the link. *And won't he be surprised by the bomb I'm about to drop on him.*

*   *   *

Commodore Bryce Suttler sat in his captain's chair and watched as the enemy force translated into normal space. In the past, such an event would be the signal for his six stealth/attack ships to get ready to engage. At this point that would be suicide. There were over a thousand ships coming, according to the reports of the Battle Fleet Scout Force. The survivors of the Battle of Congreeve. They were mad as hornets, and looking for something to smash. Since Suttler did not have orders to attack them, he decided that discretion called for him to sit and watch, and send his observations back to headquarters.

This might be my last time commanding one of these ships, he thought, wishing he did have a target he could stalk and kill. News of his permanent promotion to Commodore had come through the day before, and he hadn't been given the option to refuse. *And just how do you refuse a promotion that came down from the hand of the Emperor himself?* he thought, realizing that there really was no way to do so. But he wanted to stay in the ships, and there was no place for a commodore aboard one of the small vessels that normally operated singly, or at most in teams of two.

They promised me I could stay in command of Seastag, he thought, looking at the plot that showed the enemy ships congregating where one of their stations used to be, a station his ships had destroyed. *But I know how these things work. Contingencies of war, needs of the Fleet. I could find myself sitting a desk for the rest of the war. And it is totally beyond my control.*

"Another group is translating in," called out Suttler's Tactical Officer, Lieutenant SG Walter Ngovic. "This one looks to be mostly those big battleships of theirs."

Suttler grunted, and looked over at his Com Officer to see that worthy sending the information up the line. The first two enemy forces had been made up of mostly four million ton supercruisers, with a scattering of their scout ships. He had expected more scouts, and had informed command of his thoughts. They had told him that the enemy scout ships had taken inordinate casualties in the battle.

"How many do we have, Ngovic?" he asked his officer.

"Looks like almost a hundred in this group. Some of them are sending out abnormal hyperdrive resonances, probably battle damage, so I'm having a hard time singling all of them out."

"That's OK, Tactical," said Bryce, nodding. "We'll get a visual count on them soon. Any look like they're coming into our backyard?"

"No, sir," said Ngovic, shaking his head. "I'm pretty sure they don't know we're here. They all seem to be vectoring toward that one gathering point."

And if I were them, and came back to a system that didn't have the assets still in place that I had left there, I would be fanning out on a search pattern as soon as I could get organized. But at the moment they looked to be safe, sitting half a light hour away from the gathering point.

An hour later everything changed. "I was afraid of

this," said Ngovic, pointing to the tactical plot that showed hundreds of enemy ships starting to fan out in teams, their sensors on full power as they tried to ferret out the invisible vessels they had to know were in the system.

"Move us further out," ordered Suttler, leaning forward in his chair. "Slowly. Send orders to the other ships to do the same."

Besides *Seastag* he only had two other ships in his immediate group. The other three were five light hours away, across the system, but in instantaneous com link through the wormholes.

"Some of the enemy ships are moving out from the gathering point," said Ngovic. "We have translations back into hyper."

And that means they will be moving around the outer fringes of the system and translating back, so they can try and catch us. Suddenly Suttler was not so sure that his dispositions had been wise. That maybe they would have been better served to have sat another five light hours out, or even further.

*   *   *

Captain the Duke Maurice von Rittersdorf didn't really like the placement of his command in the screen around the Conundrum System. Not that they were close in, because compared to many of the scout force ships *James Komorov* was actually pretty far out, five light years from the star system. No, it was the orientation of his ship, and the other four destroyers that formed his part of the picket. They were on a direct path from the border region the Cacas were known to come through, all the way in to Conundrum. As such, they were likely to see a lot of traffic coming up the pike. That wasn't the problem, as it showed that the powers that be trusted him and his command.

The real problem was that his was the only wormhole equipped ship in his command, and as such the only one that had a connection back to headquarters. His other ships were spread out in a pattern to catch any signals that *Komorov* might miss. But since they didn't have a wormhole com, the only way they could communicate was by either subspace com, or by grav pulse. Subspace com was very short ranged, not more than a light month. Grav pulse could be heard out to a few light months, and gave away the presence and location of the transmitting ship.

Which meant that effectively he had the only ship that could detect and send their information up the line.

It was bitch enough sneaking in here, he thought, remembering a tense couple of days at hyper I to get to their final translation point. Then translation, then waiting several hours to see if anything had detected them and was going to jump back into hyper and come after them. They had never heard that translation, which didn't mean that something hadn't picked them up and crept away out of detection range. *It's enough to drive someone mad, all this guess work. And we live or die with good or bad guesses.*

"We're picking up ships coming in from anti-spinward," called out the Tactical Officer, giving the direction up the Perseus arm as it curved away from the Galactic disc. The direction of the Ca'cadasan Empire.

"How many do you have?"

"Looks like twenty-two. No, make that twenty three contacts. Seven of them are capital ships."

They followed the contacts for the next couple of hours, until they had moved out of detection range.

But an hour after that there were more contacts, coming out of the system and heading directly anti-coreward. "It looks like they're not going to hunker down completely," said von Rittersdorf, watching the ships on the plot. "Would have been nice if they had."

Of course the Cacas were the aggressors in this war, and were probably not comfortable going completely on the defensive. And there was still a lot of lightly defended Imperial space out there. Easy pickings for Caca task forces. *Unless the information we get to HQ can be developed into an intercept*, he thought, watching as the contacts moved away and off the plot.

"We want you to configure your wormhole into a delivery gate," came the command from headquarters later that day. "We have some special weapons for you."

Maurice sent out the order to engineering to configure the hole they used for com, after moving it to the forward missile magazine, which was almost empty after the weapons they had expended in the running battle to and from the Congreeve system.

The first of the reloads came through, only they weren't exactly the kind of missile they had already used up, the hyper VII/normal space dual drive they had used in the battle. These were slightly longer, and a little more massive.

Maurice pulled up the schematics on the missiles as they came across, a smile on his face. *These will do nicely*, he thought, looking over the specs, which included a more efficient crystal matrix battery system.

Three hours after taking the first missile aboard, *James Komorov* was deploying the first twenty of the weapons, making room for more. The missiles boosted out under minimal power, coming to rest several light minutes from the launching ship, set in a semicircle that covered most of the approaches to the system. They powered down after decelerating to a stop, the only system still working the com feed that would accept orders from its launching ship.

Now we just have to get the orders to use them, thought the destroyer force commander. He for one couldn't wait to spring the surprise on some Caca ships that wandered into the trap fat and sassy.

*   *   *

Great Admiral Miierrowanasa M'tinisasitow growled deep in his throat as he looked at the system he had made his headquarters. A system that had contained two of the giant base stations they had needed to support their conquest. One was to have moved to another system. One was to have stayed here. And now, according High Admiral Kellissaran Jarkastarin, his subordinate and rival, both had been destroyed by the cursed invisible attack ships of the humans.

I should have left a larger defensive force here, he thought, standing with his upper arms crossed over his deep chest, lower arms clasping their hands behind his back. He looked back at the armed males that were his bodyguards, scowling at their presence, here, looking at his shame. *I shouldn't have stuck my horns into that damned trap in the first place*, he thought, turning and throwing his goblet at the wall. It hit the hard alloy and bounced way, liquid flying everywhere. *And I don't even get the satisfaction of a good shattering.*

"Throwing a tantrum will help nothing," said an accursed voice from the doorway.

The Great Admiral spun and pointed both right index fingers at the other officer. "How dare you come here," he growled.

High Admiral Jarkastarin stood there with both sets of arms crossed to his front. His body language showed his challenge to the authority of the Grand Admiral. Normally that would have resulted in an attack by one male or another, if they had been lower ranking youths. As high ranking adults they were expected to keep their emotions under control, despite the pheromones that were filling the room. Even the guards were bristling at the heavy scent of male aggressiveness that was part of the genetic heritage of their species.

"How dare you come here, Kellissaran," yelled the Great Admiral, his fists clenched.

"I have every right to be here, on this ship," said the other Admiral in a cold voice. "I am, after all, nobly born, and a friend of the Emperor."

"A hanger on is all you are. And you have no authority on my flagship."

"You have failed, Miierrowanasa," said the other officer. "The Emperor gave you the sacred duty to crush these vermin, and you have failed. I warned you about trying to fight the decisive battle, when you should have simply fanned out and crushed as many of their systems as possible."

"And I told you, such a strategy was doomed to failure, as it allowed this enemy to pick and choose targets of opportunity. We would be bled from a thousand cuts."

"And look at your conquest force now, oh Great Admiral M'tinisasitow," snarled the other male, glancing at the Great Admiral's guards, who had interposed their bodies between himself and his rival. "It lies in ruins before you, the once great force, now only a shadow of itself."

"Leave me," roared the Great Admiral. "Before I have you arrested for insubordination."

The other male glared for a moment, then turned to walk away. "The Emperor will be notified of your actions, Great Admiral," said the High Admiral as he stalked away. "And I will have your position."

The Great Admiral stared down the corridor for minutes after his rival had walked away. He was tempted to send males to have him arrested. Maybe even assassinated. He gave a head gesture of negation at that thought. The High Admiral did have many friends at court, and many allies in the conquest fleet. The Great Admiral was afraid that doing anything to the powerful male might lead to a revolt in his fleet, and then there would be literal hell to pay when the Emperor found out. A commander who could not keep his subordinates in line was of no use to the Empire.

Hours later the Great Admiral was sitting at his desk when a priority com came through. "Great Admiral. We have reports of multiple hyper tracks from around the system. It appears the humans are putting a scout picket around us."

I would, were I them, thought the senior Ca'cadasan. "Are they staying in hyper? Or dropping down into normal space?"

"Dropping down into normal space, as near as we can tell," said the officer on the other end of the com. "Do you want us to sweep space for them."

"I can't see where that would do any good," said the Admiral, imagining the huge volume of normal space within light years of the system. "They will just hide, without giving off the kind of emissions we would need to find them." *And they've probably got enough of those damned invisible ships around us anyway.* "Any word on the system sweeps?"

"So far, nothing, my Lord," said the officer. "But we have to this point covered so little of the system."

"Well, keep looking." *Though I really doubt we will find anything.*

An hour later a human was brought before the Great Admiral. A young male, not an imposing physical specimen, but one with intelligence shining from his eyes.

"And what are you bringing this one to me for?" asked the Great Admiral of one of his science advisors.

"This is Doctor Ivan Smirnov," said the advisor, as if those words would mean anything to the Admiral. "He was working on the New Moscow wormhole project."

The Admiral's ears perked up when he heard that word. "The small power had its own project?"

"Tell him," said the Science Advisor, tapping the human in the back.

"Well, yes, er, my Lord," said the man in a tremulous voice. "We didn't want the Empire to be the only ones producing wormholes."

"I thought a black hole was needed to make these constructs," said the Great Admiral, leaning over his desk. Seated, he still towered over the human.

"The black hole is needed to generate the energy, my Lord," said the human. "But not for the actual generation of the hole. We were working on building up an industrial planet for the same purpose. Sort of like the generating complexes needed for supermetal production. We couldn't make as many of them in a specified time period as the Imperials could, maybe one a week. But we also found that the Imperials were using more energy than they needed to form their holes."

"How, much more?" asked the Great Admiral, clasping his upper hands on the desk.

"Twenty percent. Maybe more."

So, we could make wormholes without having to spend a century building a station around a black hole, thought the grinning Admiral, the implications of such obvious. They couldn't make near as many as the humans, and probably couldn't use them in so many ways. But a ship gate back to a major fleet system was just one of the many advantages it would give them. *We could send reinforcements through whenever we wanted, without having to run the gauntlet of the human fleet.   And instantaneous communications with headquarters.* That last could be a double edged sword, as sometimes it was better for headquarters to be months away.

"And what do you want for this knowledge?"

"Safety for myself and my family," said the human, dropping his eyes to the floor.

"Anything else?"

"I don't care for anyone else in the whole damned kingdom," said the human, raising his pain filled eyes to look into those of the Ca'cadasan. "Or the Empire or Republic. Just get me and my family to safety, and you can do what you want with everyone else."

The Great Admiral stared at the man for a moment, forcing the human to look back at the floor. It was something no Ca'cadasan would do, sell out his own people for safety. But, as he was learning, the human species was a contradiction in thought and behavior.

"Very well," said the Admiral, looking at his

Advisor. "I want this male and his family members on a ship back to the Empire immediately. With a strong escort."

"Are you sure you want to spare the ships?" asked another officer who was in the chamber.

"We need this technology," said the Great Admiral, glaring at the officer. "It may be the most important gift to fall our way, and I want to see it safely in the hands of our own scientists." *As poor as they may be*, he thought. The Ca'cadasan version of scientists were those males too old to still serve in the military. Unlike the human model, where young people with flexible minds were in the positions of discovery.

"Yes, my Lord," agreed the Advisor, giving a head nod of accent. "We'll put him on a supercruiser and get him to our space. With an escort of another cruiser."

"Double the number of cruisers," ordered the Great Admiral. "And add double their number of scouts. And they are to go through the remains of the smaller kingdom." The Admiral was well aware that some of his ships were disappearing in transit through the corridor that most of them traversed to get to the front.

"And tell them that this human is to get through, at all costs. If his vessel is taken, their lives are forfeit."

The Advisor gave a head gesture of obedience, then led the human away. The Admiral returned to his comp holo, trying to get back to his dispatches. But he couldn't concentrate on the work in front of him. His mind kept coming back to the proposition that the Ca'cadasan fleet might have wormholes. It might take some years to develop the production capacity. But once it was developed, they could continue to expand it until they had all that they needed to defeat the humans.

Maybe we should fall back from human space, he thought for a moment. *We could then come back when they aren't the only ones with the advantage of wormholes.* The Great Admiral gave a double shoulder shrug at that thought. There was no way the Emperor would allow them to retreat from the humans. And there was no telling what new advances the humans would come up with. Surely everything the Ca'cadasans had developed to date, and probably many tricks beyond.

And what should I do with the forces I have? thought the Great Admiral, looking over his dispositions, what was combat ready, what needed major repairs. *Some raids for now, without weakening the defenses in my important systems. And maybe in a month, another offensive. But this time I will strike them where they are weak, and further erode the strength of my enemies.*

Chapter Nine

Love has its place, as does hate. Peace has its place, as does war. Mercy has its place, as do cruelty and revenge. Meir Kahane

SAURON SYSTEM. DECEMBER 1ST, 1001.

"We're about to enter the Sauron System, your Majesty," came the call over the com net.

"Thank you, Admiral," said Sean, sitting at the table with Jennifer. He looked at his love, feeling sorry that she would have to go through another translation. She already looked a little pale just at the thought of translation.   "Is it getting any better?" he asked hopefully.

"Not really," she said. "Unless you are talking about my nausea. When there's nothing left in my stomach to vomit out, it's a little better. I guess I had better lie down."

"Want me with you?"

"I really hate having you see me that way," said Jennifer, shaking her head, getting up from the table.

Sean watched her walk away, his heart going out to her. *At least when she's back at Capitulum she won't have to go through this. Thank God for the wormhole network.*

Sean got up from the table and headed out the door to his quarters, his guards falling in around him. He headed for the lift bank, where one was being held for him, then rode the car up to the level of the flag bridge.

"Emperor on deck," yelled out the first officer to see him.

"At ease," yelled Sean, striding to his command

chair and taking a seat. The tactical plot in the center of *Augustine I's* flag bridge was set to a scale out to two light years, with the ship's icon blinking a couple of light months out. Sean zoomed in on that icon, and saw that they were represented as being in hyper VII, moving forward at point two five light. All around her were other ships, hundreds of them. A dozen other groupings followed, while some fairly large groups were closer to the system, and lower down the dimensions of hyper.

"It's still an impressive force," said Rear Admiral Kelso, walking up behind his Emperor.

"It was damned sight more impressive when I led it out," said Sean, thinking of all the ships and crews that did not come back.

"If you hadn't led them to their deaths, your Majesty, someone else would have," said Kelso, stepping around and sitting in the VIP chair to Sean's right. "It's the price of command. Win or lose, you have blood on your hands. Hopefully more of theirs than that of your own."

"Does it get any easier?"

"I'm just a lowly two star," said Kelso, looking into the holo tank. "You'll have to ask Lenkowski or Mgonda about that. But I believe they would tell you no. They gain some more distance, most of the time. Not in battles like Congreeve, but then, those kind of battles don't come along often, though they might in this war. No, mostly they order other lower ranking flag officers to take a portion of the fleet out and meet the enemy. They are not there. But you know what?"

"Tell me, Admiral."

"I have seen Mgonda looking over the casualty lists of an engagement, and I could swear he was barely holding back the tears. He knows what those figures mean, as cold and clinical as they are. They represent real people, humans and non, who have given their lives, their futures, their children's mothers and fathers, to implement those orders. And he feels just as responsible for those deaths if the orders originated from him, or from the CNO, or above."

"That's the way I feel, Admiral," said Sean, looking around the chamber at the men and women who served on his flag bridge. "I feel responsible for these deaths, and I was here to see them die."

"And would you feel any less responsible if you were sitting in your office in Capitulum when battle was joined?" asked Kelso, looking into the eyes of the man he had sworn oaths to serve.

"I don't think so," said Sean.

"Good. You should feel responsible, just as you should feel responsible when you pull off a victory like you did at Congreeve. It is so sad that so many had to die in that battle. And so necessary. No one wants to die in battle. But sometimes it is necessary that many die, that so many more might live. Never forget that. You are our Emperor, our commander in chief. And you sometimes must choose who to send into harm's way that the Empire might live."

Sean stared into space a moment, digesting what the Admiral had said, then looked back at Kelso. "And tell me honestly, Admiral Kelso. What kind of leader am I?"

"Not the most educated," said the Admiral without hesitation, raising a hand to stop Sean from making a defensive reply. "Very good for your age, but lacking experience. A lot of potential, just waiting to grow. You can be very immature at times, and wise beyond your years at others. But most importantly, you listen to the people who are under you. You learn. You don't always agree, nor should you. The hard decisions are yours, not theirs. And most importantly, you accept blame where blame is due. That is very important in a leader, and has been lacking in many through history. You own up to your mistakes, and don't try to scapegoat others. Now, you just need to work on accepting the credit you deserve as well."

"Jumping to hyper V," called out a voice over the intercom. The lights dimmed, and the space on the main viewer showed as the slightly less vibrant red of the dimension they were now in. Neither man showed much effect from the jump. Both were experienced spacers, with a high natural tolerance, and hyper travel would never get the better of either of them.

"Am I making a mistake, leading from the front?" Sean asked the man, who had become one of his primary military advisors. "Some in Parliament are saying that I should stay on Jewel, and keep my hands off the military."

"Parliament just wants to run the war their way," said the Admiral, shaking his head. "And that would be an unmitigated disaster. Their plan would be to fall back and protect the Core Worlds, leaving the rest of the Empire to be picked off by the Cacas, and picked clean by the other powers. As vital as the Core Worlds are to our effort, they are not all there is to this Empire. The Developing Worlds are responsible for almost twenty-five percent of our military construction and materials. Plus, most of us in the Fleet think their plan would only result in the loss of the Core Worlds as well, one by one, or a couple at a time."

"And what about my leading from the front?"

asked Sean, a slight smile on his face. "You avoided that one very neatly, Admiral."

"The, uh, Admiralty seems to have mixed feelings on that, your Majesty," said the Admiral, who was looking decidedly uncomfortable. "While some see the advantages that you bring to the table, others, uh, are uncomfortable having you in actual operational command."

"What about the Spacers and Marines serving under them?" asked Sean with a frown.

"Those people would follow you into hell, your Majesty," said Kelso without hesitation. "They think the world of a seated Emperor who puts his life on the line beside them. But there are some reservations there as well."

"They don't like seeing me on the front of the battle line," said Sean, nodding.

"That they don't, your Majesty. Being in the same system is enough for them to see that you are really one of them at heart. But they also want to feel that you are the Emperor, to be protected. It's good for morale to see you in the battle force, but bad to see you actually putting your butt on the line."

"And bad for the Empire if I get killed," said Sean, shaking his head again. "But I'm just one man. I can be replaced."

"No," said Kelso, raising his voice and pointing a finger at the Emperor. "At this moment, you cannot be replaced. If you were to be killed, then the fight for the throne would be on. There are too many people out there with a claim, none of them particularly strong. A fight for the succession is not what we need at this time. You marrying the Duchess is a step in the right direction. Getting an heir will be another, as long as that heir has a strong advisor while he or she grows up."

"So. I need to get married, knock up Jennifer, and get myself a smaller ship, so *Augustine* can go into the line of battle where she belongs, without putting the head of state at risk."

"I guess that about sums it up, your Majesty," said the laughing Admiral. "And I could suggest some people to help with your selection of a new flag. Something that would serve you well."

"Thanks for the advice, Admiral," said the Emperor, leaning back in his chair. "I've got a lot to think about. Now leave me to do just that."

"At your command, your Majesty," said the Admiral, standing and saluting. Kelso executed a picture perfect about face and walked away.

It's good to have an advisor, thought Sean, watching the straight back of the Admiral as he walked away. *It's up to me to seek good advice, and weigh it. But the buck still stops here. It's up to me to make the final decision. Though the advice about a new flagship makes a lot of sense.* Sean looked around the flag bridge of the most powerful unit in his fleet. There were only five like her in service, three of which were just coming online. It was a ship that needed to be in the line of battle, where he didn't need to be.

It took almost another hour to make it through the gradations of hyper, but finally *Augustine* jumped through the final dimensional breach into normal space. The stars were out in all their majesty, many sending their light in blazes of glory through the gas clouds of nebulae. The G0 primary of the system was straight ahead, one of the class of stars most similar to that humanity had evolved around. About twenty degrees above the ecliptic of the system, ten degrees to the right of the star, was a bright blue dot, the blue supergiant, on the fate of which hung the success or failure of the planned offensive.

Almost a hundred other ships appeared along with *Augustine I*, several superbattleships, a score of battleships, and the only other member of the Dreadnaught's class to have survived the battle. *That's a decision I can make right now*, thought the Emperor, looking at a view of *Archduke Leslie*, twenty thousand kilometers to port. *Imperium*, the third ship of the class that had been engaged at Congreeve, hadn't made it, proving that in modern war there were no such things as indestructible ships. When objects were flying around with massive warheads at significant fractions of light speed, anything that could be hit could be killed. *Superheavy battleships*, decided the Emperor. *From now on, that's what we'll be calling them.* And when they came up with a bigger class, he would pick something out for them.

He turned his attention to the tactical holo, which was updated second by second as new information came to it through the wormhole com, which was receiving information from every other wormhole equipped platform in the system. Over a thousand ships were shown on that display, superbattleships, battleships, carriers, cruisers of all classes, destroyers, even several hundred frigates, ships usually only used for patrol duties.

Several hundred icons blinked in a position a couple of million kilometers from the inhabited planet of Sauron III. Sean zoomed in on the icons, grunting with surprise as he saw the identifications below them. Not that he could pronounce any of those names, though he had enough knowledge of Crakistan from recent learning programs to read them. The reptilians had only been marginally involved in the Congreeve battle, though he had heard that they were giving a good account of themselves in Republic space. The lizard like aliens, not cold blooded at all, though they seemed like that emotionally, were staunch warriors. Fear would never deter them from a task that was called for in the heat of battle. They would fly their ships to their deaths if it was the logical decision that would benefit their species. He was happy to see them, and hoped that they were just as loyal to their allies as they were to each other.

And when the Elysiums arrive, we will have yet another ally against the Cacas. Something that will have to dishearten even those bastards. Command structure would be the problem, if only a minor one. The aliens would fight in their own task forces and battle groups, under the overall command of Sean himself. But the avians would not arrive until the ship gate was in place, and it was even now being carried by a superbattleship several light hours behind *Augustine* in the procession of warships transferring from Congreeve.

In fact, for all the thousands of ships already here, they were but the tip of the iceberg. Thousands more were on the way through hyper, and more would come by way of ship gate when it was up and running. *And when Len gets through with his little task, he'll be bringing quite a few ships here himself.* The wormholes were indeed a godsend. Allowing them to move forces at unprecedented transit times across the Empire. As long as they possessed them, there didn't seem any way the New Terran Empire could lose.

Don't think like that, Sean. There were still many

ways they could lose this war against their much more massive enemy. Arrogance could lead to several of those ways. It was best to use every asset they had to the fullest advantage, while still realizing that an enemy had plans of their own, which didn't include losing the war.

"We're being welcomed by Sauron Traffic Control," called out the Com Officer. "The Admiral commanding wants to know if you would like a pass and review, your Majesty."

"No," said Sean. "I think not." *We really don't have time for that. We need to concentrate on the business at hand.* Then he realized that it was not just about him. To these people, on these ships, it would be an honor to be reviewed by their Monarch, a much needed morale boost. "Belay that last, Com," he told the officer. "Inform the Admiral Commanding that I would be honored to review the Fleet. At his convenience."

"Aye, your Majesty," said the smiling Com Officer, turning back to her board.

And after that, me and my bride will be on our way back to the capital, and one chance at a celebration among all this turmoil.

*   *   *

SPACE TO COREWARD OF CA'CADASAN EMPIRE. DECEMBER 2, 1001.

"We're picking up eight contacts to rimward," called out the Sensor Officer, a look of alarm on her face. "Moving in our direction in hyper VII."

"Identification?" asked Commodore Natasha Sung, fearing the worst.

"Resonances are consistent with Ca'cadasan ships.

Two supercruisers, and six scouts."

It could have been much worse, she thought. While her ships were not warships, they still massed almost twenty-eight million tons each, and were as heavily armed as battleships. What they didn't have was the armor of battleships. They also carried six destroyer sized hyper VI exploration ships, which were armed much like frigates. The biggest problem with those ships was that *Nina, Pinta* and *Santa Maria* were currently cruising in hyper VII at a velocity of point nine light. They had no way to deploy those hyper VI ships, which would fall out of VII as soon as they left the hyper field of their launching ship. And that translation would more than likely destroy them.

And there's no way we can decelerate down to translation speed ourselves before those ships reach us. It might have been a near thing with a warship, or even a courier. But her ships had a hundred gravity limit on their acceleration. They had been built for the long cruise, not quick accel and decel. *And maybe the next class of exploration ships should be designed with speed and maneuverability in mind.*

"All crew to battle stations," ordered the Commodore. *"Pinta* and *Santa Maria* to battle stations. I want us arrayed in a battle line to take their attack."

"Yes, ma'am," called out the Tactical Officer. "All weapons powered up. All tubes loaded and ready."

"Pinta and *Santa Maria* are reporting all ready," said the Com Officer.

"Are you picking up any other ships?" she asked her Sensor Officer, dreading the answer.

"So far no, ma'am," said the officer. "The only resonances I am picking up at those of the eight ships in that force."

"What are you thinking, ma'am?" asked the Exec

from the secondary bridge, the only other control center on the ship. There was no CIC, the vessel not being a warship.

"They might be the advanced scout force of whatever else is out there," she said over the personal com link. "I know we can outfight these guys, even though we would take more damage that we want. But if they have some of their battleships coming after them, even one, we might find that it's more than we can handle."

And we can't even drop into normal space and hide. Not at our pitiful acceleration rate.

"Enemy ships will be in visual range in three minutes," called out the Sensor Officer.

"We have missile launch," yelled the Tactical Officer. "Twenty missiles in space. No, make that forty."

They could launch so many more, thought the Commodore. "Is this some kind of test?"

"That's what I would guess, ma'am," said the Tactical Officer, looking back.

"Order all ships to send them a volley," she ordered, staring at the tactical plot and the forty Caca missiles that were heading their way. "And fire counters when ready."

Thirty outgoing missiles appeared on the plot, accelerating at five thousand gravities toward the enemy.

The exchange was inconclusive, to say the least, as both sides picked off the missiles of the other. Sung waited for another volley to come her way, this one with more weight behind it. Instead, the enemy darted forward and back, testing the maneuverability of the human force. After an hour they fell back to a following distance that left them out of any kind of weapons range that could realistically cause them harm.

"Two of the scouts are dropping away," said the Sensor Officer, staring at his own holo. "They're starting to decelerate away."

"What the hell are they up to?" asked the Exec over the personal link.

"I think that's pretty obvious, XO," said Sung, staring at the plot. "The cruisers and four destroyers will continue to shadow us, while those two go and find help to take us down." *And there's not a thing we can do about it*, she thought. *How long do we have before those two scouts find someone to take us down?*

* * *

CAPITULUM, JEWEL.

Cornelius Walborski still found it amazing that his home address was the Imperial Palace in Capitulum. Sure, there were over a hundred thousand people living on the grounds, performing various duties, or just staying there through some entitlement or other. *And I'm just a common soldier, not even assigned to any of the Imperial Protection Details.*

The aircar took a slow circuit over the extensive grounds at his request. Thousands of square kilometers of gardens, riding paths, woods, even a couple of large playing fields, tennis courts, and a golf course. And over a thousand buildings besides the Palace itself, which, even though it was a mere ten stories, was one of the largest buildings the Cadet Lieutenant had ever seen. It had over twenty thousand rooms. *And I bet Sean hasn't even been to a tenth of those rooms in his lifetime.*

Of course, most of the chambers were quarters,

recreation rooms and kitchens for the staff that served the Imperial Family. Many others were the living quarters of noble family members and others who made up the Court. *And I'm considered part of that assemblage*, thought Walborski. *Not bad for a commoner from New Detroit, the son of a long line of commoners.*

The aircar swept over the main building and along the side of one of the extensive wings. Until he saw the area he recognized so well, the small courtyard that fronted his quarters. Nothing ostentatious, compared to those of the Dukes and Duchesses that lived here. A three bedroom, two bath apartment, a little bigger than most families would live in on New Detroit. But much more luxurious in every respect other than size.

"Cornelius," yelled the red haired woman as the aircar settled to the ground. She waited a moment until the car had stopped, and then ran out to meet her husband. Just behind her was a slim raven haired girl who was barely a teen, running after her adoptive mom to greet her adoptive father.

Walborski was out of the aircar in an instant, leaving his bags for someone else to deal with. He caught the woman in his arms and their lips met in a fierce kiss. Another body collided gently with his, and slender arms encircled both he and his wife.

"It's so good to have you home," said Devera, breaking the kiss to look up into his face. "I just wish you wouldn't be forced to save the Empire every time you moved from one place to another."

Cornelius laughed, and reached out a hand to ruffle the hair of his adoptive daughter. "You glad to see me too, squirt?" he asked the child, who was peering around him to look at the aircar, which was being unloaded by the driver. "What are you looking for?"

"Just trying to see if you brought any more children with you," she said with a smile.

"I've already gotten enough in the house," he said, putting one arm around her shoulders, the other around the shoulders of his wife. "And how is Junior doing?"

"Teething," said the child, making a face. "Up all hours."

"And I'm up with him," said Devera with a sigh.

Cornelius noticed that she was in her Warrant Officer's uniform, and probably just off a shift at the hospital. Someday she would be a full Doc, and an officer, if she decided to stay in the service. *The war will probably still be going on, if we survive that long*, thought her husband. *And she'll have to take a commission.*

"I know it's not fair for you," he said, looking into the beautiful eyes and freckled face of his wife.

"I signed up for it," she said with a smile. "No regrets. He's my son now too, and I will take care of him. And Rebecca is a huge help."

That was something Cornelius still felt guilty about. He had married this woman because he loved her. And had stuck her with the care of two children that were really not her own. But she seemed to accept them with no problem, and he couldn't think of any better parent to his children, natural and adopted.

"How long are you here for?" asked Rebecca as they walked through the French doors into the apartment, the driver following with Cornelius' bags, which the officer motioned for the man to drop to the floor.

"I was scheduled to be back by two days hence," said Cornelius, seeing the disappointment come immediately over the faces of the two women. "But they granted me an extension, seeing as how I inadvertently entered a combat zone."

"And help to save the Empire, again," said Rebecca, bouncing up and planting a kiss on his cheek.

"What's this again?" asked Cornelius with a sad smile. *The first medal I got was for taking my rage out on the Cacas in the jungle. Purely a personal mission of revenge. And the second time I took out a Caca base. Not something the fate of the Empire rested upon. Even this time, I only helped to stop one of the bombs from going off on the station. And I'll probably have to go through another damned embarrassing medal ceremony.*

"I think his Majesty will probably be able to get you an extension, dear," said Devera with a twinkle in her eye.

"If he has a good reason," said Cornelius. "But I can't see him taking the time to order more leave time for a junior officer."

"But, the wedding," said an excited Rebecca, unable to contain herself.

"What wedding?"

"Sean and Jennifer are to be married," said Devera with a smile. "I guess I mean his Majesty and the Duchess. And I am sure they will want you there."

"That's wonderful news," exclaimed Cornelius. *And about time too.* "But why in the hell would they care if I was there or not. It's not like I'm important or anything."

"You really don't have a clue, do you?" said Devera, patting his head. "You're his Paladin, his knight in shining armor. And someone he expects will tell him the truth when he asks about the ground war."

"Knight, huh. I'm just a commoner from New Detroit."

And Devera's smile in return told him there was trouble ahead.

*   *   *

"You've heard?" asked Countess Zhee, storming into the chamber.

"We've heard," said Duke Thomason, one of her remaining loyalists.

"And?"

"Not sure what we can do. He's the Emperor, and it's not like we can tell him who to marry."

"But, he should marry to improve the line," protested the Countess, who really couldn't care less about the Imperial line, except where it benefitted her. "He should marry to cement alliances within the nobility."

"I hear he really loves the woman," said Baron Nordstrom, sitting across the table from the Duke.

"What does love have to do with a dynastic matching," screamed Zhee, plopping down into an empty seat. "Did any of us marry for love? Or for the advantages the match gave to our families?"

"Leave it alone, Zhee," growled the Duke. "I swore my duly recorded oaths to the lad when he was crowned. As did you."

"And we are still the opposition," hissed the woman. "With a duty to oppose that which we think unwise in the running of this Empire."

"That's political, Zhee," said the Duke, staring into her eyes. "This is a personal matter, between Sean and his lady."

"I don't see it that way," said the Countess. "This is a matter of the Empire."

"So, what do you plan to do about it?" asked the Duke, giving her a look of pity.

"I don't know," said the Countess. "I just don't know."

"Just give it up, Zhee," said the Duke. "Don't let your feelings about the Emperor destroy you."

I can't give this up, thought the Countess, shaking her head. *Even if it destroys me, I will win this fight.*

Chapter Ten

War can only be abolished through war, and in order to get rid of the gun it is necessary to take up the gun.
Mao Zedong

FENRI SPACE. DECEMBER 2ND, 1001.

This might be it, thought Baggett, looking at the attacking force that was heading in to try and take his last defensive positions. The information had come over the com just an hour before. The hyper signature of a large New Terran Empire force had been received by Corps HQ, which still had scanners that detected such, even from the surface of a planet. Of course, the Fenri had picked it up too, and were trying to take out the human ground forces before a rescue mission could reach the planet.

Which means they're throwing everything at us, regardless of the cost.

Baggett could almost cry as he thought of what was left of his division, the unit he had inherited due to the death of its original commander, moving up from brigade command. Now it was only slightly larger than his original brigade had been at full strength, and over half of his soldiers were wounded. Wounded, in the case of most them, was not enough to keep them from fighting. Every suit was needed, no matter how off of optimal specs it was.

"All artillery," he ordered over the com, preparing himself to move to the final position held by his reduced headquarters company. "Unleash final protective fires."

He knew that command was dooming his few remaining artillery pieces. But they were all almost out of ammunition anyway, not really enough to even warrant a shoot and scoot. And they were out of the territory to move. Everything outside of his perimeter was enemy held land, Indian territory, as they used to say in the ancient writings on war.

The score or so of assorted artillery tracks put shells and missiles into the air, firing what they had left at their maximum rate of fire. The ground around the division erupted into gouts of dirt and fire, among them the battle suited bodies of hundreds of Fenri. As soon as the last round left the vehicles the crews evacuated them, moving with their light armored suits as fast as possible.

For some that was fast enough. For others, not so much, as fire rained down from the sky, kinetics targeted onto the now empty vehicles. Some of the crew in their light suits had made it far enough away to get to cover. Many didn't, and were lifted into the air by the blast waves, to be crushed against the ground, wrecked vehicles or the rubble of the structures that had once been habitations.

The Fenri continued on, through the fire that had taken some of the spark out of their attack. And into the crossed defensive fire of the heavy infantry, particle beams cutting through their armor as easily as through flesh.

A couple of kinetics came down, striking into the human positions, some of their force going into the advancing Fenri. That barrage stopped, quickly, when as many Fenri were killed as humans.

"Close with them," yelled Baggett over the com, almost sure that this would be the last command he would be able to give. He sighted with his own rifle, trying to get a clear sight picture through the obscuring haze, finally developing enough of a target to fire. The rest of the headquarters company crouched beside him and added their firepower to the mix, while the majority of the troopers moved close and fired into the approaching enemy point blank.

This was a knife fight, close up and personal. Men and Fenri were dying in each other's arms, plunging monomolecular blades through armor, firing point blank into bodies that were running toward them. The humans had the advantage in this kind of fight, with their larger, stronger suits. Which didn't mean they weren't taking horrendous losses of their own.

"Fall back," yelled Baggett, a command he really didn't want to give. To fall back meant they would give up any semblance of a tactical position. Instead, they would be fighting in small groups, often as individuals, in the ruins of the city. Until they ran out of power, protons or ammo. *If we can get out of this at all*, he thought, looking down on the swirling melee, and seeing another wave of enemy running toward it.

*   *   *

Lt. Jay Cummings gritted his teeth as two of the tanks of his reduced company fell off the com. The flat screen viewer showed the turret of one spinning through the air, the glowing point of impact showing on the side through each revolution. The other vehicle still had its turret, though jets of flame were shooting through every top hatch on the tank. The rear compartment was completely smashed, from above, the sign of a kinetic strike.

"Forward," he yelled over the com to his remaining three tanks. He could barely control his voice as he gave the command, one that would put his own precious hide in extreme danger. In fact, he doubted this was a maneuver he would come back from. But if he didn't move, the division would get rolled up by the next wave of Fenri.

The thousand ton tank moved forward, its bottom barely ten centimeters above the ground, all weapons ready. Well, all but the left side defensive turret and half of the right side turret laser cross. But all the major weapons systems were fully operational.

The tank rose up the small slope, exposing its turret to the mass of Fenri running across the flattened ruins. Many of the aliens turned toward the tank and its two mates, trying to bring their weapons to bear, while the rest continued to run forward.

"All weapons, fire as they come to bear," ordered the LT, taking control of the right side defensive turret himself, leaving the other weapons to the well trained crew of his vehicle. The small turret rose into position in an instant, spitting out hundreds of twelve millimeter rounds each second. The spray hit a concentration of armored Fenri, the high velocity rounds punching through the armor with most of the hits, ripping apart the little furred aliens within. A couple got off shots with particle beam weapons. One hit Cummings' tank, to bounce from the electromag field.

The main gun barked, sending a hundred kilograms of superplatinum and steel/carbon alloys at three hundred kilometers a second into another group of Fenri. The round splattered all of the aliens in its path, the shockwave stunning those within ten meters of its passage, damaging the suits with its wall of compressed air. The twin particle beams on either side of the gun sent out bursts of red fury, tearing into those stunned and disorganized Fenri who had been to either side of the main gun trajectory. They swung with the turret, ceasing fire for a moment as the main gun spoke again.

The lasers on the side of the turret fired as well, sending out gigawatt beams of one second duration, incinerating the occupants of battle armored suits with each strike.

One of the tanks took a hit, then another, the hypervelocity missiles tearing through the side of the turret. The tanked rocked almost over before coming back upright. The only function it was now capable of, screening the side of the company command tank.

Weapons came back at Cummings' tank, a half dozen hypervelocity missiles, four of them hitting the dirt in front of and to the side of the exposed turret. Two were hits, both to the front of the turret, where the armor was the thickest. Both bounced away, one taking out the right side particle beam projector.

Cummings wanted to order the driver to retreat. Everything in him called for that decision. The only one that could possibly save his life, even if the odds really weren't that good if he called it anyway. But to pull back meant letting that mass of Fenri get through to the division.

"Continue firing," he yelled into the com, wondering if anyone would reject the order, knowing that to stay in this position meant death.

The main gun kept up its fire, a round a second, blasting them out until it no longer had penetrators, then sending out high explosive antimatter. The particle beam fired until the system melted under its self-generated heat. Both laser crosses died, and the tank started taking multiple hits to its turret and hull. But it continued fighting. The other tank died, and

Cummings knew it couldn't be long. But the tactical holo showed that the second wave of the enemy attack was broken, with heavy casualties. He allowed himself a smile at that thought.

His last smile, as five hyper velocity missiles came in on a high arc, plunging down at thousands of gravities into the thinner top armor of the tank. The heavy armored vehicle exploded with the overload of kinetic energy, followed by the explosive power of the warheads. The crew was killed instantly, their deaths not even registering on their senses. And with it, the last armored punch of the division died as well.

*   *   *

Baggett led the headquarters company, what was left of it, into the close assault he hoped might allow the rest of the division to extract back into the ruins. His heart swelled with pride as his men and women followed him in, no hesitation shown.

Baggett ran full speed into a cluster of Fenri, all of whom were trying to bring their weapons around to target his suit. He slammed into the first Fenri, using the mass of his suit to bowl the smaller alien over. Swinging a fist, he hit another alien in the head with enough force to crack the helmet. With a swish pairs of monomolecular blades sprang from his forearms, protruding twenty centimeters past his fists. He swung one set of blades into the helmet of the Fenri he had just hit, then speared another through the chest with the other blades.

A Fenri slammed into his back, and something penetrated his suit, causing a sharp pain to his left shoulder. Baggett pivoted around, his right hand grabbing the arm of the Fenri and throwing him to the ground, where he stomped down with a left boot on the creature's helmed head, crushing it.

The General grabbed his rifle from where it swung on its carbon fiber strap and raising it toward the enemy, pulling the trigger and sending a sustained blast that he swept like a sword through the aliens, dropping eight of them to the ground with slashed suits spurting smoke and steam.

People starting cheering on the division com circuit, in clear violation of regulations. His people were well trained, so he was sure something must be going on to spark the lapse. Baggett looked past the Fenri who were running away, to see a mass of the little aliens lying in heaps on the ground about seven hundred meters away. He looked to the side, to see the burning forms of three King Tyrannosaurs, and knew immediately what had saved his division from overrun. *You people are heroes, and your families will receive your medals, if we ever get out of here. God bless and keep you*, he said in silent prayer for those crews. *May you get a hero's welcome in heaven, for no greater love does man have, than to lay down his life for his brother.*

"All troops," he called out over the com, breaking over the voices of all the others clogging the circuit. "Move into the rubble and take up positions. Dig in people," he said, looking at the retreating Fenri, and knowing that his people would soon be under kinetic bombardment. "Prepare to make those bastards pay for every inch they take."

*   *   *

"Translation into normal space in twenty minutes," called out the Fleet Navigation Officer.

Grand Fleet Admiral Lenkowski sat in his command chair and looked at the tactical holo that showed them what they knew about the system.

Which, all things considered, was quite a bit, considering that the wormhole equipped probes had just gone in over an hour before. The probes, of course, would have been picked up when they entered the system, but a quick boost at high gravity, followed by a complete shutdown of all drive systems, had made them all but impossible to detect.

And they're coming out to meet us, just like we figured, thought the commander of Operation *Surigoa*. The enemy fleet outnumbered his own, even with the losses they had inflicted to the pickets on the way in. In fact, both the fleet waiting at the hyper barrier, and that starting out from the planet that was the focus of the operation, outnumbered his entire force by themselves. *Hopefully, they won't be ready for everything we're bringing to the table, though.*

The picket certainly hadn't been. His advanced force, including a dozen ships with wormhole launchers, had taken out the several hundred ships the enemy had managed to get in front of them with the loss of one battleship and a pair of destroyers. And the enemy, who didn't have any kind of com system that would transmit from hyper to the space within a system, at least not at range, would have no idea what had happened to that force.

"Force alpha is dropping out of hyper, now," called out the Fleet Tactical Officer.

Len looked to the plot and saw that those ships had indeed translated for enough out to have avoided early contact with the enemy outer fleet. As soon as they were in normal space they started launching. Hundreds of missile icons appeared on the plot, all travelling at point nine c, fired from the acceleration stations outside the *Donut*. It would take them some twenty minutes to reach the alien fleet, and they would be coming in at point nine five light, optimum attack velocity.

Along with that force were the hyper VII carriers and their wings of inertialess fighters. They wouldn't use those ships against the outer fleet, but they still needed to be in a position to launch a strike at the inner force. All the ships in the force started accelerating inward at almost five hundred gravities, giving the appearance of attacking the enemy fleet.

Time passed, the missiles, over four thousand of them, getting closer to the enemy by the second, while the rest of his force moved through hyper on a course that would put them right next to the Fenri, moments after those missiles arrived. Len always hated the waiting, the feeling of total helplessness as they waited for the battle to actually commence. This was the time of thoughts, everyone in their own space for what seemed like an interminable period. Time for self-doubt, fear, beliefs that failure was the only option. Especially for the fleet commander, who had set the operation in motion, after approving all the deployments and planned actions of his subordinates. But eventually even time that seemed to stretch into forever had to end.

"Translating, now," called out the Fleet Navigation Officer, as the lights dimmed for a second, and the feeling of nausea came over all of the bridge crew. Lenkowski had always been an easy translator, and his nausea only lasted a few moments. By the time he recovered, the fleet was firing on the enemy ships. The missile wave was going in just ahead of them, disrupting the enemy formations, even those ships that were not targeted, as they tried to avoid weapons and their own ships, also trying to avoid those same weapons.

The space ahead blossomed with a thousand pinpoints of fire from missiles that had been intercepted by counters or beams. Radiation traces came from behind, where other missiles had been struck further out. And larger points of light flared with actinic fire as missiles broke through defenses and hit targets.

Into this the human fleet thrust like a knife, cold plasma fields at full strength, lasers and particle beams striking within seconds of firing. Over a thousand human ships in the center, four hundred battleships and superbattleships, three hundred cruisers, the rest escorts there for their counter-missile capability. To the port were the Margravi and Klashak ships, while to the starboard was a battle group made up of Elysium units. All took the closest enemy vessels under fire, concentrating the weapons of multiple capital ships on one Fenri, tearing through defenses that could withstand the power of one battleship, but not a dozen.

"Missiles away," shouted the Fleet Tactical Officer, and thousands of icons appeared on the plot. It took almost a minute before the enemy opened fire with their missiles, due in part to the shock of being struck so ferociously. What fire they did get off was ineffectual at best, attempting to get through the defenses of the specialized missile defense craft.

King Edward II shook with the hits of particle beams, and a couple of near miss missile detonations. The big ship was obviously important, and was drawing a lot of fire. Damage started registering on scores of the heavy ships, while the icons of some cruisers and destroyers completely left the plot as they were destroyed. More enemy ships were being blasted apart, and the space around the battling fleets started filling with plasma, illuminating the lasers linking the ships like ribbons of light. A human battleship disappeared from the human fleet, then another, followed by an Elysium vessel.

"Second wave translating, now," called out the Fleet Tactical Officer, and another eight hundred ships popped into normal space on the starboard flank of the enemy formation. The odds had just improved, though the enemy still outnumbered the allied fleet, and the initial shock was wearing off.

The pounding match continued for almost a half an hour, the human ships and their allies riding the tougher vessels, with slightly more advanced tech on the whole. Both sides took damage, the numbers mounting, though the losses of the Fenri far exceeded those of the allies, and grew exponentially as the fight continued.

"Third wave translating in, now," called out the Tactical Officer, and another six hundred warships, mostly smaller units, light cruisers and destroyers, translated in and began to release missiles into the flanks of the enemy formation. Missiles were not as effective at close range, and only managed to do some minor damage to the enemy force, picking off a ship here or there. It was still enough to disrupt the enemy defenses.

"We have enemy trying to break out to the port," yelled out one of the task force commanders. It was now obvious that the enemy was not going to win this fight. Despite the damage done to the allied fleet, the enemy had lost much more, over three thousand ships. Only seven hundred were left, and even the hyper-territorial Fenri could see that dying in place was not going to help them defend their territory.

"Shit," growled Len. The battle plan called for them taking out this entire force, not letting several hundred ships escape, which might, eventually, come to the aid of the other force. He linked in with the combined Klashak and Margravi force, which was still more or less intact, sustaining only minor casualties. Still, one of the ships that had sustained major damage was the Margravi flagship, which meant it had suffered casualties to the crew. Which meant that the intelligence that had controlled it at the start of the battle was no longer the same that was in charge now.

"We will comply," came back the com from the Margravi force, and they boosted for the enemy, the Klashak coming in to cover their flanks. The Margravi flagship took some near misses from missiles as the enemy concentrated on them. The Margravi Admiral in Command, who was really the composite mind of the entire crew, changed words in the middle of sentences as parts of its intellect were removed. It was disconcerting to Len, to say the least, what seemed to him was really a weakness to their military command. At full complement the Margravi flagship was a military genius. At three quarters complement about the equal of an above average human commander. At half strength, not much more than an academy dropout.

I'll have to ask them sometime how they handle command when there are more ships with higher intellectual ability than the flag, thought the Admiral.

The Margravi ships went to full power, five hundred gravities into the teeth of the fleeing Fenri task force. To the Margravi the individual didn't count, only the species, and it didn't matter how many casualties they took as long as they fulfilled the mission in front of them.   Which the insectoids did, magnificently, taking on the larger enemy force until the missiles from the human force had closed with the foe and struck them a terrific blow.   In the end there were few surviving ships from the enemy outer system fleet, a few more than a mere score of vessels.   Lenkowski's fleet had sustained casualties of a quarter of their vessels lost, many more damaged.   And there was still the inner fleet, outnumbering his and on their way out.

Maybe I should have brought everything I had with me to this place, thought the Admiral, looking at the Tactical Plot and not really liking what he saw.   Unfortunately, he had sent over a third of his force, split into a half dozen task groups, on separate missions to strike at other enemy systems where naval installations were known to reside.   Those missions were important to the overall success of the operation, but not more important than taking this system back and relieving the Army.

"Carriers are launching their birds," called out the Tactical Officer.

Len looked on as the small ships appeared on the plot, their graviton emissions showing their approximate positions and acceleration.   A moment later those icons dropped off the plot, the indication that they had erected their negative matter bubbles and effectively left the normal Universe.   They would be going into extreme acceleration in a moment, and there would be no graviton emissions to show where they were.   They were invisible, to all intents and purposes, until they dropped those bubbles.   And they would only drop those bubbles just before they went into the attack.

Enjoy your surprise gifts, assholes, thought Lenkowski,

looking at the enemy force on the holo. They had to think they had the advantage at this point, at least numerically. And they had to be pissed, after seeing so many of their own people killed.

Lenkowski had no idea as to the social structure of the Fenri. What kind of family groups they had, how they counted their relations. But, after seeing so many of their own kind killed, no matter how close or distant they were, they had to be riled up.

"Missile launch from the enemy fleet," called out the Tactical Officer.

Len looked at the holo, to see red icons blooming close to the enemy force. Lots of red icons, with more following every moment.

"Order all ships to open fire. Let's get every missile into space that we have. Might as well let them build up as much velocity as possible."

"What about the outer group?" asked the Tactical Officer.

"Are the probes in place?"

"Yes, sir," said the officer. "Outer probes are in place, inner probes still moving at point nine light."

"Very well. Order the outer force to release missiles. Let's give them a second surprise on top of the first." *And now we just sit back and watch, until enough time goes by for us to actually hit each other.*

*   *   *

THE *DONUT.* DECEMBER 2ND,1001.

Lucille looked over the films of the damage her station had taken, almost wanting to cry. She knew the vids looked much worse than the actual overall damage. After all, only one of the six cable supports had been taken out, and, according to the specs, it would have taken three to destroy her. That wasn't quite correct. If both cables to either side had been severed, the twisting forces might have pulled hard enough to have caused major damage. In that case, even the four remaining cables might not have been enough.

But they only got the one. And we're back at full operating capacity. Turning out all the wormholes the Fleet needs. Or at least trying to. With a thought she changed the holo view to a live shot of the repair work on the cable. Large robots were weaving new carbon and metal alloy fibers into the fabric of both sides of the break, then stretching them across and holding them together until the nanites could weave them together.

It would still be about five days until the cable was again in one complete piece. *And then I'll relax,* thought the Director of the *Donut* Project. *They can talk all they want about safety margins, but this thing is my baby. And she's hurt.*

With another thought she changed the view to the outside of the station. Where repair ships and men in armored work suits were toiling to replace the hull. That would take more than several weeks, though the structural components would be repaired within a couple of more days. After that, it would be cosmetic repairs. *And I wouldn't want to be one of those people for anything,* she thought, zooming in on one of the suited figures who was busy using a laser cutter to trim off some of the damage. Her eyes looked past the worker to the light halo around the black hole, almost four million kilometers away. If the worker's grabber units failed and he was pushed in that direction, it was a fall into infinity, with no chance of survival once he reached a certain distance from the intense gravitational point source that was the hole.

"We're lucky she survived," said Jimmy Chung, walking up and looking at the holo with her.

"I'm afraid it might happen again," she told the IIA Chief of Security who was also her lover.

"Security has been tripled," he said with a shrug of his shoulders. "They stationed an entire new division of Marines here, and, from what I've heard, the Army is going to put a couple of light infantry divisions aboard."

"That's still a lot of territory for an extra sixty thousand men to cover," said Lucille, switching the holo to a schematic of the station. "There's no saying that they have to hit the part of the station with the most people on it."

"We're setting up a factory on the station to crank out micro drones," said Chung, putting a hand on her shoulder. "Maybe a couple of billion of those little buggers would help to cover some of this area."

"Trillions would be more like it," said Lucille.

"The station proved it could take a major hit," said Chung, rubbing his hand over her shoulder, massaging the tight muscles. "It's going to take some serious firepower to take this thing out."

"I'll feel better when we capture that son of a bitch, O'Hara. Or whoever he happens to be now."

Chung nodded his head at that. Fleet Admiral Benjamin O'Hara had turned out to be one of the shape shifters that had been plaguing the Empire as of late. O'Hara had actually reduced station security prior to the attack.

"There's no telling where that particular agent is," said Chung. "At least we know where they come from, and the Brakakak have given us some pointers on how to ferret them out."

Lucille nodded at that. She had seen some of the new security measures employed herself. While the aliens could mimic the DNA of the human they were replicating perfectly, their mitochondrial DNA was not a match for the donor, since they still had to manufacture energy for the cells, which were still alien despite their appearance as being human. That, and the small imperfections in their retinal and finger prints, which were perfect enough to fool most scans, but not the new techniques IIA and its sister service, Imperial Investigation Bureau, were now implementing.

The security still wasn't foolproof, but anyone trying to penetrate the more secure parts of the station now had a gauntlet to run. Lucille found it a hassle herself, but one she was willing to undergo in order to keep her station safe.

"I'll still feel much better when we take some of those things out," said Lucille, looking down into the eyes of the shorter man. "Some confirmed kills, and a nice body count."

*   *   *

SUPERHEAVY BATTLESHIP *AUGUSTINE I.*
DECEMBER 2ND, 1001.

What a bloody mess, thought Commander Marc Dawson, as the shuttle carried him over the outer hull of *Augustine I*, the Emperor's former flagship. The skin of the ship was pockmarked with holes and gashes, some filled with the silver liquid metal that was made to flow into wounds and then harden. Other openings looked into the darkness beyond the hull, where machinery like electromag projectors, missile feed tubes, laser emitters and other, less glamorous but still important equipment had been destroyed.

And just like the bastards to give her to me as a first command, thought the Chief Engineer, who had spent the last several months on a station side assignment, getting Congreeve system ready as the bait. He had never served aboard one of the twenty-seven million ton behemoths, especially as head of engineering. Only a handful had, including the Chief Engineer who had been aboard during the battle. Unfortunately, she and her first assistant had been killed in the battle, and Admiral Miroslav had recommended him for the position for the foolish act of performing above and beyond his duties while under her command. Not that he didn't want the command, it being one of the most powerful warships in space and all. *Just that a mint condition one right out of the yards would have been appreciated.*

Men in spacesuits and the robots they supervised were swarming over the hull, while more moved to and fro from the eight million ton repair ship sitting a couple of hundred meters from the warship. Shuttles were going in and out of the hangars in a constant stream, bringing new machinery and materials to repair the internal damage, as well as supplies to replenish what had been used on deployment.

"What do you think, Commander?" asked Captain Javier Montoya, sitting in the other seat of the small shuttle they were using to survey the damage.

"I think she needs a shipyard," said Dawson with a grimace.

"Well, we need her in the next offensive," said the Captain, turning a frank look on his new head of engineering. "So the decision was made to repair her in place. The question is, can you do it in the specified time?   Or do I need to get another Chief of

Engineering?"

Dawson felt his hackles rise at the challenge. "I'll have the wee girl purring like a kitten, Skipper. I'll be damned if I don't." *Though I won't be getting much sleep over the next month or so. But as long as I have a ship, who needs sleep.*

Chapter Eleven

Politics is war without bloodshed while war is politics with bloodshed.   Mao Zedong

CAPITULUM, JEWEL. DECEMBER 3RD, 1001.

Samantha once again sat in the conference room, looking at more of the people who ran the Empire at the behest of the citizens. Four other people sat at the table, while four assistants occupied the smaller desks behind them, their flat comps open on the surface to their front. These people were not really important, with the exception that they were citizens of the Empire, and had the ears of the people they served.

The Regent looked over at Baron Emile von Hausser Schmidt, the leader of the dominant coalition of the House of Lords. Still young and fit, he was starting to show some of the stresses of leading the Lords in wartime. *At least we've got a man we can trust, leading the people we can trust among that nest of snakes.* That was very important, given the primacy of the senior House of Parliament. *And now with Marconi on board, and the Opposition weakened by his and his allies defections from Zhee's clique, we can expect some real support from the Lords.*

The next person along that side of the table was Laura Goolsby, the Speaker of the House of Commons. A still striking woman with ebony skin and long red hair, with only a touch of gray, she could be a staunch ally or a fierce opponent. She had been both to Sean, depending on the issue. She was an honorable woman, one who voted her conscience, no matter the consequences. She seemed to be on-board with Sean's vision of the war. Since all funding bills started in her house, that was important.

Across from Goolsby at that end of the table was Mohamed Ishner, Chief of the House of Scholars. While not as important as the other two houses, Research and Development projects, as well as the general institution of technology across the Empire, was the purview of his house. The devout Muslim was once one of the greatest theoretical physicist in the Empire. Samantha had studied the history of the brown skinned scholar's people, who had been very antiscience and extremely xenophobic on Earth. There was nothing like an alien invasion of the homeworld, and the loss of the beloved shrines of a religion, to change attitudes. All of Earth's religions had changed when it became apparent that whatever God they believed in didn't seem to care if they kept their ancestral world or not.

Sitting closest to Samantha on that side of the table was Prime Minister the Countess Haruko Kawasaki, Sean's appointment to lead the combined Houses of Parliament. It was traditional for a member of the Lords to take that position, though Sean had almost broken with tradition and appointed someone from the Commons. Until he had come upon the diminutive Asian woman, who was a staunch supporter.

They're a good group, thought the Regent. *Representative of the human race. The only thing that's missing are some alien faces.* And that was something that should have been in the room, as far as she was concerned. The Empire had always been very liberal in its treatment of alien species, even when they had joined the Empire through military conquest. They had become citizens as soon as they had, as a group, shown loyalty to the Empire. It might take several more generations before they were given their own units to join the Fleet, but eventually that happened as well. *We have aliens among the Cabinet, appointed by the Emperor. But the numbers are still too small among the totality of the Empire's population for them to have a significant presence in any of the Houses of Parliament.*

Most of the enlightened governments of the region were decidedly not xenophobic. Not the Human polities, not Elysium or Crakista. Even the Margravi and Klashak treated their minority populations well, partially due to the insistence of the Empire that was their protector and staunchest ally. Only the Fenri and Lasharans were truly xenophobes. *And the damned Cacas*, she thought with a grimace. The huge aliens only saw other species as having two uses. Slaves, and food.

And we'll be food for them before they end us, she thought, feeling her rising anger at that proposition. *That is not an end we will stand for. We'll end them first.* She was afraid that would be the only way this war would end, with one of the Empires completely annihilated. If it was the Ca'cadasans, it would herald a new era of freedom for the alien races they subjugated. If the aliens won, the Galaxy might be facing uncounted millennia of tyranny and subjugation.

At the end of the table was the one unknown in the room, a man that until the last couple of weeks would have been considered the staunchest of the Emperor's opponents. Now, he seemed to be a convert, though Samantha was not sure she trusted him fully. But the Archduke Percival Marconi, Leader of the Lords' Opposition Party, had said he was no longer on board with the program of obstructionism his party had espoused. *He seems so earnest, but can a leopard really change its spots?*

"From the reports we have received from the Fleet," said the Prime Minister, her speech tearing the Regent from her dark thoughts, "the Emperor has won a great victory at Congreeve."

"But not as decisive as we had hoped," said von Hausser Schmidt. "They still have a strong military presence at Conundrum, and still threaten too many of the core worlds."

"You were there, Percival," said Kawasaki. "What did you see? Was it so hopeless after all?"

"Anything but, my dear Countess," said the Archduke, a slight smile on his face. "What I saw was the courage of the men and women of our Empire on display. Even with an ambush, it was a very near thing. But they fought hard, without regard for their own safety, and defeated the foe. I was never so proud to be a member of the Empire as I was on that day. And not just a noble. As a citizen, among the many nobles and commoners who fought that day."

"And what of the Emperor?" asked Ishner, raising an eyebrow.

"I didn't see him at his station," said the Archduke, shaking his head. "He had a battle room that allowed him a view of all the action. But I heard him." A wide smile stretched the Archduke's face. "Over the com. Giving decisive commands to all of his task groups. Ordering his own ship and her escorts to close with the enemy. I don't know if I would have the courage to order a force I was on right into the teeth of an enemy fleet."

"Still, your Grace, you went along for the ride," said Goolsby. "That showed courage."

"Ha," laughed the Archduke. "I was on a twenty-seven million ton warship with thousands of crew aboard, none of whom were going to listen to a noble, even such as I.   Not when their Emperor had commanded them forward."

"And you think he is the right man to lead the Empire in this war?" asked Ishner, a look of doubt on his face. "Not too young, and brash?"

"Oh, he's young, alright," said the Archduke, nodding his head, then picking up the coffee cup before him.   "And brash, and inexperienced.   But he has something that so few people seem to possess in this and age. Inspiration."

"Are you saying he's inspired, your Grace?" asked Goolsby after taking a sip of her own coffee and smacking her lips.

"Maybe not as much that's he's inspired," admitted Marconi, nodding. "But that he is inspiring to others. He puts his hide on the line, as much as he can, the same as the people under him.   His people would follow him through the gates of hell." He looked over at Ishner. "Whatever hell you happen to believe in, Professor."

"So you are comfortable with his leadership?" asked Samantha, looking at the Archduke with tilted head.

"The only thing I am uncomfortable with is the way he risks his life at the front," said the Archduke with a grimace. "But, all other things being equal, and Augustine no longer living, I think he is the absolute best we can come up with. I am in his corner, and will do what you need of me to give him our support."

"And his announced wedding to a commoner?" asked Goolsby with a similar head tilt. "And, even though she has been elevated to the rank of Duchess, she is still a commoner."

"And what else are the rest of us nobles, Speaker Goolsby," interrupted Emile after a short laugh. "It's not like we have some kind of magical blood, despite what some of my colleagues believe. We have the same blood, and, in most cases, the same DNA. We just happen to be the descendants of those who took power when the Exodus III found our new home. And those elevated later on for services to the Empire. Which, truth be told, were sometimes the equivalent of the kiss ass trophy."

Marconi laughed. "My young Leader is correct, of course," said the Archduke. "I think my own ancestor was elevated for rallying the support of some townspeople to keep some others from lynching some reprobate prince or other." The Archduke took another sip of the very good coffee, then place his empty glass where one of the serving staff would realize it needed refilling. "I say let him marry the young woman, if that's his desire. It's obvious he's in love with her. Hell, my own Lady Wife was a commoner I met at University, and fell madly in love with. And it's worked out well enough these last sixty years."

Samantha felt herself smile at that last statement. With very long life spans, most human relationships didn't last a lifetime. The current average for a marriage was forty-one years, so the Archduke was nineteen years ahead of the curve. *I find myself liking this man more and more*, thought the Regent, who was only some few years older than the Emperor.

"And the so called Imperial genome that Countess Zhee and her ilk are sure to rage about?" asked the Prime Minister, pouring some cream into her refreshed cup of coffee.

"And what is that?" said Marconi with another

smile. "Some links in a couple of dozen chromosomes where both of the gene pairs must match up, recessives you know. Needed to be paired in both parents to insure that the offspring retains the Imperial advantages. So they just go into the fertilized egg and make sure that those pairs are there, and they have a child that is otherwise the combination of the traits of its mother and father."

"You know that the Countess will still scream bloody murder," said the Baron. "She will use this as a rallying cry to cause as much mayhem as possible."

"And maybe she can just, disappear," said Marconi, shrugging his shoulders.

"That will not happen, Percival," said Samantha, staring at the man. "We will not resort to getting rid of inconvenient citizens just because they are inconvenient. It simply will not be tolerated."

"Not that I would ever do such a thing, Regent," said Marconi with a slight smile on his face. "But I understand it has been done in the past."

"Not by this regime. Sean would have me jailed if he ever thought I had resorted to such. Now, let's move on to other business." *And thanks for letting me know I will have to look at you very carefully after all, your Grace.*

"We dodged a bullet with the *Donut*," said the Prime Minister, bringing up the next topic that was on everyone's mind. "If the Cacas had taken that out, we might be talking about how we were going to evacuate as much of our population as we could before we got rolled over."

"But the military and the IIA agents did save it," said the Baron, looking around the table as everyone nodded their heads. "And it's up to us to see that the security of that station remains a priority. As much as it pains me to say it, that structure is more important than any single star system in the Empire. Maybe any five of them. And definitely more important than any of us. We need to make sure that what happened the other day never happens again. Even if it means beefing up our own security forces on the other end of every wormhole that connects to the station."

"The Brakakak and the Crakista may not go along with us stationing more troops in their territory," cautioned Samantha.

"We don't have a portal connecting us with the Brakakak," said Ishner, shaking his head. "So that won't be a problem until we get them a new gate."

"We're actually shipping two to them," said Samantha, pulling up a holo on the flat comp sitting on the table to her front. "We'll be putting a ship gate into orbit around their homeworld, and another passenger gate on one of their stations."

"Why not just put it on their planet?" asked Goolsby, looking at the holo of the ship gate arrangement they were constructing about a light hour from the *Donut*, it having been agreed that such a distance from the station was a good point of placement for those gates.

Samantha looked at the plan that had been put into place by the Empire's military planners. Twenty-four gates to a flower, each about two light seconds from the center, about equidistant from each other in a circle. Between each gate was a fort, most in the process of being built, each capable of firing pentawatts of laser power, particle beams, and hundreds of missiles a volley at anything that came through the gates that was not wanted, like an enemy force. A light minute away was another flower, not quite filled with gates. Beyond that were the marker buoys of yet another, and another, until all six of the structures planned for that area formed another circle. The arrangement would allow ships to move quickly from gate to gate, while allowing enough separation that no known weapon could take out more than one. The forts provided security, along with a fleet force that was both guarding the gates, and providing a reaction force for the systems on the other side of the portals. Next would come warehouses for goods, and habitats for people waiting for their transfers to another ship.

It was thought that nothing that came through the gate could become a threat to the station. First, because all of the holes were oriented so that any ships coming through would not be on a line to the station. They would have to reorient, decelerate, and then head for the *Donut*. And in that time the defense fleet would be able to take them under fire. And second due to the distance. It would take hours for a missile to reach the station from any of those gates, and any beam weapons would be so attenuated as to be ineffectual before they reached their target.

"After what happened to their primary dock in orbit, they refuse to even discuss having a gate on their planet," said Samantha. "And considering the size of the bombs the Cacas brought through, I really can't blame them. That thing would have killed everyone on a small continent.

"And that brings up the next point," said Samantha, looking straight at Archduke Marconi. "And the reason we asked you to be here, your Grace."

Marconi's ears perked up and he raised an eyebrow.

"You are a member of the Lord's oversight committee on Intelligence, your Grace," said Samantha. "And we have a security matter that needs to be broached to at least one member of that committee."

"I'm all ears, Regent," said Marconi. "And I assume this is something you don't want discussed in front of the entire Committee?"

"We would prefer that, yes. And I would like your word that what you hear here will not go any further. This may compromise an operation that is vital to the war effort."

"With that said, how could I refuse, since my curiosity has now gotten the better of me."

"There are Caca intelligence agents in the Empire," said Samantha.

"That would not surprise me in the least," said the Archduke with a laugh. "And are the shape shifters their agents?"

"As far as we know, no. But there are other agents, members of their intelligence apparatus that are operating within the Empire, that we are well aware of. In fact, we know where several of these operatives are, at least as far as the planet or star system is concerned. And we are feeding them information."

Marconi sat up straight in his chair as the last words left Samantha's mouth. "We're feeding them information? Whose idea was that?" He stood up and stared at the Regent.

"Actually," said Samantha, holding out a hand to motion the man back into his seat. "It was the idea of their spymaster. It turns out that his species is tired of being the slaves of the Cacas. They want their freedom, and they see us as their best chance of getting it. On their recommendation, we have been feeding them false information, while they have been giving us the straight goods on their masters' dispositions and plans."

"And you're sure this information is legit?" asked the Archduke, his eyes narrowing.

"We can't tell if everything is correct," said von Hausser Schmidt. "Some of the long range stuff they have given us has not come to pass. And there is the problem of the transmission of information, both ways. But what they have told us has recently been backed up by what we have seen. I agreed with the Emperor that this was a resource we needed to cultivate. They are in the Empire anyway, spying, gathering information. We really had nothing to lose by giving them data they knew was disinformation."

"Well, your Grace," asked Samantha, "what do you think?"

"Like, as you said, a resource we need to cultivate," said the Archduke, nodding his head. "And you have my approval as a member of the Intelligence Oversight Committee to proceed. Though I'm sure my other committee members might raise holy hell to find out this had been approved behind their backs. But, as I heard said in the Fleet, it's better to ask forgiveness than permission. And you definitely have my forgiveness on this one."

"So happy to hear that, your Grace," said Samantha with a smile. *Now we won't have to make you disappear*, she thought as the smile widened across her face. *Not that we would ever really do such a thing, but there's no law against wishful thinking.*

*   *   *

"We have a go, Director," came the voice of the Regent, Samantha Ogden Lee, over the secure com.

Good thing, thought Ekaterina Sergiov, the Director

of the Imperial Intelligence Agency, the IIA. *Since we already sent the information up the line.* "That's great news, ma'am," the Chief Spy of the Empire told her surrogate boss, the one who ran the show when the Emperor was not in the loop. "So Marconi got on-board?"

"So it seems," said the Regent. "I believe he's had a complete change of heart. But I've learned over the short period of time I've been in this position not to trust anyone too much."

Something I learned years ago, thought Ekaterina.

"What did you send our friends?" asked the Regent.

"We exaggerated the damage to the *Donut*," said Sergiov, remembering the report she had approved. The Agent in Charge had wanted the Cacas to get the story that the station had been destroyed, but there were too many people in the Empire who knew that wasn't true, and it was bound to leak. "According to the information they were given, the station will be out of operation for the next three months."

"That should give the Cacas some hope," said Lee, smiling in the holo. "And probably cause some alterations in their plans."

Though I'm not sure that such an alteration would benefit us, thought Sergiov, nodding. *But I'm just the spy, not the policy maker.*

"What else?"

"We fudged the casualty figures from Congreeve," stated the spy. "We inflated them to the point where it looks like we took double the losses we really did. And the expected reinforcements from our allies have not arrived. We were able to add information about Elysium going on a witch hunt of their own people, and that causing a delay in their expeditionary force arriving in our space."

"That should lead to some over optimistic thinking among their strategists," said the Regent. "Just what we needed."

"We also gave them the other information, Regent," continued Sergiov, grimacing at the thought of what she was about to say.

"Other information?"

"You know, the straight intel we had to put in with the disinformation."

"Oh," said Lee, the expression on her face falling. "And that was really necessary?"

"It was, Madam Regent," said Sergiov, still feeling dirty from what she had had to do, feeling the betrayal of her own Empire. For the disinformation to be believed, some real information had to be sent up the line as well. Real information, the kind that led to people being killed. *Just like Coventry, on the home world, in the Second World War*, thought Ekaterina, like many in the government an amateur historian. *And I don't think Churchill felt any better than I do. Those poor people.*

"And what have our friends sent our way," said the Regent, looking very uncomfortable with the whole concept of having to betray some of her own to gain advantage.

Welcome to my world, Samantha, thought Ekaterina, as she called up the document they had received from the Maurid spymaster. "You understand that our man does not have access to all of their intel," she told the Regent. "Like us, they compartmentalize their information on a need to know basis. So, he was able to get us what he could."

"And you're sure of the veracity of this intel?"

"As sure as I can be of any intel. Most times it's

impossible to really tell how accurate intel is until it has come to pass. But it seems to match with what we already know, within the constraints of time."

And that is really a major problem with trying to run an Imperial intelligence service. All the information we receive is weeks old. The wormhole system might help, some, but we have to pretend that the information we get is still creeping along at interstellar speeds.

"And your evaluation of this intel?"

"We've got some serious problems coming up the pike, ma'am," said Sergiov, wishing for the moment that she did not know all the things she did. "I'm not sure what you people are going to do about it, but I'm glad it's not something I have to make decisions about. My job is just to get you the intel, then depend on you and the Emperor to make what you can of it."

"And sometimes I wish that I didn't have this burden placed on my shoulders," said Samantha, a sad expression on her face. "It was so much easier just being the com officer on a battle cruiser."

"Just as it was so much easier being a field agent," said Ekaterina, smiling. *For all the gut wrenching fear involved, at least the decisions were easier.*

"Let me know if anything else of importance comes through," said Lee, her face firming into a look of determination. "I may not like everything you have to tell me. But I am well aware of the importance and utility of you and your organization. Lee out."

The com died, leaving the Chief Spy with her own thoughts for a moment. They were not the kind of thoughts that she liked. *Only one way to handle that*, she thought, calling up the organizational chart of her fiefdom, losing herself in the day to day work that was the majority of her job. Soon her mind was wrestling with a way to use her limited manpower to cover unlimited possibilities. And she didn't have time to think about the hopelessness or their situation.

*   *   *

"OK," said Countess Zhee, looking at the other members of her committee, that of the Lords' Military Appropriations and Contracts. While it was true that all funding bills originated in Commons, the actual contracting of services, who would get that money and what they would do with it, was the purview of the Lords. "It's decided. The money that was going to the Gryphon conversion project could be much better spent putting more human crewed ships into space."

The show of hands was almost unanimous, all members of the committee being human, and all holding beliefs that humans should retain supremacy in the Empire. Not that aliens weren't important. In fact, most of them had from thousands to millions of aliens living in the areas that they were responsible for. In Zhees case, a region of New Hanou, in Duke von Schlieffen's, an entire continent of New Dresden. They were important, in the minds of the nobles, for their work ethic and desire to get ahead in human dominated society. But, as far as these elites were concerned, the Fleet should only be comprised of human operated warships.

Damn Augustine and the other Emperor's before him for giving the Phlistarans and Malticorans their own ships, thought Zhee. The Gryphons also had some ships of their own, and maybe three hundred vessels in the Fleet were manned by totally alien crews. Most were smaller units, though there were more than a score of battleships in that mix as well. The appropriations bill had called for funding conversions of another ten battleships to

Gryphon crews, making the vessels something that they would find comfortable as far as living quarters, food services, medical bays, etc. The shipyard was already in a Gryphon system, owned by the family of the current Minister of Commerce and Industry, Lord H'rressitor. Zhee thought there was some favoritism going on with the contracts, not even considering that every military shipyard in the Empire was now operating at full capacity.

"What about the funding of Gryphon ground combat equipment?" asked Duke von Schlieffen, nodding to the next contract on the holo. "Do you want to cut funding for them as well, Countess?"

"I see no reason to not fully fund some more divisions of the aliens for the Imperial Army," said the Countess with a sneer. "After all, they really can't do much more than fight wherever the fleet delivers them. And each Gryphon in battle armor frees a human to continue producing at home."

"I agree," said Count Warshawski, nodding at the holo. "Lord knows, I've lost enough people to the damned Army recruiter since this unpleasantness began. We brought civilization to the aliens. Let them die to defend it."

"But not in the Fleet," said Zhee, looking from face to face.

"No," agreed the Duke. "Not in the Fleet. That, as the Count calls it, unpleasantness, that happened to the Brakakak should teach us not to arm our minority populations with ships capable of killing all life on a planet. No telling what they're going to do if they get their hands on that kind of power, and the war ends." Missing was the unspoken part of that statement, but everyone in the room thought the outcome of the war was a foregone conclusion. After all, humanity had never lost a war. So why would they start the second millennia of the Empire's existence by losing one now.

"So that bill is passed to the Lords," said Zhee, who headed the committee. "With our recommendation for a positive vote." The first bill, the one authorizing conversion of ships for alien use, would never see the light of day. As far as the Lords were concerned, it had never existed.

"Next up is the appropriations bill for the expansion of the New Hanou shipyards," said Zhee, forcing herself to hold her hand down. Everyone knew how she was going to vote, since the shipyards benefited her own home system, but decorum must be observed.

"I think we can all agree on that one," said the Duke.

Especially since one of your missile facilities is coming up for an expansion contract, thought Zhee, looking at the Duke. *You scratch my back, von Schlieffen, I'll scratch yours.* That was the way committee work had always been done, and none of the members saw any reason to change it now, just because of a little thing like a war.

Chapter Twelve

We are going to have peace even if we have to fight for it.   Dwight D. Eisenhower

FENRI SPACE. DECEMBER 4TH, 1001.

"We're coming up on orbital insertion," said the Navigation Officer from the primary bridge of *King Edward II*.

Len sat in his chair on the flag bridge, watching the viewer that showed the superbattleship and eight regular battleships sliding into orbit. They weren't the first vessels to achieve orbit. There were already more than a hundred vessels in everything from low orbit, about five hundred kilometers, to past geosynch, over forty thousand kilometers. About half of the ships were logistics vessels and troop transports, and space was thick with thousands of shuttles falling into and coming out of the atmosphere.

Thank God there were still some of our boys left, he thought, looking at one of the shuttles on a zoom from the holo. It was rising up, on a heading for this very ship.   On-board was the highest ranking surviving officer from the expedition. Among the less than ten thousand from the initial ninety K that had originally taken the planet. *We got here in time to save the survivors, and we paid a price to do it*.

The Fenri had been caught off guard by the twin punch of the inertialess fighters and the wormhole launched missile swarms. The inertialess ships had hit first, coming out of their bubbles about twenty light seconds from the enemy fleet. Far enough away for the enemy to have gotten off some shots. But too close to allow them to coordinate their defense against an enemy they hadn't even known was coming. The attack craft had hit hard, knocking out almost three hundred of the enemy ships on their pass through. They had lost over a hundred and fifty of the very expensive craft. A trade off most commanders would have been ecstatic about. *But not the family and friends of those people.*

The missiles had come flying out about fifteen minutes later, moments after the first of the ship launched weapons were nearing attack range. A thousand missiles came out at an unexpected angle, traveling at point nine five light. The Fenri defenses had been swamped by the two simultaneous waves, with only a hundred and four ships surviving. Most of those surrendered, their commanders and crews in complete shock.

The fleet losses hadn't been one sided. The Fenri missile swarm had taken out over a hundred ships, and damaged twice that many. The Margravi had been the most seriously hit of any of the contingents, their penchant for sacrifice for the good of the whole causing them to take more risks than any of the other species. *But their sacrifice allowed more of our other ships to escape damage*, thought the Admiral of the courageous insectoids. *Or, is it courage, when fear is impossible for them to experience?.*

Now they controlled the system again. And, according to their intelligence, the Fenri fleet was finished as a fighting force. There were still some ships in their Empire, but no large forces. The New Terran Empire fleet had ravaged them here and in the other four systems they had struck. It would be years before they could start replacing their losses, while the Empire would take advantage of any breaks in the primary theater to keep hammering them.

Starting here, thought Len, looking at the ship gate that was being put together in high orbit. That would allow the Empire to shift whatever resources they needed to this system if the Fenri tried to surprise them. *You may have been theirs at one time, but you are ours now,* thought Lenkowski, looking at another holo that portrayed the entire system, with the icons of his fleet showing on it.

"Shuttle will be docking in four minutes," came a call over Len's personal com. "You said you wanted to know."

"Right," said the Admiral, looking at the holo that showed the assault shuttle on final approach. Most would be heading straight to the transports, and then home through the ship gate, as soon as it was assembled. There they would be used as the cadre to rebuild the terribly eviscerated divisions, until the heavy corps was again ready for redeployment. "I'll be right down."

The hangar was a bustle of activity, as a Marine honor guard and many of the ship's officers made ready to greet the VIP coming aboard. The main hatch was open, fifty meter high by fifty meter wide double doors open. Beyond the opening was the vacuum of space, the only thing between the people and it the shimmering electromagnetic field, holding the cold plasma in place that kept the air molecules from leaving the hangar.

The assault shuttle, as unlovely a ship as there was, pushed through the cold plasma field slowly, scarred nose leading. Its grabber units were glowing red with the heat of their operation, and the landing pads lowered as soon as it was in the hangar. With a clang, followed by a double as the two remaining pads thumped on the deck, the shuttle settled to the hard floor. A moment later the side hatch opened, and the naval personnel craned their necks to get a first look at the passengers.

"Commander, XXXXI Heavy Corps, on deck," called out the loudspeaker, and all of the naval personnel rendered a hand salute, while the gathered Marine company brought their ceremonial rifles to present arms. Len saluted like the rest, even though he was at least three ranks higher than an Army Lt. General. *And he's not even that,* thought the Admiral, looking up the record of the man they were saluting. *Only a Brigadier by permanent rank, brevetted to Major General to command a division when the commander was killed. And then taking over the corps when all officers above him were killed or otherwise incapacitated. But he still deserves our salute, after what he and his people have been through.*

He looks like hell, was Len's next thought as the man stepped onto the deck. He had on a fresh uniform that had been flown down with the shuttle, and looked like he had showered. His face was clean shaven, probably taken care of by his battle armor nanites. But the face was what surprised Len. It was gaunt, to say the least. Like the man had lost ten kilos of mass while on the planet. And the eyes had a stare to them, a look that seemed to be light years away. Len had seen that look before, from naval crew and Marines who had gone through the hell of extended combat. This man looked the same. The officer stood still for a moment, looking confused, then rendered a perfect return salute, dropping it and stepping forward.

"General Baggett," he said to the officer, stepping out of line and offering his hand.

Baggett snapped back to attention and saluted, and Len was beginning to think they had performed enough saluting here to last a lifetime.

"Welcome aboard my flagship. I hope you will remain comfortable here on the trip home."

"Thank you, sir," said Baggett in a voice that sounded hollow with his exhaustion. "And we're here to stay," he said, motioning toward the hangar doors, which were in the process of closing. "We lost a lot of people holding this rock, and there are a lot of Fenri slaves down there counting on us to protect them."

"When we leave here, there will be four divisions on the planet, as well as four brigades of planet based antiship artillery. That, in and of itself, may not be enough to hold the planet if the Fenri decide to commit all the ships they have left in their totally trashed fleet. But the system is only a wormhole gate away from major reinforcements."

"And my orders, sir. Will I be staying with the corps, or at least the division?"

"I don't know what your final orders will be," said Len, shaking his head and wishing he had some news to give him about his future disposition. "But I do have some good news for you, at least short term. You're going to Jewel. The Emperor has you on his list of guests, and I am so happy I was able to recover you before his wedding."

*   *   *

Major General Samuel Baggett, and the two star rank had just been verified by Imperial order, knelt in one of the chapels of the superbattleship. This one had been configured as a Reformed Catholic shrine, the largest denomination of the Empire. Baggett had not been much of a church goer in recent years, but his current experience, one that had taught him how truly fleeting life was, had convinced him that maybe it was a good time to return to the faith.

Maybe I joined the wrong service, he thought, as he took a second to look around the well-appointed chapel. *Yeah, they have to go through their own version of hell when they fight. They might not see guts splattered everywhere. Or they might possibly could. When death strikes the Fleet, it comes in fast. But, by God, they get hot meals, showers and beds. And that's sure something higher class than what we get, while we're dying in the mud.*

Shit, he thought, not the most appropriate thing to go through his mind in what amounted to a church. But the feeling of going through a wormhole was that disconcerting, and was something he had only experienced a couple of times before. There was the feeling of being everywhere in the Universe at once, as time stretched out endlessly. And then the shock of coming back to the Normal Universe, even though everything looked the same. *Because you're aboard a spaceship, genius*, thought the General, shaking his head, even barking a short laugh.

"Are you OK, sir?" asked a man in a naval uniform with the insignia of a Lt. Commander on the shoulder boards of his semi-formal uniform, and the crosses of a Christian chaplain on his lapels.

"Are you a priest?" he asked the man. Just because it was a Reformed Catholic chapel, and the chaplain had the crosses of a Christian denomination on his uniform, didn't mean the man belonged to that denomination. Military chaplains were expected to cover a number of the faiths, and it wouldn't have been very strange at all to find a Baptist minister counseling a Wiccan.

"I am, General," said the man, bowing his head.

"I've been a Fleet chaplain for the last twenty years. Before that, a parish priest. Until the New Vatican gave me orders to serve our fighting men."

"No family?"

"I had a wife, and two children," said the man, whose name tag said Martinez.

"Had?"

"They died on Cimmeria, General. Like so many others."

"I am so sorry," said Baggett, not really knowing what else to say. He thought it over for a moment, while the man stood patiently by. "Do you ever feel guilty? Surviving them, I mean?"

"All the time," said the man folding his hands to his front and looking down. He looked back up into Baggett's eyes. "But it was God's will that I survive to serve my fellow beings. As painful as that sometimes seems."

Baggett looked down himself, wondering how he was going to broach the subject to a man who in many ways had lost so much more than he had. He had loved his troops, in an abstract sort of way. *Hell, there at the end, I didn't even know two percent of them. And he lost a wife, and two of his own children.*

"Are you feeling survivor's guilt, my son," said the priest, laying a hand gently on the shoulder of the General.

"Yes, Father," said Baggett, blinking back his tears. "That I do."

"That's a normal reaction, my son. And you were in charge of a Corps?" asked the Priest, his eyes unfocusing for a moment as he went into link to gather information.

"I started in charge of a brigade," said Baggett,

shaking his head from side to side. "And I'm not even sure I was ready for that much command, since I had just become a battalion commander less than a year before. And then, people started dying, lots of them under me, some over, and I just kept getting more and more responsibility, until I got the top slot. And things just kept getting worse."

"I'm sure you did the best you could do, General," said the Priest, patting Baggett's shoulder. "And that's all God can ask of any man or woman."

"And better than most of us could do," said another voice from behind Baggett.

The General turned to see Grand Fleet Admiral Lenkowski standing behind him, changed into a duty uniform since the reception at the hangar. He still had six stars on his collar, and looked every inch the high ranking Admiral. The Admiral stepped forward and moved into the pew from the other side, sitting down beside Baggett and motioning for the General to take a seat.

"I was looking over your after action report with my Marine commander, Major General Sopworth. She felt that you did an outstanding job, considering what was facing you. I agree. A lot of men just would have given up, and hoped the enemy was in a prisoner taking mood."

"I didn't bring many people with me off of that planet," said Baggett, shaking his head.

"And I lost a third of my fleet in the action to retake that system," said Len, frowning. "I wish I could have done a better job, and brought more people home. And by people, I mean all of the sentients under my command. Instead, I lost six hundred ships, and over four hundred thousand beings, to rip the heart out of the Fenri fleet. Unfortunately for my people, it was the best I could do. And fortunately for my people, I did my best. Do you see what I'm saying, son?"

Baggett looked over at the Admiral, thinking through what he said.

"I was the one put in charge, son," said Lenkowski after Baggett didn't speak. "There might have been a young genius in my command, an ensign, or even a petty officer, who could have done a better job if given a chance. But we didn't know that, and, for all my shortcomings, I'm a known quantity. Just like you were to your own superiors. You were given command, someone else wasn't. And so you had to take the shit on your shoulders. But don't let anyone tell you that you did a piss poor job. Hell, son. Sonia Sopworth said you did as fine a job of leadership, holding out against that horde, as anyone she had ever heard of."

Baggett simply sat there and nodded his head, not knowing what to say, but absorbing the words of a man who had been a flag officer three times longer than he had been in the service, including the military academy.

"The General did have one negative comment about you though," said the Admiral. "Though, coming from a Marine, I think it was partially admiration."

"And what was that, sir?"

"She thought you exposed yourself way too much. And she had a comment about your close in blade work."

Baggett found himself laughing, and wondering how his mood had changed so quickly. *Damn Marines think they're such hot shit.*

"She also said she would be proud to serve under you any day, General. And, coming from that Marine, that is high praise indeed."

Very high praise, thought Baggett. Most of the Marines he knew, and he knew many, would cut off their right arms before praising a soldier.

"Feel better?" asked Len, patting Baggett on the shoulder.

"Yes, sir," said Baggett, getting up from his seat. "Thank you."

He made way for the Admiral to get up and get by, then moved and sat back down, kneeling from that position. He looked at the Priest, still standing beside the pew. "And Father. Thank you."

*   *   *

SECTOR IV SPACE. DECEMBER 5TH, 1001.

"Dr. Southard," said the young woman who greeted him in the hangar. "Welcome aboard the *Gringo*."

"Thank you, uh."

"Kallie Wyse," said the woman, who was dressed in an unmarked ship jumper. "I'm the third officer."

"No Naval ranks?"

"Oh, hell no," she said, shaking her head. "We're a civilian research vessel, chartered under military contract. The Imperial University at Capitulum holds title to the ship. Anyway, I'm here to show you to your quarters. One of the spacers will bring along your bags. Then we'll go and meet the Captain."

Gringo was not a large ship, only about seventy thousand tons, and capable of hyper VII travel. The hangar was only large enough for two shuttles, the one she kept aboard, and temporary stowage for the shuttle that had carried Southard from the light cruiser he had traveled into the system on.   He had wondered at the time why they were going past the hyper barrier to meet the research ship.   *Or, why the damned cruiser wouldn't go past the hyper barrier to deliver me, and instead only risked the shuttle.*   There had been a trio of destroyers outside the limit as well, and he had heard one of the ratings aboard the cruiser talk about the wormhole com one of those ships carried.

"Can ask you a question, Miss Wyse?" he asked just before they got to his quarters, down one of the two corridors that housed research personnel.

"You can call me Kallie, Dr. Southard.   You're not in the chain of command, and we don't really stand on formality here."

"Then call me Larry," said Southard, as the door to his quarters opened.

It was actually larger than he expected, a five meter square room with bed, desk, kitchenette, and two doors, one leading to the bathroom, another to a closet. He knew this kind of ship, which might go on a research cruise for a year or more, and was made as comfortable as possible for its passengers and crew.   Or as comfortable as could be, once supplies and state of the art sensors were crammed into the hull.

"And what was your question, Larry?" asked the young woman as she waved the spacer with his luggage into the room.

"Why are we so far in from the hyper barrier? Isn't that a major risk, this close to this big boy blowing its top?"

"Oh, there's no danger of that happening for at least a couple of months," said Kallie in a very cavalier tone.   "We'll move out behind the barrier well before anything can happen."

"And why do you believe that nothing will happen for at least two months?"

"That's what Dr. Tashiga told the Captain," said the Third Officer. "He said that, based on his theories of stellar evolution, this star will continue burning neon for at least two months before it goes into oxygen, and then silicon burning, causing a collapse."

"It's already burning neon?" Southard asked in alarm. "How long has that been going on?"

"About five days," said the Third Officer, her eyes widening at the scientist's tone. "Why?"

"We don't have much time," said Southard, storming from the room. "Where is your Captain?"

"The Captain is off duty at this time," said Kallie. "The First Officer has the con at the moment."

"And Dr. Tashiga?"

The woman went into link for a moment, something Larry couldn't do on this ship, not having yet been granted access. "He's on the observation deck."

"Then take me there."

Moments later the Scientist was led onto the so called observation deck, with was really a very complete scientific observation suite, with multiple stations and over a dozen holos, including one very large 3D viewer where the normal *window* would be on the deck.

The view in the largest holo was spectacular, the roiling surface of a supergiant star with over fifty sols of mass. Once two blue supergiants that had been in an unstable orbit around each other, they had fallen into a single mass that was a thousand times brighter and hotter. And one whose lifespan was much reduced over what the two individual stars would have enjoyed. Those stars had already entered the carbon burning stage that produced neon, about two hundred years before, and doomed them to supernova about four hundred years down the line. Now, because of their increased mass, that cycle had ended, and the star was burning neon, fusing it to oxygen. Huge prominences arched from the surface of the star, some curling to splash back onto the brilliant surfaces, others to continue flying out into space.

Another holo showed a schematic of the twenty close in observation platforms that were arrayed around the star at ten astronomical units, about one point five billion kilometers out. Even at that distance they were still absorbing fierce amounts of stellar radiation. They were, of course, getting their information on the star over one and a half hours from the time it was happening, due to the light speed limit. The plot showed *Gringo* was two light hours further out, way too close, to Southard's way of thinking. They were using a subspace relay from the satellites, and getting their information ten minutes after the fact, still a great improvement over the light speed limit of normal transmissions.

Southard's eyes glanced over the other holos until he came to the one that was of the most importance, the main sensor scan of the star. Spectrographs, deep radar, subspace pulses, they were combined on this holo to give a picture of what was going on in this star. And he didn't like what the star was showing him. It was still burning neon, at a much reduced rate, and oxygen was starting to fuse in the core. By his estimation, based on eyeballing the star, oxygen would be used up in a little over a week and a half, and silicon would become the dominant substance. The silicon would fuse, resulting in the production of iron in the core, and the collapse that would cause a supernova. The last stage would probably last a couple of hours.

"There you are," said Dr. Yoshi Tashiga, turning in his chair to stare at Southard. "I told them you weren't needed here. That your theories were wrong, and I was right."

"And still a pompous ass, eh, Yoshi," said Southard, glaring at the man who was his prime rival. "I guess it's a good thing I got here, then."

Chapter Thirteen

Politics have no relation to morals. Niccolo Machiavelli

THE *DONUT.* DECEMBER 6TH, 1001.

"Welcome aboard the *Donut*, your Majesty. My Lady," said Dr. Lucille Yu, smiling as she bowed at the waist.

Two score of Marines in their ceremonial red uniforms performed a rifle salute at the same time. The other fifty Marines in the chamber were in full battle armor, the medium suits normally worn for shipboard actions, where maneuverability was paramount. The Imperial Secret Service and the Imperial Intelligence Agency were also here in force, over forty agents in the room, all trying to look nondescript in the business suits their operatives normally wore. And all failing miserably, as those suits, of a very conservative cut, were all that was needed to give away their function.

There were scores of newsies in the room as well, the select few of the thousands who had wanted to be here. Sean knew that all had direct mind uplinks to their networks, and that everything they saw and heard was being cast on their home planets, if near enough, or recorded for later playback. Dozens of small drones floated through the air, adding to the footage, and all carefully programed to stay clear of the Imperial couple, who had a security field around them projected by their closest battle suited Marine guards. Any unauthorized device that entered that field would be deactivated, if not destroyed, and its owner would find him or herself the center of questioning as to their intentions.

Sean held the arm of his Fiancé within the curve of

his own, her left hand resting lightly on his forearm. He looked at her face for a moment, seeing her nervousness at appearing in front of such a large gathering. She looked up into his eyes, swallowed, smiled, then composed herself and nodded her head. *Good girl*, thought Sean, nodding back, then stepping forward to shake Dr. Yu's hand. He knew that Jennifer would never relish the public eye. As long as she could tolerate it in small doses, everything would be fine.

"Thank you, Director Yu," he told the woman in front of the cameras. "And I am very happy that the *Donut* is still here for me to be greeted on."

"Amen to that," whispered Read Admiral Kelso, who had just come out of the wormhole in time to hear the last comment.

"We have set up a stand over here to allow you to speak to the press, your Majesty," said Yu, waving toward a heavy faux wood structure set toward the near end of the gate room.

Sean glanced at Jennifer, and she nodded once again. He had told her there might be questions, and it was his job as the Supreme Ruler of the Empire to talk to the press. Especially since Samantha had made a deal with the press, allowing them access to him at times like this, in return for them getting on board with Sean's other policies, like giving the war effort a positive spin. But another part of the deal was that Jennifer was not fair game for their questions. Until and unless she agreed to an interview.

The couple walked over to the stand, which had seats arranged behind it. Sean helped Jennifer into one of the chairs, then took his place behind the podium and started to receive questions. A few of the reporters still tried to direct questions to Jennifer, but for the most part Sean deflected them, and passed over those reporters. Until finally a question came that he hadn't been expecting.

"Zoe Chan," said the Asian woman who had waited her turn patiently. "Galactic News Network. Is it true that we have a new method of detecting the shape shifting aliens that have caused so much trouble?"

Sean froze, a troubled expression on his face. *How in the hell did they find out so quickly?* was his first thought, followed a second later by, *this is supposed to be top secret information. If it's leaked, we lose a big advantage in trying to catch the bastards.*

"I am sorry, but I cannot say anything on that subject," he told the reporter, smiling, trying to disarm the situation.

"If you can't, your Majesty," asked the reporter, "who can? After all, you are at the top of the intelligence heap. If there's an answer out there, you must know it."

"Oh, I know the answer," said Sean, motioning to one of his security staff, then linking to that agent's com. "I just don't think I can give you an answer at this time." *Make sure that none of this gets out to the public,* he sent over his implant to his Chief of Detail. *Remove any mention of this topic from the casts, and take Ms. Chan into custody at the end of this interview. I want to know where she has gotten this information.*

Yes, sir, came back the reply, and Sean could see agents already on the move to make sure they were near to Ms. Chan.

Zoe Chan saw the movement, and seemed to have realized that she had asked the wrong question. The young woman sat down and tried to disappear, but the damage was already done. Now it was damage control, making sure that none of these people spread rumors that caused as much damage as a disclosure would.

If the damned shifters know we have new ways of detecting them, they will go to ground, and avoid penetration of secret facilities. They will attack us where they can, more assassinations and bombings, only the targets will be those we can't properly defend.

After another hour the press conference was over, and Sean couldn't wait to get back to the front, where he didn't have to deal with such things. Most of the questions had dealt with the military situation, and the recently concluded Battle of Congreeve. Sean was happy to answer those questions, as one of the reasons for that battle was to raise the morale of the Empire, and what he had told them could only bring hope. *And hopefully, Bagration will raise it more.*

"Those are all the questions we have time to answer," said one of the Emperor's Press People. "We have data chips for all of you that you might find interesting."

Sean was on his feet in an instant, leading Jennifer away from the stand and toward the exit from the chamber, his armed guards and entourage forming up around him. Lucille Yu walked with him, filling him in on the state of the station, and all of the new construction going on in the local space. Sean was careful to not give her any information she was not privy to already, since there were many things going on that she did not have a need to know.

The Emperor looked with approval on all the military personnel he saw on the way to the tram, then on to the next gate room. Most of the soldiers, Marines and spacers were in soft uniforms, though all were at least carrying side arms. Every single one of them, all looking very alert so soon after the attack on the station. One in every four soldiers, and half of the Marines, were wearing battle armor, and were heavily armed. There were also many more than he remembered from his last trip, and linking into the station computer, he was gratified to see that the military presence had doubled since the attack, and that more were scheduled to be assigned.

The next gate took them directly to the portal at the Hexagon, the closest one to the palace, and one of two that had now been installed in the capital city. Sean decided he really didn't want to have to deal with the public any more this day, so he and his party took the lift into the depths of the building, kilometers down, into the hidden, secret rooms of the structure. From there they took the private train to the palace, itself debarking into the Imperial refuge far beneath the main building on the grounds.

"I am so happy to be home," said Jennifer as they finally reached the private quarters of the Emperor and his family, which at the moment consisted of a couple score cousins and Sean's soon to be wife.

"We have a dinner scheduled with Samantha, the Prime Minister and some of my cabinet," said Sean, linking into the palace computer. "Are you up to it?"

"Not really," said Jennifer, her expression one of extreme fatigue. "Can I skip out."

"Of course," agreed Sean, sitting down next to her on the bed and putting an arm around her. He kissed her tenderly, then forced himself to get up from the bed. "I need to get ready. I'll be back soon. And I've scheduled a special ceremony for tomorrow. One I don't think you'll want to miss."

"We'll see when tomorrow comes," she said, walking toward the master bath. "I'm going to relax, then catch some sleep. Wake me when you get back here, and I'll have a special ceremony for you as well."

Dinner was in the Gold Room, a formal dining chamber used for occasions of state. Only one of the thirty tables in the room was occupied, though it was seated to capacity with all the members of the Cabinet, the chiefs of the military, the Prime Minister, and, of course, the Regent. Only a few security personnel were in the room, their eyes constantly roaming, even in this supremely secure location.

"Jennifer will be staying here after the wedding," said Sean, looking at Samantha. "She says she has had enough of going into combat."

"Smart girl," said Samantha. "So, she will be Empress after the ceremony. And I can leave this job."

"Sorry," said Sean, after taking a sip from his wine glass. "Jennifer really doesn't have any experience with government, and she has no idea how to deal with some of the snakes we are inflicted with. I will depend on you and Haruko," he gestured at the Prime Minister, "to teach her the ropes."

"That could take some time," said the Prime Minister, frowning, then taking a sip of the vintage reserved for the imperial line.

"Then take the time. I really don't expect for her to become a master manipulator. She doesn't have the upbringing to become one of us. Or, to put it frankly, the heart."

"Then, perhaps your Majesty should consider marrying someone who has been raised for the role," said Lord Halbrook, the Minister of the Exchequer.

"I love this woman, my Lord," said Sean, glaring at

the man. *He means well, and has turned out to be a better ally than I thought. But dammit, this is my decision.*

"Then keep her as your mistress," said Lord Garis, the Minister of State. "It's been done before, and no one will even care."

"No one except me and Jennifer," said Sean, resisting the urge to smash his glass on the table top. "And we're the only ones who count in this matter."

"Only a suggestion, your Majesty," said Garis, holding up a hand. "I meant no offense, as I am sure Halbrook did not."

And we will be hearing more and more of this in the time leading up to the wedding, thought Sean, making the decision to hurry the process up to reduce the complaining to a dull roar. *After all, once it's a fait accompli, the naysayers will be drowned out by those who will want to wish us great happiness.*

"I want the wedding scheduled for Saturday," said Sean, looking over at his Regent. "Get your people on it."

"That only gives me five days," said Samantha with a frown.

"Any reason it can't be done?"

"No, Sean. It will inconvenience some people, and some others may have their feelings hurt when they can't get here in time. But getting it done is not a problem."

"Good. And I want Cornelius here, by tomorrow. I have something in mind for that boy."

"He's already here, with his family," said Samantha. "We extended his pass, since a good portion of it was spent dealing with the enemies of the Empire."

"I figured we could let him finish up his training with the class that started just after his," said Grand

Marshal Mishori Yamakuri, the Army Chief of Staff. "It only seems fair, especially since you already expressed your wishes for him to be at the wedding."

"He's finished with his class," said Sean, looking into the eyes of the head of his army. "As of right now, he is officially a second lieutenant."

"That's quite irregular, your Majesty," protested the Grand Marshal. "There may be rumors of favoritism that follow him around through his career."

"I know all about that, Mishori," said Sean, nodding. "After all, it was something I had to deal with when I was at the Academy. But in his case he earned it. I looked over the after action report. He led a combined force of Army and Fleet personnel into an assault that took one of those big bombs away from the enemy. And then was instrumental in getting the device off the station. I would say the young hero passed his leadership exam with flying colors. So he's a second lieutenant as of now, date of rank to be the day he stepped out of the wormhole on that station and into battle."

"Yes, sir," said the Grand Marshal with a smile. "How can I argue with that. And where would you like us to station him? After the wedding is over, of course."

"Preacher asked for him," said Sean, thinking back to his conversation with Major General Walther Jodel, the man now in charge of all Special Ops forces in Sector IV. "I'm sure he can come up with something for the young man to do."

"The Cacas are going to hate you, your Majesty," said the Grand Marshal with a laugh. "Preacher and Walborski. They might surrender immediately."

The dinner was productive, Sean being able to get

his wishes across to all those present. While not giving many orders, his suggestions would carry almost as much weight. It waited until the end of the after dinner conference before the question came up he had been sure was coming.

"Do you still intend to lead from the front, your Majesty?" asked Grand High Admiral Sondra McCullom, the Chief of Naval Operations. Everyone at the table leaned forward, waiting for his answer.

"It would make all of us feel much better if you ruled from the capital," said Field Marshal Betty Parker, the Commandant of the Imperial Marine Corps. "The Empire needs your leadership, and cannot afford to lose you at this time."

All the heads at the table nodded in agreement with what the Field Marshal had said. Sean looked around the table, knowing that these people, the ones he depended on to keep things running smoothly, were not going to like what he had to say. *Well, tough. This is why I get to wear the crown, so I can make these decisions.* He thought for a moment before giving them his answer.

"I had one of the dreams," he said, seeing the interest increase in all of their eyes. "Yes, you all know what kind of dreams we have in my family. And I seem to be one of the most powerful with the curse that some call a gift in generations."

"And what did you see in the dream, Sean?" said Samantha, who as an Imperial Cousin was well versed in the lore of the gift.

"I saw myself, much older, and worn by long decades of war, walking the bridge of a warship like no one would believe. Looking down on the home world of the Cacas. We had won."

"That's wonderful," said the Prime Minister,

clapping her hands.

"And what does that have to do with you going back to the front?" asked Lord Garis.

"You have to be leading the Fleet," said Samantha, immediately understanding the import of the dream. "If you are not in the lead, it will not come to pass."

"Yes," Sean said with a cold smile.

"But, the dreams don't always come true, do they?" asked Garis, looking uncomfortable about the whole subject of prophecy.

"No," said Sean, shaking his head. "They don't. But if I don't play the part shown me, they definitely won't." He didn't tell them about the other part of the dream, the feeling of loss he experienced when thinking of Jennifer. *That could be decades in the future as well. And what the hell am I supposed to do? Sacrifice the entire human species for just one person, no matter how important to me.*

"You could still get killed before any of this comes to pass," said McCullom, raising an eyebrow.

"All kinds of things could happen," said Sean, nodding. "Still, I intend to lead from the front, and pray that the dream comes to pass. And I will listen to no arguments to the contrary."

It was very late before Sean could pull himself away from the conference and seek his bed. Jennifer seemed to be sound asleep when he curled up next to her. A moment later she had turned to face him and had her arms around his neck.

"Are you tuckered out after your long meeting," she said after kissing him.

"I'm not that tired," he said with a laugh, his hands roaming over her smooth skin under the sheets.

"Good," she said, her smile growing. "Because I'm fertile tonight, the nanites have been sent to bed, and I think it's time to make you an heir."

*   *   *

The Yugalyth, who considered himself the Prime of the spy ring the Knockermen had set up in the Supersystem, stared at the holo as it put more nourishment into its now oversized eating orifice. The holo was currently showing a replay of a news show that one of its human operatives had recorded when it had first aired live, just before it had been yanked by the Imperial authorities.

And it was lucky that the stupid human reporter asked the question, it thought, taking a large swallow of the meat it was using to feed its metamorphosis. *Otherwise, we would never have known, and I would have lost more agents in trying to penetrate their heavily guarded installations.*

"We have the reporter here, sir," said the voice of one of his human operatives over the intercom.

The Yugalyth looked up from the holo, taking stock of the large room it occupied. Fourteen subunits were growing from its body in a radial pattern, each now a small copy of a nondescript human, though the skin was pure Yugalyth. When they reached full sized, they would be ordered to find, kill, and imitate a particular human. At that point they would have been assigned penetration missions. Not anymore. Now they would be used purely for terror, in areas that were unguarded.

The door to the large room opened and the woman was shoved in. She stood there for a moment, looking confused, her eyes adjusting to the shadows. She saw the creature looming from the shadows, and hissed in a breath of shock. Even in a culture that dealt with many different alien forms, the Yugalyth was shocking to look at.   It hadn't completed its metamorphosis yet, but would soon be a queen of its kind, its only task to make clones of its genetic material, to produce as many of its kind as possible in the shortest time. Now it looked like a huge lump of flesh sitting on the floor, only its head and arms actually appearing human. Almost. The head was too large, the mouth too wide, and full of an alarming array of teeth. One of the large hands held a piece of meat that look very much like a human leg, and the sharp teeth took another large hunk out of the thigh area.

"You are the woman who asked the Emperor the question about detecting my kind?" asked the Yugalyth through another orifice that had formed on its chest.

"I, am," stammered the woman, her eyes wide with shock. "And you are one of them?"

"I am," said the creature in its deep voice.

"And you are allied with the Ca'cadasans?" asked the reporter, her voice shaking.

"We are not allied with those creatures. We are allies with those in the region who see your ascendance as an error that will cost us all. An error that must be corrected."

"Then why are you helping them?"

"Because they are against you," growled the creature. "But I did not bring you here to answer your questions, but for you to answer mine. Where did you hear about these new tests to find my kind?"

"I have a source in the government," said the reporter.

"I know you have a source, human. What I want to know is, who is it?"

"I cannot divulge that information."

"You think you have rights here," laughed the

Yugalyth, while its upper mouth tore another chunk out of the leg it was devouring, adding to its biomass for the production of its kind. "I will kill you when I will, and no one will ever know what happened to you. Now, give me the information I want."

The woman shook her head, tears in her eyes, fear shutting her down. The Yugalyth reached forward with its other arm and grabbed the reporter around the neck, lifting her toward it while it dropped the half eaten leg to the floor. The woman rose up to its eating orifice, and the teeth clamped down on one of her thighs and tore out a bite.

"Please," screamed the woman. "Don't kill me."

"Give me the information I want, and your pain will end."

She stammered a name and a position, enough for the Prime to have his agents locate the person. *The great thing about humans is that they will sell out their own for enough money*, it thought, staring into the eyes of the terrified woman. *And if money doesn't work, terror will.*

"Please," she stammered again. "It hurts."

"Then we will end your pain," said the creature, pulling her close again. The Yugalyth did not consider itself a cruel creature. It only did as it must to complete its mission. And part of its mission now was to get enough biomass into its system to spawn more of its kind.

The Yugalyth pulled the woman to its eating orifice and pushed her head in. A swift bite and it decapitated the woman, then chewed a few times to completely pulp the skull, tearing apart the nutrient rich brain. The woman felt nothing after that first bite.

"I need more food," he told one of his fellow

Yugalyth over the com.   "And I want this person brought here before me. I must know what measures they are about to take against us."

*   *   *

"At least two dozen people have been reported missing within this circle in the past week," said the briefing officer, getting the undivided attention of all the detectives in the room.

Capital Police Lieutenant Ishuhi Rykio sat there with them, looking at the ten kilometer wide circle where all the disappearances had occurred. While it was not unusual for people to come up missing in the city of over two point three billion, that many in one small area was something to raise concerns. *I wonder if the shifters have anything to do with it*, thought the former Naval commando turned detective, who was also now working for Naval Intelligence undercover.

Rykio had been instrumental in breaking up one ring of the Yugalyth, those responsible for the murder of two Prime Ministers, and maybe having a hand in the assassination of the last Emperor. *And everyone thought the threat was over when we took those bastards down. I thought not, but everyone had victory disease, and preferred to think that we had gotten rid of the problem.*

The Detective called up information on the victims on his implant while the briefing officer, a captain, continued to speak. Again, there were always disappearances in a city this large. Mostly people who just wanted to leave a family, or get away from people they owed money to, which included the organized crime of the city. There were plenty of murders as well. Not anything like what had occurred in pre-space society, maybe a couple of hundred a day in the largest city of the Empire by an order of magnitude. The society allowed people to carry weapons for self-defense, and by the laws of Jewel all such weapons alerted the police when they were used. But no such signals had been received in any of these disappearances, save one.

And they're all pretty nondescript people, he thought. *No master criminals, no people that might have pissed someone off. Just ordinary people.*

"Are we boring you, Ishuhi?" barked the Captain.

"Not at all, sir," said the Detective, swallowing his retort. His Fleet rank was commander, far loftier than that of the captain who led a homicide precinct. *But I can't let him know that*, thought the Detective, who used his position on the police force to keep Naval Intelligence abreast of any problems they were having in the city.

"Well, what did you find? Don't keep the rest of us in suspense."

"Just that there was no reason for any of these people to disappear. And that maybe one or two of them going missing might make sense, coincidence and all. But all of them. No way."

"A wonderful example of deductive reasoning," said the Captain with a sneer, evoking laughter from the other men and women. The Captain turned back to the holo for a moment, then looked back out over the room. "I want all of you people to hit the streets. To ask every one of these people's neighbors if they know anything. Anything at all, no matter how silly. I want to get whoever it is that's doing this to these people. Now get to it."

And I need to let Intelligence know what's going on here, so they can also, 'get to it'.

*   *   *

DECEMBER 7TH, 1001.

Cornelius was not really sure what was going on, only that he had been ordered to report to one of the rooms of the palace, someplace he had never been before. Devera and Rebecca had tried to hide smiles when he told them, but would not tell him what they thought was going on. Now he was walking down the corridor, the brand new gold bars of a second lieutenant on the collar of his dress uniform, beret under a shoulder flap, as it was supposed to be while indoors. Every military member, of every service, that he saw gave him a salute first, even the higher ranking officers. The ribbon with diamond stars on his left breast pocket was the reason they so honored him. The Imperial Medal of Heroism, the highest award that anyone in the Empire could be awarded, military or civilian. The diamonds indicated that he had won the award twice, a rare achievement, as the act of heroism to win any single medal was usually enough to kill the one so honored. He had been told in no uncertain terms not to wear the medal itself, and the ribbon that went around his neck, what he would normally have worn with his dress blues. That was also an unusual enough request to raise an eyebrow.

I hope it's not another damned medal, thought the Ranger, already feeling uncomfortable enough with the two. *If it is one, please, dear God, let it be a lesser award.*

Two Marines in ceremonial red rendered a rifle salute as he approached the door to the chamber. An Army Colonel saluted as well, then stopped Cornelius to give his uniform a once over, making sure everything

Doug Dandridge   224

was in place. "Perfect," said the Colonel, after inspecting the Ranger's uniform. "Now do us proud, Ranger."

I wish I knew what I was doing us proud about, he thought as one of the Marines opened a large wooden door and gestured for him to walk in.

Cornelius almost stopped in shock as he saw that room. Only because he was already moving did he continue. The room was filled with people, civilian and military. The military people were all field grade and above, with a preponderance of flag officers, Generals and Admirals. Cornelius recognized some cabinet ministers, and a couple score men and women wearing the clothing of nobles. Almost all of them were wearing a decorative plate on their upper chests, suspended from a platinum chain around their necks. Cornelius thought the decoration looked familiar, but he could not recall what it was.

A red carpet stretched ahead, leading up to a low set of stairs that led to a raised dais. Sean, in his Commander in Chief's uniform, eight stars on his shoulder boards, stood there, Jennifer by his side in a blue dress that set off her red hair perfectly. A man stood near Sean, a Brigadier with the same decoration hanging from around his neck, a long sword sitting on a pillow he held in both hands.

"Cornelius Walborski," said Sean in a strong voice. "Come forward to be recognized."

Cornelius swallowed, then marched forward with a straight back and leveled shoulders. He caught sight of his wife and adopted daughter out of the corner of his eye. Both had wide smiles on their faces, Rebecca holding both of her hands to her chest. The Ranger walked up the steps, afraid that he was going to fall flat on his face because of the ceremonial sword at his side, something he was not used to wearing.

"Kneel," ordered Sean, and a voice on his implant told Walborski to kneel on the cushion just in front of the Monarch.

Oh shit, thought Cornelius, understanding dawning. *They can't be serious.*

"We are here today to welcome a brave man to our ranks," said Sean, reaching for the sword on the cushion, then holding it up into the air. "One who has shown his total devotion to the Empire, through his deeds, in defense of all we hold dear. He has proven his worth before, as can be seen by the double award he wears on his breast. He deserves another such. Instead, we have decided upon another honor."

Sean looked into Cornelius' eyes, a smile on his face that was soon replaced by the stern look that the ceremony called for. "All knights are nobles. The very act of being made a knight enobles the blood of the recipient. But not all nobles are knights. Only those found worthy by deed are inducted into our ranks. You, Cornelius Walborski, have been found such, and it is my pleasure to make you one of us."

The Emperor placed the blade of the sword on Cornelius' left shoulder and let it rest there for a moment. He raised the sword over the head of the Ranger, then placed it on Cornelius's right shoulder. "I name you a Knight of the Empire, with all the rights, privileges and responsibilities of that title."

Sean looked Cornelius in the eyes, and the Ranger could see the heartfelt love and respect the man had for him. "Arise, Sir Cornelius, Knight of the Empire."

Cornelius got slowly to his feet, still shocked at what had just happened. Physically, he didn't feel any different. But he knew that now he was thought of in a different way by the people in this room.

Sean placed the sword back on the pillow and accepted one of the pieces of metal from Jennifer, who also gave Sean a wide smile. Sean motioned for the Ranger to bow his head, then placed the chain and the decoration around Cornelius' neck. "Take your place with your brothers and sisters, Sir Cornelius," he told the Ranger, offering his hand for a shake.

Cornelius' implant signaled him to walk back down the steps and to the side, to a place between a couple of other officers with the knight symbol hanging from their necks. As soon as he had taken his place, another man entered the room and walked to the front. This one was also wearing an Imperial Army uniform, the symbol of Heavy Infantry on his collar. The twin stars of a Major General were prominent on his shoulder boards.

I know him, thought Cornelius, looking closely at the familiar face, which seemed much the worse for wear, especially the eyes. *Baggett. From Sestius. But he was only a colonel then. And now he looks like he's been through hell.*

Sean repeated the ceremony with the General, adding another member to the knighthood. After he was through with Baggett, Sean knighted one more man and a pair of women, two of them Fleet, one a Marine.

"Refreshments await in the Platinum Room," said Sean after the last new member had joined the ranks. "Welcome our brothers and sisters into our fellowship. And to our new members, tonight there is no rank, only the companionship of equals."

Rebecca ran up to Cornelius after the Emperor left the dais, her face alight with happiness. "Does this make Devera a lady?" she asked breathlessly.

"She was already a lady," said Cornelius, pulling his wife into a hug. "But now she gets the title."

"It is so good to see you, Sir Cornelius," said Jennifer, walking up to them, putting a hand on Rebecca's head. "And so good to see you with a family."

"Thank you, your Grace," he told the woman, snagging a couple of glasses of champagne from a passing tray, handing them to the two women, then grabbing another for himself. "I think you honor me too much."

"You deserve all that Sean has granted, Sir Cornelius," Jennifer said with a head shake. "If not for you, we might be looking at the swift conclusion of this war. And not a conclusion that we would like."

Cornelius felt himself blushing from the compliments.

"Enjoy them while you can get them, honey," said Devera with a laugh. "God knows, when you become a General someday, they'll be screaming for your head."

Jennifer laughed, a musical sound that turned heads their way. "She may have something there. But now, I have a message from Sean. Enjoy the party, but afterwards, he wants to have a word with you."

Cornelius did enjoy the party, rubbing elbows with people who were so far above him in the rank structure that he had trouble seeing them in the great distance between them. All seemed generally welcoming, though he was also sure that all would send him to his death in a heartbeat if the Empire needed them to. Not that he held that against them, as he might have to do the same with people under his command.

He was led to Sean when he asked one of the staff

where he was. Sean was seated behind a desk, looking over several holos, including one that showed the extent of the enemy incursions into the Empire. He was on his feet as soon as the Ranger entered, holding out his hand. "I want to give you a personal handshake, my friend. And a personal thank you for saving our asses."

"Just doing my job, your Majesty. It seemed like something that needed doing, and I was there."

"Sometimes I wish someone like you were sitting on the throne, while I was out commanding a destroyer." Sean shook his head, a wistful smile on his face. "Unfortunately, the job is mine."

"I'm just good at breaking things, your Majesty," said Cornelius, taking the offered chair and pouring himself a cup of coffee.

"Very good at breaking things," said Sean with a laugh. "I have to make sure you get more and better tools for breaking things in the future." Sean looked down for a moment, then over at the holo, before returning his gaze to Walborski. "You're going into Preacher's command. Not sure where yet, since he controls the entirety of Sector IV's special ops. But he requested you, personally. Not that I had any doubt that you would be going to the prime sector of battle."

"I am honored that the General asked for me, your Majesty."

"But that can wait until after my wedding," said Sean with a smile. "After all, I had the honor of attending yours, and I wouldn't want you to miss out on mine. And, I have a favor to ask."

"Name it, your Majesty."

"I would like you to be my Best Man at the ceremony."

"Are you sure, your Majesty?" asked Cornelius in surprise. "Surely you have more senior people to give that honor to."

"Well," said the Emperor with a twinkle in his eye. "None of them have your talent for breaking things. And that kind of ability must be cherished and nurtured."

Chapter Fourteen

If you are going to sin, sin against God, not the bureaucracy. God will forgive you but the bureaucracy won't.   Hyman Rickover

OUTSIDE CONUNDRUM SYSTEM. DECEMBER 9TH, 1001.

Doctor Ivan Smirnov stood on the observation deck of the Ca'cadasan supercruiser and watched as the ship opened a hole from normal space into hyper I. The ship was one of four of the four million ton vessels, along with their escort of eight scout ships. *I'm glad they feel we're important enough for a strong force*, he thought, looking over at his wife and children as they sat anxiously watching the big aliens who took up much of the chamber. Ostensibly those big males were there to guard them, though he was sure they would also kill him, and his family, on orders from above, without the slightest compunction.

At least we're safe, for now, thought the New Muscovite scientist. *And we'll remain safe, as long as I deliver on my promise.*

That he could deliver he had no doubt, as long as the aliens followed his directions. It might take a year or two, but they would have wormholes, at least enough for command and control, and moving some ships from points across long distances. *And maybe I can get some more humans off the targeting reticle*, he thought, shaking his head at the stubbornness of his species. *They have to know they can't win this thing. The Ca'cadasan Empire is just too damned big. All they're doing is delaying the inevitable.*

He looked once again at the holo of the space around them that was displayed in the chamber, hoping that he saw nothing that looked like an Imperial ship. *If they catch us, we're dead*, he thought, looking over at his wife, who returned a resentful stare. *I couldn't let that happen, dear, and someday I hope you'll get over it.*

She had let him know that she did not like the idea of his turning traitor, of betraying his own species. She couldn't seem to take the realistic view, wanting to resist, even if it cost her life and that of her children. *Well, I can't allow us to die. Not if I have the means of keeping us alive.*

"Is everything OK, Dr. Smirnov?" asked one of the humans who had grown up around the Ca'cadasans, proof to the scientist that the big aliens didn't mean to exterminate the species after all. Why would they keep humans around if that was their intention? No, they meant to conquer humanity and add them to their own Empire, not the best outcome for the human race. And far from the worst, truth be told.

*   *   *

"We're picking up alien ships moving along in hyper VII," said Lt. SG Lasardo, the Tactical Officer of the James Komorov. "At the extreme range of our sensors, and coming this way."

"Identification?" asked Captain Maurice von Rittersdorf, the commander of the hyper VII destroyer.

"Looks to be a quartet of their supercruisers, along with six, no, eight, scouts."

The Captain looked at the tactical holo that showed the enemy ships, in hyper VII and accelerating at five hundred gravities, up to point seven light relative to the dimension. He knew that according to Caca doctrine the aliens would get up to point nine five light, using their superior shields to ward off radiation, and nothing the Empire had would be able to catch them.

Calling up a holo of that area, von Rittersdorf noted that he had three missiles stationed very near to where those ships would pass. Almost directly in their path, which veered just a bit from the course that most Caca ships took to leave the Empire. *It's got to be important, whatever they are carrying. The number of ships. The heading, out of the Empire, maybe, unless they're on their way to that little corner of the Sector. Smart money would bet they are carrying something they don't want us to intercept. But what? And does it really matter, as long as it's important to them?*

"When do we need to send a subspace signal to those missiles to achieve an intercept?" he asked Lasardo, walking over to the tactical station.

"Within the next ten minutes, forty seconds," said the officer, doing the calculations quickly on his board.

Subspace signals traveled twelve times faster than light, going through their own dimension that was a twelve to one correspondence with real space. The Cacas were traveling in hyper VII at point seven c, giving them a pseudospeed of twenty-eight thousand times the speed of light. If *Komorov* were not well ahead of them in space it would already be too late to send the command. And if the missiles translated into hyper VII after the aliens had passed them, they would never catch up before they ran out of power and translated back into normal space, in the form of particles.

"Send the signal," ordered the Captain, looking over the holo one more time. "We may not get more than one of them, even if we're lucky. But the one we get may be the one we need to get."

The Captain took a few steps over to the com station, to stand behind that officer. "Connect me with the Commodore. I think he needs to know about this."

*   *   *

"I understand, Captain," Commodore Edward Lacy, the Admiral's fill in while she was on a short leave for the wedding, told the young man on the wormhole com. *I see higher rank in your future von Rittersdorf*, he thought. He had approved of the Captain's actions at launching some of his weapons at the Cacas. "I don't see what else we can do at this moment. Most of our assets are spread as a net between Conundrum and the inner sector, or the pathway back to Caca space. Anything I cut loose to send after them will never catch them."

"You could send my force, Commodore," said von Rittersdorf, his anxiety plain on his face.

Not a very good choice if you want to live out the war, thought the Commodore, smiling at the young man. *But I appreciate the offer.* There was no way von Rittersdorf and the six destroyers in his force could take on that many Cacas vessels and survive, even if by chance they could catch them. The odds of them even getting through the scouts to the supercruisers were nothing short of astronomical. The only reason the missiles launched ahead of the Cacas had a chance was because they would seem to come out of nowhere, right into the paths of the enemy ships. *Now if you were in a better placement*, he thought, looking at the holo. *You could empty your magazines into them before they could react. But you are not in the proper placement.*

"No, Captain," he told the courageous officer. "I don't see any reason to just throw you and your crews away on such a forlorn hope. We'll let the Admiralty know what we saw, and if they want to try and do anything about it, they can."

"Yes, sir," said von Rittersdorf, the relief clear on his face. "We'll keep tracking them as long as we can, in case they happen to change their course within our sensor envelope. Any other orders, sir?"

"I think it might be a good idea to put some more missiles on that path, in case they try something like this again." *Because it looks like they are reacting to the losses of so many of their couriers by trying something new. Though, with a force that size, I wouldn't think they would have a problem running the Slot back to their homeland*, he thought, using the term they had come up with for the area outside the border of Sector IV space, lying between the New Terran Republic and the Kingdom of New Moscow. It was a term that had been used in the South Pacific in World War II, when the Japanese had run ships through a sea lane between several islands.

Of course, now that the New Terran Republic and the Crakista were attacking ships in that region, it might seem a good idea for the enemy to avoid it. *But they can't know about those operations here, can they?*

"And if they do try to do it again?" asked the Captain.

"Then hit them with everything you've got, as long as it doesn't risk your command. You're more important on picket duty, giving us notification of their movements, than in trying to stop a force larger than your own. Still, I'm going to ask the Admiralty for more of the remote attack missiles for your area. I might not be able to get many, but I will make sure you get as many as I can steal."

"We're about thirty seconds from attack," said von Rittersdorf, looking off the holo.

The Commdore kept the link open as he waited for the firing, on the edge of his seat as he held his breath.

Hoping that they would get some good results from the impromptu ambush.

*   *   *

"We have translations ahead," called out the voice of a Ca'cadasan from the bridge.

What the hell? thought Dr. Ivan Smirnov, his head turning quickly back to the holo that showed the region they were traversing. *How the hell could they have known I was aboard? Or even what I was going to do?*

Three objects appeared on the holo, only seconds away from the small force.   Acceleration figures appeared under the missiles, ten thousand gravities, Smirnov's implant converting the Caca script into something he could read. If they had been coming in from just about any angle they could not have caught the Caca force, which was now accelerating at five hundred and twenty-five gravities, building up its velocity in hyper.

The Caca ships opened fire, their lasers aiming on the juking weapons. Particle beams were useless, their matter dropping back into normal space as soon as they left the hyper fields of their firing vessels. And the weapons were too close, coming in too fast with the combined closing velocities, for counter missiles to be deployed.

One of the missiles dropped off the plot, flaring briefly in the space a couple of light seconds ahead of the Cacas before the plasma fell back into the normal Universe, leaving behind only the photons of electromagnetic radiation to spread, some striking the Ca'cadasan ships, with little effect.

Two of the missiles struck, one each to a scout ship, with a combined closing speed of point seven one light. Both scouts ships, five hundred thousand ton vessels, blew apart under the combined kinetic and antimatter energies. A moment later the plasma was gone, translated back into normal space.

Smirnov stood before the observation deck holo for many minutes, waiting for more missiles to appear. When they didn't, he breathed a sigh of relief and looked over at his wife and children. *We're still alive, for now. But what else are they going to send after us?*

*   *   *

SEVERIDE SYSTEM, SECTOR IV. DECEMBER 9TH, 1001.

"Prepare to match velocities and be boarded," came the signal over the com.

Prestor Johnson looked at the com board as if whoever had sent that signal would magically appear over it. He linked with the com and ordered the signal to appear on visual, and the person who had sent the signal did appear over it, a youngish looking woman with the uniform of the Fleet, a busy bridge behind her.

Just my luck, he thought. *Enigma*, his thirty thousand ton personal yacht, had translated into the Severide system, home of a developing world on the edge of Sector IV space, bordering on Sector III. He had thought he would outrun any mention of himself to this system, which, as far as he knew, didn't have a wormhole connection. Or any reason to have one.

And here he was, facing a one hundred and eighty thousand ton destroyer, actually within her beam weapon envelope. While it was an older vessel, the *Naginata* was definitely more than a match for his luxury ship, as technologically advanced as it was. And the holo showed four other ships closing on his location, all smaller than the destroyer. All capable of blowing his ship out of space.

"Acknowledge, *Enigma*," said the woman on the holo, her transmission coming across three light seconds of space. "Acknowledge our transmission and your compliance, or we will open fire. All of our lasers and particle beams are locked on, and any attempt to jump into hyper or subspace will result in the destruction of your vessel."

Prestor removed his hand from the control panel button he had just been about to push, the one that would have opened up the subspace portal. The destroyer would have picked up his graviton emissions almost instantaneously. It would have taken his ship almost five seconds to open the portal into subspace or hyper, and he would have taken two seconds of laser fire in that time period.

"I acknowledge, *Naginata*," he said into the com. "I am ordering my ship to match velocities with you."

"Don't try anything, *Enigma*," said the Captain of the destroyer. "As far as I can tell, you have done nothing to warrant the death penalty, or a mind wipe. And I would hate to have to execute you for no reason."

But you would, you fascist, thought Johnson, as he watched the destroyer draw closer, both ships now communicating with each other and making sure they matched courses and velocities so that boarding could occur.

Ten minutes and some odd seconds later an assault shuttle left the hangar of the destroyer and flew the short distance between the ships. *Enigma* did not have a hangar that could handle the craft, so the shuttle linked to her by way of mating tube to one of the small vessel's airlocks. As soon as the shuttle docked Prestor hit a panel on his com panel.

Try to stop that, he thought with a smile, as his com system broadcast all the information he had collected in the Congreeve system, including how he had been unlawfully detained, and how, on the Emperor's orders, a planetful of singular sentients had been endangered. His original plan had been to try and sneak into a system that hadn't received an alert about his fleeing the Imperial authorities at Congreeve. A system much like this one. And to get a message through to some ships, possibly those owned by one of his companies, and eventually get it on the hyperwave circuit that still covered more systems than the wormhole net. It took days to transmit messages through the stations that stretched between star system, versus the almost instantaneous transmission through the wormholes. But it also wasn't monitored like the wormhole system, as information could pass the outer relay of a star hours before it was actually seen by the major bodies of that planetary system.

But now I just have to hope that every ship in this system gets this message, and that someone moves it further up the line. Hopefully one of the news outlets I own. They'll transmit it to the public, no matter what those bastards in the government try to do.

"Keep your hands where we can see them," called out the first armored Marine to burst onto the bridge, a heavy stunner in his hand.

"What do you think I'm going to do?" asked Johnson sarcastically, putting his hands up in the air. "Fight a squad of heavily armed Marines."

A man in a naval officer's armor followed another pair of Marines onto the bridge, about all that it could handle. "What are you doing there?" asked the officer, pointing to the com board. The officer was silent for a moment, and Johnson was sure he was talking to his ship. And the ship was listening in on the signal he was sending out.

"Turn that com off," said the officer to the first Marine, pointing to the board.

The Marine reached out with a gauntleted hand and pushed Johnson to the side, none too gently. He reached over and hit a couple of panels on the board, but nothing seemed to happen.

"Turn it off," yelled the officer, and the Marine brought down a hand with all the strength of the suit onto the panel, smashing through. Sparks flew for a second, and the board went dead.

"We're taking you off this ship," said the officer, waving two of the Marines off the bridge, allowing two Spacers to move in. "You will give control of your vessel to these people, and then you will be taken aboard the *Naginata.*"

"And if I don't think it's in my best interest to give you control of this ship?" asked Prester in a growl.

"Don't make this any worse than it has to be, Mr. Johnson," said the officer, glaring at the trillionaire. "If you don't give over control, we'll have a frigate take her under tow with magnetic grapples. That might cause more damage than either of us would want."

Prester nodded, then linked with the ship and told it to give the access codes to the spacers. After, he was hustled aboard the shuttle and taken to the destroyer, where he was locked in the small brig.

It took several days to deliver him to the station in orbit around the habitable planet, where he was again hustled aboard, this time with his hands in restraints. He was led to a lift and then down a corridor, until he was deposited at the office of the Commodore in charge.

"Mister Johnson," said the Commodore, whose nameplate over his desk said McCaffrey. "You've caused a lot of problems for a lot of people, including yourself. I hope you're happy."

"You have no right to detain me," said Johnson, trying his best to appear fierce, and failing. "I'm a private citizen."

"The charges against you could land you in confinement for quite some time, Mr. Johnson," continued the Commodore, as if he hadn't heard a thing that the trillionaire had said. "Don't you know that we're at war? And that you were in a combat zone, and therefore subject to the laws governing conduct within that zone, civilian or not?"

"And what are you planning to do to me?" asked the deflated trillionaire, looking at the magnetic restraints on his hands.

"I would like to put you on a target drone and give my boys and girls some weapons practice," said the Commodore, glaring at Johnson. "But orders from the top have given me the parameters of my responses."

The Commodore called up a holo over his desk that showed *Enigma*. "Naval Intelligence thinks that what you have developed here is a nearly perfect spy ship. Capable of sneaking into a system through subspace, which almost no one scans for in this day and age. The only thing missing is a wormhole heat sink."

"And what does that have to do with me?"

"We want the names of the people who developed this vessel. All of them, so we can pick their brains and make ships like this."

"And *Enigma*? Do I get her back?"

"I'm afraid not, Mr. Johnson," said the Commodore, shaking his head. "Consider her a donation to the war effort, to go along with your other donations."

"What donations are those?" asked the trillionaire with a bit of trepidation.

"The fines that will be levied against you," said the Commodore with a predatory smile. "I think the figure mentioned was a hundred billion, to be taken in manufacturing capability of need to the Empire."

"You can't do that?"

"We can and we will. Unless you want to find yourself confined to Purgatory for a couple of decades."

"Put that way, I guess I can part with some of my wealth. It's only money, after all." *And the news I broadcast will still hurt them. There's really nothing they can do to stop it from spreading.*

"Oh, and that broadcast you made from your ship before we captured you," said the Commodore as Johnson was being led from the office. "I just want you to know that the Emperor already told everyone about his error in staging the battle in the Congreeve system, and the way it endangered the Mucanoids that lived there. And you know what? Nothing like a victory to gain the positive attention of people." The Commodore laughed at the expression on Johnson's face as he was led out, while Johnson thought over the proposition that he was not so smart after all.

Chapter Fifteen

Vote for the man who promises least; he'll be the least disappointing.   Bernard Baruch

SAURON SPACE. DECEMBER 11TH, 1001.

Marc Dawson looked at the engineering control panel once again, marveling over the fact that it was his. *I never dreamed I would have this much power under my control,* he thought, looking at the holo of the power bars to the six matter antimatter reactors the ship carried. All were running at peak power, putting out more than twice the energy of a fifteen million ton battleship. *Augustine I,* now wearing the moniker superheavy battleship, was almost twice the size of the standard model, and generated two point two times the energy. And most of that energy could be funneled into the laser rings and particle beams, giving the ship more than twice the punch of the smaller ship, even without the addition of her wormhole fed weapons.

"Preparing for jump to hyper," called out the voice over the com, letting him know that the bridge was expecting the energy they needed.

Augustine was still undergoing repairs from the battle of Congreeve, though all of her major systems were working at full capacity. The outer armor had been repaired as well, and a new coating of nanofiber had been added, making her much more resistant to beam weapons. There were still a lot of repairs going on under the skin, but nothing that couldn't be continued while the ship tested her main systems.

"Jumping to hyper I," called out the Helmsman over com.

The MAM reactors spiked slightly, more power being fed to the hyperdrive projectors as they converted energy to gravitons and opened a hole between the dimensions. There was a moment's nausea, then the graphs dropped slightly as the hyperdrive throttled back to the energy needed to remain in hyper I, less than half that needed to enter.

"Jumping to hyper II," called out the Helmsman. They were operating far outside of any gravity well, and all dimensions of hyper were open to them here. The captain was just testing all systems by performing one jump after another. Again the graphs moved up, to over four times their peak during the previous jump. The system still had major capacity left over, even at the rates the reactors were working.

The ship continued up through the levels of hyper, until it reached hyper VII, at which point the reactors were working at ninety-five percent of capacity, dropping down to sixty after completing the jump. The ship started to accelerate after that jump, reaching its safe capacity of four hundred and ninety-five gravities, pulling as many gees as it could while grabbing for more velocity.

And still the reactors are only at eighty-one percent capacity, thought the Chief Engineer, checking all systems on multiple holo displays. The reactors were now producing enormous amounts of heat, like small stars radiating in their magnetic bubbles within each containment capsule. The heat radiated into the magnetothermodynamic generators that converted it directly to electrical power, with very little waste. What waste there was transferred through superconductor cables to the radiating surfaces of the skin, where supermetals, the most efficient heat radiators known, pushed it into the vacuum of space. Before the discovery of the artificial produced elements, heat buildup was a big problem on large ships. Now it was just another problem solved.

"Powering up weapons systems and electromag field," called out the Tactical Officer over the com. A moment later the power graphs on the reactors went up again, to ninety-nine percent capacity, while new holos appeared showing the power status of the thousands of electromag field generators, and the charging of the laser rings by their multiple emitters.

"Everything appears to be holding together," announced Dawson to the Captain. "All systems are go."

"Very well," said Captain Javier Montoya from his bridge station. "We'll maintain current power configuration for the next hour, and see how she holds up."

"Yes, sir," acknowledged Dawson, looking over at some other screens that showed his men and women manning their own stations, monitoring all aspects of the engineering section, making sure that no problem was ignored while it was still small, and possibly becoming big.

He checked on the sections working near the reactors themselves, each crew member wrapped in heavy suits of augmented shipboard armor. *Everyone is working well*, he thought, happy at the teamwork his people had achieved.

An hour later they powered down the peripheral systems, lasers, all of the electromag screening save that needed to protect from charged particle radiation. They started on a curving decel profile that turned them while they stopped, then started them on a path back to the system.

"Good job, Engineer," said the Captain to Dawson as they reentered normal space at the hyper I barrier. "The performance of your division was to my complete satisfaction today."

And hopefully it will be when we enter combat as well, thought the Chief Engineer, patting the hard surface of the disengaged panel. *But you won't fail us, will you girl?*

*   *   *

CONUNDRUM SPACE.

Commodore Bryce Suttler looked through the holo viewer at the system he had basically been ejected from. The enemy had persisted in their search, and it had been a close call for several of his vessels. On his orders they had all repaired to points ten light hours from the star, well outside the system's hyper VII barrier. The space out there was vast enough to hide just about anything, especially ships that radiated almost no infrared.

They still had a good view of the system, with the ability to keep tabs on the enemy fleet. Even if everything was ten hours after the fact. *At least we can still get almost instant notice of hyper translations*, he thought.

"There's that convoy we were told about," said Lieutenant SG Walter Ngovic, the *Seastag's* tactical officer. "Too bad we can't put some missiles into them."

"Yep," said Bryce, staring at the icons that had appeared on the plot. "But they might as well be across the Galaxy for all we can do about it." *Except send acknowledgement back to Fleet that the Caca convoy they knew was coming here, that they had tracked for the last twenty light years, did, in fact, make it here. What a bunch of bullshit.*

"We're getting a transmission from headquarters," called out the Com officer.

"Eyes only?"

"No, sir."

"Then put it up on the holo."

The face and upper body of Vice Admiral Sheila Mtwambe, the commander of all stealth/attack forces in Sector IV, which meant most of them at this time, appeared in the holo.

"Suttler. We have a tasking order for you."

"Yes, ma'am. What's the mission?"

"You are to relocate your ships to these spots outside the system, then reconfigure your wormholes to cargo gates."

"For what kind of cargo, ma'am?" asked the curious officer with a thrill, pretty sure he already knew what was coming.

"These," said the Admiral, and her form left the holo, to be replaced by what looked like a small version of their own ship.

Not really our ship, thought the Commodore, leaning forward in his chair to look at the thing he guessed was a weapon. It had the same flattened surfaces as *Seastag,* angled to reflect active sensor probes away from the transmitting ship, the same flat black, light absorbing material. It looked like a missile of some type, but the grabber fins were tiny as compared to any missile he had even seen.

"Something new from R & D?" he asked. The woman appeared on the holo once again, the missile in the background, with people around it to give it scale. It appeared to be the same size as a standard missile, like those carried by the stealth/attacks.

"We call it, the Viper," said the Admiral, nodding. "It strikes from the dark, without warning. It's been under development for the last three years, originally as a weapon against Lasharan incursions. It was to be placed near inhabited planets, activated when enemy ships drew near, then launched into its attack profile. The first the Lasharan ship would know it's there would be when it went into final attack acceleration within ten thousand kilometers of the target.

"Those grabbers look a little small for much acceleration," said Suttler, bringing up the original view of the weapon on a side holo.

"They generate ten thousand gravities, same as your standard attack missiles," said the Admiral, referring to the weapons carried by the stealth/attack, used for short range high acceleration attacks. "But only for that very last ten thousand kilometers. The heat generated is enough to burn off the grabbers in a little over twelve thousand kilometers, so they can't accel very far off their optimal attack pattern"

"Amazing."

"You are to load one hundred missiles each for the six of your craft, pushing them into space as soon as they arrive to make room for more. And from there, you are to program all the missiles for a long, slow run into the system, looking for Caca targets."

"You really think we'll get any of them with these things?" asked Bryce, liking the idea in theory, wondering about it in practice.

"I don't know, Commodore. I kind of wondered that myself. Their success depends on their getting in really close to ships with very good sensor suites. And the first one that strikes an enemy ship will cause the others to ramp up their efforts at detecting them. But if we have to spend six hundred expensive missiles to damage one even more valuable ship, as well as making the Cacas more paranoid, they will have served their purpose."

"And why do you want them released from those specified points?"

"That doesn't really have anything to do with the attack by these missiles," said the Admiral with a cold smile. "You are also to download three hundred mines, to emplace in those areas. From there you will monitor incoming and outgoing enemy ships. And you will keep us apprised of those comings and goings. On our command, you will launch the missiles from the mines at ships moving toward them in hyper."

"And just what kind of ships are we looking for?"

"Just send us the intel, Commodore," said the Admiral. "And we will decide when we attack them."

Which means she really doesn't know what they're looking for themselves. Wonderful.

"No problem, Admiral. We're here to serve."

"Good man, Suttler. And I understand you wish to stay on deployment, despite your promotion to true flag rank. Most unusual, but appreciated. It's nice to have someone who thinks outside the box at the pointy end. And also someone who knows how to follow orders, without being completely idiotic about it."

Bryce nodded and smiled, realizing that her comment needed no reply. After all, while they were Fleet, they were also considered some of the elite of that Fleet. Not to be sacrificed for no reason, depended upon to give a return for the investment of their lives.

"Mtwambe out," said the Admiral, and the holo died.

"Helm, get us to those coordinates, slow and easy. We don't want to be spotted. Com, send those orders to the other ships as well." The crewmembers went about their duties, leaving Suttler to settle back into his chair and think, sometimes a blessing, sometimes a curse.

*   *   *

"We need to get back on the offensive," growled High Admiral Kellissaran Jarkastarin, red eyes glaring across the table at the Great Admiral.

I wish I had sent you and your force off to the nether regions before calling this meeting, thought Great Admiral Miierrowanasa M'tinisasitow, glaring at the slightly younger male who was his military inferior, and, unfortunately, his social superior. He looked around the table at his gathered high admirals, the males who ran the conquest fleet at his command. Up until a couple of weeks prior, his had been the largest conquest fleet in the history of the Empire. The only larger was the one fighting on the other side of the Empire, and that was not a conquest fleet. That was an armada, trying to take down the greatest threat the Empire had ever encountered. *The kind of force we need here.*

"We are too weakened from the human offensive to go on the attack," said one of the other High Admirals, he whom the Great Admiral saw as his voice of reason, even if other males called him a coward to his back. That he had killed scores of strong males in fair fights was one reason they would not say such to his face.

"We only advance the goals of the Empire in the attack," shouted out a third male. "We are here to destroy these people, to grind them into dust, to be forgotten by the Galaxy. We do not do this by sitting here in this system."

And we are too damned aggressive as a species, thought the Great Admiral, looking down at the table and thinking. *Maybe I should send my more aggressive males off on a strike. Either they'll be successful, or they'll be destroyed. And either way, I win.*

"We are only a shadow of the conquest fleet we were," said the cautious High Admiral. "We should wait for reinforcements from the Empire. Or at least until the ships from their Republic get here, even if it doesn't bring us back to full strength."

And those ships were due within a couple of weeks, if they had left the Republic as soon as they were contacted. *That is why we need those wormholes, more than any other reason. I have no way of knowing what is the current location or status of my forces outside of this system. And it still takes us six months to get new ships from the Empire to here. Hopefully that human scientist will pan out, but that will still be years in the future.*

"We have enough of a force here to take out several of their core systems," argued Jarkastarin, staring at the Voice of Caution. "Reduce their industrial capacity by a significant percentage, kill some more billions of these humans." The High Admiral shifted his gaze back to the Great Admiral. "Accomplish what we were sent here to accomplish. Not cower like zagratta in the shadows."

No, we are not zagratta, thought the Great Admiral, thinking of the small vermin that tended to infest most Ca'cadasan farming concerns. *But neither are these humans. They are closer to sliggothra.* He pictured in his mind the huge predators that had been the bane of early Cacada, before the early hunter gatherers wiped them out. Now they only existed in zoological gardens, recreated from their ancient DNA. *Just as someday we might recreate humans, which, in my opinion, would be a major mistake.*

"The humans will track your force, Jarkastarin," said the Voice of Reason. "They will move forces in with their damned wormholes, overwhelm you, and we would just lose more of our fleet for no return."

"Then perhaps it is time to resort to hit and run attacks," said Jarkastarin, hunching both pairs of shoulders. "Strike from the edge of the system. Come out of hyper, launch, then go back in. The ships they bring in by wormhole would arrive too late to do anything to us, they couldn't catch us in hyper, and we would move on to the next target. And if they don't have a wormhole gate in that system, we could move in and totally destroy the human presence there."

"And in that case, you might get ambushed after you poke your nose too far into the system to back out in time," said the Voice of Reason.

"Then we will just hit and run," said Jarkastarin, looking like he wanted to call the other Admiral a name, then thinking better of it. "We fire in spreads of missiles and take everything of value out at long range."

"You must not hit their planets with those missiles," cautioned the Great Admiral, wondering if this idea might be just what he needed to get the recalcitrant male off his back, and raise the morale of his fleet.

Jarkastarin's expression showed what he thought of human planets, and the creatures that lived on them, even nonhumans. "Of course I will not harm their precious planets. I will only target ships, mining stations, antimatter production facilities and the like."

"Very well," said the Great Admiral, giving a head

motion of acceptance. "You may take your personal force, and another hundred ships." He looked around at the other High Admirals. "I will authorize two similar forces, to the first two High Admirals who ask for command. But no more than a third of the fleet here gathered is to go out raiding. I mean to hold this system, and by that I include the planet that the humans still infest. All ground combat males are to remain here, so that they can be used to reduce the Conundrum planet."

"I must protest that order, Great Admiral," said Jarkastarin, slamming a heavy right lower hand onto the table. "What if I need ground combat males to take enemy ships."

"Then you will destroy those ships, and not risk any of yours in trying to capture them. You will not risk having them project antimatter onto your ship, by whatever means they do so. Is that clear?"

"But…"

"Is that clear, High Admiral? Because if it isn't, I can just keep you here in this system, and let another commander go in your stead."

The other officer glared for a moment, then gave a head motion of acknowledgement.

"Good. Then this meeting is over. The three commanders who will lead raiding parties will present to me their proposed orders of battle for my final approval. And no stacking your task groups with battleships. These will be balanced forces."

The Great Admiral stormed out of the room, not really caring if his subordinates approved of his decisions or not. The Emperor had put him in command, and as long as he held that position, he would command.

*   *   *

"Admiral on deck," shouted a voice over the hangar intercom.

Admiral Chuntao Chan was torn between smiling and crying as she looked over the officers and Marines gathered on the utility hangar deck of the HIMS *Akagi*, the flagship of Task Force Four, her first, and probably, last major combat command. *At least the Emperor gave me the chance*, thought the woman, who was widely thought to be one of the greatest minds of the Empire.

That was the reason she was being relieved of command of this group of six hyper VII Fleet Attack Carriers, which, along with their defending escorts, comprised the Task Force. Those, and the six wings of inertialess attack fighters they had launched into the battle, the whole reason for their being.

"It was a pleasure serving with you, Admiral," said a tall, blond Captain with the insignia of naval aviation on her collar.

"The pleasure was all mine, Svetlana," said the small Asian woman, returning the salute, then shaking the other woman's hand, looking up into ice blue eyes. "Your wing performed admirably. They, and the others, were instrumental in our victory."

The other woman, Svetlana Komorov, returned a sad smile at the praise, and the flag rank scientist realized what she must be thinking. *Almost half of your force destroyed was a heavy price to pay, even if extracting a hundred times the cost to the enemy. But that doesn't matter when they're your people.*

"If you would like, I could get you a berth in R and D," offered the Admiral. "I could use someone like you to run herd on the pilots we will need."

"My place is here, Admiral," said the Captain,

shaking her head. "If you order it, I will give it my best shot. But I'm not a genius, like you are. They need you back there, that's for sure. Just like they need me here."

Now it was Chan's turn to shake her head. "I will not order you to leave your command. The offer is genuine, and you would be an asset. But I will leave it up to you. You are also an asset here, and you will have your hands full rebuilding your wing before the next offensive."

When those ships would be coming was anyone's guess. The Empire had plenty of six hundred ton insystem fighters, and one thousand ton attack fighters. But not fifteen hundred ton inertialess attack fighters. The production lines for them were still in the process of ramping up, and there was only so much negative matter around, and too many priority uses for the substance.

"Just get us what we need to win this war, ma'am," said the Captain with a smile.

Chan nodded and turned, walking toward the shuttle that was waiting for her. *I'm not the mind that creates*, she thought as she stepped aboard the armed assault shuttle. *I'm the brain that refines, that finds the flaws and corrects them. I'm important, but not as much as those scientists who do the theoretical work, the creation, the initial engineering.*

As soon as she was in her seat, and the cabin attendant, a young warrant officer, had checked on her, the shuttle raised from the deck and boosted toward the cold plasma field that kept the atmosphere inside the open hanger. They put on the acceleration as soon as the shuttle cleared the carrier, heading for the ship gate that had been erected just inside the hyper barrier.

The Admiral watched the task force recede behind

them on her seat holo, zooming in to look at her flagship. *Akagi* was easily distinguishable from the standard hyper VI fleet carrier. It massed twelve million tons, two more than a regular carrier. Most of that extra mass went into the more robust hyperdrive projectors, and the reactors needed to power them. About half a million tons went into the larger than normal hangars, and the missile magazines needed to rearm those ships with the hundred ton weapons they carried.

The ship, while armed with lasers and some particle beam projectors, as well as a quartet of missile launchers, was not made to enter into close combat. She couldn't stand up against any other type of capital ship in a beam fight or missile duel. Most had doubts the ship could even hold out long against a couple of heavy cruisers. That was not her mission, and the dozen light cruisers and thirty destroyers in the task force were there to defend her and her sisters from enemy missiles, and to sacrifice themselves to protect her against larger enemy vessels closing on her position.

She zoomed out the holo, changing it to a tactical view. Icons sprung up all over the plot. Not only her task force, but the other hyper VII carrier group. Hundreds of battleships, a thousand escort and supporting vessels. What had gathered so far, and only a fraction of the strength that would soon be stationed here. A lot of ships from the last battle had gone through the ship gate on their way to Central Docks, for repairs and upgrades. There were many more that had gone off on the strike on Fenri space, scheduled to be back in a week. And…

"We're being ordered to steer clear of the gate for the moment, ma'am," said the shuttle pilot over the com. "We have priority traffic coming through from the other side."

Must be high priority, thought the Admiral, as her shuttle veered away from the gate while putting on deceleration, and vectoring in a curve that would lead to a position where they could again make a gate approach, when the time came.

She zoomed the holo on the gate and gasped as the nose of a ship poked through, soon followed by the rest of the fifteen million ton battleship. It was not of human design, a more elegant, beautiful form that probably gave up a little bit of toughness, while gaining acceleration and maneuverability.

Elysium Empire ships, she thought, admiring the lines of the big warship as it pushed through the gate, then accelerated away to its fleet staging area. A moment later another ship came through, followed by yet another. Altogether, the shuttle was put on hold for two hours, while over three hundred ships from the Elysium Empire came through. They were a welcome reinforcement in her eyes, and a sign that the humans were not in this alone, not anymore. There were already some Crakistan ships in the system, with more scheduled to arrive any day. The next battle against the Ca'cadasans would feature the three strongest empires in this region of space standing shoulder to shoulder against the aggressor.

"We're clear to go through," said the pilot, and the shuttle started to accelerate toward the gate.

I really don't like this part, thought Chan, who had been in on the original tests of the portals. The feeling was like nothing she had ever experienced, ranked as a nine on a scale where puking her guts out after a college party was a five. The shuttle plunged through, and the feeling of being stretched across space and time almost overwhelmed her. Time seemed to tick with agonizing slowness, and then she was through, catching the breath she had been starting to take when they had first penetrated the mirror surface.

This is new, thought Chan, looking on the holo that showed the outline of the ship gate flower that had been put together since the last time she had been there. The shuttle accelerated, changing its vector to head toward the gate that led to Central Docks, where she would transfer through the passenger gate system to her final destination. The icons of forts blinked on the holo, as well as those from over a hundred ships, the defensive force that would keep an enemy from coming through one gate and attacking the industrial base of the black hole. Since only one ship could come through at a time, two if the attacker wanted to take greater risk, the fleet would pretty much immediately overpower any enemy. Or at least it was so hoped.

Chan expanded the holo, zooming out, until the icon of the *Donut*, and all of the myriad of ships and stations in orbit around the black hole, filled it. From Central Docks she would be taking a passenger gate back to the *Donut*, cutting five hours off of the route heading straight from here to the station on her shuttle. They could also head to one of the forts, and jump to the station, but that portal was actually much further from her connection than the one coming from Central Docks.

Amazing, she thought, trying to wrap her mind around the new reality of galactic travel. *I actually travel eighty light hours out of my way to save twenty minutes of transit time. Our ancestors would think we had lost it if we mentioned such a thing.* But this was the new reality, at least for the humans and their allies. And, hopefully, never for the enemy.

*   *   *

"Your Empire has won a great battle against the invaders," said Klorasof, one of the Ancients that Xavier Jackson was familiar with, its red and gold striping distinctive. "And even more significantly, they are forging a mighty alliance with the other peoples of this sector."

"Then you think they are going to win this thing?" asked Commander Xavier Jackson, the *guest* of the legendary Ancients since they had rescued him from space.

"It is too early to tell," said the creature, waving its six arms in the air in a complicated dance of communication that the human still had trouble reading. It moved across the room on its belly cilia, reaching an arm for a drinking container. "The enemy you fight is strong, and stubborn. The odds of your people winning are less than thirty percent, according to our best estimate."

"And you can change those odds," said Jackson, launching into the same argument he had tried so many times with these creatures.

"We can fight one battle," said the Ancient, its mouth wrinkling up in distaste at the last word. "After that, we are no longer a factor in the Galaxy."

The aliens had explained to Jackson, many times, that the Baby Universes they used for power could not be replenished without a generating facility like the station the humans had around the black hole. Once they were empty, the creatures would have to depend on fusion, or matter antimatter, both much too feeble for their needs.

"Then fight that battle and help us to win. And maybe my people can charge up some more of those bottles for you."

"Eventually," said the alien, an expression on its mouth which Jackson had come to associate with wistfulness. "Eventually. But not now."

Chapter Sixteen

The power to wage war is the power to wage war successfully. Charles Evans Hughes

CONUNDRUM SYSTEM. DECEMBER 12TH, 1001.

"Something's happening, sir," called out Ngovic from his tactical station.

"What do you have, Tactical?" asked Suttler, moving up behind the junior officer's chair.

"Over four hundred enemy ships, heading away from the fleet," said Ngovic, pointing to the movement on the holo over his board, tracked by their graviton emissions. "Accelerating away as one force for the moment."

"Shit," said Suttler, staring at the holo. "This really isn't what command wanted." *And we depended too much on the enemy doing just what we want. The most basic of military axioms. The enemy never does what you want them to.*

They watched the holo in silence for some minutes, Suttler looking over at the Com Officer at one point to make sure the data was going out.

"We're getting some separation in the groups," said Ngovic, his finger pointing to the body that was showing some gaps in two places. "Looks like three equal groups, all moving to jump on different courses."

Maybe they'll be back in time to catch some of our gifts, thought Suttler, thinking of the four hundred missiles they had sent accelerating at a leisurely twenty gravities toward the system. At their small size, the distance, and the low graviton load, they would be completely undetectable by the enemy on the way in. They would cut acceleration at point two light, and coast the rest of the way, making minor course corrections to bring them to their targets and their final runs.

Right now, that attack was no longer the priority. That had been overtaken by what looked like three strong enemy raiding parties heading out to cause damage to the Empire's industrial base.

A moment later all of the enemy ships had jumped to hyper I, and their courses had diverged from each other even further.

*   *   *

"Shit," cursed Admiral Mara Montgomery, watching the plot that was being relayed from one of her scout squadrons.   She really couldn't think of anything else to say, and that one word seemed to be most appropriate to this situation.

Three goddamn raider forces, all heading for different targets, and we won't be able to track them once they get past the pickets. Not without our ships giving themselves away, which will probably lead to the enemy destroying them.

The problem was all of her ships were on picket duty, tracking the comings and goings of the enemy. They were able to do that without giving themselves away, since they were sitting in normal space.   If they were to pursue the enemy, they would have to jump into hyper, giving away their positions, and then try to either catch the enemy, or guess where they were going and get there first. Either way, if the enemy didn't want to be tracked, they could break off a smaller force from their raiding parties to pursue and destroy their trackers. Or she could try to move other scouts into position by guesswork, never the best of solutions, but maybe the only one she had.

No, I'm going to have to order some of my pickets to pursue. Not really fair to those crews, but necessary. And just who are going to be the lucky bastards that get chosen for that mission?

Montgomery looked over the holo that showed the disposition of her forces and picked out the two task forces that were closest to the enemy's courses. *That's their job*, she thought of the two task force commanders. *Not really fair of me to put this on them, but it is their job to choose the ships they want to pursue. Or am I just coward enough to give them that responsibility?*

Most of the people in Sector IV would have looked at Mara Montgomery in disbelief if they had heard those thoughts. She was counted as one of the most audacious scout commanders in the Fleet. Of course, it was easier putting herself and her ship in danger, than ordering others to do it for her. She had done just that in the past. A good example of that was when she had ordered ships into danger to cover her own while the Emperor was aboard. She hadn't liked it then, and she still didn't.

"Get me Commodore Lacy on the com," she told her Com Officer, dreading the need to give the order. But this was one she couldn't duck.

*   *   *

"Well, shit," growled Commodore Edward Lacy after the com terminated. *Shit really does roll downhill.* He hated the order. He especially hated the part of the order that said he was not to take himself and his ship on the pursuit. *So I get to tell off some of my subordinates to go on what could very well be a suicide mission. And I don't have any time to waste.*

The Commodore looked over his dispositions and made a quick decision. He needed at least two ships with wormhole coms, and preferred at least one battle cruiser. He looked over his possibilities and made his choices, five ships to form a pursuit force. *And now for the hard part*, he thought, ordering the com officer to connect him to those officers, through the wormhole where one was available, relayed through a wormhole com equipped ship where not. All the time wishing that the Admiral was back from her leave to make these decisions.

*   *   *

"Captain Yurik will be in command of the squadron," the Commodore told von Rittersdorf over the com. "*Lisboa* is the largest ship of the force," he continued, naming the hyper VII battle cruiser. "She also has a wormhole launch system, so will carry the most firepower. Captain Yurik has been given instructions to use his ship as the contact vessel, while yours will be tail end Charlie, so we have a guarantee of a com link."

Maurice felt relief at those orders, and shame on top of the relief. His ship would be outside of the sensors of the enemy. The chances of his ship coming back had increased exponentially. That was not true for the battle cruiser, the light cruiser or the two other destroyers tasked with this mission.

"I understand, Commodore," he said, trying to keep his voice steady.

"We need for all of you to grab the enemy and hold on. We have to know what their target is. If you can keep them under observation, even halfway to their target, we can probably get ships in front of them. Good luck, Captain."

The holo went blank, and a moment later the Captain of the *Lisboa* was on the com. "We'll meet here, von Rittersdorf," ordered the senior captain, as a map came up on a second holo that showed the rendezvous point for all the ships. "Right now I plan to stick to them on their port flank. But we'll have to play it by ear the whole way. Any questions?"

"No, sir," said von Rittersdorf, looking at the proposed meeting point and finding no fault with it, or the strategy. *Other than it would be nice to have a dozen battleship squadrons with us.*

"Then we'll see you there. Make sure your ship stays out of Caca sensor range. Yurik out."

And that's one order I will be glad to obey, thought the junior Captain, ordering his helm to put them on a course toward the meeting point.

*   *   *

SECTOR IV SPACE.

"We have some more information to feed your bosses," said Sonia Rupert, trying not to stare at the orange striped creature standing before her. This was her tenth meeting with the creature, a Maurid, ostensibly a client species of the Cacas. *But not as subservient or reliable as the damned big aliens think.* The Maurid still intimidated her, despite being genetically augmented herself. The way the creature moved, the way the muscles slid into place under the fur, the razor sharp claws and teeth, all bespoke the deadliness of the creature.

She handed over the data chip and waited as the operative put it in a reader and scanned its contents. "Smart of you," said the Maurid who had been asked to be called just that, the Maurid. "It might arouse their suspicions to receive information that the station was destroyed. Two years, huh. That should help them to regain some of their arrogance."

"That's what we're hoping, at least," said Sonia,

nodding, then wondering if the creature even knew what the gesture meant. *She's a damned spy, so she must know.*

"And what have you got for me?"

"A real gem," said the creature with a toothy smile. "I'm not sure you're going to like it, but as far as I can tell, it's genuine."

The Maurid passed over a chip similar to the one she had just given the creature, the kind of nondescript memory that was used in millions of different machines. Only this one would dissolve in human saliva. If she popped it in her mouth, it was gone in moments.

Sonia placed the chip into a slot on the small reader she carried, looked over the screen, then sucked in a breath. "Are you sure about this?"

"As sure as we can be," said the Maurid. "This really isn't in our area, but one of our agents overheard some talk that shouldn't have been going on in public. A quick search, a little hack, and there you have it."

"Shit. This is not good."

"I think the process the human is talking about is not on the same level as what you use. The Ca'cadasan Empire will always be behind you in that respect."

"Any advances they make in that direction are totally unwelcome," said Rupert, scrolling down the info. "Any chance we might be able to intercept this human. It would be worth the loss of a battle group to keep him from getting to your Empire."

"Not my Empire, human. And no, he has left the Conundrum system by now, on a roundabout path back to the Empire. If you haven't intercepted him by now, you won't.

"And we understand you are about to go on the

offensive again," said the Maurid after a moment's hesitation.

Rupert stiffened, not sure what to say. "I'm not at liberty to discuss that at this time."

The Maurid laughed. "Quite understandable. Don't worry. We have already developed this intelligence, and my spies think I have already sent it up the line. Which I will, of course, only not in its entirety."

Sonia nodded her head at that. The Maurid had to pass on some straight information, if only to keep her bosses satisfied that she was actually spying for them, and not instead working as a double agent.

"The Great Admiral is expecting some reinforcements as well, both from the Republic, which you probably already know about, given those wonderful wormholes you use in such abundance. But also more from the Empire, which you will not know about for several more weeks, when they penetrate the *Slot*. You'll find that on the chip as well, and a profile of the highest ranking officers of the conquest fleet. Maybe that will help you to kill more of the assholes."

"And some of your people as well?" asked Rupert. "Doesn't that part bother you?"

"Sacrifices must be made, if we are ever going to get out from under the subjugation of the Ca'cadasans. We would prefer that others make the sacrifices, but if some of us must die, so be it. If further generations are to gain their freedom, even if it's within your Empire, it will be worth it."

"Thank you," said Rupert with a head nod. The creature did not like being touched, as Sonia had learned at an earlier meeting. "I'll be in touch."

"One other piece of information, that we learned

from our friends, the Knockermen," said the creature, her lips sneering as she said *friends* and *Knockermen*. "The shape shifters are in your capital, in force. They are planning to strike, to try and take out a head of government. During some kind of celebration."

The Imperial Wedding, thought the IIA agent in a panic. "I have to get this information to where it can do some good," she told the Maurid, turning and starting to walk away. She looked back for a moment, and the creature was already gone, disappeared into the shadows.

* * *

SECTOR IV SPACE.

"Dr. Tashiga disagrees with you," said the Captain Walter Orendorf, the commander of the *Gringo*, looking at Dr. Southard over his glasses.

And what the hell are you trying to do with those eye glasses? thought Southard, staring at the Captain. Nobody suffered from impaired eyesight, not for the last thousand years. The genes for those kind of defects had been removed from the gene pool. Only people trying to achieve some kind of fashion look wore them, and the scientist could think of no reason someone aboard a research ship would need to pursue such an affectation.

"Dr. Tashiga is wrong," said Southard, his voice rising, unable to believe this, officer, was unable to listen to reason. "Look. I am acknowledged as the foremost expert on supernovas in the Empire. Dr. Tashiga is not. That should settle the question, here and now."

"And Tashiga says your theories are out of date,"

said the Captain, continuing to look directly at the scientist.

And he had over a week to convince you that he was correct, and I was wrong. Is there anything I can say to change your mind?

"What good does it do us to stay here, within the hyper barrier? After all, our remote platforms can gather all the data we need."

"Dr. Tashiga disagrees with you on that as well," said Orendorf, pulling his glasses off and sticking one of the earpieces in his mouth. He chewed for a moment, then looked back up at Southard. "Tashiga believes we will get some better readings with the ship's sensors. And the closer we are, the better."

"And that's crap," said Southard, slamming a hand down on the table.

"Dr. Southard. I would thank you to refrain from these kinds of displays in my cabin."

"I'm sorry," said the scientist. "It is just frustrating that you lend so much credence to that, man. And you will not listen to reason."

"So, Dr. Tashiga thinks we have two to three weeks before the star blows. And you think it will detonate in what? Five or six days. Tell you what. I'll compromise. Give Dr. Tashiga another eleven days, then we'll move out beyond the hyper barrier. Will that be satisfactory."

"This isn't politics, Captain," said Southard, shaking his head. "Compromise will not change the facts. That star will enter silicon fusion in five to six days, iron will build up at the core, and the stellar furnace will die. Seconds after that the star will explode. And we will not be able to outrun the heat and radiation wave to the hyper barrier. By the time the particles of matter reach us, we will be gone. Well before that, really."

"You have my answer, Dr. Southard," said the Captain, putting his glasses on the desk. "Take it or leave it."

"Then I request permission to leave this ship."

"I think not," said the Captain, shaking his head, then putting his glasses back on. "You were assigned here under reserve officer activation, and here you will stay, until we receive orders to the contrary."

"Very well," said Southard, turning and storming from the room. *The idiot thinks this is some kind of game, that he is in charge. Just wait until fifty solar masses of star explodes in his face.* Southard made his way back to his cabin, sitting down and logging into his personal terminal. *I've still got some friends*, he thought, sending a personal message through to one of the destroyers that was sensibly sitting outside the hyper barrier, the one with the wormhole com. He didn't know if it would help, or if he would get a reply back in time. But it was the only thing he could think of doing. *No, not the only thing*, he thought, pulling up the program that showed the ship's systems, and seeing if he could get the codes to the shuttle.

They might court martial me for this. Or at least bring me up in a civilian court for theft of government property. But if it gets me out of this stellar furnace, they can do whatever they want.

* * *

CAPITULUM, JEWEL. DECEMBER 11TH, 1001.

The Yugalyth Prime squatted in the chamber and looked over her spawn. It would never move from this place, not unless assisted by many of the mobile members of its kind. Its only job now was to grow those mobile forms. Now over forty of them clustered into the chamber, not to move the Prime, but to receive their final mission instructions.

It does not matter that they die, thought the Prime, who now had another dozen extrusions from its mass that were growing into human form beings. It looked at the mobile units, all of which were different, some men, some women, all as average and ordinary looking as could be. These were not configured to try and get through any high security areas. The one who had been configured that way had left days ago. These were made to strike, strike hard, and do as much damage as possible.

And now all we are waiting on is the special equipment. That was not something it could provide. The contacts it had with the Knockermen network in the capital, which did not include any of those aliens for obvious reasons, and through them the underworld, was supposed to give them what they needed. If they didn't come through there were still targets his minions could strike, but none like the one that was presenting itself the next day.

"You have your orders," he told the lesser Yugalyth through his speaking orifice, while his eating mouth continued to feed. "After you receive your equipment, you will go to your rallying points and await the hour."

The Yugalyth thought for a moment about why it was doing this, sending so many of its own kind to their deaths, even while it risked its own existence doing so. The Yugalyth had not always been gifted with all of the attributes they now enjoyed, though they had always been a very plastic race. The Ancients had done this to them, and made them the intelligence operatives of their Empire. Then those same Ancients had played with time and space, and lost many of their star systems as a result. One of those systems had been the one had birthed the Yugalyth species, who had never again found a home. And the humans were embarking on the same disastrous path.

"The equipment is here, sir," said one of the human mercenaries over the com. The humans did not like to enter this room, probably feeling that they would also become food. They delivered those they had kidnapped to the door and shoved them in. Once in the room there was no escape, except down the digestive system of the Prime, where they were converted to Yugalyth biomass.

"Very good," it said over the com. "Make sure everything works." It cut the com and turned back to its mobile units. "Now is the time. Gather your equipment and strike. The humans must learn that they must not tamper with time and space the way they do."

*   *   *

"We think we've got something, Lieutenant," said the Detective First Class, walking into Ishuhi Rykio office.

The Lieutenant was looking at a holo map of the city, the overview of the disappearances, which had spiked once again. The case was Priority Alpha for the police department. And what they didn't know was that it was also Naval Intelligence Priority Alpha One, the highest. Someone in Fleet intelligence thought this had something to do with the Yugalyth, and rooting out those creatures here in the capital system couldn't be any more important.

"Tell me," he said, looking up at that big man who

had just interrupted his thinking. Detective First Class Ramirez was also ex Naval Intelligence, and though he had not been reactivated, he knew the scoop. The man closed the door behind him and walked up to the desk.

"One of our informants reported being chased through the streets by men he said looked at him like he was a side of beef," said Ramirez, pointing a finger at the map holo and indicating a point near a large park. "He didn't know who they were, but he was sure that they meant him no good. The snitch, who is an expert at getting his own hide out of trouble, was able to lose them."

"I guess that's wonderful for him," said Rykio, not really seeing how this helped them. The area indicated was large, and almost a third of the disappearances had occurred in that region. Which meant that two thirds of them hadn't. Which meant that area might not be the center of whatever was taking those people.

"This is where it gets interesting," said the Detective, ignoring the sarcasm from his officer. "The informant followed the men after they gave up chasing him. I know, crazy. But my guy realized this might be worth some real money. So he decided to take a chance. And he caught them, red, making a snatch and grab, right here." The detective pointed to a spot, which then glowed on the map.

That's about three kilometers from where they tried to grab the informant. Interesting. "Did he see what direction they went."

"Better than that," said the smiling Detective. "He saw them put their victim, this time a young woman, into an air van and take off. My man was able to call a taxi just before they took off, and had the cabby follow them, to here."

"Shit," blurted the Lieutenant, zooming in the map to look at a large warehouse that occupied most of a block. *What an unlikely bunch of circumstances*, he thought. But unlikely circumstances were how people with the perfect plan often got caught, given enough time.

"Do you know who owns that building?"

"A holding company that first went into business about six months ago," said the other Detective. "The records on them are kind of sketchy."

"We have them," said Rykio, pumping his fist into the air. "Get together a team, while I kick this upstairs. I want to get these people before they have a chance to relocate." Unsaid was the fact that Naval Intelligence would also be brought in, something both men knew, and the higher ups in the department would find out soon enough.

Chapter Seventeen

A diplomat is a person who can tell you to go to hell in such a way that you actually look forward to the trip.
Caskie Stinnett

CAPITULUM, JEWEL. DECEMBER 12TH, 1001.

The day of the wedding dawned warm and clear. Weather control had long been a dream of mankind. Unfortunately, it had never been obtained, except in the grossest of manners. Heat could be pumped into an ocean system to spawn storms, and sometimes rains could be generated in the same manner, though there was always the risk of it getting out of control. Clear weather, not so much.

So Jennifer felt as if God was blessing her marriage by sending them such a fine day. She patted her flat stomach, imagining the life that was already growing there. She would not show for many weeks, but the seed was planted, with the Imperial genome intact. It was a boy. Not that it really mattered, the heir could very well be female. But she knew Sean would be thrilled to have a son.

Oh Glen, she thought, seeing the big Marine in her thoughts, blinking back the tears. *We had planned on having children, of raising them on a frontier world where there was air to breath and wilderness to explore. But now those worlds are at risk, and the only safe place, if there is one, is here, on the capital. The Cacas would have to go through the entire military of the Empire to threaten my child.*

"What's wrong," said Sean, moving up beside her and holding her in his arms. "You're crying."

"I'm just so happy that this day is finally here," she

told her fiancé. That was the truth, and a lie. She was so very happy to be marrying the man in front of her, and saddened that her last love hadn't survived.

"I want to see you smile," he said after kissing her. "I want this to be the happiest day of your life. Because, after this day, you will be first among women of the Empire."

"As far as I'm concerned," she said, smiling, "I already am."

"With me you already are," said Sean, stroking her hair. "This will just make it official for the rest of our wretched minions."

"You." Jennifer laughed and punched Sean in the chest. Her fist met iron hard muscle, a part of Sean's genetic heritage. *He never works out, except some of those martial arts he enjoys, and he's built like an athlete.*

"Ready, your Majesty?" asked Phyllis Clarke, the woman who had been designated as wedding planner, for a ceremony that promised to be much more complicated than any other in the last couple of decades.

"Born ready," said Sean, smiling, his eyes never leaving those of Jennifer. "You?"

"Nervous as hell," she admitted. "But yes, I'm ready."

"Then it is time to go, your Majesty. My Lady."

The lift took them up to the roof of the main building, where a half dozen transports waited. All looked alike from the outside. The one they were ushered inside was as much different from the others as a mansion was from a barracks. The inside was as luxurious as Sean's aircar, with plush seats, state of the art holo systems, a small bar. Sean and Jennifer sat in the back seat, with Phyllis sitting in the facing seat with one of the Secret Service Agents on the security detail. Senior Agent in Charge Catherine Mays and two more of her agents took the seat in the next compartment, right behind that of the Imperial couple, while a further pair sat right behind the pilot's compartment.

One of the other transports was packed with twelve Secret Service Agents, while the other three had infantry from the Imperial Protection Division, wearing medium combat armor, ready to deploy. As soon as everyone was aboard all six of the ships jumped into the air, where another six troop carriers and twelve gunships formed up around them. Overhead was a squadron of atmospheric attack craft, while even further up was a squadron of orbital fighters. And on this day a small squadron of Fleet warships hovered in low orbit over the capital, on the lookout for anything that might come from space to interrupt the ceremony.

Traffic was still coming into Constance the Great Spaceport. Even such an event as this couldn't stop the traffic that was constantly coming in and out of the capital. The only restriction was a pinching of the air corridors, with shuttles cautioned to not deviate under severe penalty of law.

We're really doing this, thought Jennifer, wondering if she was going to wake up from this dream after all, and find that she was still a frontier world doctor. She looked over at Sean, who was looking back with that charming smile on his face, and knew that this was reality.

*   *   *

Sean couldn't stop looking at Jennifer. The smile on her face was radiant, and he was sure he had made the right choice. *She's beautiful*, he thought, looking at her perfectly made up face, her red hair flowing down the back of her dress, held in place by interlinked chains glittering with precious stones.

Sean had seen more beautiful women in his time in the Universe. Most altered by nanite molding or other surgical methods. Jennifer was all natural, and to him that made her much more desirable than any artificially enhanced woman. And she had a fine mind as well. Maybe not on his level, but not too far behind.

The com signal in his link chimed, the kind of sound that only accompanied a priority message. He looked at the signature stamp and saw that it was his chief spy, Director of the IIA, Ekaterina Sergiov. *I would have thought that she would be at the cathedral already. It must be really vital for her to chime through at this time.*

He connected through his link, using his thoughts to communicate, so as not to alarm Jennifer. Most people preferred to actually speak, and to look at the person they were speaking to on holo. There was always the risk with mind link that something might be *said* that wasn't meant to be.

Your Majesty, came the voice of the Director through the link. *We have notice from one of my agents about an attack on the capital. Involving the shifters.*

Where did this intelligence come from?

Striped Wolf, said the woman, using the code word for the Maurid double agent. *We think the intelligence is good. The source says that it comes from the Knockermen themselves.*

Any idea of the target? asked Sean, giving Jennifer a worried glance, seeing a frown come over her face.

Not by name, your Majesty. But today is your wedding day. I can't think of a better target for someone who wants to make a statement.

And your suggestion, Ekaterina? Should we call off the

wedding? He felt heartsick as he said the last, looking at Jennifer, imagining the disappointment she would feel.

By no means do I think you should call off the wedding, your Majesty. These people, or whatever they are, are now terrorists. And letting them have their way is the same as letting them win. The wedding must go on. I am mobilizing everything I have, including Capitulum police, to cover all avenues of approach on the ground. I suggest that you alert the military, or give me the authorization to do so. We probably need more top cover, unless I miss my guess.

You have my authorization, Ekaterina, sent Sean, looking out the window at the city passing underneath, the huge towers they were flying over, and the even taller buildings off in the distance. *Every barracks, planet wide. But tell them to not interfere with the wedding, or the guests, unless it becomes necessary. I don't want us causing lot of alarm over what might turn out to be nothing.*

I might suggest employing a distortion field around you and the Empress, said Sergiov after a moment's hesitation. *It might just cause an assassin to miss.*

The com link died, and Sean continued to stare out into the city, until soft arms encircled him.

"What's wrong?" asked Jennifer.

"Some last minute military preparations for the offensive," he said, feeling guilty at having to lie to her.

"Are you sure that's what it was? You wouldn't be holding something back?"

And it's not a good way to start off a marriage, thought Sean, looking into her concerned eyes. *Especially when we are going to be a governing partnership.* "Ekaterina thinks there may be an attack by the shape shifters." He cringed a bit as he saw her eyes widen. "It might be during the ceremony. Or soon after."

"Should we, postpone it, then," she said, her eyes

starting to mist up. "Maybe we can have a small ceremony at the palace."

"The Emperors of this Empire do not marry in small, private ceremonies," said Sean, shaking his head. "To back out now sends the wrong message. And, since we know it's likely coming, we're prepared."

Jennifer nodded, not looking happy with the idea that her wedding day might be interrupted by terrorists. But he could see by the set of her chin that she was determined to see it through.

"We're preparing to set down now, your Majesty," said Senior Agent in Charge May from her station. "Let the soldiers deploy first, then my people will form up around you and escort you into the cathedral."

"Don't crowd me too close," said Sean, knowing that the woman would have by now received the warning from Sergiov, who was also her boss. "We want the people to see the happy couple."

Thank God we're dressed for the occasion, thought Sean, running a hand over the shoulder of Jennifer's blue gown, which covered her from her neck down to her ankles. The dress was as elegant as could be, and was also made up of impact armor cloth with a reflective undercoating. It could handle any small caliber round that wasn't launched by a mag rail cannon, and several seconds of medium intensity laser fire. But he couldn't guarantee that they would not be shot at by more powerful weapons than the clothing could withstand.

Sean himself was wearing his naval Commander in Chief's uniform, with the same ability to withstand fire as Jennifer's gown. He also had a ceremonial pistol belted to his waist, that was actually a very serviceable particle beam weapon. On both forearms, hidden under his sleeves, were laser projectors of the same power capacity as military grade pistols. He thought that if it came down to using those weapons to defend himself and his bride, he was really fucked. But having them made him feel better.

The area in front of the cathedral was cleared for the landing. The huge plaza that extended from the bottoms of the steps for kilometers to the outer wall was packed with millions of adoring citizens. Huge holo projectors set up for their viewing showed the transports coming in for landing. As soon as they entered the cathedral the view would switch to inside. Billions of people across the planet were also watching, from homes, bars, restaurants, even stadiums and arenas set up for this purpose. And, for the first time in history, over three hundred billion people, humans and aliens, would watch a ceremony from the capital city in real time, through the wormhole net.

Sean also noticed all the troops in that plaza, soldiers and Marines in battle armor arrayed around the outside borders. A hundred more on the landing stage. And in the air, hovering on their suit grabbers, hundreds more. Not seen were the sniper and heavy weapons teams occupying vantage points on the cathedral roof and towers, and all the surrounding buildings. Outside of the perimeters of military personnel were thousands of Capitulum police, mostly equipped for crowd control, though their heavy alert teams were also present.

"If you please, your Majesty. My Lady," said May, opening the door and inviting them out.

The plaza reverberated with the roar of millions of people, cheering for their Monarch and his bride. Sean was popular once again, after his victory at Congreeve. People had hope once more, and this ceremony was a symbol that the Empire would go on, and humans would still have a place in the Galaxy. Sean and Jennifer both waved to the crowd, basking in the adulation.

"Ready?" asked Sean as he held out his arm for his bride.

"Ready," she agreed, taking that arm and letting herself be led into the cathedral.

The large doors opened, and the Emperor and his bride walked through, while the hundreds of thousands of heads within the Reformed Catholic Cathedral of St. Marks turned and craned to catch the first sight of the Imperial couple. Large holos on the side walls showed the sight to those who could not see them across the huge cathedral.

"See you in a moment," said Sean, kissing Jennifer, then walking toward the front on the long carpet. There waited the Patriarch of the Church, Pope Julius Komo, his ebony face shining under his Mitre of office. Forward of him stood one of the newest knights of the realm, Second Lieutenant Cornelius Walborski, looking handsome in his dress uniform, even if his expression was decidedly uncomfortable.

Too bad, boyo," he thought of the young hero. *I stood at your side when you married, now you can do the same for me.* The other people serving as Men of Honor, nine of them, stood to the side of Walborski. They included three cabinet Ministers, two Admirals, and a Field Marshal, as well as three other nobles, including Major General Sir Samuel Baggett. One of the *men* was Lord T'lisha, the Phlistaran Minister of Security, looking splendid in the formal clothing of his own people, cloak over his shoulders. The Minister looked as uncomfortable as the Best Man did, though for different reasons.   He was in charge of all security services in the Empire, and had to have been informed of the possibility of an attack. *And surely he wishes he were in the command center. Or, knowing the old barbarian, with one of his people's great axes, charging and enemy, just like his ancestors.*

The Emperor looked up and around for just a moment, his eyes taking in the hundreds of drones that filled the air.   Some were from the news services, getting high definition 3D images of the ceremony. Some were from the security services, scanning every face in the cathedral, sniffing the air for particles that might have DNA samples, then triangulating on any that might be of interest. And there were drones tasked with knocking down anything in the air that tried to get too close to the couple.

Sean walked to his place, aware of all the eyes on him, waiting for the moment when they would all be drawn elsewhere, as his were at this moment.   The music started, and Jennifer walked down the aisle, her own proud looking father holding her arm, her ten Maids of Honor in a line behind her. And, just as Sean predicted, every eye left him, drawn to the radiant beauty who was walking forward to join her life to his.

"You do have the ring?" he asked Cornelius out of the corner of his mouth as the procession walked down the aisle. "Tell me you have it, so I don't have to order you on a suicide mission to the Caca home world."

"I have it, your Majesty," said the Ranger, patting one pocket, then another, then acting like he was about to panic.

Sean almost burst out laughing in a relief of tension as the young man reached into the first pocket he had pretended to check and pulled out the box.

"I guess the Cacas are safe, for now," said Cornelius. His face broke out in a smile, and Sean almost broke out into laughter again.

Straighten up, he thought as Jennifer walked up to stand beside him. *This is big boy stuff now, and you need to act it.*

The party all faced the Patriarch, who started to recite the ceremony that had been old when humankind left the Earth. "My brothers and sisters," intoned the deeply resonate voice of the man who had served in the priesthood for over a hundred and seventy years, rising to the pinnacle of his profession. "We are gathered together, in the sight of God, to celebrate the joining of two people into one. Sean and Jennifer have proclaimed their love for each other in their betrothal, and now they will affirm that love with their joining. Let us pray."

The ceremony seemed to fly by to Sean's perception, while proceeding with agonizing slowness at the same time. There were the two readings from the book that had guided the Christian faith for thousands of years. That book, no longer considered the inerrant word of God by the space faring race of humans, was still considered the basis of the religion. One reading was from the Old Testament, and Sean was not even sure what it had been about when it was finished. The second was the timeless story of Jesus and the wedding feast, and the changing of the water into wine.

Did any of this ever really happen? thought the Emperor as the words were read. He had not been the most religious of adults, though raised in the church, like all in his family. Appearances had to be maintained, and so he had attended services whenever possible. At this time his belief or disbelief was not really all that important. Many of his subjects believed, not all in the way of the Reformed Catholic Church, but in traditions close enough, even if that similarity was only that they had also originated on the planet of the species' birth.

And then came the part that everyone was waiting for. Jennifer's father symbolically gave his daughter to the man who would be her husband and protector, the rings were produced, and it was time to say the words.

"I, Sean Ogen Lee Romanov, take this woman, Jennifer Conway, to be my lawful wedded wife. To have and to hold, in equal partnership in all that I do, for better or for worse, for richer or poorer, in sickness and in health, till death do us part." Sean slid the ring on her finger, then presented his own left hand for her to hold.

"I, Jennifer Conway, take this man, Sean Ogen Lee Romanov, to be my lawful wedded husband. To have and to hold, in equal partnership in all that I do, for better or for worse, for richer or poorer, in sickness and in health, till death do us part." She slid the ring onto his finger, symbolizing their joining.

"Then in the name of God, the Almighty, through his son, Jesus Christ, I name you man and wife. May no man break asunder what God has joined."

Those last words had always struck Sean as silly, since the divorce process in the Empire, and even in the Church, was simplicity incarnate. But looking at his bride, his heart beating faster, all he could think was *we can make this last a lifetime*.

"You may kiss the bride," said the Patriarch, whose own wife was looking on from the chorus with a beaming smile.

Sean wasted no time in taking Jennifer into an embrace, and kissing her tenderly for all to see. The kiss went out all over the news nets, and hundreds of billions of citizens saw that, for the first time in over a year, a couple again sat the thrones of the Empire. And with that couple, could an heir be far behind?

"I present to the congregation, the Emperor Sean, and the Empress Jennifer. May they share their love through the decades, and may that love be brought forth in their wise rule."

The crowd erupted into a deafening roar that lasted for minutes. It quickly died off as the Patriarch again spoke, and the ceremony continued with the Eucharist.

Sean and his new Empress walked back up the aisle while flowers flew through the air. The doors opened, and the double line on Fleet, Army and Marine officers appeared, stretched from doorway to the stairs, forty meters away. All held swords overhead, forming an archway of blades for the couple to walk through. The pair had taken the first step outside the church when something exploded off in the distance, and the angry humming buzz of particle beams reached through the air over the screams of the crowd.

Chapter Eighteen

When the war of the giants is over the wars of the pygmies will begin.   Winston Churchill

CAPITULUM, JEWEL. DECEMBER 12TH, 1001.

"Everyone ready?" asked Detective Lieutenant Ishuhi Rykio over the com. The acknowledgements started coming back quickly from all the elements of the operation.   Higher ranking members of the department were also on the link, monitoring. But the operation was his, and he meant to strike hard.

The Lieutenant looked over his dispositions on his link. He had snipers on every rooftop, teams of SWAT in heavy armor waited across the street from every entrance, while other troopers crouched on those same rooftops, ready to spring into action. There were even teams set up in every known underground passage beneath the building. *And we scanned down there thoroughly*, thought Rykio. If there was a still hidden tunnel down there, it wasn't because the police hadn't tried to find it.

OK, he thought, taking one last look at the building, then back at the team behind him. "Go, go, go," he said into the com, running into the street with ten other men on his tail.

Everyone was dressed in combat armor, the light type worn by police during raids, and much like the Army version used by their light infantry divisions. It enhanced their strength by about three times, and gave them protection from moderate sized projectile weapons, and just a touch of laser fire. The com and sensor suites were almost on par with the much larger medium and heavy suits worn by the Army and

Marines. The two men closest to the Lieutenant were wearing the same type of heavy suits used by the SWAT teams. Their function was a little different than that of the other cops.

"Take it out," shouted Ishuhi over the com, pointing at the heavy warehouse door.

The two men in the heavy suits ran flat out into the door, the strength of their armor smashing the steel alloy barrier off its hinges and into the room. They followed after, pulling their laser rifles off their backs and sweeping the large room with their light enhancing sights.

A shot rang out, a chemically propelled weapon, such as used by many civilians, including members of the criminal underworld. The round sparked off a wall, and one of the heavy suits fired his laser into the area where he had determined that the bullet originated. A scream echoed across the mostly empty room, and more shots followed.

"This is the police," yelled Ishuhi over his suit speakers, feeding into all the other suits of the raiding party. "We have this building surrounded, and you are outgunned. Drop your weapons, now, or we will be forced to fire on you." *First with stunners*, he thought hopefully. *I would rather have this crew alive than dead. Or at least with intact brains, where we can get something from them.*

We give up," called out one of the men in the shadows. A chemically powered assault rifle clattered across the floor, out into the light. Pistols followed, until a dozen weapons were laying on the plasticrete floor."

"Move into the light with your hands up," called Rykio over the speakers. "Fingers laced behind your heads."

Men and women started to appear, coming into the light, and the Lieutenant began to think this might be a fairly bloodless operation after all. He was still thinking that when a pair of particle beams, angry red, came lancing out of the dark to strike one of the men in a heavy suit.

The suit could withstand the hit of a particle beam rifle for several seconds before the armor failed. Two beams struck at the chest, within a centimeter of each other. In less than a second they had eaten a hole through the armor and vaporized the thorax of the man within.

"Shit," yelled the Lieutenant, dropping to the floor with his stunner out. "Bring them all down."

The room filled with the sound and vibrations of sonics, and the people who had already surrendered fell limply to the floor. That didn't stop the pair of particle beams from lancing out again. One hit a wall and burned a deep runnel into the plasticrete. The other hit a cop in the arm, slicing through the alloy and vaporizing the limb underneath. The cop fell to the floor, screaming in agony.

At least he's alive, thought Rykio, checking the man's status on his HUD. It would take some weeks to grow back the arm, but when it was done, he would be good as new. A thought flashed through the Detective's mind of the days when that was not true, and losing a limb, or several, was considered a tragic loss.

"Open fire on those people with the particle beams," he ordered over the com. "Full powered lasers."

A moment later the lasers lanced out as well, visible through the air that was cloudy with the smoke of vaporized biomass. The police swept the beams through the darkness that hid the criminal gunmen, several moving at ankle level, a couple more at waist, and still others at chest level. One particle beam came back, barely missing one of the cops. Another sweep of lasers and the return fire stopped.

"Hit that area with some stunners," ordered the Lieutenant. He fired the grenade launcher under his own rifle, loaded with a sonic stun grenade, which impacted along with several others in the corner. By the light of the flash the grenades put out he could see a pair of bodies, one laying at an angle that showed it was missing a head.

"Cover us," he told the rest of the cops, designating one to move up with him. Police doctrine called for them to stick together. Rykio was having none of that shit. He had been a Naval Commando, and in his experience it was always better to keep the possible targets separated. He waved the other man to the far side of the room while he moved to the other, then they both walked toward the downed criminals, in some cases stepping over the prone bodies of the stunned humans.

"And these aren't human," he said over the com as he looked down at the headless being. The skin on the neck looked human, but the next layer of flesh under that didn't. And the spine looked alien in the extreme. "We have shape shifters here. Everyone be careful." *And I'm calling the Fleet in on this one*, he thought, linking into the Naval Intelligence circuit and sending out the call.

"We have some people trying to leave the building," called out one of the rooftop teams.

"Try to take them down with stunners," he told the team leader. "If they don't go down immediately, kill them.   And don't let any escape.   They might be shape shifters."

As he received the acknowledgement he waved the rest of his team forward.   Men moved out to search the warehouse, while others secured the criminals with magnetic restraints.

"Over here," yelled one of the men, and Rykio ran to see what was going on.   "There's a door here, sir," said the officer, pointing at what looked like a very heavy barrier in the frame.

Rykio tried to open the door, but it would budge. "Get over here and see if you can bust this down," he told his remaining heavy suit man.

After two minutes of hammering on the door it was readily apparent that it was not opening by force. Lasers burned into the metal alloy, which was similar to what was used on warship hulls.   They didn't burn through enough, and the door stood here and mocked them.

"We need demolitions in here," he called out over the com.   "Now."

*   *   *

Prime was having trouble believing that the humans had found him.   After all, hadn't his people only gone out late at night, being very careful to make sure that they were not followed.   Or at least his own kind had, but could the same be said for the humans he had hired?   They were only criminals, after all, only in it for the money.   And not the brightest of people.

My mobile units should be striking at their Emperor and his reproductive unit now.   If they are successful, this Empire will have been decapitated.   If not, we will still have had an effect on them that they will have trouble recovering from.   Now, I must make sure there are more of us here, on their capital world.

The twenty growths attached to his body were not ready yet. Half of them were still in the early stages of formation, no larger than human children, missing even the limbs they needed to walk. The other half were about a day from being ready. *But they must be used now, so I can guarantee that my kind survives here. One or more of them can become a Prime.*

The Prime sent a thought through his body into the half of the mobiles who were almost ready, waking their brains, turning control of their bodies to the newly awakened consciousnesses. The mobiles started to move, pulling themselves away from the Prime, ripping the last strands of biomass holding them to their progenitor.

Go, signalled the Prime to his progeny through a release of pheromones. *Leave this place. Seek dark places, mature, and grow more of you.*

The mobiles started for the door, looking like incomplete humans. They would be spotted immediately if they were to go out into the open. They could only survive by hiding, until they could capture some of the genetic code of a human and make themselves over.

The creatures had almost matured mentally, with the capability of thinking for themselves. As soon as they were through the door they scattered, heading into the sub-basement, where half a dozen tunnels led from the complex.

Defend me, the Prime ordered the smaller, less complete mobiles. Those creatures, with the mental capacity of a human toddler, pulled themselves away as well, breaking off, then crawling with their partially developed arms toward the walls of the room. Reaching them, they scrambled up the surfaces and onto the ceiling, secreting a resinous compound to hold them to the surface. There they waited for a target to appear.

*   *   *

"Fire in the hole," yelled out the demolitions specialist, a woman from the Fleet who had come with the force that had responded to Rykio's call. With a bright flash the door blew off its hinges and out into the warehouse. Smoke swirled for a moment, then cleared, revealing another room.

"Hold up," order Rykio, reaching out his hand to stop his men from advancing. "You guys, stay up here and make sure nothing comes out."

The Lieutenant followed the other people through the hole, a team of Naval Commandos sent by the Fleet, eleven in all. Rykio, also augmented as a former commando, made twelve, and the men moved quickly and silently into the room.

One of the commandos waved and pointed, and half the men turned that way while the others kept up their observation of the other surfaces in the room. The doors looked like a lift, something that was on the schematic of the building that Rykio called up on his HUD.

"This leads us where we want to go," he said to the Lt. Commander in charge of the team. Since Rykio was a full Commander in the reserve, he was in charge of the party, and the other officer nodded and waved one of his men forward.

A few moments later the doors slid open, revealing an empty shaft that plunged down about ten meters, ending on the top of the lift. Two commandos jumped the short, to them, distance down to the top of the lift, then opened the top hatch to go through. *It looks clear,* sent one of the commandos over a com link. Two more commandos leapt down, then another, until all of them were through the car and into the basement on the other side of its door.

The men fanned out and searched the basement. At one point a man was found, holding his hands out and making sure that they knew he was unarmed. "It was only a job," said the man, stammering. "I didn't know what kind of a monster I was working for. You gotta believe me."

"Who the hell are you?" asked Rykio, walking up to the man whom the commandos had already put restraints on. "And what do you mean, monsters?"

"That damned thing in the subbasement. When I found out what it was doing, I wanted out, but I saw what the damned thing did to my buddy, Gavin. No one should be torn apart like that."

"And where is this, thing?" asked Rykio, not really interested in what happened to Gavin.

"In the room, under the subbasement," stammered the man. "Go into the subbasement and look for another lift at the northeast corner. It goes down about fifty meters, then it's a maze down there."

Police started coming down into the room, SWAT troopers in heavy suits. The backup that the Lieutenant had requested. "Let's go, people. We've got a monster to hunt."

It was easy enough to get into the subbasement, as the lift they had found in the basement went down there. Two men rode the lift down, then the rest jumped down onto the roof a pair at a time. The other lift was a bit more difficult to find, hidden as it was behind a false wall. A couple of the commandos carried deep radar sets, and after a complete sweep of the northeast corner the door was found and pulled open.

"The lift is not here," said one of the commandos, looking down the shaft. "And too far to jump."

"Then we go down the old fashioned way," said the Lt. Commander

The commando he was talking to nodded, then pulled a slender cable from a side bag. The man pushed the end of the cable against the plasticrete wall, let the nanites on that end bond, then pulled the cable to test it. Satisfied, the man went down the cable, rappelling against the wall. A moment later he was joined by another commando, coming down a second cable. They hit the roof of the lift and one started to open the top hatch. He only had it partially opened when a particle beam sliced through and came close to spearing him. Only his augmented reflexes saved him, and the two commandos blasted through the top of the lift with their own particle beams, firing until their proton packs were empty.

With a nod one of the commandos lifted the ruined hatch again while the other threw a stun grenade into the cab of the lift. Both men grabbed their cables and pulled themselves up the wall a bit. The grenade went off, partially lifting the hatch. The men jumped back to the roof, one opening the hatch while the other dropped through. The second man followed, and two more rappelled rapidly down to the roof, then into the cab.

The buzz of a couple of particle beams came up the shaft, and Rykio cursed that he wasn't down there. "We're taking fire," said one of the commandos over the com. "No one hit, but we're returning fire."

Two more commandos headed down the cables,

dropping onto the roof, then through the hatch in swift motions. The firing intensified, the angry buzzing noises growing in volume as more weapons added their fire.

"I'm going down," said Rykio, grabbing hold of a cable.

"Wait a moment," said the Lt. Commander, putting a hand on the Detective's shoulder.

"Clear," shouted out the Chief Petty Officer from below.

"Go ahead," said the Lt. Commander.

Rykio nodded and started down the cable. *Haven't done this in quite a while*, he thought as he rappelled down, the cable feeding through his gloves. In a moment he was on the roof, then sliding through the hatch, hoping that the way was truly clear, and he wasn't walking face first into enemy fire.

The scorched meat smell hit his nostrils as soon as his feet hit the floor of the lift. One commando waited for him, the others had fanned out across the room, taking cover positions that let me see and aim down the three openings that led into the chamber.

"There were three of them," said the Chief, pointing over into one corner of the room, then another.

"That doesn't smell quite right," said Rykio, gagging slightly.

"They weren't quite human," said the Commando. "They burned just fine though, once the protons sliced through their outer covering."

Rykio nodded and stepped out of the lift. A moment later the Lt. Commander and another Commando came down, followed by the last pair just moments after.

"We've stopped a couple of them from getting through," came the voice of the SWAT commander over the com. "They were coming up some of the tunnels, moving quietly as you please. Not quietly enough."

"And prisoners?"

"No, Ishuhi," said the other man, also a Police Lieutenant. "They didn't seem to be in the mood for being captured. And I wasn't about to risk my men trying to bring them in alive."

"Fair enough. Keep an eye out for some more. I believe the only way they can get out of here is underground. Or so they'll believe."

"We're ready to move out, Commander," said the senior commando officer. "Three men down each side tunnel, four down the larger central one with me. And we'll depend on your SWAT for backup."

"I'll go up the central one with you, Commander," Rykio told the officer. He turned as something heavy landed in the lift cab, to see the first of the SWAT heavy suits had arrived.

"Let's go then," said the officer to his men. "The sooner we get done here, the sooner we go home. If the attack on the Emperor isn't still going on."

"The Emperor?" blurted Rykio, his eyes widening. "He's under attack?"

"He was when we came down here," said the Lt. Commander, nodding.

"Then why aren't you there?"

"Look, Commander," said the commando officer, looking like he would have wanted to be there if possible. "There are over twenty thousand people there already, between the Fleet, Marines, Army and police. The eleven of us really aren't enough to make a difference, and it's also important to get these bastards." The man stopped and looked at his three men. "Let's move out."

*   *   *

Prime did not really feel fear as most sentient beings did. He knew he was but one cell in the greater organism that was the Yugalyth. His end was regrettable, but as long as some of his kind got out of here, it would be OK. Unfortunately for him, he had no way of knowing if any of his progeny had escaped. His kind did not communicate by radio frequencies like the Margravi. Telepathy was a fantasy, as far as anyone knew. He could communicate through pheromones when his kind was close. Otherwise, he had no means of contacting them, as the use of communications devices, even highly encrypted ones, would give away the location of their users.

The sound of particle beam weapons came down the tunnel and through the closed door. The sound rose, and the Prime knew it was because the enemy had brought more warriors into the fray. He knew he didn't have any more to commit, as he knew that there was only one outcome possible for his outer defense. It would be overwhelmed.

After a few moments the buzzing stopped, and there was only one explanation for that as well. Prime waited, a particle beam gripped in one of its many arms. The others were grown into claws, weapons it could hopefully use to rend its enemies. Unless they were wearing battle armor, in which case the claws would prove useless.

It took some minutes before it heard something at the door, moving the manual opening lever after the electronic lock didn't open it. The door swung open, and Prime went into action.

*   *   *

"Be careful," said Rykio to the Commando at the door. "There's definitely something behind that door." He looked at his HUD, which showed a chemosense trace coming through the door, which was not airtight.

"Opening," whispered the Commando, who then turned the handle and jerked the door open, two other men right behind with weapons ready.

None of them were ready for the clawed tentacle that came through the opening and grabbed the Commando around the shoulders. The man had time for one brief cry before he was snatched into the room.

"Kill it," yelled the Commander. The other two Commandos raised their rifles, but hesitated to fire with their compatriot in the way. Another tentacle came out, reaching for another victim.

Rykio didn't hesitate. He jumped through the door, batting aside the second tentacle, twisting in the air to dodge the particle beam fired by the one human looking arm on the, thing, that squatted in the room. Whatever it was, it was like nothing he had ever seen before. It must have massed several tons, with claw tipped tentacles waving around it, two moving toward him. There was a head like appendage on the top, and the thing was dragging the Commando it had grabbed toward a wide orifice with large, sharp teeth.

First things first, thought the Detective, whose mind had gone into combat overdrive, his mental processes running several times faster than normal. He fired his particle beam, vaporizing the arm that held the creature's one high tech weapon. The thing's particle beam rifle fell onto its mass, and a tentacle tried to grab it, failing as its clawed digits were unable to find the right grip on the weapon.

The creature pulled the Commando to it and popped the rating's head into its eating orifice. The Commando was wearing a soft suit of impact armor, including a high collar, and a tactical helmet. What he didn't have was anything protecting his upper neck, and the creature's teeth sheered through to decapitate the man. It tried to chew the head, but failed because of the tactical helmet, and swallowed the man's head whole.

"Goddammit," yelled Rykio, raising his rifle and aiming at the creature's head. He wasn't sure if that was where its brain resided, but it was worth a try. Before he could get off the shot, something fell from the ceiling, grabbing his rifle and jerking it out of his surprised hands. He caught sight of something about the size of a child, malformed, with no legs, rolling off the mass of the creature and trying to control the rifle. Then two tentacles grabbed him and pulled him toward the eating orifice as well.

*   *   *

The mobile unit waited until its two brothers were slaughtered by the SWAT cops before it made its move. It knew the hunters had chemosensors, which were probably flooded by the scent of the two Yugalyth they had just killed. If it could only move silently enough. With a slow move it was through the opening, and into the sewers that ran under the building. This was a main, a meter and a half of filthy water and waste running through a two meter wide channel.

The Yugalyth crawled into the water, careful to not make a sound. The gills on its neck extended as soon as it was under, and it allowed the current to pull it along. Within minutes it was a kilometer away. In no hurry to leave the sludge, it rode the current until it got almost to the treatment plant, then crawled out and looked for a worker it could take into the darkness, eventually to impersonate. It would take time, but it had time, and eventually it would make more operatives for this planet. And then the humans would pay for killing the Prime, as a new Prime went to work.

*   *   *

Rykio struggled against a creature whose strength made his augmented abilities look like those of a child. It pulled him toward its eating orifice, popped his head in, and bit down. While the commandos were wearing only soft skinned impact armor, and had exposed flesh that could be rended, the Detective was wearing the same kind of combat armor as that worn by light infantry. It was hard but flexible alloy, much too tough to be penetrated by teeth, no matter how large. The creature's teeth splintered as it bit down, and Rykio grabbed the sides of its mouth with his gauntlets and ripped into the flesh.

The creature started to scream, the sound coming from another orifice lower down, while the eating orifice writhed in agony. The smell coming through his nostrils, brought in by the openings in his helmet, was strong and sickening, and the reason the creature was in agony. The tentacles whipped him through the air and against the hard wall, where he fell stunned to the floor.

Now he could hear the hum of particle beams, a continuous sound, competing with the hiss of vaporizing flesh. Rykio looked up to see the creature in a frenzy, tentacles waving, first one, then another seared off at the root. He backed himself into the corner, pulling his mag rail pistol from its holster and adding his fire to that of the commandos.

Suddenly the creature, or what was left of it, stopped moving, its remaining tentacles flopping onto its body.

"Cease fire," yelled the Lt. Commander.

"Continue to fire," yelled Rykio. "It might be bluffing, and I want this thing dead."

The other officer acknowledged, and the beams started eating into the creature again, which screamed and started lashing again with its remaining tentacles. After a few more minutes, and a change of proton packs for all involved, the creature and all of its half sized minions, picked off as they tried to get at the commandos, were broiled, what hadn't been vaporized.

We got it, thought the Detective Lieutenant, shaking his head. *But we didn't get it in time, did we?*

Chapter Nineteen

War should be the only study of a prince. He should consider peace only as a breathing-time, which gives him leisure to contrive, and furnishes as ability to execute, military plans.   Niccolo Machiavelli

CAPITULUM, JEWEL. DECEMBER 12TH, 1001.

Sean reacted immediately as soon as he saw the flash of red out of the corner of his eye, well before the sound of the beams reached his ears. He grabbed Jennifer by the arm and flung her back into the church, then ducked down and tried to get a bead on whoever was attacking him. A half dozen of the officers who had formed the archway were down, one missing his entire head and torso. The sickening smell of scorched flesh reached his nostrils, and he knew that the odor was made up of particles of people he knew.

Beams were coming down all around, a dozen of them, ripping through the people nearby. Citizens were screaming, trying to push away from the crowd in a panic. Marines in heavy armor were flying over the crowd, getting themselves and their better protection between the shooters and the Emperor.

He looked back to see Jennifer trying to get out the door and to him. She was cradling her left forearm, and he was pretty sure that he had broken it when he threw her. *Better that than letting you stand here and get killed*, he thought, looking in approval as Cornelius grabbed the new Empress and carried her back from the entrance. *She'll be safe with him if with anyone*, he thought with approval, then turned his attention back to the immediate threat, the people shooting at him, and hitting his people.

Something exploded high up in the air, followed by another. Over a hundred armored soldiers boosted into the sky, some on a direct path toward, something. The others forming into a shield to protect those below. Particle beams came lancing down, most hitting the electromag fields of heavily armored soldiers, all of whom were now firing back.

"What's going on, Colonel?" asked Sean, running in a crouch toward a regimental commander in heavy armor who had established an open air command post on the top of the steps.

"Your Majesty. Some men in combat armor flew over the plaza with their full stealth packages on. We didn't even know they were there until they opened fire. Stingships got a couple, and my soldiers got the rest."

"All of them?"

"I think so, your Majesty. But we can't be sure right now. It would be better if you and the Empress didn't try to fly to your reception until we do a complete sweep of the area. If they have missiles?"

The Colonel didn't have to complete that last sentence. If someone was hanging in the sky, stealthy, unnoticed, they could bring down a transport with a missile.

Sean looked out over the plaza, at the clumps of people who had been killed or wounded, emergency personnel clustered around them. He felt the shock of the attack finally coming over him, his hands shaking as he thought about what almost happened to himself and his bride.

"It might be a good idea to just cancel the reception, your Majesty," said the Colonel, retracting his faceplate and looking at his Monarch.

"Not on your life, Colonel," said the Emperor, shaking his head. "That reception is more for our people than for myself and the Empress. They deserve the celebration, not the cloud this act will cast over the event. If I give in to terrorists, they have already won."

Sean could see the combination of concern and admiration on the officer's face. He couldn't really care less about the admiration. He was not doing this to look the hero, but because he had meant what he said. They could not postpone things because of acts of terror. He looked at the closest clump of casualties, cringing as he saw the half body of a child. *We're lucky they didn't deploy small yield nukes*, he thought.

"It's clear, your Majesty," said the Colonel.

"Did you get them all?"

"We're still not sure about that, your Majesty. Some may have gotten away. But we're sure there are no more in the area. Complete close range, full power sensor scans have been run over all the nearby buildings up to ten thousand meters."

And why wasn't that done before the attack, thought the Emperor, holding back the words. *Because we didn't expect such an attack like this, we were lax, and now we paid the price.*

"I must check on the Empress," said Sean, getting up from his crouch and running into the church.

*   *   *

Cornelius had been quite a bit back from the Emperor and Empress when they had walked through the door. As far as he was concerned, his part in the ceremony was over. He and his family were expected to be guests at the reception, both the public one at the nearby civic center, and the private one at the Palace.

His enhanced hearing had no problem picking up

the angry buzzing of particle beams just outside the church, along with the screams and shouts of people. The Ranger didn't know what was going on, but it didn't take a genius to realize that there was trouble out there, and his friends were right in the middle of it.

A woman came flying through the entrance, instantly recognizable by her red hair and light blue ankle length dress. She hit a man, hard, both going down, and Cornelius knew where he needed to be.

The Ranger shoved people out of the way as he pushed through the crowd. A few tried to shove back, and found themselves losing to his enhanced strength. Most glanced at him, and realized that he was going where he was going no matter what they wanted. Some higher ranking people started to protest, but he ignored them as he fought his way to Jennifer.

The Empress was getting back to her feet, helped up by some of the men nearby. She was cradling her forearm, which was hidden under the sleeve of her dress, but the angle of which foretold a bad break. She turned back to the door and started forward, just before Cornelius grabbed her gently by the shoulders.

"He wants you in here, your Majesty," said Cornelius in her ear. "He wouldn't have thrown you in here like that if he didn't think it was important to get you under cover."

"But, he's out there," she said, her voice quivering.

"He's a warrior, and he has warriors around him. Let's get out of this crowd, and I'll get someone to look at your arm. Just come with me, Jennifer."

She nodded and let him pick her up. The Ranger moved into the church, gently pushing past anyone who got in the way. A lot of people were crowded near the exit, many of them military, men and women trying to get out of the church to help their Monarch, and just getting in the way.

Cornelius looked around, trying to find a quiet place to take the Empress. He found a pew in an alcove that was set aside for small services that was empty and led the way into it, sat her down, and unbuttoned the sleeve that was over her forearm. He glanced for a moment at the statue of the saint, he wasn't sure which one, looking down on them from the wall of the alcove.

"That's a bad break," he said, looking at the bent forearm.

"I should make that diagnosis," she said, wincing as he touched the arm.

"And what diagnosis would you give," he said, as he put a pain patch on her neck taken from the small med kit he always kept with him.

"It's really fucked," she said as the pain medication rushed into her system.

"Not as fucked as it's going to be," said a sibilant voice from the entrance of the alcove.

Cornelius looked up to see a nondescript man standing there, a chemical pistol in his hand pointing at the Ranger. "If you move I will shoot you," said the man, looking into Cornelius' eyes. "Then I will shoot her."

"And if I don't move?"

"Then I shoot her, and leave," said the, creature.

For some reason Cornelius didn't think the *man* was human. It was just something in the tone of his voice. Like he had tried to mimic a human being, but was not far enough along in the process. *A shifter*, thought Cornelius, his mind moving into overdrive, his thinking speed tripling. *How in the hell did it get in here?*

He thought he knew how. Guests were scanned for weapons, and given cursory ID when they entered the church. But with hundreds of thousands of people coming through the doors, there wasn't time to give everyone a complete scan, especially any of the new procedures. How he got the gun in was another matter, and one he would worry about later.

That's not right, thought Cornelius, his mind working down several paths at once. *If he hasn't completed his change into someone well known, he never would have gotten through.* Then the time for thinking was over.

The gun shifted, the shifter taking aim at the Empress, and Cornelius made his move.

The hand that was on the seat, resting on a hymnal, grabbed the book and threw it at the gunman. It sped through the air at high velocity and hit the gunman in the head. Cornelius cursed. He had aimed for the gun, but in the stress of the moment had thrown it too hard, with not enough follow through. The gunman shifted his weapon and shot at Cornelius, also missing through a combination of the Ranger moving too fast, and his vision blurred from being hit in the head by the heavy book.

Cornelius needed a weapon against something whose capabilities he really couldn't guess. His pistol was simply ceremonial, it didn't even have a magazine inserted. Which left him with only…

Thinking was action, and his right hand grabbed the sword grip on his left side, while his left hand pushed Jennifer down onto the pew. The sword swished out of its scabbard as the gunman aimed and fired again, striking Cornelius in his left shoulder. The impact armor of his uniform stiffened, enough to stop a low velocity round. Not enough to stop the high velocity pellet that came out of the gun. Still, enough to slow it down, so it only ripped through his shoulder like a normal bullet, and not the body destroyer it was made to be.

The Ranger grunted in pain and brought his sword up, then down, onto the wrist of the creature's gun hand. The sword was ceremonial as well, with no edge, and came down like a club on the wrist. The creature hissed, and the gun arm dropped, but he retained control of the weapon, and started bringing it back up immediately.

There was only one thing the Ranger could do. He lunged forward, using the point, which, while still not the duty edge of a real weapon, was enough, with the strength of the Ranger behind it, to push through the throat of the creature, coming to a stop against the spine. The eyes of the creature went wide, its breath rattled, but it still brought its weapon up to aim at the Ranger once again. Cornelius pushed harder, hoping to push through the spinal column and into the cord, but the bone was too tough.

Maybe I saved the Empress, was the thought of his sped up mental processes as he waited for the round that was going to end his life. The sound that came was not what he was expecting, more like the hissing spit of a mag rail pistol, and the head of the creature exploding in front of him was definitely not what he was expecting.

A huge figure appeared behind the fallen body of the assassin. A dracocentauroid, holding a huge mag pistol, lips curled back, revealing his carnivore's teeth.

"Lord T'lisha," said Cornelius, recognizing the Imperial Minster of Security. "Thank you."

"Thank you, young man," rumbled the large

sentient. "It is to my shame that such as this made his way in here in the first place. I could not bear to think that he might have killed my Empress."

Cornelius nodded, then sat down, feeling a little light headed from blood loss, his sword sliding out of the shifter's throat. People were around him in an instant, including several doctors, one to treat him, one to treat the Empress. Cornelius closed his eyes, knowing that everything would be alright.

*   *   *

Sean glared down at the creature that lay dead on the floor, sans head, which was missing thanks to the impact of a fifteen millimeter round from his Minister of Security's personal weapon. The neck told the story. The *man* was nothing such. It was a Yugalyth, plain and simple.

"How in the hell did it get in here?" asked the Monarch, looking at his newly wed spouse, lying on the pew, her arm being put in a soft splint. The bone had been set back into place, after a nanite pain block had been inserted. He felt shame at the thought that he had been the cause of that injury. That it had been sustained through his getting her quickly to safety, before a particle beam reached from the sky and vaporized her entire lovely body, did not matter. He had caused the injury, and in his mind, he was totally at fault.

"We found where he was hiding," rumbled Lord T'lisha, a decidedly uncomfortable expression on his long snouted face. "In an opening on the base of that statue over there." He pointed to the figure of another saint. "A human couldn't have fit. Not even a Malticoran. But those things can dislocate, and even bend bones.

We thought we had the church covered. We checked their invitations, which were supposed to be secure, against their prints and surface proteins. And they were scanned for weapons. We scanned the entire building for weapons the day before the ceremony, but somehow that one was sealed in something that spoofed them."

Sean looked over at the being that was his head of all security services of the Imperial government. The IIA, IIB, Imperial Constabulary, Marshals, Secret Service. All of the intelligence and security services save those of the military, which still reported their findings to the civilian organizations by law. *It's not really your fault, my friend*, he thought, shaking his head, realizing that the being would need to castigate himself for a time. *We'll all learn from this. We thought they would only strike as strategic targets, forgetting that myself and Jennifer are strategic targets. Now, no target is safe, and we will have to change things. Which is a win for them.*

He looked past Jennifer, to the man who kept doing things for him and his Empire. Cornelius lay across the same pew, his jacket and shirt off while a doctor sprayed his wound with nanites. The little robots would go after the bullet in the shoulder, disassembling it in place, then making repairs to the bone and tissues. *Saving the* Donut *was probably his greatest accomplishment, and more important than saving either of us. But this action will always be closest to my heart. I guess a knighthood was not quite a high enough reward. I'll have to look into whether or not we have a barony vacant on Jewel.* Sean smiled a moment at a thought. *Or maybe New Detroit.*

"I will have my resignation in the system as soon as I can compose it, your Majesty," rumbled T'lisha, breaking into Sean's thoughts.

"You will do no such thing," said Sean, looking back at his Security Minister. "You are the only being I want in that position, Lord T'lisha. And you will retain that post. Do you understand me?"

The great head nodded, and Sean looked back at his bride. The doctor had stood up and nodded to the Monarch, who quickly took the medic's place by her side.

"I am so sorry," he told her, putting his arm gently over her shoulders. "It's all my fault that you got hurt."

"It's not your fault," she said in a sleepy voice. "You were trying to get me out of the line of fire."

"And into the frying pan," said Sean, shaking his head, feeling the tears beading up in his eyes. He looked at the cast, which was now a hardened piece of plastic, setting her arm and protecting it. *Should be good as new in a couple of days*, he thought. *The physical injury. But what did it do to your sense of security? What did it do to the sense of security for all of my subjects?* "As soon as you're cleared here, we'll go back to the palace."

"And the reception? What about all the people there, expecting us?"

"I'm not really sure we need to attend," said Sean, looking back at all the people still gathered in the church, many of them still in shock, changing his mind from his earlier stance. "It would be an insult, having a party over the bodies of those who died here today."

"This isn't just our celebration," Jennifer said with a sleepy smile. "As soon as I wake up from these drugs, we are going to give them one. A celebration of life, and the continuance of the Empire, despite what these bastards tried to do today."

Sean sat there for a moment, not sure what to say, his thoughts a roil. *If we do this, some people are going to say that I only care about myself, just another noble of privilege. If I don't, some will say I am a coward, despite what I have done in the past. There really is no good decision here.*

"Can the Ranger make it to the reception tonight?" he asked the doctor who was working on Cornelius.

"I'll answer that one, your Majesty," said the man in question, craning his neck to look up. "Damned right, I can be there. And I want a dance with the Empress, with your permission, your Majesty."

"You deserve one, Baron," Sean said with a smile.

"Baron?" blurted Cornelius, trying to sit up and cringing with pain. The doc put his hand on Cornelius's chest and pushed him down.

"I'm not sure of what yet, but we'll think of something."

Several hours later Sean and Jennifer danced alone on the wide floor of the civic center, before the ten thousand guests who ate and drank at the tables. And, through the wormhole com system, a hundreds of billions of other citizens across the Core Worlds. Jennifer's arm was immobilized by her side, and Sean held her carefully as they moved across the floor. A wide smile was on her face, erased every once in a while by a wince. Sean saw her bravery. The Empire did as well, and all thoughts about the suitability of this woman as the co-ruler of the Empire was erased in the minds of reasonable people.

The dance music stopped, and other people started to make their way onto the floor.

"I beg your indulgence, Lords and Ladies, Citizens," said Sean, his voice amplified over the center's speaker system. "My lady wife has promised a dance to a very special man. The one who saved her life today, and mine as well, through saving hers."

The people moved back to the edge of the dance floor, while Cornelius Walborski, in a fresh uniform, walked out onto the floor, his left shoulder stiff and unmoving. He took Jennifer by the hand as the orchestra started in on a slow waltz. They pirouetted around the floor, both obviously injured, both just as obviously determined to complete the dance. A few people started clapping, then more, until the entire crowd was voicing their approval of the courageous Empress, and the man who the news would trumpet as the bravest soldier of the Empire.

Their dance over, the two repaired to the Emperor's table, while the other celebrants crowded onto the floor to take advantage of the music, and their drink lowered inhibitions. There would be no more dances for the Empress, despite what tradition called for. The Emperor availed the wishes of some of his ladies, as few as he could get away with, so he could spend the rest of his evening with his love.

*   *   *

"We will crucify them for this," said Countess Zhee, sitting at one of the noble tables with her husband. "How dare they make a spectacle of themselves after so many people died. This is a disgrace."

"You should leave it alone, my dear," said her husband, technically a count, though she was the titular ruler of her county. "You will just damage your cause even more by attacking him now. Those two can do no wrong with the people, at least at this time."

Zhee sat there in silence, unable to respond. Her reason told her that her husband was correct. But her emotions ruled, as they had since she had felt insulted by this same Emperor. *I will find a way to destroy him*, she thought, taking another sip of champagne.

Chapter Twenty

Conquered, we conquer.   Plautus

SECTOR IV SPACE. DECEMBER 15TH, 1001.

Here we go, thought Captain Maurice von Rittersdorf, watching the tactical holo. *James Komorov* was well away from enemy sensor range, moving through hyper VII at point nine three light.   The electomag field was being pushed to its limit.   Rads were still getting through, and people were getting sick. Medical had its hands full making sure everyone got their dose of antirad nanite boosters.

The plot of the out of range enemy ships was coming from *Lisboa*, as the hyper VII battle cruiser clawed space to stay within range of the enemy.   That enemy was almost out of range, and once they were, they would be lost, their destination unknown.

And here we were, sweating that they would attack us, wipe us from the face of the Universe, and instead they outrun us. I guess I shouldn't be too disappointed, since we're going to survive. But either way, they still get away.

"Something's happening," said Lieutenant Lasardo, looking at his board holo, then back at the main holo. Half of the enemy ships were already off the plot. Some had accelerated well ahead of the force before dropping off the plot. To scout ahead? No one really knew. But they had forged ahead for some purpose.

"Shit. Just when we thought we were going to get away with this," said the Helmsman.

Ten of the enemy ships were decelerating, dropping behind the main force. The deceleration was slow, a gentle thirty gravities. *It makes no sense*, thought the Captain, watching as a few more enemy ships dropped off the plot to the front. *The rest of them are forging on, and these are dropping back. Why? To attack us? Then they should be deceling to hell and gone. To force us to decel and lose the main party? That might make sense.*

"What do you think is going on, von Rittersdorf?" asked the Captain of the *Lisboa* over the com.

"I really don't know, sir," said von Rittersdorf, shaking his head. "This really doesn't make any sense. The only thing I can think of is that they are trying to chase us off. But, why wait so long to do that, when they could have tried the same thing at the start of this chase?"

"Desperation?"

"And why would they be desperate, sir? They are on the verge of losing us. And they always had the firepower to drop back and kill us if they wanted to." *Just like we feared the whole time we've been chasing them.* "What are you going to do, sir?"

"Since I'm not a complete fool, I'm going to start decelerating at a much higher clip, and hope they're satisfied. I'm…"

"We have a hyper translation," called out Lasardo. A trio of icons appeared on the plot, light minutes ahead of the *Lisboa*. Which meant they were light seconds in hyper VII.

The com holo to *Lisboa* went dead, a moment later its plot dropped off the net, along with the two of the new contacts. One continued on, by its acceleration figures a missile.

"*Komorov*," came the call over the com. "We've lost contact with *Lisboa*. Do you have any idea what happened."

You saw the same thing I did on the plot, thought von

Rittersdorf, knowing that they were feeling the same thing he was, panic. *Not quite the same thing, since they're back in the Supersystem, safe and sound.* "They're gone," he said quietly into the holo. "The Cacas fired missiles at them from normal space. They're learning." ·

"Do you know the dispositions of your other ships?"

"The last destroyer in front of us is still on the plot. We don't know about the other ships."

"Roger that," said the controller back in the Supersystem.

We should have all been equipped with wormhole coms for a mission like this, thought the Captain. The only problem was there were not enough to go around. Even with the *Donut* pumping out thirty a day, they still would never have all they really needed. And the loss of *Lisboa* meant they had lost two of the wormholes, along with a hyper VII battle cruiser and over three thousand crew.

"We have three more launches," yelled Lasardo, panic in his voice. "Target is the *Ling*," he continued, referring to the next ship up the line, the only one they still had contact with. Which meant.

"The other ships are gone," said von Rittersdorf, staring at the plot in shock. *Ling* dropped off the plot as he said that, and in a rush of fear he realized they were next.

"Helm, course eighty-five degrees spinward, sixty degrees up ecliptic. Full emergency power. Now."

The Helmsman was well trained, and didn't hesitate when a command was barked at him in that tone. Lasardo was an instant behind the Helm, hitting the warning klaxon. Full emergency power was ten gravities above what the inertial compensators could handle. The maximum it was thought that the crew could handle for any length of time outside of the tanks. And there was no time to get into the tanks.

Komorov boosted at five hundred and thirty-five gravities to the spinward direction of the galaxy, and up to the ecliptic, the top of the disk of the Milky Way. She was still moving forward at point nine three light, but using the boost to change her vector. The bridge crew were pushed back into their chairs, blood pushed from their brains, eyes starting to blur, reaching into a blackout stage. The new, improved humans were able to handle more of those kind of forces, while their skin suits helped to push the blood out of their legs and back up their bodies. Still, it was hell on the bridge crew, and any others who had been able to get into acceleration couches.

Those who hadn't gotten to their couches in time, almost half the crew, were not so lucky. They were thrown in the opposite direction of the boost at ten gravities, their bodies only stopping when they ran into something they could no longer continue through. The skin suits were also light weight impact armor, stiffening, providing some protection. Still, there was a spate of broken carbon reinforced bone, torn muscles, some skull fractures. Even a few deaths that could be reversed if they were treated in time. Altogether, an unpleasant experience. But better than being turned into vapor.

The Captain was barely able to see the plot as the three missiles translated into hyper and oriented toward the destroyer. *Link, dammit, link*, he thought, trying to get through to the ship's computer system. His thoughts were blurred, unclear, the acceleration trying to pull him into complete darkness. *Link*. And then he was in, immediately recognizing the minds of several others of the crew. Not many, but hopefully enough. Including his Tactical Officer, who was already starting the defensive systems to firing.

The missiles, if they had been coming straight in, as planned, would have hit the destroyer head on seconds after launch and blown her out of hyper. As it was, the missiles, despite their acceleration advantage, were coming from a slow start, no more than point three c, the limit of Caca translation technology. Now they were heading past the destroyer, and would need to change their vectors and pursue, not the easiest of tasks for a missile. One went off on closest approach, more than five light seconds away, too far to physically damage the destroyer, only able to send the merest hints of radiation into the *Komorov*. Her lasers fired, four blasts, eight, twelve, and the other two missiles detonated in hyper, their plasma quickly fading in catastrophic translation back into normal space.

The Captain maintained weapons alert status while he tried to maintain his connection with the ship. He waited several minutes, about as much as his people could stand, before sending the order to reduce acceleration to maximum normal, five hundred and twenty-five gravities. The relief as immediate. He could breathe again, really breathe. His muscles were sore, but a few movements proved they still worked. There was some bruising on his hands, blood accumulation from the accel that should soon clear.

"Medical," he said over the com. "Report."

"The Surgeon is out, sir," said the Chief Pharmacist's Mate over the com. "Skull fracture. We're stabilizing him now."

"We have casualties all over the ship, Chief. I need

to get those people taken care of."

"We're on it, sir," said the Chief.

And you're undermanned, with too much work ahead, thought the Captain, looking at the holo, waiting for the next missiles to appear and strike them down. *But you'll do the best you can, which is all any of us can ask.*

The bridge crew waited with sweating faces and anxious expressions as the ship continued to change its vector, accelerating here, decelerating there, getting the hell away from the enemy. Minutes passed, with no further signs of the Caca.

"Get me HQ on the com," said the Captain. A moment later the holo showed a middle aged woman, a single star on each of her collars. "We've lost contact with the enemy, Commodore. I think the Cacas are using one of our tricks against us."

"I guess we couldn't count on them to be stupid forever," said the straight faced woman. "Much as we would have liked."

"What are your orders, ma'am? Do you want us to try and regain contact?"

"No, Captain," said the woman, shaking her head. "The only thing you could accomplish now is to give us a momentary location, and then they would take you out. We've got another force waiting ahead of them. We're hoping they'll gain contact."

"And us?"

"You are to report back to the Conundrum screen. And be careful."

The Commodore didn't have to say why. One ship, in space that was mostly still under enemy control, with enemy patrols. The odds were against them. *And it's not like we haven't been through this before.*

*   *   *

CAPITULUM, JEWEL.

'Well, we expected they would start learning some things from us, just like we have with them," said CNO Sondra McCullom, looking up from her flat comp into the eyes of the Emperor.

"Not really what I wanted to hear," said Sean, knowing that his wants had nothing to do with the reality of the war. "Do we have any idea what they did?"

"From the little bit of data we retrieved from the *Lisboa,* and the more complete records from the *Komorov,* we think they dropped mobile launch platforms, much like the mines we used against the Fenri. Some of their ships moved ahead of their main force, dropped these platforms, which decelerated to translation velocity, dropped out of hyper, and waited. They tracked our ships coming in and launched when the vessels were right on top of them. Our ships didn't have a chance."

"And the ships they dropped back?"

"We believe they were a combination decoy and tracking force. Our ships were looking at them the whole way, and they got the chance to pick up data about their new weapon."

"And now we have to rework our own tactics for scouting out the enemy. Shit. And we're sure to lose a lot of ships before we get it right. At which time they develop something new."

"That's war, your Majesty," said the CNO with a shrug of her shoulders. "It's a shit deal, but it's what we have. We just have to keep developing new weapons and means of deployment faster than they do."

"And that's all there is to it, Admiral?" asked Sean, shaking his head. "We also have to keep throwing the best people our Empire has into the meat grinder, and for what? People converted to plasma, or blown to bits on the surface of a planet."

"We possibly get to keep our species as a going concern," said the Admiral, pointing her finger at the Emperor and emphasizing her point. "We get to keep our Empire, and the civilization that supports it. Not guaranteed, but even a good chance is better than none. And if you run out of people who are willing to put themselves into the crucible, look no further. I'll step down from here and head up a battle fleet in a heartbeat. Hell, I would lead a task force, even a battleship if that's all you can give me."

"I need you here, Admiral McCullom," said Sean, giving her a quick smile. "Someone has to listen to my complaints, and you are it."

Sean looked at the holo being projected by his flat comp. "So, how are we standing as far as fleet replacements are concerned?"

"Everything we can get ready will be good to go by the time of the offensive," said the Admiral, pointing to her own comp holo. "That's assuming that the damned star actually lights up in a month or more. If it goes off sooner, we will of course not have as much ready."

"And the allied fleets?"

"Crakista and Elysium forces are all at their staging points already, though we are expecting some more ships for each force. We have assigned them to task groups with their own commanders, as per their requests, and your orders. In two cases this has resulted in groups that are mostly either Crakista or

Brakakak, in order to give their high admirals a command commensurate with their rank."

"Good," said Sean, reaching for his glass of soda. "I want their commanders to feel that we trust them. And what about the Margravi and Klashak?"

"We have passed some of their task forces through to the *Donut*, while they upgrade their systems to our standards." The Admiral looked away for a moment, chewing her lip in thought. "Are you sure you want them included in this operation. My staff feels they would be better suited to continued screening of Laharan and Fenri space, and letting us withdraw more of our own units for operations against the Cacas."

"No. I want this to be an alliance operation. I want the Cacas to realize that they are not just fighting us, but most of the governments of this region. I want them faced with a united front. So no, they stay."

"Yes, sir. You're in charge."

Yes, I am. And I will be blamed if our allies let us down in combat.

"Anything else?" he asked, looking at a holo of one of the new superheavy battleships. "I hope we have three more of these ready to go."

"Those three will be ready for combat at the end of this week," acknowledged McCullom. "I would like more time for shakedown, but I understand the need. In another month I can get you three more, and then we have to wait for another four months for more to come off the lines. By then we will be into full production, a hundred ships a year."

A hundred of the most powerful units either side has deployed so far in this war, thought the Emperor, wondering if that would still be enough. *But it will have to be, while we keep commissioning battleships and superbattleships.*

"And we have word about the pirate operations going on in Sector VII," said McCullom, her expression grim. "It seems they are capturing humans, as well as our cargo, and selling them to the Vergasa."

"Shit. Now those assholes." Vergasa was a smaller star nation, not more than fifty inhabited systems, sitting a hundred light years outside of human space toward spinward. The large, furry creatures did not allow anyone else in their territory, and were said to use slaves for much of their grunt work, much like the Fenri. "What can we do to get them back?"

"The only thing I can think of is an expeditionary force. Invade, take out their military, and take our people back."

"And get us into another war?" said Sean, grimacing. "As if we don't have enough to handle already. Even if they are a small fry."

"I think the only other choice would be to see if the Ministry of State can buy them back," said McCullom. "Then, if we win this war we're already in, we can go in there and take back what we couldn't purchase."

"I really hate the idea of letting our people rot in slavery," said Sean, closing his eyes and trying to come up with something he could do. "Let's do this. I want our ships in sectors VII, VIII and I to keep on those pirates. But I also want them interdicting any traffic across their sectors heading out into unincorporated space. They are to search any ships they come across, even those with Imperial registry. And any with stolen goods and people aboard are to be impounded."

"That might cause some trouble with our allies," said McCullom. "If any of the ships happen to carry their registry."

"The Ministry of State will deal with that. I'll personally apologize to anyone we inconvenience. But I want these orders followed, to the letter."

"Yes, sir."

"In fact, I have a meeting with the Cabinet in one hour. So anything else of vital importance before I leave?"

"No, your Majesty," said the CNO. "And may I ask how the Empress is doing?"

"She's doing fine, if still a little shook up," he said, still troubled by what had happened on their wedding day. "The arm has almost healed completely."

"Will she still need the position at the Medical Center?" asked McCullom, raising an eyebrow.

"No. I think not," said Sean, shaking his head. "She has another job now. Full time, unless I'm mistaken."

"Very good," said McCullom with a smile. "Then we will not hold that position open for her."

She's not doing anything but be the Empress, thought Sean, walking from the room. Which was OK with him, since he trusted security better when the bystanders could be controlled, unlike a hospital, even a military one.

The underground tram took him to the office building a block down from Parliament. The megascraper had one of his public offices, and was near to most of the government office buildings that housed the headquarters of the major departments. Offices were also assigned to the ministers in the building, as well as to key subordinates. Underneath resided the massive databanks of the civil government, fed by the processing offices in the building.

Sean moved from the basement to one of the cabinet meeting rooms on the upper floors, accompanied by his augmented security detail. He was getting used to the security, much as his father and mother must have. And, after what had just happened, at the wedding, and at the *Donut*, he was happy to have it.

The Ministers were already waiting for him when he walked in the room, only a pair of his security agents coming through the doors with him. There were already guards in the room, as well as the complete security details of everyone involved in the meeting on the floor.

The Ministers all came to their feet as he entered. Sean stopped for a moment, looking out the huge steelglass window that overlooked the city, giving a view of the river all the way down to the coast, and all the huge buildings built along the banks. Fifty kilometers out in the bay was the long shape of Peal Island, home to the Naval Academy that he had graduated from. It was almost lost in the mists of distance, but was still as familiar to his vision as the day he had walked to the landing field as a newly minted ensign. *Things were so much simpler back then*, he thought with a slight smile on his face. *The whole Universe was in front of me, and I had the hopes of every ensign as they walked from those halls.*

"Please be seated, ladies and gentle beings," he said, nodding to the gathered Ministers. All of the high rankers in the room took a seat, Lord T'lisha lowering his bulk onto the special bench built for his species.

"Samantha will not be joining us today," he told the gathered Ministers. "She will be spending more time with the Empress, preparing her for her duties.

She will resume her duties as Regent when I return to the fleet."

The heads nodded at the table. No one questioned his leading the fleet on the next op. He had already explained to them about his dream, and by now everyone in this room was a true believer in his gift.

"Even though Samantha has done a fine job as my Regent, I am still the Emperor, and all decisions must originate with me." *And it frees Samantha of any blame of anything goes wrong, the least I can do for her.* "So, let's get it clear right now. If there is anything I need to know, bring it out now, so I can sign the paperwork."

"I have received a message from the Admiralty," said Lord Garis, after looking around the table to see if anyone had needed to speak first. "Are you sure you want to stop the shipping of our allies? They might see this as an insult."

"I want to interdict any possible slave trade of our citizens," said Sean in a forceful tone. "That is why I want your Ministry to make it clear to them that we are not trying to insult them, but only to protect the citizens in our space. They all have to know that not every one of their freighter skippers is a saint."

"The Crakista might just be," said Garis with a smile. "I have never met a harder bargaining people, but honest to a fault."

"But not all of their skippers are Crakista," said Sean, pointing a finger at the Minister. "Even their leadership must realize that. They allow their minority species to conduct themselves within the laws of their Empire, and they must know that not every sentient in the Empire is a, saint, did you say. I will talk with their leadership over wormhole com, if necessary, but I will not allow their ships free passage without checking them out."

"Understood, your Majesty. I just wanted you to be aware of the difficulties we might encounter."

And that's why you have the damned job, thought Sean, looking at the older man. *Though I have to admit that you're damned good at it.*

"Lord Halbrook," said Sean, looking over at another middle aged human, one who had served his father for many years. "What can you report on the income front? Is our income matching our expenses?"

"Of course not, your Majesty," said the man with a frown. "With a war of this size and intensity, there is no way that we can pay for everything. We still haven't paid off all the bonds on the *Donut*, and now we are tasked with finding the funds to pay for an unprecedented military expansion."

"So we will be running in the red for a while?"

"Maybe more than a while," said the Minister. He looked over at Lord H'rressitor, the Gryphon Minister of Commerce and Industry. "Despite the Minister's efforts at increasing our industrial capacity, and the goal of reaching full employment within the next five years, we can only raise so much in taxes. We are in danger of going bankrupt."

"And if we don't win the war, going bankrupt will be the least of our worries," said the Emperor. "Raise corporate income taxes if you must."

"They're already at fifty percent," said Halbrook, grimacing. "The owners and shareholders are going to raise hell."

"They'll raise more hell if we lose this thing. I remember reading one time that on old Earth, taxes reached as high as ninety percent during wartime. And the industrialists still made a fortune. They'll pay more taxes and love it, as the wealth comes rolling into their coffers. So raise the corporate taxes to seventy-five percent. And sell more bonds to the workers. With more people working, they can afford to give up some of that income. And see about investing some more of my assets into production. The Emperor's largess is doing no good sitting around in banks, or in untapped resources."

"And do you want to pay seventy-five percent tax as well, my Lord?" asked Halbrook.

"No. I'll pay one hundred percent tax. I don't need any more money, and the Empire sure doesn't need for its leader to become even wealthier. So take all my profits, and plow them back into war production."

"And of course publicize that you are doing that," said Halbrook, his grimace turning into a smile. "I'm sure that will play well with the public."

"I really don't care if it plays well with the public, Lord Halbrook," growled Sean. "I only care about how it aids the war effort. Now, if it can shame some other nobles to do the same, great. If not, then we have to come up with another way to tap their wealth. After all, having great holdings doesn't do them any good either, if they are vaporized, or sitting in the belly of some Caca.

"OK. Anything else. Lord H'rressitor. You look like you are about to be ill. What's wrong?"

"I'm not even sure if I should mention this, your Majesty," said the big male of a species that was probably closer related to dinosauroids than avians, but due to the beak and feathers was put in that classification by most people outside their race.

"Mention it, Lord H'rressitor. If it doesn't reach

my ears, there is really nothing I can do about it."

"It concerns a minor bill, your Majesty. One of no real importance, except to my people. A small spending bill to allow conversion of ships already being built in our shipyards to be crewed by my people."

"I was assured by Baron von Hausser that the bill would pass when it got to his House," said Sean, a look of confusion on his face. "And the funding has already passed the Commons."

"But the bill never made it out of the Lords Military Appropriations Committee," said the being in a choked voice. "And if it never passes the committee, it can never be voted upon."

And the idiots on that committee insult one of the most loyal species of the Empire, he thought, looking at the distressed Minister. His people had been considered loyal citizens for the last seven hundred years, after a hundred years of proving their loyalty. They had proven themselves in war and peace, offered freedom from their former oppressors and a future with the liberators. Not all species joined the Empire in such circumstances. Some were the conquered, the past oppressors, who had resented the humans. After several generations of assimilation into the Empire, while retaining the roots of their own cultures, even they became enthusiastic partners. But not all humans thought they deserve a fair shake.

"I am signing an order right now to pull that bill out of committee and onto the floor of the Lords," said Sean, linking in with the building computer, and through them the comp at the Parliamentary Lords Office Building. He looked over the bill, gave the order, and affixed his electronic signature to it.

"Will that not incense the Lords?" asked the

Minister.

"I really don't care how the Lords feel about it," said Sean, standing up and looking over the table at all the ministers. "I am trying to restrain myself from instituting martial law, but they keep trying my patience. We are at war people. A real war, to the finish. And that makes me the dictator of the Empire, if I so wish. I don't wish, and they will bow down to me in this matter, lest they find themselves with little in the way of power. Am I understood? If Parliament ever interferes with your business in this time of trouble, I want you to let me know."

The heads nodded around the table, as Ministers looked at him with wide eyes.

"You are your father's son," said T'lisha, a smile on his long face.

Sean nodded, smiling at the compliment, then sat back down so they could get back to business.

*   *   *

RUBY, SUPERSYSTEM. DECEMBER 18TH, 1001.

Bagget looked up at the dim orange star in the sky as he stepped onto the reviewing stand. The gravity felt normal, as would be expected on a planet with a one point zero one field. The local vegetation was variations of purple and orange, the terraformed life of Tau Ceti, mostly orange out here on the grasslands.

I haven't been back here since I graduated from Sandhurst, thought the officer of the Imperial Army Academy that was located on this, the major army training planet of the Empire, orbiting around the star Umber. Sanctuary D-IV was the official nomenclature for the planet, it went by the common name Ruby, and it was one of the major land warfare bases of the Empire.

He reached the top of the reviewing stand and looked out over the open field, on which was arrayed the prize that the Emperor promised him. The First Heavy Infantry Division, one of the oldest and most decorated of the Empire. Over twenty thousand men and women standing in their armor out in the cool sun. *And it's all mine. Hopefully, I can lead some more of them back than I did from my last unit*, he thought. That division was also on Ruby, receiving replacements, rebuilding. In another three months they might be combat ready again. Then again, it might take longer.

The three close combat brigades of the division were arrayed toward the front, each with three rectangles of heavy armor suited infantry, almost eight hundred to a group. Behind them was each brigade's armored battalion, thirty-two of the one thousand ton King Tyrannosaur heavy tanks, and fifteen of the smaller Velociraptor light scout tanks, a mere two hundred tons. Standing behind the tanks was the headquarters battalion, including the actual HQ company, and companies of engineers and antiair.

Back behind the line brigades was the combat support brigade, with the division headquarters company, as well as three artillery battalions and a heavier ADA battalion. Also attached to this unit was a heavy engineer battalion, with all of the various machines needed to help dig the unit it, or an enemy out. And the specialized jamming and countermeasure companies that would help to obscure the unit from space.

Two aviation battalions were also assigned to the division, and their ground crews stood to the side of the combat support brigade. Their vehicles, twenty four ground attack craft, fourteen heavy transports, and a dozen air superiority fighters, were hovering in the air above the division.

"The unit is ready for your review, sir," said Brigadier Dagni Thorwaldsdottir, her regrown leg still in a supporting cast while nanites and stimulation reconstituted its strength. She had also received a promotion, and Baggett had requested her as his exec. The original division commander had been promoted up to corps command, while the exec had been given another division.

"I trust they are all in order," said Samuel, smiling at the beautiful warrior, who would be cleared for suit duty in another week or so, it was hoped.

"You can count on it, Sir Samuel," said the woman with a return smile.

Baggett nodded and stood as the unit passed in review, the first of the heavy infantry brigades marching out of their rectangles and along the front of the stand. The brigade commander, battalion and company commanders all saluted as they passed, their helmeted heads turned toward the stand. The tanks followed in a line. As soon as the first brigade passed in review the second marched out, and then the third. Combat support command and the aviation battalions followed suit, until the entire division had passed.

"We will be deploying in a week, from what I have heard," said Baggett to his exec, after the last trooper had marched away.

"Combat drop, or slow and easy?" asked the woman, referring to a safe shuttle landing.

"I think they have something else in mind for us and the other corps."

"Corps, as in multiple?   Just what are they

planning?"

"We're going to take back our planets, Dagni" said Baggett, looking off into the sky. "While our Fleet is blasting the damned Cacas out of space, we're going to kill every damned one of them we can catch on the ground."

Chapter Twenty-one

Wars have never hurt anybody except the people who die. Salvador Dali

SECTOR IV SPACE. DECEMBER 21ST, 1001.

"Oh shit," said Dr. Larry Southard, looking at the most current scan of the blue supergiant. Most recent, in that it was over three hours ago in real time. *We're dead*, he thought, looking at the spectrograph that showed the star was starting to fuse silicon. Millions of tons of silicon a second, piling up the same mass of iron in the core. And when enough iron accumulated the star would stop putting out energy, it would collapse inward, until it reached the pressures were it couldn't collapse any more.   And then it would rebound.

"Captain," he called out on the com.

"I see it Doctor," said that officer, his voice still calm. "We're boosting for the hyper barrier right now. We should arrive in seven hours. Dr. Tashiga assures me that we will still have plenty of time to make the jump."

"Dr. Tashiga couldn't assure me that he knows where his ass is, Captain," said Southard. "I think we better get in the tanks and put on all the acceleration we can. And the destroyers need to be warned, now, so they have a chance of escaping."

"This isn't supposed to be happening," protested Tashiga over the com. "It wasn't supposed to be burning silicon for at least another week."

"Unfortunately, Tashiga," said Southard in his best sneering tone, "the star decided not to listen to you."

"All crew," called the voice of the Captain over the com, his voice echoing over the speakers as well. "All crew, report to the acceleration tanks. We need to move, people. Emergency accel in three minutes."

Normal procedure called for a five minute period between the warning and initiation of emergency boost. That the Captain was cutting it short meant he was taking the threat very seriously. *If only you had taken it seriously enough when we weren't in danger.*

Southard was in his designated tube in two and a half minutes. He hoped the other crew had made it as well, though he really didn't care if Tashiga was in his or not.

"Emergency boost in twenty seconds," came the voice over the com. When the clock ticked down, *Gringo* went into her emergency max of five hundred and twenty gravities, thirty-two above the maximum her inertial compensators could handle. There was no more reserve available. If something happened to the compensators, they were all dead.

An hour passed, then another, while the ship piled on the acceleration and clawed for the barrier. If all they needed to do was to get there it would be one thing, but they also needed to decel to a low enough velocity to make a jump, or the heat and electromag radiation from the supernova would still burn them out of space. Southard was linked into the ship's sensors, and through them the transmission from the satellites. Not that the satellites would do much good, as their signal would reach the ship about the same time as the thermal wave.

"We have major graviton fluctuations," said the voice of the computer over the com. "Graviton emissions are off the scale."

Which means the star has collapsed, and is now exploding.

Three and a half light hours away that was what was happening. The star exploded, sending a trillion trillion trillion trillion trillion trillion tons of high temperature matter out in a globular blast that would spread for thousands of years at a high fraction of light speed. Running ahead of it was the wave of heat and light. Everything in the system that got in its way was vaporized, to be added to the plasma from the star that would eventually form a stellar nursery.

The explosion of the star itself was forging elements far heavier than iron, the only way these substances could be created in the natural Universe. They would help to enrich the planets that would form around the new stars, and could possibly be of use to whatever life developed on those worlds, if any.

This was of no interest to the people aboard the research ship. They were counting down the arrival time of the thermal wave, and finding no hope in that countdown. The clock was off by several seconds, the people aboard surviving for just a bit longer. Dr. Southard's last thought was he hoped the explosion actually did what the Empire wanted it to. Then he, like the ship around him, was converted into a fine hot plasma that was later pushed along by the material wave of the explosion.

The destroyers picked up the graviton disturbances as well, and their captains made the proper decision. The ships fired up their hyperdrive projectors and attempted to open up the holes into the higher dimension, sure that the superhot matter would pass them by. Unfortunately for them, the projectors could not open those holes. Space and hyperspace was roiling from the explosion, and this close to the blast hyper was not available. The destroyers and their crews suffered the same fate as the research vessel. The one equipped with a wormhole com was able to get out the message that the star had exploded, fulfilling that part of its mission.

Gravitons sped off from the explosion through all dimensions of hyper, in VIII at a pseudospeed of a hundred and sixty thousand times the speed of light. Hyperspace became inaccessible for several light years around the former star converted to expanding nebula. And for hundreds of light years in every direction the dimensions reverberated with the blast of gravitons. No instrument capable of tracking ships through the dimensions could hear through that noise. Just what the Empire had been counting on.

*   *   *

THE *DONUT*.

"My God," blurted out the com tech on duty in the Fleet Command Communications Center. "They're gone."

"What are you babbling about, Sheila," said Lt. Commander Tosh McIntosh, walking over to the Tech's panel.

The room was filled with people, sitting at over a hundred stations, one of scores of such chambers across the *Donut*. Their job was to keep track of all the myriad ships and commands that used wormhole coms.

"It was the *Minimoto*," said the Tech. "One of the ships watching that star that was about to blow. They shouted 'it's blown up', then dropped off the net completely." The tech started checking her diagnostics, then looked up at the Commander with wide eyes.

"The wormhole link has been severed, sir."

Did they mean the star had blown. There couldn't really be any other explanation, could there? "Link up with the nearest wormhole equipped ship from that star. I want a report from them."

"Yes, sir," said the Tech, getting to work.

"I'm going to kick this upstairs," said McIntosh. "I know they've been waiting for this, but I don't think they figured it would be this soon."

McIntosh sent up the com request to his immediate superior, all the time hoping that there had been some mistake. Otherwise, three destroyers and their crews had died in a manner in which no human ever had before.

* * *

CAPITULUM, JEWEL.

"Your Majesty," said the voice through his priority com. "It's happened."

Sean opened his eyes, looking at the sleeping form of the woman beside him. Her arm was now healed, and as far as he could tell she was settling into the position of Empress just fine. Not that she had any really pressing duties, since hers was more one of an ambassador of goodwill to the people on the Homefront.

"How long ago?" he asked, not even needing to ask what the woman on the other end was referring to. Senior Agent May knew better than to disturb him at night about anything that wasn't of the utmost importance.

"Initial report came in to Fleet twenty minutes ago," said the Agent. "It was verified fifteen minutes later by another wormhole equipped ship about five light years from the star."

"Why did it have to be verified? What did the ships on the scene say?"

"This is Admiral McCullom, your Majesty," came the voice of the CNO over the com. "We lost contact with our ships after the first report. I am afraid that the destroyers and the research ship might not have made it away in time."

Sean closed his eyes, feeling the pain of losing yet more people, in a situation he really hadn't thought there would be that much risk. *Why couldn't they jump to hyper before the thermal wave reached them?* He dismissed the thought he didn't have time for. *We weren't ready for it to happen so soon, but it happened when it did.*

"What are your orders, your Majesty?" asked the CNO. "The clock is ticking."

I realize that, Admiral. It seems the damned thing never slows down. "Alert all commands. We will move as soon as possible."

"Yes, your Majesty," said McCullom, her voice showing anxiety and eagerness both. "The joint chiefs will be meeting within the hour to finalize our deployments."

"I will be there, Admiral," said Sean, sitting up in bed. "Sean out."

A hand touched the Emperor on the back. "What's going on?" asked a sleepy voice.

He turned to see Jennifer propped up on one arm, her other hand rubbing across his shoulders. *And I've got to leave you again. But better you stay here, safe, so I have one less worry while I'm out with the fleet.* "The star blew up," he said, turning, putting the back of his hand against her cheek and caressing her.

"I thought it wasn't going to go supernova for another week or two?"

"Unfortunately, the stars don't ask when they can do what they want," he said with a sad smile. "We're going to have to jump off faster than I expected."

"Just make sure you come back to me."

"Oh, I'll be back after the meeting with the Joint Chiefs."

"You know what I mean," said Jennifer, sitting up and kissing him. She broke the kiss and touched his face. "No matter what, you come back. No heroics. Lead, but don't go charging into the fray like some damned knight on horseback."

"Yes, ma'am," agreed Sean, kissing her, then getting up from bed. "Now, I need to look presentable before I appear before my levymen. You know how they think their Emperor is always ready."

She laughed. "At least you're always ready in bed, my love. And that's where I want you, when this operation of yours is over."

Sean returned the laugh, then headed into the bath to get a quick shower, sending orders through his link for his personal steward to have a uniform ready for him, then a signal to his security detail to ready the underground tram to the Hexagon.

*   *   *

SECTOR IV SPACE.

"The star has gone supernova," said Grand Fleet Admiral Len Lenkowski over the com holo.

"It wasn't supposed to do that for another two weeks," protested Grand Fleet Admiral the Duke Taelis Mgonda, sitting up at his desk. The two admirals were in different systems, separated by twenty light years.

There were still gaps in their projected orders of battle. Gaps they expected to have filled in the coming weeks. *Now I guess that won't happen*, thought the Duke.

"I said that very thing to Sondra, and she just told me the insubordinate son of a bitch just went off on its own, without her permission."

"So we go," said Mgonda. "Ready or not."

"Oh, we'll still have a couple of days before we have to boost to the targets," said Len. "That will give us a chance to get some more of our logistics ships in place, if nothing else. And get the Emperor on board."

"I still don't like the idea of having him with the Fleet," said Mgonda, raising a hand in protest before the other admiral, his true equal in rank, could speak. "I know. He's good for morale. The boys and girls will follow him everywhere. And he's finally getting enough sense through his thick head to listen, and balancing that with the judgment to take command when he needs to. I just worry that an errant missile will get through, and we'll have a crisis of succession on our hands, just when we don't need it."

"He's like that star, Taelis," said the other Admiral with a smile. "He's going to do what he wants, no matter what we try to do about it."

Len looked off the holo for a second, then back with a grimace on his face. "I've got to go, Taelis. We're expected to attend the conference at the Hexagon by holo. And you know how I feel about that."

Mgonda laughed as he thought, knowing exactly what the other admiral was thinking about. *Once we were our own lords and masters while deployed, days or weeks away from command. Now they're on our ass all the time.*

*   *   *

RUBY, SUPERSYSTEM.

"It's on, Sam," said Lt. General Lishnir, the Phlistaran commander of the Third Heavy Corps, which exercised command over Baggett's division. "We need to get you deployed to Massadara post haste."

"I thought we had another week," protested Baggett, sitting up in bed, looking at his clock and realizing that he had only gotten three hours sleep. *No rest for the wicked*, he thought. *But I'm a good boy. Or at least that's what my momma used to say.*

"Looks like the star had other ideas," said the Corps Commander. "I just hope we have enough resources after this is over to keep that blast from sterilizing the nearest inhabited star systems."

Baggett nodded, thinking of the damage those fast moving charged particles would cause to the beings of a living world. Since the nearest inhabited system was seven light years from the star, they had eight or nine years before the radiation wave reached it.

"Dagni will be disappointed," said Baggett, thinking of his Assistant Division Commander. "She just got cleared for suit training, but not for combat."

"Do you need her?" asked the Lt. General.

"Of course. And more importantly, the division needs her.

"Then bring her along on deployment, but keep her back at HQ, preferably with your logistics train. But start your boys and girls through the wormhole within the hour. It will take quite some time to get your entire combat strength through. Twentieth division will follow as soon as your last combat trooper is through."

"And when do we fight?"

"You hide for now. And strike as soon as the first Fleet vessels make it into the system. And Samuel."

"Yes, sir."

"Once you start, don't stop. For anything. You give them hell, and kick their slimy asses off that planet. You take it back for the Empire. It's ours, and they need to learn that."

"Yes, sir," said Baggett with a smile, putting on the skin suit he would wear under his armor. "That's a command I will be very happy to obey. As will my boys and girls." *And I'm finally in the main fight. No more sideshows, Sam. This time you get to pay the bastards back for Sestius.*

*   *   *

"You're going back to Sestius, Hunter," said Major General (brevet Lt. General) Walther Jodel, The Preacher.

The Hunter, thought Second Lieutenant the Baron Cornelius Walborski, trying to keep the smile off of his face in front of his old mentor, and the current commanding officer of all special ops forces in Sector IV.

"How much training time will I have with my platoon, sir," said Walborski, almost slipping up and calling the man Preacher. He wasn't sure how well that would go over, a brand new second Louie calling a general by his nickname.

"One day," said Preacher with a grimace, raising a hand to derail any protest. "I know. It's not really enough time to learn your command, or for them to learn about you. But they know your rep, and I can bet they will be very glad to get an experienced Ranger to lead them, and not some shavetail whose only experience is some training."

"Yes, sir," said Cornelius, still not sure about leading forty Rangers, some of them long term NCOs.

"Look, Hunter. From what I read, you led Chief Petty Officers on the *Donut*, who all gave you glowing recommendations in their after action reports. The Naval Commandos are a rough bunch, and if they thought well of you, I don't see how your own could think less. Just lead like you did on the *Donut* and you'll be fine."

Sestius, thought Cornelius. *The Freeholders are still holding out there.* His thoughts ran to his farm, his wife, his future. And then, her death in the jungle at the hands of the Cacas. *And now I get to play in that jungle again. Not quite as bad as Azure, but bad enough.*

"Can do, sir," said Cornelius, snapping off a picture perfect salute.

*   *   *

CONUNDRUM SPACE.

"We have new orders from headquarters, sir," said the Com Officer.

What the hell now, thought Suttler, coming to an instant awake state in his cabin. "What do they want us to do now?"

"Mostly just watch, sir," said the officer. "And listen to hyper. They want to make sure that hyperspace is just a screwed up as they thought."

Bryce sat up in his bed. "The supernova went off," he exclaimed. "Kind of early, wasn't it?"

"Command acknowledged that point, sir. They said it couldn't be helped."

Bryce almost laughed when he heard that last

statement. *Of course it couldn't be helped. It's a damned supernova. Not like we had any control over it.*

"They also want us to keep tabs on the reactions of the Cacas, sir. And any signal intercepts we can achieve."

"Very well. Do it." *And I bet the Cacas shit in their pants when they find they can't track shit in hyper. And I'll be happy to watch that bowel movement.*

Chapter Twenty-two

A pint of sweat, saves a gallon of blood.   George S. Patton

THE *DONUT*. DECEMBER 22ND, 1001.

"I hear we're getting a new second Louie," said Private First Class Everett Linsk, looking up from his cards. "I wish they would just let you lead us, Sarge." He pointed with his cards at Sergeant First Class Rupert SanJames, the man who had been their platoon sergeant for the last six months. They had been missing their officer all that time, since the new platoon leader they had just received at that time had stepped in front of a Caca particle beam.

"This one might just surprise you, Linsk," said the Sergeant in question. "I heard that Preacher has the highest opinion of him."

"Great. So the Preacher likes him. What the hell is that supposed to mean?"

"He was a militiaman on Sestius when Preacher was there," said SanJames, pointing a finger at the PFC. "And a Sergeant on Azure."

One of the other men whistled at that. "That was some bad bush on Azure," said the man, Corporal Quan Lee. "Everything on the planet trying to eat everything else, including us." Lee looked down at his cards for a moment, then gave the Sergeant First Class an intense look. "What's the name of this guy, anyway?"

"Cornelius Walborski," said the SFC with a smile.

"Shit a brick," exclaimed Lee. "Looks like we hit the jackpot this time."

"So who the hell is he?" asked Linsk. "The name doesn't ring a bell.

"Just the only man to win an Imperial Medal of Heroism as a civilian slash militiaman, then another as a Ranger. And he was on Azure alright. Took out an entire Caca command post by himself, with a little help from a nuke tipped rocket."

"Fuck me, you say," blurted out the PFC.

"I think my wife would take exception to my doing that, Ranger," said a soft but strong voice from the doorway.

"Attention on deck," called out the first man to turn and see the new platoon leader standing there.

Damn, but he's quiet, thought SanJames, jumping up to attention.

"At ease," said the officer with a smile. "I don't really hold with that chicken shit so called courtesy when we don't have to. And that means, when I'm the only officer here, I'm just like the rest of you. Only what I say goes. Understand?"

"Yes, sir," said every man in the room, all ten of them.

"And what's your opinion on cards, sir?" asked Linsk, his eyes looking over the uniform of the officer.

SanJames was making that same inspection, seeing the double award of the Imperial Medal of Heroism, a few lesser medals, and the emblem of knighthood hanging around his neck. The most important thing to the SFC was the combat infantry badge over his left breast pocket, that and the Ranger tab on his left shoulder.

"I'm fine with cards, as long as you deal me in," said the officer, gesturing to the empty chair at the table. "No better way to get to know the people under me, I say."

"Watch out, LT," said Lee with a smile. "Linsk cheats."

"Then he's my kind of man," said the Lieutenant with a broadening smile. "A man that doesn't play to win has no business looking after the backs of his brothers."

The night whiled away, the enlisted men drinking with their new officer, the bonding beginning, about the only bonding they would get, since the battalion was shipping out by wormhole in the morning.

*   *   *

CONUNDRUM SPACE.

"We are experiencing problems with hyperspace, Great Admiral," said the Low Admiral in charge of the conquest fleet's logistics.

"What do you mean, problems?" asked the High Admiral, not liking the sound of that at all.

"Ships are disappearing off the track while entering and leaving the system."

"Destroyed?" asked the Great Admiral, a queasy feeling in his stomachs.

"Not as far as we can tell, Great Admiral. Incoming vessels are still coming through, but we are not tracking them by the usual means. Hyper seems to be reverberating with graviton noise. Nothing that moves can be tracked through it."

"By the Gods," hissed the supreme leader of the fleet. "Then we will not be able to track the human ships?"

"Nor they, us," said the lower ranking male, giving a head motion of agreement.

"I don't really care if they can track us," growled the Great Admiral. "Because we are not leaving our systems while this phenomenon is going on. Not until we know what is going on."

"We are running a database search right now," said the Low Admiral. "Hopefully, we will come up with a solution."

The holo went blank, leaving the Great Admiral with his own thoughts. He called up the holo of the distribution of his fleet, looking anxiously at the icons of his ships that were being accounted for as in transit. *But are they still in transit? Or has something happened to them.*

"My Lord," said another voice over the com. "We have just had a catastrophic translation at the hyper VII barrier."

"One of ours?"

"Actually, my Lord, it involved seven different vessels in a formation, based on the dispersion of the signals, which were damped almost to indetectability."

What in the hell is going on? Some ships are coming in just fine, while others are unable to translate down before they hit the barrier. Is this some new human weapon. A chill ran up his spine as he thought that. *If the humans have a weapon that powerful, we are doomed.*

"Great Admiral," came the voice of the Low Admiral over the com. "We have found precedent. From the early days of the race plying hyperspace."

"And what was it? Speak up. I need to know, now."

"There was a supernova near the edge of the early Empire, about a hundred light years out. None of our worlds were endangered, but several inhabited planets were sterilized, one with intelligent life."

"And what does this have to do with our current

situation?"

"Ships of that day had trouble tracking other vessels in hyper for almost a week after the explosion."

"Anything else?"

"No, my Lord."

Then this is only a temporary phenomenon. A supernova, one which we did not know about. But this is human space, so they had to know it was coming. But did they know the effects of such a blast on hyper. The smart way to bet is yes, which means they will have something planned. But what?

Several hours passed before more information came.

"One of the outgoing ships has returned," said the officer in the com center of the flagship.

"Why did it do that?"

"They stated that when they tried to translate up into hyper VII from VI, something prevented the translation. They thought that was unusual enough that they deceled and returned."

"So we aren't able to get into VII at all." *And I wonder what happened to ships that are still in hyper VII? They simply can't translate out, which would explain those ships that ran into the barrier. Or something worse.*

"Orders, my Lord?" asked the officer.

"I want all ships to move into the system, as soon as they can," ordered the Great Admiral, imagining a human fleet popping into existence at the hyper I barrier and bringing all his ships under fire before they could react.

"How far should I order them in, my Lord?"

"Fifteen light minutes should do it," answered the Great Admiral, thinking that he could launch as soon as they appeared on visual, which would still be a quarter hour after they saw his ships, but still hours before the enemy missiles would arrive. "And station some light units right at the barrier. I need someone to tell any incoming ships what's going on." *Except, if they're already in VII, they aren't coming here until this disruption is over. A week? Or longer? Whichever, it can't be good for us.*

*   *   *

SAURON SYSTEM, DECEMBER 24TH, 1001.

"Permission to come on board, Captain?" asked Sean, stepping out of the shuttle onto hangar deck three of the heavy cruiser *Manila*, his new flag. The ship had all of the command and control capabilities of the *Augustine I*, the superheavy battleship that had been his flag on the Congreeve operation. What it lacked was the combat capabilities, which was fine with the Admiralty, as they did not desire for their Monarch to go into the thick of things, like he had at Congreeve.

"Permission granted, your Majesty," stated the Captain, the only response possible when dealing with the supreme commander, who could walk onto any ship of the fleet whenever he wanted to. The skipper of the ship saluted the Monarch, waited for the return of his salute, then offered his hand to the Emperor. "Welcome aboard, your Majesty. I am Captain Bertha Littletree."

Sean shook the tall woman's hand, taking in her coppery skin tone and straight black hair. *Native American descent*, he thought.

"Your Steward and your pet are already aboard, your Majesty. I hope you will find your quarters satisfactory."

"I'm sure I will," said Sean, nodding his head. He already had a good idea what the quarters were like, since he had given the orders for their configuration himself. The cruiser was built as a cruiser squadron flag, the lead ship of six heavy cruisers. As such, she had a commodore's stateroom, which had been fine with the Emperor, who didn't see the need to have opulent quarters for himself aboard a warship. The Secret Service and the Fleet had insisted on some modifications, which were supposed to be minor, and specifically intended to increase his security.

"I'll look at my quarters later, Captain. For now, you can get under way whenever Len gives the signal that his force is boosting. And I would like to see the command center, if I might."

"Yours to command, Majesty," said the Captain, motioning for a man to come over.

"Good to see you again, Jacobs," said Sean, accepting the bow of the ex Senior Chief who was now his shipboard Steward.

"Your Majesty. It will be my pleasure to serve," said the man, straightening from the bow. "And welcome, ma'am," he said, giving a short bow to Special Agent Mays, the head of the Emperor's security detail.

"I take it the Marines are already aboard?" asked the Secret Service Agent, speaking of the company of Sean's personal bodyguard that would be traveling with him.

"Yes, ma'am. And I'll lead you to the control center now, if that is your wish, your Majesty?"

"It is, John," said Sean, following the Steward off the hangar deck and toward the nearest lift bank. "And how is Killer."

"All legs and tail, your Majesty," said the smiling man, who was also the cat sitter of the expedition. "Last stages of kittenhood. And I'm sure he'll be glad to see you."

Of course he will, thought Sean, not really sure how he thought of the imprinting that was used on the cat to bond him to his master. To Sean, who had grown up around dogs and cats all his life, it seemed like cheating, when the loyalty of a pet was supposed to be earned through pleasant interactions. *But I have to admit, it's good to have the little guy come running when I enter my quarters.*

After a short lift ride they arrived at the augmented flag bridge, with over fifty com stations arrayed around the large central holo tank. All stations were manned, and all of the crew and supervisors were on their feet when the Emperor entered.

"At ease," said Sean, looking around the bridge, his eyes stopping on Rear Admiral Kelso, his Flag Captain. "Tell your people to not bother with that ceremony from here on out," he told the older man. "Not that I don't appreciate it, but they have better things to do."

"Yes, sir," agreed the Admiral. "And your station is through that door to the front.

Sean nodded and headed that way with a smile on his face. The room he entered, about twenty meters cubed, did not seem all that impressive at first. Until he linked into the computer and the room came alive, projecting the Universe around him in breathtaking detail.

"Get me Len," he said into the interface, asking for a com opening that was provided immediately. "Your people ready, Len."

"Ready and willing, your Majesty," said the Grand Fleet Admiral. "All systems seem to be operating to specs. Including the wormholes."

Sean nodded, glad to hear that last. That had been a major worry with this operation, that the turmoil caused by the supernova might also have an effect on the wormholes. Either making them hazardous to traverse, or even collapsing the holes altogether. Mathematically, it had seemed safe enough. The Emperor was happy to see that it had also worked in the real world.

"Any major problems?"

"It seems that we can't use hyper VII, for the moment," said Len, his eyes narrowing. "In fact, our ships within forty light years of the blast can't even use hyper VI."

"What do you mean, can't use?"

"We can't open holes in the dimension of hyper VII at all," said Len. "Any of our ships that are within hyper VII can't leave, and nothing can enter."

"Are the ships in VII in any danger?"

"Not unless they run into a hyper barrier. The ships in VII can remain there for a couple of weeks, or whenever the turmoil is reduced enough to allow translation again. All wormhole equipped ships have been warned, and told to warn whatever other ships are with them in hyper that don't have wormhole coms."

"I really didn't expect us to be denied the use of VII," said Sean, his mood sobering.

"Neither did anyone else, your Majesty," agreed Len. "But it is what it is, and we have to accept what we can do. And remember, the Cacas also won't be able to use VII, graviton communications are almost shot, and we know what we're doing, while they don't."

"Put that way, Grand Fleet Admiral Lenkoswki, I guess we have nothing to worry about. This thing ought to be a walk in the park."

"Except the park is still filled with carnivores, your Majesty," said Len with a slight smile. "Always remember that."

"Oh, I will, Admiral. And I'm going to make sure they know it too."

*   *   *

REPUBLIC SPACE. DECEMBER 25TH, 1001.

President Julia Graham studied the tactical holo that showed her forces in relation to the enemy they were chasing. Technically, they weren't exactly chasing them out of the Republic. The Cacas were retreating on their own, trying to get back to their main base in the New Terran Empire so they could reinforce their primary battle fleet, which had recently taken a pounding at the hands of the Imperials.

Unfortunately, even as it took them out of her Republic's territory, it also took them out of range of her own fleet and the forces of their Crakistan allies. All of the Caca ships, every single one, was a hyper VII vessel, while less than five percent of her own forces could navigate that dimension. The Cacas could cover space four times faster than her own ships, and there was no way around that. Her only hyper VII ships were battle cruisers and light cruisers.

At least we don't have to worry about them right now, she thought, standing on the flag bridge of the heavy cruiser that had just jumped into the New Washington System, once the home of the Republic's capital. That was good, since her force, the cruiser and ten destroyers, really weren't enough to stand up to any kind of Caca raiding force.

"We killed four of the enemy supercruisers," said the voice of the Crakistan Admiral who went by the designation of Admiral in Charge of Republic Third

Battle Fleet. The reptilian beings face looked out of another holo, not showing the least inkling of emotion.

They like for everyone to think they're cold bastards, thought the President, looking into the eyes of a reptilian predator. *And they sure act like they are. But underneath they still have feelings, even if they have suppressed them with their logical thinking.*

"Unfortunately, we were only able to get the one salvo off in passing, and they moved by too quickly for us to get a second one in."

And that's the problem, thought Graham, nodding her head. All of the ships were carrying the new hyper VII capable missiles, as the prewar stockpiles of VI weapons were almost gone. The hyper VII missiles, while capable of opening a hole into the highest transport capable dimension, did so at the price of having a lower range than the VI missiles. They could be launched at oncoming targets and get in one approach, as long as the enemy was coming toward them. If the enemy was at high acceleration, there was no way the VII missiles could catch them from behind. And the only way to get a head on solution was to launch on a Caca force with perfect timing, which only happened when they had been spotted ahead of time, by a wormhole com ship that could send the signal to the ambushing force.

Which means that nine times out of ten we don't get an effective shot, and half the time when we do, we still don't accomplish as much as we would wish.

"What are your orders, Madam President?" asked the being who was the first alien to be put in charge of a Republic battle fleet.

"What are our options, Admiral? Can you get into Imperial space in time to help Sean against the forces leaving our territory?"

"Unlikely, Madam President. While I cannot say for sure that we would arrive before the Emperor initiates his offensive, since we have no way of knowing when the requisite supernova explosion is to take place. But, given the most recent prediction, we would not arrive in time to be of aid. The other possibility would be to marshal our forces within your Republic, and await developments."

And that would be the very definition of ingratitude, thought the President. The Empire had given her Republic almost immeasurable aid, including several thousand ships that, while they might have been of an obsolete design, still possessed state of the art electronics and power generation capabilities. *They need us now, as we needed them before. But where can we be of use to them.*

"Madame President," came a call over the com. "I think you need to be aware of this."

"Excuse me for a moment, Admiral," she told the Crakistan female.

Another tactical holo sprang to life beside the original. This showed a region outside her space, stretching between her borders and those of the no longer extant New Moscow. There were two lines of ships indicated on the holo, one, two hundred light years from the New Terran Empire border, made up of ships from that military. And two hundred light years further out from them was a task force made up of ships from her own fleet, one light cruiser and five destroyers.

And a number of icons were approaching that outer picket. A number that she really couldn't count, due to so many icons being right on top of each other.

"Are you seeing this, Madam President?" asked the voice of Commodore Natasha Romanov, the commander of the outer picket, on board the light cruiser *Orleans*.

"Yes, yes I am, Commodore," answered Graham. "How many of them are there?"

"We're counting at least five hundred of them. It looks like a major reinforcement effort. From their heading, it looks like they are on a course directly into the Empire."

"I need to issue some orders, Commodore," she told the picket commander.

"Hopefully something to discomfit this enemy," said Romanov with a tense smile.

"You might say that," she told the Commodore, just before blanking the com. She looked back at the holo of the Crakistan Admiral. "You saw that, Admiral?"

"I did indeed, Madam President. My tactical staff are plotting their location and probable future locations along a time frame."

"The question is Admiral, can you do something about them?"

"I can have a battle force in their way in a day and a half, if that is what you mean, Madam President. We should be at stop before they get within detection range of our hyper. And," the Admiral looked off holo for a moment, "I believe we can have wormhole equipped scouts well enough ahead of them to give our force targeting information."

"Then those are your orders, Admiral. Get in position to light them up. And good hunting."

The reptilian smiled, a predatory grin that showed more emotion than Julia was used to seeing on those visages. But one she had seen before. She had given the alien a hunt, one of the few things the carnivores truly enjoyed, as long as there was a logical reason for it.

*   *   *

SECTOR IV SPACE. DECEMBER 26TH, 1001.

"The five trailing ships in our force just, blew up, my Lord."

"What?" gasped High Admiral Kellissaran Jarkastarin, looking up from the holo he had been studying of the system they were about to enter. "How do you know?"

"We picked up faint graviton emissions that could only mean a catastrophic translation. Five of them, directly behind us."

"What about the rest of the force?"

"All safely in VI, as far as we can tell," said the Tactical Officer who had first spoken.

"What do you mean, as far as you can tell?" *And what did he mean by faint graviton emissions? Those ships translating catastrophically should have been the loudest things on our sensors.*

"We are having trouble tracking the other ships, my Lord."

"But, they're right with us. How can you be having trouble tracking them?"

"Right now hyperspace if full of random graviton fluctuations," said the Tactical Officer. "I've never seen anything like it. It defies explanation."

"So you have no idea what's causing this. Could it be some new weapon of the humans?"

"If so, my Lord, we have already lost this war. The amount of energy that would be needed to produce this kind of distortion would be nothing short of astronomical."

"We're getting ready to drop to V, my Lord," said the Helmsman. "Orders?"

"Drop to V, you dolt. Or did you plan on pushing us through the barrier?"

"Yes, my Lord," said the chastised male, looking back at his board.

The ships dropped down through V, IV, III, II, I, and then prepared for the final jump to normal space. On each shift the crew became more and more ill. Ca'cadasans were among the hardest hit of species during jumps, which made for excruciatingly hard translations. The High Admiral sat in his command chair, clenching his fists and holding his breath, trying to get over his nausea as he waited to see how much of his command he still had with him. The hole opened, the ship made it through with the normal horrible nausea. The Admiral tried to get himself back under control, while waiting for the report of his younger Com Officer.

"They all seem to be with us, my Lord," said the Com Officer. "All except the five that didn't make the transit back to VI.

And if whatever had caused this had happened a few minutes earlier, we all would have run into the barrier, and my force would be gone.

"What do you have on the system?" asked the High Admiral of his Tactical Officer, looking over at the male, then back at the central holo tank, which showed, nothing.

"We are not tracking anything in this system, my Lord," said the Tactical Officer, looking over his shoulder with a confused expression.

"What?"

"Nothing, sir. No heat signatures. No graviton emissions. Nothing."

"And the planet? The one we came to smash?"

"It's on the other side of the star, my Lord," said the Tactical Officer, pulling up what they knew about the system on his over the board holo.

"By the Gods, so we know nothing about what might be in this system."

"Do you want to decel back out and go into hyper, my Lord?" asked the Helm Officer. "We could get around the star much quicker that way."

Jarkastarin looked at the other male as if he had grown a second head, and both were now babbling nonsense. *I would rather stick my head in the mouth of a Janaka*, thought the Admiral, thinking of the large predator that lived in the seas of the homeworld.

"No. Put us on a straight line course for the planet that bends us around that star. Just keep us far enough away to be safe." He looked over at the Com Officer. "And order all ships to keep on the alert. I have a bad feeling about this place."

"Then maybe we should just leave, my Lord," said the Tactical Officer.

And have these vermin think we are afraid of some unusual stellar phenomenon. Not on your life, Tactical. Or mine, or the entire force's. "Follow my orders, Helm. You too, Tactical. I believe there is human life on that planet, and I intend for there to be none when I leave this system."

* * *

MASSADARA, SECTOR IV SPACE.

"Welcome to Massadara, General," said the Liaison Officer to Baggett as he stomped out of the wormhole in his heavy combat armor. The armor itself massed a ton, and five hundred kilos of munitions, batteries and rations had been added. Every man and woman of the division was carrying extra gear, every vehicle was loaded down with everything they could carry. They were here to stay, and to fight, and though resupply would be coming through the hole, no one wanted to take any chances that they might get cut off and run out.

I finally made it here, thought the General, looking around the cavern, which, he had to admit, was not a very good view of the planet. Massadara had been the original destination of his then battalion, a light infantry unit that had been upgraded to medium armor. But they had been sidetracked to Sestius, and had written their history on that planet instead.

"Thank you, Colonel," said Baggett to the officer. "I was told to report to the planet commander when I arrived."

"Yes, sir," said the Colonel, pointing to an open area of the cavern. "You might want to ditch the suit before you go into the chamber he's in. It can get kind of crowded in there."

Baggett nodded, walking to the indicated area, and ordered his suit to open through the link. Nanites first opened the seams on arms, legs and body, while his helmet retracted onto the back of his suit. Within seconds the seams existed where solid alloy had before, and the suit hinged open under its own power. As soon as it had opened completely he stepped out, his hard connections popping out of his lower spine and skull. The General walked forward in his skin suit, the ubiquitous garment that members of every service wore under their armor. His had the patches of his unit, and his rank on the breast and sleeves, so there would be no mistakes.

"Lead the way," ordered Baggett, glancing at the wormhole, where more of his men were coming out quickly. It would take hours for all of the infantry to come through. The heavy units would wait until they were just about to start their offensive, and the wormhole had been moved outside and expanded. He had reservations about starting operations without his armor, artillery and aviation assets, but understood the need to secrecy until the particle beam bolts started flying.

Baggett recognized Colonel General Mich Sapatra the second he entered the room. The tough as nails officer was probably the shortest person in a room that included many women. He looked like a fireplug, all thick muscle. He had been Baggett's first battalion commander, so many years ago. The man looked up from the map and smiled as he saw the Major General step into the room.

"Good to see you, General Baggett," said the man, walking away from the table and returning Baggett's salute, then offering his hand in a fierce grip. "I always knew you would go far. Even when you were a shavetail Louie."

"I'm happy I could prove you the prophet, sir," said Baggett, following the man over to the table.

Sapatra laughed, a deep rumbling sound that surprised people coming from such a short man, until one remembered that his chest was that of a much taller body builder. "If I were a prophet, I could wish that I saw this shit coming," said the four star General, shaking his head. He pointed to the table, which showed a large continent.

"This is the main landmass of this world, and the one we think the Cacas will be landing on when our ships enter the system," said Sapatra.

"And why is that, sir?" asked Baggett, reaching out and moving the map over to see the continent across the ocean. "Since they still have some people on the ground here, wouldn't they try to land there."

"And get themselves blown into space by orbital bombardment?" said Sapatra, moving the map back. "No. I think they're going to land here, and try to close with us, wherever they can find us. They would hope they could delay our bombardment, hopefully until they could get a relief force here to kick us out. But they won't know about you, or the other two divisions of your corps. So I want you to set up over here, on the coastal plains."

"Shouldn't the Corps Commander pass this down to me, sir?"

"Oh, he will still have operational control of the corps," said Sapatra, pulling a cigar out of his pocket, offering one to Baggett, and, after refusal, puffing his into ignition.

Baggett looked askance at the burning tube of vegetation that was pumping fragrant smoke into the air. He thought the habit of smoking nasty, even though so many military people indulged without any ill effects.

"He and the other two divisions will be located around the other coast and their mountains, and he might have some command and control problems with your division. So you will be taking orders from this headquarters. Understood?"

So we'll be on our own over there, except for whatever support Sapatra might be able to give us from what he already has. "I understand, sir."

"Now I don't want you playing it safe once they are down," said Sapatra, putting a finger through the holo and onto the hard surface of the table. "I want you to hit them, and hit them hard. They will be exposed down here, and your heavy infantry should be able to rip them a new one."

"Do you think they'll really come down here, sir? Seems to me that they would try to blast their way out of the system."

"From what I understand, they will see a force they can't really blast through. I fully expect them to evacuate their logistics ships and those troop transports of theirs to the surface, since those ships will just be easy targets as they try to break out."

And they will hope for an eventual relief force for their ground forces, thought Baggett as he nodded. *The wonderful thing about their not having instantaneous communications. They'll likely think this is a local operation, and not know that there is no help available.*

"We're going to ship one of the two wormholes up to you prior to the attack. I want you to get all of your heavy assets out and under cover, which means I don't want them being spotted from space. So minimal power, and no crossing open spots."

"How long do we get to keep the hole?"

"No more than two days, so get everything through that you think you will need. I know, you won't get everything you think you need, like a year's supply of everything. But get as much out as you can. Then ship the hole back here. I've got some other uses for it."

"And when will they attack, sir?"

"We were expecting the ships to get here in five days," said Sapatra, frowning. "But it seems that hyper VII is unavailable, so maybe eleven days." The General turned the frown into a smile. "Which may not be a bad thing, since the Cacas won't be able to use VII either, or so we hope. And we'll have more of our own ships coming to the party."

The General stared at the holo for a moment more, his nostrils flaring as if he were already fighting the battle in his mind. He looked over at Baggett. "I know you won't let us down, Samuel. So get your people in position and get ready to kick their asses."

"Yes, sir," agreed Baggett, rendering a salute and turning to leave.

"And don't let me hear about a major general getting into hand to hand combat, Baggett. The Empire has too much of an investment, and you're too much of an asset, to risk you killing a couple of Cacas eye to eye."

"How?"

"After Action Report, Baggett," said the smiling Planet Commander. "We see all, we know all. Now don't act like a second Louie, and make sure the bastards pay."

*   *   *

SAURON SPACE. DECEMBER 27TH, 1001.

Captain Svetlana Komorov watched as the last ship in her wing came aboard, standing on the side of the hangar deck as the fifteen hundred ton inertialess attack fighter poked its nose through the cold plasma field that kept the atmosphere in. The ship cruised slowly along the open area and stopped, then vectored sideways into a slot between two other ships.

"All craft are aboard, Captain," she told the commander of the *Akagi,* watching as the heavy hangar doors slid shut. She was of equal rank with the ship's commander, who was in charge of the care and feeding of the carrier, while Komorov was in charge of the aviation wing. There was a commodore aboard who exercised operational control over both parts of the combat team.

The carrier was fully crewed. Unfortunately, her wing was not. With two more hyper VII carriers to assign fighters too, and losses across all the wings on the Congreeve operation, as well as some minor losses against the Fenri, there just weren't enough ships to go around. Or, maybe more accurately, not enough negative matter to make all of the ships operational.

The fighter she had been watching settled to the deck with a triple thump of landing gear. The engines powered down, and moments later a pair of hatches, one forward, one aft, slid open as the debarkation ladders dropped from craft to deck. The crew started coming out, the four bridge personnel and two engineers, while the ground team ran forward, looking over the outer skin of the ship, one climbing the top, making sure the fighter would be ready for combat when needed.

"Welcome aboard, Commander Humphrey," she told the officer leading the crew away from the craft. He was replacing one of the division leaders she had lost at Congreeve, and would be in command of forty-three fighters, nine less than he should have.

"Thank you, ma'am," said the young man who had also survived Congreeve, and earned a command slot by taking over for his then wing commander after that Captain had been killed on the first pass of the Caca ships.

"How's your division shaping up?" was her next question.

"I wish I had some more time to get the newcomers straightened out," he said, looking back at some of the other fighters in his division, half of which occupied this hangar. The other half were in the other port side hangar, while those of Second Division were in the starboard hangars.

"You and everyone else who's in a command position," said Komorov with a laugh. "I think you dispersed them as well as could be expected." There had been some hard decisions to make with those dispersals. They had intact teams that had performed well at Congreeve. They hadn't wanted to break them up, but it also seemed cruel and unusual punishment to send people into combat who hadn't been through it before, without the leavening of experienced crew. *The Admiral settled that*, thought the Captain of the officer who commanded *Akagi* and two of her sisters.

"Not a one of your original crews had any combat experience before Congreeve," had said Rear Admiral Condalisa Perez. "The same as your new people. Your old hands," and the Admiral had smiled at calling people who had been through one battle such, "have developed trust in their teammates. So I suggest, and a suggestion is all it is, that you keep the old teams together, and assign new teams in equal measure to each squadron."

And that's what we did, thought the wing commander, who considered it the best choice of a bad position to be in. The best would have been for everyone to survive Congreeve. An unrealistic outcome, just as it would be unrealistic to think that everyone would survive the coming battle. *That's what this war is going to be about. Go into every fight, lose crews, then rebuild, just to do it again. Should have gone into battleships. At least there, when the ship comes through, so do most of the people. And when the ship doesn't come through, it's a total loss.*

"Prepare for jump to hyper," called a voice over the intercom. The ground crews kept about their business, experienced spacers to which a translation was not much of anything. The only change was the people on top of the fighters getting down fast, so they wouldn't fall if they happened to catch a bad reaction.

"We have a staff meeting in ten minutes, Commander," said Komorov after checking her implant clock. "The Admiral has passed down our targeting information, at least what there is of it. I want both the divisions ready, so you guys can drill your people on the simulators on the way."

The lights on the hangar dimmed for a moment, and the slight nausea of jump sat in Komorov's stomach. They were on the way. Next stop, Massadara.

Chapter Twenty-three

Ten soldiers wisely led will beat a hundred without a head.   Euripides

SESTIUS SYSTEM, DECEMBER 28TH, 1001.

"Grandfather," yelled the young man, running into the hidden cavern that was the Freeholder guerilla movement headquarters on Sestius.   "The Hunter is back."   He ran further into the cavern, to one of the smaller side caverns that were used as personal quarters.

Former Marine Sergeant Major Montano Montero, the Patriarch of his clan, and leader of the Sestius resistance, looked up from the his meal to see his favorite grandson standing in the door of the cavern. *Hell, one of my few surviving grandsons*, thought the man who at one time had counted them in the scores.   He put down the unappetizing meal, which consisted of military rations, not too bad in and of themselves, until you had to eat them every day, and stood up.

"You talking about Walborski?" asked the Patriarch, walking to the entrance of his quarters and out into the main cavern.   Fifty meters further back into the cavern was the wormhole, used to bring supplies in to people who could no longer farm and ranch, since those activities attracted attention from orbit, which normally was a terminal error.

"Hello, Mr. Montero," said the young man in Ranger's passive cammo, a heavy chemical propelled rifle over his shoulder.   Another, older man stood beside him, and a line of similarly clad men filed past.

"Walborski," said the Patriarch, a smile on his face, which turned to a frown when he saw the tan bars on the collar of his camo suit. "And you had to go and let them make you an officer. What a waste of a fine soldier."

"Sergeant Major," said Walborski, using the rank for emphasis. "This is Colonel Tomas Suarez, my regimental CO."

"Colonel," said Montero, holding out his hand. "And it's retired Sergeant Major. So don't expect any bowing and scraping."

"The Lieutenant told me all about you, sir," said the Colonel, taking the hand. "He neglected to tell me that you were a condescending son of a bitch." Suarez laughed, and Montero joined in.

"And what are you here for, Colonel?" asked Montero, not sure why so many men, and they were still coming out of the wormhole, would come to Sestius. Especially special ops infantry, who really couldn't do much about the Cacas in orbit.

"We've come to clean out your infestation of roaches," said the Colonel.

"We don't have many on the planet. And the ones we do have are holed up in the mountains, in hardened facilities."

"Then that is the first place we take out," said Cornelius, looking at the Colonel, who was nodding.

"Right you are, Lieutenant. And I think Captain Freemont's company would be perfect for the job, don't you."

Walborski smiled, and Montero didn't need to be a genius to realize that Walborski was probably part of that unit.

"And then we wait for the rest of the roaches to come down, where we can get at them."

"And how are you going to do that, Colonel? Did

you bring a bunch of surface to space missiles with you? Long range?"

"Nope. I'm leaving that up to the Fleet. They ought to be here in about eight days or so. Then we'll see how many of them bail out of their logistics ships and troop transports."

Montero thought about that for a moment with a growing smile. "Will you need guides? I have the best people around for showing you the sights."

"I would appreciate that, Mr. Montero. And, first of all, Captain Suarez could use someone to show him that hardened facility in the mountains. Do you have someone in mind."

"Why, yes, Colonel," said the old man, who was still in top shape from living on a planet where survival required fitness. "I think I'm up to it. Don't you, Lieutenant?"

*   *   *

REPUBLIC SPACE.

"We did what we could, Madame President," said the Crakistan Admiral, her unemotional face looking out of the holo. "We struck their force with as much might as possible, but still half of it made it through."

"And your losses, Admiral?" said Graham, not really wanting to hear the news.

"We sustained one third losses, Madame President. That includes the ships that were totally destroyed, as well as the percentage damage to our surviving ships."

Julia nodded, at a loss for words. She had followed the battle on holo while it was occurring. The ambush had seemed to go off perfectly, with missiles jumping up to hyper VII and hitting the oncoming force. The only problem was the lack of missiles capable of getting to VII. They were still scarce in the Republic, with the Empire giving all they could spare, which was nowhere near enough.

And then the enemy force, missing over a third of their number, did the unexpected. They decelerated, turned around, and came after the combined human/Crakista force. They had plenty of missiles they could launch in hyper VII. Dual purpose missiles were the only ones the aliens carried. And launch them they did, just before jumping down to normal space and closing with the Republic force.

We were lucky to get any of our force away, thought the President, looking into the face of the Admiral, still expressionless. *And you don't feel anything because of it. No sorrow, no regret.* She shook that thought away, knowing that it was unfair. The Crakista had lost just as high a percentage of the ships of her own people as she had the human vessels.

"Orders, Madame President?"

"Bring your force back into Republic Space. I want all the heavily damaged ships to head to the New Rome naval yards. That includes the ships of your people, Admiral. All other vessels are to report to the logistics train at Mesa's Star."

"Very well, Madame President. And who should take over command of the combined fleet?"

"You are to retain command, Admiral. You fought a force almost as massive as your own and inflicted heavy casualties on that force. I don't see how any of my people could have done better."

"Thank you, Madame President," said the Admiral, the words coming out of her mouth as if she was tasting them for the first time.

She's learning how to deal with us emotionally flawed creatures.

"And what about the ships that got past us?"

"They're the Empire's problem now. The Emperor knows they are coming. And the Cacas might be surprised when they move a little further into the Empire." *Like they might have problems dropping out of hyper VII, if what Sean told me is correct.*

"Meanwhile, I leave it up to you to reorganize your fleet and prepare to go on the defensive, for now. I'm sure the Cacas will be back, and I want us to be ready for them." *Because I'm tired of losing so many of my citizens to the genocidal maniacs.*

*   *   *

SPACE TO COREWARD OF CA'CADASAN EMPIRE. DECEMBER 29TH, 1001.

"They're closing on us, Commodore," said the Science Officer who was the acting Tactical Officer.

We really didn't think we would need someone to run a battle for us when they built and crewed these ships, thought Commodore Natasha Sung, looking at the tactical holo that showed two groups of ships coming after her squadron. They had not been able to get away from the Caca force that had been tailing them for the last couple of weeks. And now another, larger force was coming up behind that one. With similar resonances as the following force.

I should have slowed, she thought, considering the actions she could have taken weeks back. *If we had slowed enough to translate into VI, we could have released our scout ships.* Those ships were of similar size and capabilities as destroyers. Lightly armed destroyers, true, since they had been designed and built to scout the environs of the Galactic core, or the Magellanic clouds. They were science vessels, not warships, but they were better than nothing. Of course, with the three large mother ships in VII, the hyper VI ships were less than nothing

The other course of action would to have been to have decelerated back down into normal space and found some place to hide. The problem with that solution was she didn't know how many Caca ships would eventually be vectored to their location. Enough, searching long enough, and they would be sure to find the big, twenty-seven million ton vessels. *And, dammit, I'm not accomplishing my mission if I'm sitting hiding in some gas giant moon system or nebula. The longer I hide, the longer it takes to get in touch with the people I'm supposed to see.*

The other possibility would have been to slow to under point ten light, and bring more hyper VII missiles through the wormholes, configured as cargo gates. Enough missiles could take out any force, as long as it wasn't a fleet. Instead, she had decided to keep to hyper VII and her top speed, and now she was about to pay the price.

"Force Alpha is accelerating, Commodore," said the Tactical Officer. "They are closing to missile range."

"And force Bravo?"

"Still coming on."

And when they get within missile range, we're totally screwed. They'll swamp our defenses and blast us out of space.

"We have missile launch," yelled out the Tactical Officer. "Missiles in space and accelerating at ten thousand gravities."

"What about force Bravo?" asked the Commodore just before the vector arrows appeared on the plot. She felt her mouth fall open as she saw the vector arrows, and how they were not pointed at any of her ships.

"Missiles were fired from force Bravo," called out the Tactical Officer, a confused expression on his face. "They fired on Alpha."

The ships in Alpha launched everything they had, aimed at Bravo.

"Are you sure Bravo is Caca?"

"Their resonances are similar, ma'am. But I can't tell you they are an exact match."

So, feuding Cacas? Or someone else? And if someone else, are they friendly? Or are we trading one threat for another?

Whoever they were, they were at least as advanced as the Ca'cadasans. The exchange of missiles blew all the Caca ships out of hyper. And three of the strangers were taken out as well, leaving nine of their ships still closing on the Imperial exploration vessels.

"We have a visual on the unknown vessels, ma'am," said the Tactical Officer, putting the view of the approaching ships on the holo.

"Definitely not Caca," said Sung, studying the clean lines of the unknowns. They were slender, much more so than any warships the Commodore was familiar with. They looked like some kind of martial weapon themselves, fragile and tough at the same time. Estimates of two million tons mass each came up on the sensor analysis.

"We have a message coming in," called out the Com Officer, looking over at the Commodore. "We don't have a translation yet, but the signal is being sent to the linguistic banks. Do you want to send our language primer over to them."

"Of course," said Sung, waving her hand at the Com Officer. "Get it to them, as fast as possible."

The Com Officer nodded and worked her board, sending the information. "We're receiving a burst transmission from them as well," said the Com Officer. "I think they're sending over their standard language programs. Feeding it into our computers now."

Sung looked at the holo of the approaching ships, frustrated that she couldn't talk to them, yet. Not knowing their intentions as they closed on her vessels.

"We have a basic translation going, ma'am," called out the Com Officer. "And they are within visual com range."

"Send them a visual of our bridge," she ordered, looking over at her Tactical Officer, who was shaking his head. "Any other suggestions, Mr. Fujardo?"

"I don't know if it's a good idea going visual yet, ma'am. Not when we don't know their intentions."

"And those ships could probably blow all of us out of hyper if they wished," said Sung. "I'm sure seeing our faces isn't going to change their minds."

She waited a few minutes, until the com holo came alive on her own bridge, showing a golden skinned being sitting in a command chair.

He's almost human, she thought of the alien, then amended that thought immediately. Superficially the alien did look human, to a point. Similar shaped skull, a pair of eyes, golden in color, with slitted irises like those of a cat. Neck was thick, shoulders well developed. Even the proportion of the upper arms and forearms were similar, if not quite exact. The hand only had three digits, two fingers and an opposable thumb, all tipped with hard, claw like, nails.

The nose was broad and had a single nostril on the

end, while the hair was a mass of golden curls, looking much like the mane of a lion. She was sure the interior of the creature would not show many similarities. Convergent evolution tended to work more on exteriors than on internal organs.

"Greetings," said the creature in a melodious voice, the words not really matching the lip movement.

Because it's a translation, thought Sung. "And greetings to you from the New Terran Empire. And thank you for attacking the Ca'cadasans."

The creature showed a predator's sharp teeth as it smiled. "They are vermin, with no honor. We exterminate them when we can, since they seem to eschew the honor of fair battle."

"We are at war with them," said Sung, wondering if this could be another ally. A true one, unlike the Megeda, who had seemed to be the ultimate mercenaries.

"Ah, a martial species," said the being at the other end. "Would you like to battle?"

"Excuse me?" said Sung, not sure the translation had come through.

"I asked if you would like to fight?" said the creature, its lips curling back to reveal the double row of sharp teeth.

"We are not here to fight," said Sung, shaking her head, then realizing the alien might not know what the motion meant. "We only fight when we must."

"That is unfortunate," said the alien. "We find combat to be most enjoyable, and we would only engage to first damage."

"I think they mean like counting coup," said the Tactical Officer. "Like the Amerinds. They fight until someone touches the other with a lance. Or in this case, with a beam weapon."

"So you fight for enjoyment?" asked Sung.

"Of course," said the still smiling alien. "Unless it is with such as the ones we destroyed. Only a fool does not strive to win when the stakes are life and death. But among honorable opponents, it is enough to prove skill."

"We are involved in a fight with the ones you destroyed. Back in our home space. And there is no honor involved in that fight. They mean to destroy us, and we don't intend to be destroyed."

"I like the spirit of your people," said the alien, whose designation for himself came up on the holo beneath him. *Grilyon*, she thought, wondering if she was pronouncing it correctly in her mind. "But why were you running from these creatures? You outmassed them by a factor of three."

"We are not warships. We are explorers, looking for allies against the Ca'cadasans. Until you came along, these were following us just out of missile range. And we thought you were the force the others of them had been sent to fetch."

"There are others of these things coming?" asked the Grilyon commander, his ears perking up and rotating to the front. "Many of them?"

"We don't know how many, Captain. Only that they would bring enough to destroy us. They came upon us almost two weeks ago, sometime after we met with the Megeda."

"You met with those dishonorable thieves," said the Grilyon, making a motion that swished his mane around his head. "And they sold you out to the Ca'cadasans. You should never have trusted those …."
The word that came was not translatable, but Sung

would have been surprised if it wasn't derogatory.

"If you seek allies, we might be convinced to be on your side.   But first, we must go and find these Ca'cadasans that are following you, and bring them to glorious battle.   And we do not fight to damage with such as they. We crush them."   The three fingered hands opened to reveal its sharp claws. "We destroy their vessels, and let the bodies of those not incinerated float through the cold of space, forever."

"And when you have taken care of them?"

"Then we will come back for you, and escort you to our nearest base.   We would learn more of you people, as I am sure you would learn more of us. And perhaps we can come to an understanding."

"I don't think these are the folks we were sent to find," whispered the Tactical Officer.

"I really don't care.   They seem to relish fighting, and it we can turn them fully against the Cacas, we might just take some of the pressure off of our front. I would call that a win for us."

"And the other power we are being sent to contact?"

"Maybe these guys know about them. And, if not, they will still be there in the extra couple of months it takes us to negotiate with these new guys."

She turned back to the holo. "Do you want us to steer a certain course, while we are waiting?"

"One of our ships will accompany you, while we pick up others of ours on the way to the enemy force. They will show you the way."

The holo went blank, followed moments later by a com request from another of the vessels.   Sung felt better than she had in weeks, with a strong ally to help guard them in the unknown section of space.

*   *   *

REPUBLIC AND OUTSIDE SPACE, DECEMBER 30TH, 1001.

"We have another large force of enemy ships heading our way, Madame President," announced the Crakista Admiral in Charge of Republic Battle Fleet Three.

Really more of the commander of the entire Republic Fleet, thought President Julia Graham, looking at the face of the Admiral on the portable holo her aide carried around so she would be in constant contact. The holo was linked into the wormhole com aboard the heavy cruiser she was using as her transport.

The President looked up from the holo to the cityscape she was touring. *Or, maybe that should be the ruins of a cityscape*, she thought. New Washington, the capital city of the Republic, on a world of the same name, had once been her home, both her birthplace, and the central location of the government she had been the leader of. Now she stood on a hill made up of the smashed rubble of the downtown business district, looking over the crater where her residence and office used to stand.

Until those bastards came, she thought, glancing up to the sky.

The New Terran Republic had fought wars before. Against the Crakista in the far past. Against the Klang, frequently. Even one against the New Terran Empire. And never before had they seen such destruction among their own core worlds.

The city of New Washington had once been the home of fifty million people. Now it was the home of no one, except the stray dogs and other vermin that stalked the streets, trying to feed their starving bodies. The planet had once boasted a population of ten billion, the most densely populated in the Republic. Now there were a mere twenty million survivors. Fifteen million had been evacuated before the enemy had blockaded the planet. Most of the rest had died from the orbital bombardment, nine billion of them, followed up by the landings and the slaughter of hundreds of millions more. And then had come the round up to the camps.

Graham almost vomited as she thought of the tales she had heard from some of the survivors of those camps. About how the Cacas entered on a daily basis to select their victims, slaughtering them in front of the others, then field dressing them and hauling away the meat for their own consumption.

And then the Caca fleet had left, leaving a skeleton crew of warriors behind to continue the harvest, to stock the larders for their eventual return. *Only we got here first*, she thought, staring at the ruins that stretched to the horizon. *Savages. Even the Klang don't eat us. Filthy barbarian savages.*

"What are your orders, Madame President?" repeated the Crakista female who was their ranking officer in this space. "Most of my fleet is still in the early stages of moving out of the region. We are still in position to intercept them."

"How large is the force?"

"At least four hundred ships, Madame President. You should have already received the report from your picket."

"Of course I have," she replied, reaching down and picking up a child's plastic man that had ended up somehow on top of the rubble.   *I just wanted your confirmation.* "Can you hit them?"

"We can. But I must warn you that we will take casualties, even if we ambush them. After all, they can also send missiles between dimensions."

"Can you hurt them worse than they hurt you, Admiral?"

"While I can guarantee nothing, I believe the odds are in our favor, Madame President."

"Then hit them, Admiral," she said, looking at the small toy that had once portrayed a soldier of her Republic. "Hit them with everything you have. Keep hitting them until you don't have anything left to fire. I don't want any of the bastards to ever see the stars of their home. Understood?"

The Crakista Admiral looked taken aback by her display of emotion. She looked like she wanted to say something, then straightened and saluted in the human manner. "Understood, Madame President. We will avenge the children of your people."

*   *   *

SECTOR IV SPACE.

"We are picking up nothing from the planet," said the Tactical Officer, looking back at the High Admiral.

By all the Gods, what is this? thought **High Admiral Kellissaran Jarkastarin.** "This is supposed to be one of their developing worlds, with over a hundred million of the humans infesting it," he growled. "They couldn't have all escaped."

"We are picking up no signals from the planet, my Lord," said the Tactical Officer, shrugging both shoulders. "Nothing on any of the com channels. No indication of intelligent life."

"Lights? Heat sources? Graviton emissions?"

"Nothing, my Lord. But remember, we are looking at the day side of the planet, so we would see no lights. And heat sources would have to be very strong and robust for us to pick them up."

"And graviton emissions? What of them?"

"With all of the static through hyper, I am having trouble picking up the emissions of our accompanying ships, my Lord. Much less anything else. There are a few irregularities near the planet, but I cannot get enough of a fix on them to tell what they are."

"Com Officer," said the High Admiral. "Transmit orders to three scouts on each of our flanks. I want them to change their vectors enough that they see at least a sliver of the night terminators of that planet. I cannot believe there is nothing there."

He looked at the tactical plot again, which basically showed him all the larger bodies of the system, and his own ships. And nothing else. "Tactical. I want that planet watched continuously with visual scans. If there is a pebble in orbit reflecting any sunlight, I want to know."

Hours went by, the High Admiral sitting on his bridge, watching the viewer that showed the planet, his eyes shifting every few moments to the tactical holo.

"Scout ships are reporting no lights at the terminators," called out the Com Officer. "No heat sources at all, save for one volcano in eruption."

"Tactical. Anything in space?"

"We have tracked a couple of small objects in low orbit around the planet, and that is all, my Lord."

"They couldn't have evacuated a planet with over a hundred million beings on it," growled the lead male.

"Not when they didn't know we were coming. That's impossible, even if they had a wormhole to take them off the planet." He thought some moments about that idea, dismissing it as soon as it came. It would have taken months to get that many beings off of a world, marching them as fast as possible through the wormhole all day and night.

"Orders, my Lord?" asked the Helm.

"I believe we should be cautious, my Lord," said the Tactical Officer. "We do not know what is on that world."

"Bah," spat Jarkastarin. "There are no ships in orbit. No forts. We cannot even pick up defensive platforms. If they are there, they have turned off everything on the surface and are cowering in underground shelters." He pointed a finger at the viewer. "They are there, and I mean to blast them out of their hiding places."

"We could launch missiles at the planet from where we are now," advised the Tactical Officer.

"I advise against that, my Lord," said the Helm Officer. "It is forbidden to kill living worlds, unless they are terraformed. And according to our spectral analyses, this is not a world with predominantly Terran life."

"Bah," said Jarkastarin again. "We do not need missiles to chase them from their burrows. We will go into orbit and pound them with kinetics."

"All of us, my Lord?" asked the Helm, his posture showing that he was not enthused with that idea.

"Send a couple of pods of scouts into orbit first," said the High Admiral after some thought. "They can drop some kinetics on the planet, and see if the vermin are stirred from their lairs. Once they have established that there is no threat to the rest of the fleet, we will move closer to add our firepower."

"Yes, my Lord," echoed the Com Officer and Helm Officer in unison.

"Time to orbital insertion of the scouts?" he asked the Tactical Officer.

"Approximately three hours, my Lord."

The High Admiral looked at his Com Officer. "Order the rest of the force to come to a rest five light minutes from the planet. We will come in after the scouts have cleared the way."

"What if they have ships on the other side of the planet, my Lord?" asked the Tactical Officer. "Waiting for us."

"Then the scouts will find them while they orbit. And we will come in and destroy them. Any other indications that there might be ships in orbit."

"No, my Lord," answered the Tactical Officer. "We are still picking up some anomalies, but nothing we can pinpoint."

In three hours the two pods of scouts, twenty of the five hundred thousand ton vessels in all, slid into orbit around the planet. They held at ten thousand kilometers above the surface, and completed six orbits before they started dropping kinetic weapons on the cities that looked totally deserted below. Bright pinpricks flared on the dayside, brighter on the night. And still no reaction.

"It looks like the planet was inhabited, my Lord," said the Tactical Officer, playing back the scenes of the surface as transmitted by the scouts. Several very large cities, and hundreds of smaller, were scattered across the world, along with many thousands of villages and almost countless single habitations. And still no sign of life. A dozen KE weapons landed on one of the cities, blasting large sections of it to rubble, and still nothing.

"Move the rest of the ships in," said the High Admiral. "Start landing the ground warriors as soon as we are in orbit. I will want a thorough search of this world while we demolish the empty cities. They are down there, and we are going to get them."

An hour later the entire force was in orbit, from five thousand kilometers to as far out as twenty-five thousand. Shuttles were scorching their way in through the atmosphere, delivering a platoon of armored ground warriors each per trip. And still no sign of the humans.

This is infuriating, thought the High Admiral, staring at a holo of the globe that was blossoming pin points of blinding light as the kinetic weapons continued to fall.

"Sir," called out the Tactical Officer, a look of alarm on his face. "We're picking up power readings. Heat spikes, electromagnetic fields."

"Where, fool?" growled Jarkastarin, glaring at his officer. "Can we get a fix to target them?"

"Everywhere, my Lord," said the wide eyed officer. "And they will be easy enough to target, if we have anything left to target them with."

The High Admiral stared in disbelief as the planet bloomed first with energy spikes, then disappeared under a wave of generated static. He was about to give the order to boost away, to leave the orbit of the planet, to get them far enough out that they could lob high relativistic missiles in at the world. As he opened his mouth to shout orders the flagship shook and shuddered under the strike of a powerful particle beam.

Moments later high velocity missiles started to rise from the surface, pulling hundreds of gravities through the atmosphere, then pushing ten thousand gees after they had left the gas envelope behind.

*   *   *

The common wisdom of space warfare was that ships had the advantage over planets in all respects. Planets could be armed enough to make a conquest more expensive, but they could not beat an invasion fleet. But that presupposed that said fleet would take out the orbital defenses from range, then target what shore defenses they could locate on the way in.

The planet would, meanwhile, try to obscure the sensors of the opposing ships to give their weapons a little more time, always saving some to shoot at the landing shuttles when they made their inevitable appearance. This didn't take into account that the enemy ships might not find out about the defenses until they were all in orbit of the planet, and within range of all of the weapons.

This was an Imperial Army show. Thirty two brigades of mobile shore artillery had been transferred to the planet through the wormhole that had been brought there recently. Ninety-six battalions, two hundred and eighty-eight batteries. Each battery had ten of the one thousand ton mobile shore defense guns. About a third of the battalions were made up of hypervelocity projectile cannon, with secondary laser weapons. Another third carried heavy particle beams, while the last third were equipped with high power lasers. Eight hundred and eighty-eight guns, all fired at once, concentrating their firepower on the most appropriate targets among the enemy ships.

The high velocity cannon fired one hundred kilogram penetrators with nuclear warheads at point two c. The rounds tore through the atmosphere as almost instantaneous streaks of fire that hit the enemy ships in low orbit, punching through electromag fields as if they didn't exist, penetrating several meters of armor before their warheads detonated. The guns were specifically designed to take out ships in medium to low orbit, ones that would not be able to react in time to weapons the fields couldn't repel, and the outer layer of their armor couldn't withstand.

The twenty scouts ships in low planetary orbit were taken out in an instant, each struck by scores of one megaton warheads. Half shattered, leaving swarms of debris flying around the world. The other half was killed just as well as if they had been blown apart, all of their grabber systems taken out, adrift with no functional weapons systems, doomed to eventually fall back into the atmosphere.

The next layer of ships, scouts and a number of supercruisers, were also targeted. The first salvo toward them all hit the ships that were not prepared for their fire. The second volley had similar results, if not quite as spectacular. By the third volley the ships were taking out about half of the rounds with counter fire, lasers, particle beams and close in defensive projectile weapons. Hundreds of rounds disappeared in bright pinpoints of nuclear fire, while the others continued on to strike their targets, which didn't have time to maneuver out of the way.

The cannon immediately lifted on their own grabbers, using the shielding of the planetary defensive jamming to move to new locations. Over ninety percent of them made it. Ten percent took either severe damage from close misses, or were totally destroyed, their locations plotted from the trajectories of their shells. As soon as they had located new positions, they reacquired the closest targets and opened fire again.

The particle beam equipped batteries took aim at both the ships in medium orbit and many of those further out. The beams, traveling at point six light, packed a punch, though not in the same range as the hypervelocity projectile cannon. They still ravaged the hulls of the target ships, eating holes in the outer armor, burning through grabbers, knocking out laser rings. The electromag fields attenuated them somewhat, but at this range the beams held together well, and achieved about eighty percent of mass on target. The guns fired for ten seconds, keeping their protons on target, then ceased fire as the projectors started to overheat. The guns lifted at this time and moved to new positions, sustaining about the same casualty rates as the projectile batteries.

Lasers concentrated on the furthest vehicles out. They were not as effective against ships with strong electromagnetic fields as the other weapon types. But they still did some damage. And while all the batteries were firing, prepositioned missiles rose from the surface and headed for the enemy ships.

*   *   *

"Get us out of here," yelled the High Admiral, feeling his flagship shudder underneath as particle beams struck. The ships in low and medium orbit were dropping off the plot at an alarming rate, or losing power and all acceleration. "Order all the force to move away from the planet." *We'll move out of their range, or at least the range of their shore batteries, and lob missiles at them until this duplicitous world is dead.*

The ship shuddered again, two different motions, that of being hit by streams of fast moving protons, and the shift caused by launching counter missiles. The force was getting some intercepts, but the volume of fire and the close range was not allowing enough. The High Admiral looked on a side viewer to see one of his battleships hit by a missile, actinic fire blurring the view of the hull for a moment. It was not a large warhead, none of the missiles seemed to carry the gigaton range weapons that warships employed. While in the low megaton range, they were still enough to cause considerable damage, even to the tough supercruisers and battleships. Enough damage to allow other missiles to strike, until enough had hit to take the ships out of action.

The Ca'cadasan ships pulled away at their maximum safe acceleration, pushing crews heavily into their couches as they accelerated at well over five hundred gravities. It wasn't fast enough to take them away from their killers, as the shore batteries continued their tactic of fire and move, shoot and scoot. The High Admiral railed as his force died around him. Until they had finally got out of effective range of the weapons, five light seconds away. Naval weaponry would still be effective at this range, but not the smaller weapons of mobile shore guns, firing through an atmosphere.

"Report," said the High Admiral, looking over at his Tactical Officer.

"Twenty-three ships made it away from the planet," said that male, turning a frightened eye toward his commander. "Thirty-four still remain in orbit of the planet, unable to boost."

"Where they will die," whispered the High Admiral. He watched on the viewer as one of those ships exploded, hit by more of the nuclear tipped shells.

Missiles were ignoring those close in vessels now. Another exploded, and bright flashes ran over the hulls of some more. *I will avenge you*, he thought, now watching as the planet launched missiles reached for his remaining force. His ships were now cycling missiles at a prodigious rate, their laser rings sending off beam after beam, knocking most of the enemy weapons out of space.

There were some hits, several dozen. The small warheads really didn't do much damage, but to ships that were already in dire straits and trying to get away, it was enough. One battleship had taken so much that a strike by one small megaton warhead hurt enough to cause an antimatter breach aboard, and the twenty-five million ton vessel went up in a flare of spreading plasma.

"Take us to a light hour out, and we'll make them pay," he told the Helm Officer.

"We're picking up incoming objects," called out the Tactical Officer. "Over two thousand of them. Accelerating in at over ten thousand gravities."

"Where in the hells are they coming from?"

"It looks like that moon over there," said the Tactical Officer in alarm, as the main holo switched to a view of said body, an eight hundred kilometer diameter rock sitting in orbit four million kilometers from the planet. Along their path of retreat. And it was firing missiles from surface batteries that were on an intercept course with the force.

"Turn our vector," shouted the High Admiral. *Two thousand missiles. And what kind? The same as were fired from the planet? Or ship killers?*

"We're picking up ships coming from that moon, my Lord," called out the Tactical Officer, his tone one of panic.

The Admiral leaned forward in his chair to take in the view of the central holo, a close up of the edge of that rock, and what looked to be a hundred vector arrows coming around it. The kind of vector arrows that indicated ships.

"They're calling for our surrender, my Lord," called out the Com Officer.

"No," growled the High Admiral. He glared at the Com Officer, until a flash at the corner of his eye attracted his attention. He turned back to one of the holos in time to see another of his battleships explode.

"Get us out of this. We can't let these vermin take us. You can't let these vermin destroy me."

"There is no way out, my Lord," said the Tactical Officer, his expression changing from fear to disgust. "We have two choices. We can surrender, in which case the humans will take us prisoner, and our fate will be in their hands. Or we can continue to resist against a force that we cannot defeat, and we can die."

The High Admiral stared with wide eyes at the holo, then back to his Tactical Officer.

"They have called for our surrender again, my Lord," said the Com Officer. "They want an answer."

"Missile impact in three minutes," called out the Tactical Officer. "Orders, my Lord?"

The High Admiral sat in his chair, staring at the holo with wide eyes, a low growl in his throat.

"Order the force to surrender," the Tactical Officer said to the Com Officer.

"You cannot give that command," said the Com Officer. "Only the High Admiral can command while he is alive."

The Tactical Officer gave a head nod of

agreement, then stood up from his chair, fighting the increased gravity of acceleration on spread legs.   He staggered over to the Admiral, who didn't move a muscle. The Tactical Officer reached out, grabbed the older male by his horns, and threw him out of his chair. He let his weight fall on the other male and brought both hands up, then pummeled the High Admiral in the head, all four fists striking, two at a time. The Admiral tried to grab the younger male's hands and failed. The Tactical Officer grabbed the hilt of the ceremonial dagger out of his leader's belt sheath, brought it up in an overhand grip, and plunged it down through the throat of the High Admiral.

"I am now in command," the Tactical Officer told the bridge crew. He looked over at the Com Officer. "Signal the force to surrender. And tell the humans we have given up."

Moments later the incoming missiles started to self-destruct, while the human force grew closer.

*   *   *

Of the other two forces that had gone raiding, one had fought an indecisive action with a human force and was compelled to withdraw without hitting the developing world they had been tasked at destroying. The other made it to its target system, which was found to be lightly defended.   They left a smashed world behind them, two hundred million dead, all cities and industrial concerns crushed.   They left the system behind and headed back to one of the Ca'cadasan bases at hyper VII. Later, as they closed on the base system, they found they were unable to jump back down when half the force ran into the hyper barrier, the Galaxy taking revenge for their actions.

Chapter Twenty-four

There is no instance of a nation benefitting from prolonged warfare. Sun Tzu

SESTIUS. JANUARY 5TH, 1002.

At least we're not burning up in the heat, thought Cornelius as he clambered up the side of the mountain. Like all the men in his platoon, he was wearing an unpowered skin suit that gave him a bit more protection than soft clothing, or bare flesh. The suit would stop low velocity projectiles and a moment of laser fire. Against particle beams, it was not much protection. It had a passive cammo coating that helped it to blend in with its surroundings, and when the pores were closed it trapped most of the body heat within. Everyone also wore a cloak that helped to hold in more of their heat, making the Rangers as near undetectable as possible to heat sensors.

Of course, like all of them, that cloak was now rolled up on his back, over his rucksack, since none of the men really wanted anything interfering with their ability to climb the rock. The pistol on his side, a low velocity liquid chemical weapon, was snapped into place, his rifle, similar to the pistol with the exception of its muzzle velocity, was strapped over his back. *And at least I don't have to carry a rocket launcher, or any of the heavier shit,* he thought as he wedged his fingers into a rock crevice while looking for his next point of contact. As an officer, he wasn't required to hump more than his personal equipment. Of course, not being a complete ass, he was carrying extra ammo and grenades that might come in handy for the rest of the platoon.

It was cool out, this high up, but not as cold as the higher snowcapped peaks that surrounded them. The fort was built into the rock of a plateau that allowed the Cacas good observation of all the valleys around them. And protected them from assault from anything but troop carriers, which they could shoot down before they got within attack range of the plateau. Or so they thought.

Walborski shifted a foot, reaching up and placing the toe into the rock. Like his gloves, the soles of the boots utilized nanotech to bind to the rock. Still, he was careful to maintain three points of contact at all times. It was almost a thousand meters straight down if they fell off the face. No one wore antigrav vests. If one was activated, the enemy was likely to know they were there, which would compromise the mission. And no one expected someone equipped with one not to use it if he fell, so the temptation was removed. They did carry a light parachute below their rucksacks, for their extraction if needed, but it was a risk deploying an old fashioned chute in mountains so close to a rock wall, especially with the winds that were rushing past.

Only a hundred meters to go, thought the Lieutenant, looking up at the two point men who climbed before him. His Platoon Sergeant had suggested that the LT let the entire first squad precede him, but he wasn't wired that way. He wanted to be one of the first to the top, after the scouts, so he could get a look at what they were dealing with

Off in the distance came the crack of explosives, the rest of the company on their diversionary attack. Hopefully attracting all of the attention hereabouts. From the noise echoing through the mountains, it sounded like they were in the next valley, when it fact they were two valleys over.

The first man climbed over the lip of the cliff and crouched low, looking around for a moment, then waving for the rest of the people to come on. He disappeared as he moved further in, and the second scout took his place, serving as the link between the first scout and the still climbing platoon.

Walborski pulled himself up over the lip of the cliff, aided by the scout, then turned to help the next man up. The second scout moved away, and the LT signaled for the man he had helped to stay in place. The man nodded, and Cornelius moved in a crouch toward the group of rocks the scouts were sheltering behind. The LT couldn't understand while the rocks were there. He would have had them removed, and could only put it down to arrogance, or laziness. Both of the scouts were on their bellies, looking around different sides of the rocks, their glasses trained on something. Walborski went to the left and tapped that scout on the shoulder. The man crawled back and Cornelius took his place, looking first over the scene with his own enhanced vision, then bringing his field glasses up to get a closer look.

There were a hundred meters of open ground between where he was and the outer works of the fort. A hundred meters of killing field. There were towers at each corner of the blockhouse that was the fort, in each tower a firing slit that allowed whomever was in them to cover all the approaches.

"We're all here," said Sergeant First Class Rupert SanJames, his platoon sergeant, indicating the entire forty man unit had achieved the plateau. "Orders?"

"We wait," said Cornelius, not really liking that part of the operations order. The longer they sat here, the more likely they were of being discovered. But without the go ahead, they were at risk from the orbital assets.

Cornelius checked the old fashioned watch that all Rangers wore, watching as the seconds ticked down. Of course, there was no guarantee that the Fleet would arrive on time, or be spotted by the enemy on time. But they needed to move while the enemy warships, what there were of them, were leaving orbit, and the shuttles from the two transports up there started on their way down.

"Get the launchers ready," he ordered his platoon sergeant, then watched as the older man went to the four Rangers equipped with the weapons and told them to prepare. The men in question extended the launchers, getting them ready to launch, though still powered down.

The deadline ticked by with no signal, and Cornelius wondered if they would be sitting here until someone spotted them, and brought down kinetic weapons from orbit. *I don't know why they think those troop transports aren't equipped with dropped penetrators. If they were my ships, they would sure have them.*

Something flared bright in the air far above, a smaller second sun in the sky. A small tactical nuke that was the signal. "On my command," he whispered to the men nearest him, who transmitted it in low voices down both sides of the line. SanJames was at his side a moment later.

"Don't even think about it, LT," said the Sergeant First Class.

"What?"

"You're an officer now. Follow me is a good motto, but you don't need to be the first man into the open."

"I'm their leader."

"Then lead. But don't put your ass on the line just to prove how brave you are. These men know about your history. You don't have anything to prove to them."

And your job is to make sure I live long enough to actually lead Rangers, thought Cornelius, looking into the Sergeant's eyes. He nodded.

"And don't stick too close to me," cautioned SanJames, waving a finger in the air. "It wouldn't be good for the both of us to be cut down."

There was another boom in the sky, another bright flash high up in the atmosphere.

"Aim launchers," he ordered, watching as a pair of the men went around the corners of the rock formation, lining up their launchers and looking through their sights. "Arm."

The men, all four of them, hit the switch on their launchers that sent power into their systems. It was just a trickle of power, which might have been detected, but the chance was slight in the moments before they were deployed.

"Fire," yelled Cornelius.

Both men in position pulled their triggers in that instant. Now the launchers would be very detectable by any systems the enemy had. The rockets were propelled out of their tubes by magnetic propulsion, the same as used in mag rail weapons. They shot out to twenty meters, then ignited their engines and rushed at their target, pulling hundreds of gravities of acceleration. In less than one tenth of a second they struck their targets, the towers. The warheads detonated, small nuclear devices of two hundred ton yield.

The blasts sheared off the tops of both towers, killing whatever was in them. The Rangers hunkered down behind the rocks, all but the two rocket gunners, who rolled as fast as they could behind the rocks, while the one of the remaining two stood and leveled his launcher at the front of the fortress.

As soon as he had his target in sight he fired his rocket at the heavy doors of the fort. The rocket flew slowly toward the door, programed to give the gunner time to get under cover, and no longer threatened by the anti-rocket weapons that had been in the now truncated towers. This was a one kiloton warhead, which blasted the heavy alloy door off its supports and into the fort.

The last rocket gunner counted to ten, then raised up and put his warhead into the opening that was now revealed. It too went off in the thunderous blast, actually blowing out part of the door that had just been blasted in.

"Now," yelled Walborki, and the first squad jumped over the rocks and ran full speed toward the breached entrance. Nothing fired at them while they ran, and one team entered the fort to secure the entrance, while the other remained outside. Second squad started off, the LT with them, and made it halfway across the hundred meters without issue. That was when a particle beam reached out from the rooftop and hit one of the Rangers, vaporizing a large hole in his torso.

The Rangers knew better than to stop, and accelerated toward the door. More beams struck out, most misses, one taking off the arm of a Ranger. Third squad opened fire on the roof, their liquid chemical propulsion rifles sending high velocity rounds at the partially hidden Cacas. Each Ranger also launched a grenade, while the two dedicated grenadiers fired bursts of full auto thirty millimeter on arching paths that brought them down on the roof.

Walborski armed a hand grenade, then pitched it onto the roof at the same time as two other Rangers. All hunkered down for a moment, while the much more powerful explosives of the hand grenades detonated on the roof. Then they headed into the fort, leaving third squad to handle the remaining Cacas on the roof.

There was very little resistance on the first floor, the mininuke having done its job. Most the Cacas, without armor while thinking they were secure, had been killed by the blast. Those who had survived were either badly wound from shrapnel, burned by fire or radiation, or dazed out of their minds. They were taken prisoner with ease.

First squad worked their way down to the next level, where there was resistance, though not much. Second went up to secure the level above, then the rooftop, while third leap frogged first and went further down.

In less than fifteen minutes the fort was theirs, for a total of six killed and eleven wounded. Light casualties for such an operation, as they had killed forty-six Cacas, and captured another thirty-one. The cost still bothered Cornelius, unlike the casualties of any other operation he had been in. These were his men, and he had expected to bring them all through. SFC SanJames must have known something. Or maybe it was just his experience.

"Good job, Lieutenant," he told Walborski,

motioning for the man with the com to unpack it and turn it on, since there was now no threat of being detected.   "I think you're going to go far in this human's army."

"I wish we could have done it with a lesser cost to ourselves," he said, turning his haunted eyes on the Sergeant.

"Oh, give it a break, sir," said SanJames. "We are the pointy end of the stick. And we are expected to take our objective, to fulfill our mission. We are not expected to all return. Some of your people died today. People I know, Linz, Garcia, Bogart, the others. But we took the objective, one that personally scared the hell out of me. And we did it with casualties far lower than any reasonably intelligent person would expect."

"The Captain wants to talk with you, sir," called out the man with the com set.

"Give it here," he told the man, taking the compact set from his hand. "What are your orders, sir?"

"Just sit tight for now," said the senior officer. "If they have any transport up there, prep it. The Cacas are on the ground, and more on the way. As soon as we know where they all are, we'll assign targets. And Lieutenant, good job."

The com went off, and Walborski handed the set back to the man tasked to carry it. He had a smile on his face as he looked back at his Platoon Sergeant. *Then we get back into the jungle, and the hunt is on.*

*   *   *

MASSADARA SPACE. JANUARY 7TH, 1002.

"Prepare to launch," said the voice over the

intercom. "All ships, prepare to launch. Five minutes and counting."

Captain Svetlana Komorov acknowledge the order, sitting back in the command chair on her fifteen hundred ton inertialess fighter. Her small bridge crew of one other officer and two ratings looked at each other with a bit of anxiety, normal before action, even though the next four or five hours would probably be pure boredom. She looked at the screen to the tiny engineering control compartment, where a Chief Petty Officer and a rating were monitoring the power source of the ship, its fusion reactor.

"All offensive systems are ready," said the Petty Officer who was also the weapon's officer of the craft.

"Inertial navigation system online," said the Pilot, looking back at his commander. He would have much more responsibility than the other pilots of the wing, as his commander, who was also the wing commander, would have the entire wing to think about. "All drive systems nominal."

"Engineer. Anything to report on the reactor?"

"Reactor at fifty percent, ma'am," said the Chief, looking out of the viewer. "Testing now."

The power dials on the reactor, visible from the bridge, went up to ninety percent, then peaked at one hundred, before dropping back to fifty.

"Reactor is nominal," said the Chief. "Negative matter containment at one hundred percent."

And that's all we can do here in the hangar, thought the Captain. They would have to wait until they launched before they could test the electromag systems, which were integral both to their particle shielding and the negative matter bubble needed for their inertialess drive.

"Launch in one minute," called out the controller from the ship's aviation control center.

"We've finished uploading the targeting data, ma'am," called out the Pilot.

Svetlana nodded, looking at that data herself. The *Akagi* had been in normal space for eight hours, accelerating toward the star until she had built up to point eight light. With the turbulence in hyper they were not picking up the graviton emissions of any ships within the Massadara system. Of course, theirs were not being picked up either, which was a two edged sword. Fortunately for the attackers, them, they knew where to look for the enemy ships, while the enemy had no idea where they would be coming from, or that they were even there.

The ships had been scanning the space ahead with their visual sensors, picking up any sign of an object, no matter how faint, and matching it with the known bodies in the system. And they had found most of the enemy, if not all. They were gathered in two groups, one well within the system, near the habitable planet. The other just a half light hour in from the hyper barrier. There might have been other ships in the system, but probably not in any large groups.

I think we have their measure, she thought, looking over the groups. Her wing had been tasked to hit the inner group. The other wings from the two accompanying carriers were targeted on the outer group. Neither attack was thought to be enough to take them out. But they would cause damage, and confusion, and the odds of the missile launching ships destroying those groups would increase exponentially.

"First Division checking in," called the commander of that half of the wing. "All ready."

"Second Division. All ships are ready."

"Acknowledging," she said, watching as the clock in her implant ticked down, until.

"All fighters, launch, launch, launch."

The oversized doors to the hangars were already open, and the first layer of ships lifted off the deck and boosted out at twenty gravities. As soon as they were clear the next layer lifted and followed. It only took three minutes for all of the vessels to leave both hangars, where they altered their vectors onto the heading toward their target.

"OK, people," said Komorov over the com, not really worrying about the enemy listening in on their signal. They would outrun the light of their com lasers, which were not aimed into the system in the first place. "Form up into the attack pattern. Then we'll make sure we have the most up to date data and bubble up."

It took about a minute for the ships to all get into place, First Division on the port, Second on the starboard, while Komorov and her command group, hers and two escorts, took the center. She really wasn't sure why she needed escorts. There really wasn't anything they could do to protect her if someone shot at her ship.

"On my command, raise bubbles and boost for the target," she said into the com. "Raise bubbles, now." On the ninety fighters, electromag shields ramped up to full power, while the twin negative matter containment tanks released their materials through magnetic conduits that ran into the field that englobed the ship. A moment later all of the ships were cut off from the normal Universe, all radiation, including gravitons, excluded from their space.

"Boosting ahead, now," said the Pilot, taking his

cue from the program that every ship was running that would time their trip to the attack. "One thousand gravities. Two thousand gravities. Five thousand. Ten thousand. Fifteen thousand. Twenty. Twenty-five. Thirty. All systems nominal. Velocity, point eight c. Time to light speed, three point four minutes."

And time on target, after we achieve our maximum velocity of two c, five and a half hours. Now there was basically nothing to do for the next five plus hours. The crew would look after the ship. She pulled up the information they had on the enemy ships, their systems and her own weapons, studying information she already knew by heart, just in case there was something in there she had missed previously. She might not find much, but anything that could get her and her people through the shit would be worthwhile.

*   *   *

OUTSIDE CONUNDRUM SPACE.

"What does the objective look like, Commodore?" came the voice of Grand Fleet Admiral Len Lenkowski over the wormhole com.

"No change, Admiral," replied Commodore Bryce Suttler, looking at his tactical plot which showed the Conundrum system, with the visual plots of all enemy ships. *Sure made it harder to track them*, thought the Stealth/Attack Ship commander. Graviton emissions were just about unreadable at this time, thanks to the supernova. So everything was visual, which left something to be desired. First off, it was not near real time, like graviton tracking. Second, it was easy to lose individual ships at a distance, especially when they were sitting dead in space and not putting out huge amounts of waste heat.

The Cacas had received reinforcements the day before, not unexpected, and not what the Cacas had been expecting. *They had been expecting many more, but the Republic came through and took quite a few of them out.* For some reason the outer Caca force had moved further out, closer to the barrier, as it they were planning something. And there had been some ships that had left the system some days before, or so it seemed. Even with the interference, he had been able to visually confirm that they had jumped to hyper I. But from there, because of that same interference, he had no idea. Not that they were really able to do anything out there, not as few as they had been.

Suttler looked over at the other holo, which showed the approaching Imperial fleet. His sensors were, of course, not picking them up. And so neither was the enemy. Instead, he was getting the fleet's own track from the wormhole com of the flagship. And it was an awesome sight, even if it was not the entire thing.

Hundreds of ships moved through hyper VI on their way in, still far from the first barrier. To the side of them was another formation of hundreds of vessels. And behind them were more, and even more behind those formations. The Commodore knew the assigned order of battle, and it was still awesome.

"Our first ships are getting ready to drop down to V," said the Grand Fleet Admiral over the com. "Let me know what you detect."

Suttler nodded and pointed at Ngovic, letting the Tactical Officer know he was up. He glanced back at the tactical holo, noting that the formations were stretched out, one ship after another, each a light second back from the vessel ahead. It took three seconds to jump, and at their current velocity of point two light, they would be jumping one after the other at five seconds intervals, which would keep them from making the overwhelming noise of hundreds of simultaneous translations.

"First ship jumping now," said Lenkowski. "A destroyer."

Ngovic looked up and shook his head. "Nothing Admiral," said Suttler. "We're picking up no trace of translation."

Another destroyer jumped, then a third. Normally this would be setting off every alarm in the system, but the sensitive pickups on the *Seastag* were not showing a trace.

"This one's a light cruiser," said Lenkowski as the next ship jumped.

"Still not a trace, sir."

"Heavy cruiser up next."

That ship jumped without a trace. As did the next ship, a battle cruiser. After twenty more vessels it was the turn of a battleship, then a superbattleship. And finally, the last test, a superheavy battleship, twenty-seven million tons of warship. *And if this doesn't set off the detectors, nothing will,* thought Suttler as the huge vessel jumped.

"We are registering a slight indication of gravitons," said Ngovic, looking over at this commander.

"That registered a bit, Admiral."

"Enough for them to detect us insystem?"

"No, sir," said Ngovic, running the trace through his system. "I doubt they will pick anything up in the system."

And the jumps down to lower levels should generate even less noise, thought Suttler, looking at the Admiral. "Looking good, Admiral. I think you're going to get in clean."

"Thank you, Commodore," said Lenkowski. "Now, I'll turn you over to one of the com techs. Keep monitoring."

The holo went blank, coming back to life over the Tactical Officer's board. Suttler continued to watch the procession of ships on the holo, one after the other jumping, until all were in V. Minutes later the front of the line started to jump to IV. When they were through the next line was jumping to V, a perfectly choreographed dance where no two ships were changing dimensions at the same time, minimizing their signature, slipping through under the hyper interference of the supernova.

*   *   *

"We're jumping into normal space, your Majesty," said Kelso over the com.

"Thank you, Admiral," said Sean, looking at his own tactical holo. His command room was itself the holo, and he was standing within it, looking at all of his units as they arrayed themselves in normal space outside the Conundrum system. There were still two lines of ships, a Margravi detachment and part of the Elysium fleet, coming in behind them, one still in I, the other in II.

He switched the holo to a real time visual of the system, a composite of the feeds from every wormhole equipped ship in the fleet. The bright point of the star was ahead, the dots of planets ranging out. There were some glints near the planet, more toward the outer system just inside the hyper I barrier. Sean zoomed in on the glints, which revealed themselves to be large formations of Ca'cadasan ships.   Of course, he was seeing the outer group as they were six hours ago, the inner group over two and a half hours later still. Supposedly, they were still in position, not knowing that an enemy fleet had just appeared outside their system.   At least, according to Lenkowski, there had been no appreciable translation signal.   All of the ships were in stealth mode at the moment, their skins set to absorb all photons impacting on them, their grabbers propelling them inward at a sedate twenty gravities. At that rate they were producing very little heat, most of it projected into space behind them, where there were no observers.   The enemy would have to know exactly where they were, then use their most intense light gathering visual sensors on a slow track to actually see them.   And the odds against that were merely astronomical.

Sean zoomed in on his own task group. His heavy cruiser, the *Manila*, was surrounded by a trio of specialized missile defense light cruisers and a dozen of the same kind of destroyer. They were tucked in close to a task force of hyper VII carriers, which, unfortunately, had not been able to use the higher dimension for travel. *That's one we didn't see coming*, he thought. They had lost some ships that had tried to translate down from VII, and there were still half a hundred vessels trapped in that dimension. It had been an expensive lesson, and he was glad that his fleet hadn't been traversing VII at the time the star had exploded, or they would have been trapped for two weeks, or longer.

The carriers were starting to launch their inertialess fighters, which would sweep in just ahead of the missile storm to strike at the enemy, hopefully causing a lot of confusion. The main fleet, in six different formations, were now launching their missiles, the weapons moving in at five hundred gravities to avoid detection. The inertialess fighters would continue in at fifty gravities, waiting until they got much closer to the system before they raised their bubbles and moved at full acceleration.

Next, Sean switched the view to the tactical readout at Massadara, watching as the ships started in, and the estimated positions of their inertialess fighter force. Then to Sestius, all through the wormhole coms of the ships involved. He stayed on that one for a moment, thinking of the people that had elected to stay on that world he had visited soon after being informed that he was the Emperor. He didn't know how many were still alive, and could only hope that some were.

He cycled through all fifteen of the systems his fleet was hitting, every place they knew the Cacas had a strong presence. Sean had studied a lot of old Earth history. To him, this was like being in the mid twenty to late twenty-first century, when naval wars across the globe were still pretty common. And an Admiral might have control of ships across millions of square kilometers of ocean. That had been the effect of radio, followed by satellites, on the way they made war. And wormholes were having the same effect. Prior to wormholes, it was more like warfare from the days of sail. Fleets were sent into battle, the results not known for weeks, sometimes months. Emperors sat in fear for their navy when they went to war.

I could have stayed in the palace and gotten the same information I'm getting now, thought Sean with a smile. *But it wouldn't be the same. This way I'm actually in the battle, even if I am hanging back with the rear echelon.*

In three the attacks had already finished. The

Cacas had been swept away by the stronger Imperial forces. Casualties were still high, but the systems had been freed, washed clean with human blood. Six still in various stages of battle. Four were going the human way, but two were not. The human forces were fighting hard, but it didn't look like they were going to snatch victory from the jaws of defeat that were clamping down on them.

He shook his head. There was nothing he could do in any of those fights, no miraculous commands that could turn the tide. Right now he had to concentrate on this fight, even though he had pledged that he wouldn't try to micromanage. But he still intended to exert overall control of the fight.

And here we go, he thought, watching as the inertialess fighters started to pull away from the carriers. This fight was in its early stages, but as far as he was concerned, they were committed to this battle. The Counterstrike was on, and this next couple days would either see them kick the Cacas out of the Empire, or prove they couldn't.

Chapter Twenty-five

You must not fight too often with one enemy, or you will teach him all your art of war.   Napoleon Bonaparte

CONUNDRUM SPACE. JANUARY 8TH, 1002.

"We're picking up some anomalous signals from outside the system," reported the Fleet's senior Sensor Officer over the holo.

"What kind of anomalous signals?" asked Great Admiral M'tinisasitow, glancing over at the system holo that showed only his own forces. *And we can't even track ships reliably in real time, due to that damned hyper turbulence. When, by all the Gods, will it finally stop?*

"We really don't know, my Lord. They match nothing I have ever seen, or anything in the data banks. I surmise they could be human ships, jumping down through hyper dimensions, or into normal space. Unfortunately, the turbulence is too severe for us to hear through it.   But, as we are expecting them to strike, I think this could be a sign of it."

"I agree," said the Great Admiral. "Good work. And keep listening for any other signs." *Not that he's likely to hear much. That was probably their ships dropping down into normal space, and we'll have the Gods' own time trying to track them by grabber emissions.*

"All ships are to go to maximum readiness status," he said next, tapping into the general com system that would go all over the ship, including his com specialists. "I believe the humans are on the outer edges of the system. All ships, ready all weapons and raise cold plasma fields to maximum. Active scans to cover all possible approach lanes."

He stopped talking and the com link severed. His voice continued to speak in the background, as it would on all of the ships for the next several minutes, so that every warrior would get the message.

He looked back at the system tactical holo, highlighting what he thought were the most likely avenues of approach for the humans. He had done this very thing almost a week before, when the hyper distortion first manifested itself. And he had arranged for some surprises to be placed well out of the system near those avenues of approach. *This hyper phenomenon is something the humans hope to use to surprise us. But it works both ways, and we can use it to surprise them as well. Probably not enough to win the battle, but maybe enough to shock them into making mistakes.*

*   *   *

GRILYON BASE SYSTEM.

The *Grilyon* Admiral raised a drinking horn into the air and shouted out a toast in his own language. The thousand males and females in the great hall echoed his toast, which played back in Teranglo in Commodore Sung's portable translator. All of the males and females were robust, muscular, and equal in every way in the Grilyon society. All were warriors, a people who reveled in combat. In fact, she had seen blood drawn a dozen times this evening. But merely blood, shed with their own claws. She had not seen anyone seriously injured.

To them it is sport, she thought, shaking her head, then taking a bite of the roasted meat on the plate before her. *The entire society seems to be made up of people who love to fight.*

She had been challenged a couple of times herself tonight, but the Admiral had stepped in each time and defused the situation, explaining that the humans were guests that did not understand their ways. Most of her crews had been left in the ships that orbited this class M world. She had foreseen that there might be problems with these cantankerous creatures. So she had only come down with her other captains, some of the anthropologists, and a few of her Marines.

She looked up to see another of the aliens staring at her, a behavior that normally presaged a challenge. She glanced over at the Grilyon leader to see him studying her intently. *He wants to get our measure*, she thought. *To know if we can fight with honor. But I wouldn't stand a chance against their weakest female.*

"Perhaps I should accept their challenge," said Major Saul Briggs, the overall commander of her Marine detachment.

She looked over at the man, who appeared to be as tough as any human she had ever seen. *He ought to be*, she thought of the former Force Recon trooper. Very few of her people were augmented. He was one of the few.

"I would prefer we not get in a fight with these people," she told the Major.

"And that might be just what we need to do," said Dr. Hau Quon, the chief anthropologist of the squadron. "After all, these people come from a society which holds martial prowess in high regard. And so far we have not proven that we have any."

That's nothing less than the truth, thought the Commodore. When the Gilyons had found them, they were running from what looked like a lesser force. *They have no reason to believe we aren't weaklings. And why would they want to ally themselves with weaklings?*   "We're explorers, Dr. Hau. Not warriors."

"And we're still members of his Majesty's Fleet," said Briggs, fingering the Star of David he wore around his neck. "On a mission to forge alliances. And these guys look like they would make some damned good allies."

Sung had to admit that the Major was correct. The Grilyons were individually a strong people, even if they didn't control that large a fleet. And they were not bullies. Not really, despite their genetic predilection for combat. They weren't conquerors. Weaker species they left alone.

"I would challenge our new friends," said the male who had been staring at the Commodore. "I would test their courage and their spirit. What say you, humans?"

Sung looked over at Briggs. "Do you think you can take him? Or at least put up a good enough fight to gain their respect?"

"Hell yes, ma'am," said the Major, looking at the large Grilyon, who was a strong looking warrior even among their fit looking people.

"My Chief of Ground Warriors accepts your challenge with great honor, Warrior," she told the male.

Everyone at the tables stood up and hurried toward the fighting ring. Not every match had gotten this kind of attention, but this was something every one of the thousands in the hall had been waiting for. The big male Grilyon stood on one side, taking off his weapons' belt, then his upper fur and scale coat. He was barefooted, as were all of his people when not wearing full, high tech combat gear.

Briggs sat down and pulled off his boots, then stood up and took off his shirt. Sung had to admit that the Major was a fine specimen, with muscles rolling under his tight skin. He did a couple of stretches, amazing her with his flexibility. *And I'm not sure why I'm surprised. He's a fighter, and leader of fighters. It's his business to stay in fighting trim.* Her eyes moved between the human and the alien, and she wondered again about the wisdom of letting the Major fight.

"To first blood," called out the leader of the aliens, raising his hand in the air. The Grilyon warrior moved a couple of meters into the ring, and Briggs followed his example. The leader dropped his hand, and the grinning alien warrior charged forward.

Sung was sure she had never seen anything move so fast from a standing start. The warrior covered ten meters in a second and bound into the air, claws on his feet extended, hands gripped into striking fists. Aimed right at the Major, who moved out of the way in a blur that made the alien seem downright slow in comparison.

The Grilyon hit the ground with a frustrated growl, then swung a backhand at the human. Briggs caught the swing on a double forearm block, his feet sliding in the dirt from the force of the blow. The alien jabbed with his other hand, catching Briggs in the chest and driving the air from his lungs. The hand that had struck first came back, opening into striking claws, and came down at the Major's face.

Again Briggs was not there, sliding to the right and hitting the Grilyon in the back with a flurry of punches, so fast they looked like a blur to the spectators. There was the sound of intaken breath, and cheers for the Major. The warrior grunted from the strikes, that weren't enough to take him down.

With a roar the warrior spun on his heel and

jumped forward, right into a left legged side kick into his stomach that drove the breath from the creature. As it staggered back Briggs slid forward, launching another flurry of blows, punches, backhands, chops, striking the alien about the head and shoulders. Sung knew her Marine didn't know the soft spots of this creature, and was trying to defeat him with sheer number and strength of blows.

The male reached out for the Major with a clawed hand, trying to grab the Marine's shoulder. Briggs dropped lower to the ground in a crouch, under the claw, and pummeled the ribs of the Grilyon male with a series of short sharp blows. The thudding of the fists on bone sounded across the ring, and many of the spectators sucked in another breath at the display of martial prowess.

Briggs stepped back, looking over at Sung. The male stood there, trying to catch his breath, and she was fairly sure that the Grilyon had a broken rib or two, or whatever passed for them in his species.

"When will you call this fight?" she asked the Admiral, looking over at his predator's face.

"It ends at first blood," he said, grinning. "Not before."

And now she saw the fatal flaw in this challenge, as far as her man was concerned. The Grilyons were made to draw blood. And Briggs had nothing on him that would penetrate that leathery hide. *Maybe he can just take a superficial hit*, she thought, wondering how she could get that idea to the Major. It was obvious to all that Briggs was punishing the alien, and could probably kill him, given time. And that was another result that the Commodore did not want to think about. The Grilyons saw fighting as an enjoyable pastime, but she wasn't sure how they would react to one of their own being killed by an outsider.

Briggs ducked under another blow, then blocked a second, then threw a wheel kick into the warrior's face. The alien's head snapped back, and blood spurted from his mouth.

"First blood," yelled the alien leader, stepping into the ring and laying a hand on Briggs' shoulder. "You are the victor, human."

The large warrior wiped the blood from his mouth with the side of a hand, then stepped forward to put his other hand on the Marine's opposite shoulder. "You fought well, human.   I would be proud to fight beside you, and call you brother."

"As would all of us," echoed the leader, looking around the pit to see head motions of agreement. He looked over at the Commodore. "We will fight beside your people, Natasha Sung.   Against the honorless vermin you now battle."

Sung looked over at her smiling Marine Major, now arm in arm with the warrior he had just battled, lifting a mug of their strong ale into the air. *Not the way I would have gone about forging an alliance. But hell, whatever works.*

*   *   *

MASSADARA. JANUARY 8TH, 1002.

"How are things going at your end, Baggett?" asked the Planetary Commander from his HQ. The com was coming through a couple of thousand kilometers of fiber optic cable, allowing them to talk without giving their positions away to the ships in orbit. Most of which were moving out of orbit to deal with the threat that was now striking at their force in the outer system.

"We're ready to go, sir," replied the commander of the First Heavy Infantry Division, his massive suit leaning against one of the holo projectors that would soon be employed to mask the surface of the planet. The fifty ton unit was currently powered down, waiting for its chance to project a holographic image into the sky that would obscure the visual observation of the surface. There were four hundred of the units in his area of operations, along with several hundred jammer sets that would mask the electronic signatures of every Imperial unit as soon as they powered up.

"In fact, the boys and girls are chomping at the bit, General." He looked over at the King Tyrannosaur tank that sat under its high tech passive cammo covering, making it look like a small hill under the canopy of tall needle leaf trees. The tank was also powered down, the crew aboard, ready to get her up and running in seconds when the order was given. *And they know exactly where to strike*, he thought, pulling up the tactical map of the area, and the large force of Cacas who had recently landed and were frantically setting up defenses. More of their shuttles were landing every minute, ferrying the troops down from the almost helpless troop transports still in orbit, at least giving the soldiers a fighting chance, and not just making them targets of warships they couldn't fight.

"Almost," said the planetary commander.

The clock inside the heads of both men's implants ticked off the seconds. Until, right as Baggett's hit zero, the voice of the commander spoke. "Roll them out, Baggett."

"Yes, sir," shouted the General into the com, then

switched to the broadcast circuit for his brigade commanders. "The word is go," he said into the com, listening to the jubilant acknowledgements that came back.

Not very professional, he thought with a smile, not about to castigate anyone for the feelings he knew were going through his commanders. *They want payback, for family, friends, even the strangers they had taken oaths to protect.* Thoughts of Sestius, of his losing battle against the Cacas, giving ground as his attached units, his people, bled out. As the civilians he was supposed to be protecting died by the thousands. *And now we get some.*

The holo projector came to life, rolling into position beneath an opening, then firing a powerful blast of laser light in a wide cone up into the sky. The clouds overhead flared with bright light, the clear areas with a canvas of colors. The other projectors added their light, until an area of hundreds of thousands of square kilometers were no longer under visual observation from space.

The electronic jamming commenced at the same time, each unit putting out megawatts of static across all frequencies, blotting out enemy communications, covering up the electronic emissions of Imperial battle suits and vehicles. The division's main battle computer, secreted in a secure cavern, was keeping track of all the changes to the electronic jamming, switching the division's com through frequencies that were clear for seconds at a time.

At the same moment the ground based equipment powered up, a hundred hypervelocity rockets flew into the air, pulling a thousand gravities. A couple of seconds after launch, over fifteen kilometers into the sky, the rockets detonated. Two thirds of them blew out clouds of particulate matter that added more obscuring potential to the atmosphere. Thirty-two of them detonated with the flash and crack of nuclear warheads, ionizing the atmosphere, adding even more *junk* to look through.

The shore guns fired next, sending up their shells and beams to hit the bombardment ships that still sat in orbit. As soon as all the obscurants were in place they lost target lock, and continued to fire on where the targets were predicted to go in the next several minutes.

"Artillery, open fire," was the next command over the com net. The hundred and twenty tubes of division artillery opened fire, sending their one hundred millimeter shells on shallow high velocity arcs into the enemy targets. Most of the shells had warheads in the kiloton range, rippling with nuclear fire across the Caca positions. Some were heavier rounds, carrying hundred kiloton warheads meant to ravage fortifications and destroy armored vehicles, their preferred targets.

The tank behind him rumbled into life, lifting on its grabbers, its electromag field coming up in a shimmering bubble. The tank moved forward, between the trees, knocking down one that got in the way.

Baggett walked away from the projection unit and back to his command bunker. It was not his role to close with the enemy, that was only a desperation move, with no place in this battle. His job was oversight, to make sure his brigades were doing what he wanted them to do. As it was the brigade commanders' jobs to see to the dispositions of their battalions, to accomplish their missions, while the battalion commanders saw to the employment of their companies.

Still, the division commander stared at his HUD as

he ran to the bunker, worried about his plan, and the people under him, who would be fighting and killing, or fighting and dying. And the Cacas, who would not roll over and die, no matter the odds. They were still living creatures, no matter their sins. And it was his job to make sure than none of them ever saw home again.

*   *   *

Captain Svetlana Komorov sat in her command chair with her eyes locked on the her tactical display. *Two minutes until we drop our bubble*, she thought, her stomach flip flopping with anxiety.   Up to this point they had been all but invulnerable, forging into a war zone, the only real risk that they might run into something solid on the way. When they dropped the bubbles they would again be less than a hundred very small ships, attacking a group of over two hundred that were heading their way.

"All weapons armed and ready," said the Weapons' Tech.

"Preparing to raise cold plasma field," came the call from back in engineering.

Which will protect us for about a hundredth of a second against a full power warship beam. Don't get cold feet now, Svetlana. You know you're going to hammer these assholes.

The two minutes seemed to simultaneously stretch into forever and run like a speeding animal. It almost caught her by surprise when it ticked to zero.

"Dropping bubble, now," called out the Pilot. The magnetic field pulled the negative matter back to the side pylons of the ship, where it was sucked into storage. A second behind the cold plasma ejected into the strengthening magnetic field, and the fighter had as much protection as possible.

"What the hell?" blurted out the Weapons' Tech as

something flared on the screen to their port.

The Captain looked over in time to see another of her ships flare into plasma as something struck. She looked forward, seeing the ships they had come to strike, forty-five light seconds ahead, fifty-six seconds at their current velocity of point eight c. And those ships were already firing on them, when they couldn't possibly be seeing them for another forty-five seconds. Radar was picking up millions of small objects in flight, projectiles fired from close in weapons systems, exploding as they traveled from between ten and twenty light seconds from the firing ships. The electromag fields were able to repel the metallic objects that were under a gram. Anything larger, at the speeds the fighters were traveling, and they would have a pellet ripping through their ships at point nine five light closing.

There were one hundred and ninety-seven enemy vessels, about what they expected. And every one of those ships was putting out every beam weapon they had in sweeps across the space from a position about ten degrees to port, and forty-five degrees in a circle around that position. Which meant that every one of her ships was in that cone of fire. The only thing saving them now was that the cone covered such an immense volume of space.

Another fighter exploded, this too far to the side and rear for her to see, only noticed as its icon blinked twice and disappeared. *And a hell of a way to mark the deaths of brave crew.*

"Fire first volley of missiles," she ordered. "Send that command out to all ships."

The Weapons' Tech looked at her in surprise. Doctrine called for them to fire when they had entered the visual range of their enemy, at the point where they were seen, still forty seconds away. *But we may not last that long*, she thought, as the ship bucked under her slightly from the release of the short ranged missiles, which boosted at ten thousand gravities while they acquired their targets.

A trio of weapons exploded ahead, hit by the enemy defensive fire, their huge warheads filling space with heat and radiation. More objects exploded, including some more of her ships, and she cried inside at the damage her command was taking. The Pilot was now maneuvering frantically, trying to avoid the objects their sensors were showing in their way. The ship's computer was helping immensely in categorizing and prioritizing targets. They bore in closer, the ships now adding vector to carry them over the enemy formation, it now considered much too dangerous to punch through as originally planned.

Warheads started to explode among the enemy ships, some direct strikes. Some near misses. But not enough kills. "Fire second salvo," she ordered, and the fighter again bucked as two more missiles were released. Moments later the other ships of the force released.

We're going to make it, thought the Captain as her ship's vector pulled on a course that would take them over the enemy force at five light seconds range. There were only forty ships left in her command, disastrous losses, and another ship blinked off the holo as she watched. But the second salvo was savaging the enemy vessels.

We're going to make it, she thought once again, an instant before a laser from an enemy battleship swept through her ship. Only a thousandth of a second contact, and all that was needed to convert the fighter into exploding plasma, some of which disappeared as it contacted the now freed negative matter which cancelled it out.

Thirty-one ships made it past the enemy formation, leaving behind only forty-one fully functional enemy vessels, a score of drifting hulks, and the plasma remains of the rest.

Chapter Twenty-six

I am tired and sick of war. Its glory is all moonshine. It is only those who have neither fired a shot nor heard the shrieks and groans of the wounded who cry aloud for blood, for vengeance, for desolation. War is hell. William Tecumseh Sherman

CONUNDRUM SPACE. JANUARY 9TH, 1002.

Sean stood on the deck of his command holo room, looking over the remains of the battle for Massadara space. There were very few enemy ships remaining. Most of those were drifting hulks, in the process of being boarded. Always a risky proposition, as the ships could be ordered to self-destruct while the humans were aboard. But there were always some captures, and hopefully some Caca tech to examine.

"How is your ground offensive going, Colonel General Sapatra?" he asked the commander of the Massadara planetary ground forces on the com.

"Splendidly, your Majesty," replied the General, his face appearing on a com holo. "We are rolling them back on all fronts. It helps that they didn't have the time or the transport to bring their heavy equipment down when they abandoned ship."

Sean pulled up a tactical holo of the planet. All of the fighting was raging over the largest continent, the one that had been the primary habitat of the colonists. There were Cacas on the other continents, maybe a couple of thousand, but nothing that couldn't be taken care of later, after the main continent was secure. "Let me know as soon as you have taken all objectives, General. Sean out."

He switched the tactical holo back to the Conundrum system, the focus of this day's action, and the battle that would decide whether the offensive was success or bust.

"The first of the inertialess fighters should be going in any second, your Majesty," came Kelso's voice over the com.

Sean looked at the holo, cursing under his breath that he wasn't getting the real time info he was used to. Not at that remove. That was part of the price of using the cover of the supernova. They were picking up almost nothing on graviton emissions, which meant they had no idea what was happening outside the range of the visual sensors of his wormhole equipped ships. Or at least not at any time scale that made sense.

"Are the subspace com links up?"

"Not at this time, your Majesty," stated Kelso. "Subspace is not degraded quite to the point of hyper, but it's bad enough where transmissions are almost completely static. Garbage."

"Keep me appraised of any changes Admiral," said Sean, not really expecting any, and not really knowing what else to say."

He switched to the feed from the closest of the attack/stealth ships to the strike, cursing again as he saw the lag time between it and the enemy force, seven light minutes. That frustrated him to no end, so he switched to the forward force, coming in on a forty-eight degree angle to the spinward ecliptic from the main enemy force. Over seven hundred vessels, they included all of the Elysium ships in this prong of the attack, as well as a hundred Klashak vessels, and two hundred human ships. They were on his plot in real time, their information transmitted through the wormhole coms of the several equipped ships of the task group. And they were locking on, or as well as they could without graviton tracking, and releasing swarms of missiles into space on a heading toward the same enemy force the fighters were about to strike. After several salvoes, fourteen thousand missiles, they took aim at the force further into the system, releasing twenty-one thousand more weapons.

So, they have to know that force is here, as well as the one Lenkowski is about to hammer them with. But the rest of us are still from minutes to hours away from visual detection. Everything seemed to be going perfectly according to plan, which really worried him.

He switched the view once again, this time to the tactical holo of the Sestius system, a place still near and dear to his heart. The place he had met his wife, who was now the Empress. There was also a space battle going on there, ships of both sides pounding each other at long range with missiles. Right now it looked like his side was going to win that fight as well, though they would be hurt in the exchange. And there was a land battle going on at the surface of that world as well. But a very different one than that going on at Massadara and Conundrum.

*   *   *

SESTIUS.

Walborski raised a hand in the air and pumped it down twice, signaling the other men to go down on a knee in front of him. The jungle was quiet, unusually so. And hot, which was not unusual in the least.

The Ranger in front of him turned and starting moving his fingers, signing the information he was passing on from the forward scouts. *Fifteen Cacas in a clearing, around a landed shuttle. Seem unaware that we're here.*

Cornelius signaled back, ordering the man to move up to the scout and let him know that the platoon was moving into position. The man nodded, turned, and moved in a crouch, careful to not make any noise. The Lieutenant motioned to his first squad leader, who dropped back for a second, then came up with the other two squad leaders.

The LT motioned to third squad leader to take his men to the right flank, then for second squad to go to the left. He would take first squad up the center with himself, while SanJames stayed in the rear with the two men from platoon headquarters to secure their rear.

Cornelius moved slowly and quietly through the brush, his thermal covering over his head, sweat pouring from his face. His men moved beside him just as quietly. They came up on the scouts and went prone, pointing their weapons into the clearing.

The Cacas were all armored up, the look of ground warriors about them. The shuttle was down in a clearing it had made when it crashed through the jungle canopy. Several large trees had come down with it, and there was still smoke rising from a few small fires.

The Lieutenant raised his rifle to his shoulder, looking right and left to make sure that the men on either side were doing the same. After a nod he looked through his scope, aiming for a weak point on the armor, where it covered the throat of the Caca in flexible plates. He put some tension on his trigger, let out a partial breath, and squeezed. The rifle pushed hard into his shoulder, and a hole instantly appeared at the striking point of the twelve millimeter round. Cornelius put two more shots into the creature from his suppressed rifle as it was going down, all of its fellows following it to the ground.

Cornelius leapt to his feet and ran for the shuttle, jumping over a couple of obstacles in the way, two other men on his flanks. He turned and slid his back against the side of the shuttle to the right of the hatch, dropping his rifle to hang by its strap while he pulled the monomolecular blade from its sheath on his thigh. A Caca came running out of the hatch, to catch the blade in the back before his off foot had made it outside. The Ranger on the other side of the hatch prepped a stun grenade and tossed it into the shuttle. As soon as it went off two Rangers ran into the ship, while the rest of the platoon got up from their positions and fanned out, looking for any of the Cacas they might have missed.

The first Ranger came out of the shuttle. "It's clear, sir. We got all of them."

"Mark the ship for recovery," he told his com specialist, who was carrying the small beacons they would use to tag recoverable alien equipment. "Then we move out." He took the com from his specialist and activated it, looking at the electronic map of the area, noting that there was another shuttle down twelve kilometers to the south. *So we have an opportunity to kill some more before nightfall*, he thought with a smile. That last thought troubled him just a bit, as he wondered how his wife and family would think of him if they knew of the darkness in his heart.

*   *   *

CONUNDRUM SPACE.

"Prepare to jump," called out the Helmsman's

voice over the com.

Commander Marc Dawson looked over the power graphs of the reactor systems. They were at fifty percent of capacity, what was needed for transit through hyper I. The power graphs rose to sixty percent, and the lights dimmed slightly as almost all of that energy was transferred to the hyperdrive projector that opened the hole between hyper I and normal space.

And if everything works properly, we'll be only light seconds from the enemy force, he thought, closing his eyes and looking at the tactical holo that was coming in over his uplink. There was some guesswork involved, and so some chance that they might come out much farther from the enemy than predicted, or even possibly within the Ca'cadasan formation.

"All reactors to full power," he called out over the engineering command circuit, more for the information of the people working around those energy generating devices than to order anything. He controlled the process from this board, and with the push of some panels he had the system up and running at one hundred percent power.

All combat systems across the ship were already fully charged, all batteries at one hundred percent capacity. But that energy would be sucked down in minutes without the matter antimatter reactors pushing more power into the system.

"Electromag fields at full power," called out the Tactical Officer over the com. "Cold plasma injection commencing. Laser rings locking on to targets."

Dawson closed his eyes, pulling up the plot his link was feeding to his occipital lobe. *Shit*, he thought. *The laddies at the top actually got this one right for a change.* They were within five light seconds of the enemy force, which had not been able to track them through hyper. Targeting data was beginning to flood the tactical plot as sensors picked up information on the enemy force. *And they've already been stung a wee bit*, was his next thought, as he saw that some of the icons were blinking orange, the indication that they had taken battle damage, some of them red for severe harm. The harm caused by the attack of the intertialess fighters, and the missiles launched from the task force to spinward.

Augustine shuddered slightly, releasing missiles, firing her on board particle beams. She was also letting loose with all six of her laser rings, which had no recoil, but would still be doing severe damage to whatever targets they hit at the range they were striking from.

And then the superheavy battleship shook some more, the recoil of the wormhole fed particle beams ripping out at point nine nine nine five light, imparting their antimatter loads into the hulls of two target ships.

"Reactors are handling the load just fine," Dawson reported to the bridge, as the liaison officer in that compartment asked for verification of the readings they were getting. "Number four is fluctuating a wee bit, but I'm adjusting the feed manually to smooth that out."

Augustine shook again, this time in a different way. She had been hit by particle beams, a number of them, ripping gouges in her thick armor, here and there penetrating into the areas below. A laser ring went offline as two of the emitter units were destroyed, with three breaks in the circular focuser itself. A missile detonated nearby, one of her own, struck by a laser when only thirty thousand kilometers outside the tube.

One of the enemy ships exploded, a particle beam

eating deep into the superbattleship and causing onboard antimatter to breach containment. It was followed by a scout ship, then a human destroyer that got in the way of a couple of incoming missiles that had targeted a standard battleship.

Now the forces were intermingled, moving past each other, letting their enemies have the full power of their broadsides, every weapon aboard capable of hitting an opponent's ship. The enemy force was moving outward at point one c, while the allied force was moving at point two c in the opposite direction, and decelerating at their maxim rate to keep proximity as long as possible. Still, they were only intermingled for ten seconds or so, and then the ships were moving away from each other.

Augustine shook again, this time with a heavy hit. Dawson caught a flash out of the corner of his eye on a side holo, turning just in time to see the entire crew of the number six reactor cut down, turned to ash and steam by a particle beam that ripped through the hull armor, machinery, and the redundant armor of the reactor compartment. It shouldn't have been possible to get that kind of penetration. By chance a dozen beams had hit that area of the hull, blasting through, leaving an opening for another, capital ship beam to slice through the open space, which hadn't self-repaired yet, and hit the armor of the reactor compartment.

The crew all died, and the reactor itself was hit. It was a tough piece of equipment. It had to be, to handle the reaction of matter and antimatter. But the casing took damage, severing many of the incoming power leads, welding metals together, totally trashing the compartment.

"Containment breach imminent," called out the

voice of the computer that monitored all engineering operations. "Containment breach imminent." *Which means the damned system can't tell me when it's going to blow.* "Captain. One of the reactors is about to blow. I'm going to have to jettison it."

"Go ahead, Chief Engineer," said Captain Javier Montoya, the expression on his face over the holo showing a man who was already handling all he could. "Do what you need to do, just keep giving me power."

"That's a roger," said Dawson, pulling up the control panel that allowed him to fire the reactor capsules out at high velocity into space, in such a case as was going on at this time. He touched the panel for number six, which expanded on the board, then placed his thumb over the identification panel, which read both his print and his DNA. After that, he pushed the jettison panel, which changed color, first blinking red, then going steady. He pressed down on the panel, looking at the schematic of the reactor, waiting to see the representation move up through the top of the ship and into space. The outside hatch blew open, and Dawson waited for the ejection. And waited, as nothing happened, and the computer voice kept telling him that his death, and that of everyone else aboard, was imminent.

*   *   *

The Great Admiral stared in disbelief at the tactical holo. First, he had been hit by the impossible fighters of the enemy, which had resulted in his losing over a hundred ships. He had punished them as well, his people having learned from the Congreeve engagement what to look for, and when to throw up a blockade of fire. The fighters also gave off some kind of signal when they returned to normal space, a subspace surge that they had barely detected through all the interference. It had been noted at Congreeve, and, while it wasn't much, it did give them just a bit of warning. They didn't have a lock though the signal, but they did have a general direction, and a time, so they had fired everything they had, and had destroyed at least two thirds of the attacking fighters. *And how many ships would I have lost to them if we hadn't perceived that signal.* He knew, of course, that the humans would learn from this, and come up with a new strategy to again give them the edge.

Then he had been hit by the incoming missiles by the enemy task force that had gone around them to spinward, thousands of missiles seeming to come out of nowhere, not even picked up until they were less than a light minute away, and that by active radar and lidar. That also had seemed unfair. So much of modern warfare was based around being able to detect an enemy and his missiles through graviton emissions at long range, and that resource had been swept off the table for this fight. They had gotten lucky in one area. If they couldn't track the missiles by gravitons, neither could the missiles they. His ships went into evasive maneuvers, putting out as much fire as possible, and he had only lost another hundred ships to that strike. He almost expected the enemy to start a vector change and come after him, but it appeared on visual that they were continuing into the system to attack the ships near the inhabited planet, a force the foe outmassed four to one. He had sent a signal to those ships insystem, but he wasn't sure what good it would do, except to tell them their doom was coming. *Maybe they could get away*, he thought for a moment, then dismissed that notion. Of course the enemy would have the system ringed with ships, waiting for his insystem force to do just that.

His fleet had taken a pounding from the human force that had just passed through it. He had at most four hundred ships that were combat capable. And there was sure to be another enemy force on the way in to hit him. Maybe more than one. Any way he looked at it, his force was doomed. So the next thought on his mind was what to do about it. The honor of the Race called for them to die fighting, to never surrender. *But they didn't have a situation like this in mind*, he thought, imagining the almost one million Cacada that were still under his command. *And what kind of treatment can we expect from the humans*, he thought, sure that it wouldn't be good.

I might have a few more minutes to decide, he thought, staring at the holo again, wishing his thoughts could change it. But it was reality that was staring him in the face, and there was nothing he could do to change that. Even his surprise, waiting out in the dark, would not be enough to do more than hurt the enemy some more.

*   *   *

"What's the problem with *Augustine?*" said Sean into the com, looking at the tactical holo zoom of the battle that had just occurred.

His former flagship had all of his attention. He knew many of the people on board that vessel, including the Captain.

"They're reporting problems with one of their reactors," said Kelso over the com. "From what I understand, they're working on it."

Sean used his command override to look at the operating system of the ship in question, coughing as he saw what the problem was. *They're going to blow up*, he thought with a start. A ship like the superheavy battleship might even survive one reactor breach, tough as she was, and especially if they were able to reduce the antimatter feed. But if one reactor went, it might set off others, and the stored antimatter used for all the reactors. Best case scenario, half the crew killed and the ship crippled. Worst case, everyone died. And from what he was seeing, no one was abandoning ship at this time.

"We have missiles on approached," called out an almost panicked voice on the com. "Estimated impact in one minute ten seconds."

Sean switched the holo from the part of the fight he had been watching, to see the icons of thousands of missiles heading his way. *Where in the hell did they come from*, he thought, his attention taken by the fact that his life, and the lives of everyone in the task groups around him, were in deadly danger.

Chapter Twenty-seven

I am not afraid of an army of lions led by a sheep; I am afraid of an army of sheep led by a lion.   Alexander the Great

MASSADARA. JANUARY 9TH, 1002.

Major General Samuel Baggett moved with his security detail on a tour of what had been the front lines. It had been, before the general collapse of the Caca forces. Now it was a field of death and despair, mostly for the aliens. There were bodies everywhere, most of them in the distinctive ground combat armor worn by the Ca'cadasans that, while giving decent protection, seemed to have lesser capabilities than the human version. *That will probably change in the future*, thought Baggett, recalling that the Cacas had surely captured many human suits, and were just as sure to reverse engineer them in the near future.

Many of the suits had large holes burned through them, acrid smoke still rising, the victims of particle beams. A line of suits nearby were literally torn apart, obviously hit by a high velocity projectile, probably from a tank. One of the thousand ton vehicles sat on a hilltop with its gun leveled on a large cluster of Cacas who were prisoners, reminding them of the futility of their position. The prisoners were sans suits. Actually sans all clothing, standing with bowed heads under the guns of heavy infantry troops.

An explosion sounded in the far distance, a short dull crump. There was still some resistance, the Cacas being a stubborn people. The ones they had under guard had taken enough between the artillery and infantry supported tanks, and had gone from fiercely resistant to cowed in an instant.

Something flew over with a sonic boom. Baggett looked up into the clouds, now their natural color as the holo projectors were off line. Now it was to human advantage to have unobstructed vision of the surface, and clear communications. A pair of atmospheric fighters flew over, just off the assault ships that had inserted into orbit. There were four of the ships, with a hundred of the fighters each, as well as their ground troops, which were being shuttled down.

There would still be scattered resistance for the next couple of days, but the humans would be the ones to call down strikes from orbit. *We paid our cost in blood too*, thought Baggett, looking at the line of troopers that were laying on the ground, sealed into preserving cryo containers that would keep their remains intact until interment. That interment would be here, on Massadara, the place they had fought and died for. That was the tradition of the Army, for all but nobles, who would be sent back to their home planets for burial. He knew there were several of those as well.

"It's always sad to see the aftermath, isn't it?" asked Brigadier General Dagni Thorwaldsdottir, the Assistant Division Commander. She had been cleared for combat just before the start of the campaign, but had spent her time in the command bunker, as per Baggett's orders.

"It sure is, Dag," said Baggett, looking into the pretty face revealed by her retracted faceplate. "At least it wasn't the bloodbath it was back in Fenri space."

"And what will happen to them?" she asked, motioning with her chin at the hundred odd prisoners gathered below.

"They'll be fed, interrogated, then used to get whatever information we can about their strengths and weaknesses."

"In violation of the Accords?" said Dagni with a tone of distaste.

"They didn't sign the Accords," said Baggett, looking over the ruins of what had been a human town of ten thousand, his mind's eye seeing the destruction of Cimmeria, and so many other densely populated systems. He spat. "And they sure didn't follow the spirit of them. So let them suffer, I say. The bastards deserve whatever they get."

"We're getting a com from Grand Fleet Admiral Mgonda," came a call over the net. "On the general circuit."

"Put it through," he told the tech. "Put it through to the whole division."

"To all units in the Massadara system," came a voice over the net. "Stand by for a cast from the System Commander."

There was dead air for a few moments, then the deep voice of a man used to command came over the com. A voice everyone in this sector was familiar with.

"To the valiant Spacers, Soldiers and Marines in the Massadara system. I was proud to send a message to the Emperor moments ago. That message was, 'we have met the enemy, and he is ours'. I am happy to say that all organized resistance in the system, in space and on the ground, has ended. The commander of the Ca'cadasan forces in the system has called on his people to surrender to us, unconditionally. We are in the process of rounding up the last of the Cacas not in our custody. They have been ordered to surrender, to come out into the open without weapons, with all hands raised into the air." There was a moment's pause. "And if they do not come out into the open, to relinquish their persons to our custody, they are to be destroyed by whatever means necessary. I would not have any of our people killed by the dastardly actions of an enemy who had already capitulated. Mgonda, Commander Imperial Forces Massadara System, out."

Cheering rose all around as the soldiers of the First Heavy Infantry Division digested the message. They had survived the battle, the Cacas had been defeated, and the Empire was well on the way of throwing the murderous bastards out of its space.

Baggett linked into the command circuit to get the rundown of the battle as told by its casualty figures. While his division had rolled over the enemy, the other two had hit much stiffer resistance. They had still won, but at a higher cost, if nothing like what Baggett had seen in his last posting. And the Fleet? They had won, with heavy casualties. They had destroyed over three billion tons of Caca warships, at the cost of three point six billion tons of their own. More importantly, they had lost over a million spacers, which made the land battle losses seem like nothing. *Not nothing,* he thought. *Every one of those people is someone's spouse or lover, brother or sister, son or daughter, maybe even a parent.*

He looked again on the naked Cacas, shivering under the guns of his soldiers, and wanted to give the command to shoot. But that would destroy his career, and, more important, his humanity. With a shake of his head, he turned away, walking to the sounds of a distant firefight, wanting this madness to end while he still had a soul.

*   *   *

SUPERHEAVY BATTLESHIP *AUGUSTINE I.*

Dawson grabbed the laser cutter head from the tool locker, then ran into the lock leading to the reactor chamber. The outer door to the lock was set into the containment vessel that the reactor compartment sat in. The inner was set into the reactor compartment itself. Both doors were of heavy construction, barriers to the radiation within the compartment.

Four engineers ran into the lock with the Commander, closing the door behind. Dawson activated the inner door and stepped into the compartment, hauling the heavy cutter head that the strength of his suit allowed him to carry.

The radiation meter on his suit went off the scale, and he saw why immediately. There was a large hole in the side of the reactor, and the chamber was flooded with neutrons. That was not the only damage apparent. The chamber was a complete disaster, gashes through alloy supports and control runs, systems melted, a seemingly hopeless wreck. *And I've got almost no time to get two systems online, and the damage cut away that's holding this bitch in place.* A wave of nausea passed through him from the radiation, which was another concern. But not more of one than the reactor that was threatening to go critical.

"Get on that feed there and cut off the antimatter going in," he told off one engineer, then pointed to another. "And see if you can start the hydrogen feed going." That would take care of one problem. There was raw anti-hydrogen sitting within the fluctuating magnetic field of the reactor, and no hydrogen for it to react with. The reactor was no longer in vacuum, and some air was getting into the containment field, hence the radiation from the minor reaction. But not enough to clear it.

Dawson took a look at the ready antimatter containers, attached to the outside of the compartment, and used to heat up the volatile substance as it was fed in from the outside stores, before feeding it into the reactor. And from what he was seeing on the schematic on his HUD, it was still feeding anti-hydrogen into the reactor through the nonfunctioning regulator valve, adding to the problem.

If the reactor blows it's not really that much of a problem. But if the ready antimatter goes with it, and it's almost sure to, then we have real problems. And the feed from the ready tanks was also jammed, no, in reality, gone, so there was no way to evacuate the tanks.

"Cut those supports through," he told the other two engineers in his team, pointing at the two heavy structures holding the reactor to the chamber wall. They had been hit hard by the particle beam, and sections had pushed through the skin and welded to the outer compartment, holding the containment cell in place.

As those people headed for that task, he moved to the control run that led to the ejection charges and grabbers, that were here to push the reactor out of the ship. The charges were only there to start the fifty meter tall compartment on its way, at which time the grabbers would accelerate it out into space and away from the ship.

Dawson opened the control run and found the superconducting cable inside was gone, totally vaporized by the beam that had struck it. He continued to open more of the run, until he found the still intact end, then back the other way until he found that terminator.   Reaching into his bag, he pulled out a spool of superconductor and attached it with nanite spray at the severed end closest to the internal switching. He then ran the cable to the other end and attached it.

"You should have control of the ejection process now," he told his Assistant Chief Engineer in Engineering Central Control.

"I'm not getting any signal," she said into the com, her voice controlled, but quivering on the edge of panic.

"I've cut the antimatter feed," shouted the engineering rating working that task.

Too late, thought Chief Engineer, monitoring the buildup in the reactor.

"The hydrogen feed is gone, sir," said the other rating. "We need a new unit."

Shit. We don't have time. "How's it coming on those supports?"

"We're almost through the second one now, sir."

"Everyone else out of here," he shouted into the com. "Now."

The other ratings ran to the lock and cycled through, while the man with the cutter continued to work. Dawson cut the run from the far end, then pushed the cable into a remote control box. He checked the unit, saw that everything was in working order, and turned his attention to the man still cutting away.

"It's free," yelled the man.

And I'm sorry, Spacer, he thought, pushing the button on the control box.

The charges went off underfoot, and the grabbers immediately took over, accelerating the capsule up and out at over a thousand gravities. Death for Dawson and his engineer was instantaneous, as they were crushed within their suits by the hundreds of gravities overload.

Two seconds later, with the capsule over twenty kilometers above the ship, the reactor breached, followed by the breach of the ready stores, a gigaton blast that turned every bit of the capsule into fast moving plasma and radiation. *Augustine* took her share of the heat and radiation, but the ship survived, still decelerating for her return to action, and another go into harm's way.

*   *   *

HEAVY CRUISER *MANILA*.

"Missile impact in three minutes," called out the voice of the Tactical Officer of the *Manila*. Klaxons were going off all over the ship, including the control room where the Emperor stood.

The tactical plot showed the incoming missiles, spread out in formations that would distribute their attack over several minutes. Not the best of formations for an attack, but they had the advantage of having closed before detection, making counter missile engagement short and indecisive. The plot also showed all of *Manila's* escorts moving at best emergency speed to get between the missiles and the heavy cruiser. A moment later all of the escort ships for the carriers started to move away from their charges, frantically trying to join the other light cruisers and destroyers in the screen. And leaving their hyper VII fleet carriers unprotected, except for their own defensive fire.

"We need to get you out of here, your Majesty,"

said Senior Agent Catherine Mays, the head of his protection detail, putting an armored hand on Sean's shoulder. "Please. We have to move."

Sean looked at her for a moment, wanting to protest, to demand that he be allowed to stay at his post. *But my post is nothing in this battle. Everything has run fine without me.* Sean nodded and let her lead him away, the other men and women of the detail forming up around them in the corridor. There were some Marines in the corridor as well, looking all directions to ward off any threat to their Emperor. The corridor was otherwise empty, everyone else on the ship at their battle stations.

"We need to hurry, your Majesty," said the woman, keeping him moving until they got to the sealed hatch near his quarters. At least it had been sealed, up until this moment. Now it was wide open, as was the hatch inside the three meters of open space. And inside of that was his special ejection capsule, with three acceleration couches waiting.

"In you go, Sir," said the woman. "And hurry."

"Missile impact in two minutes," called out the voice over the intercom.

Sean patted the woman on the arm. "Thank you, Catherine. And get your people to their own pods."

Sean walked into the capsule and fell into one of the couches, letting it strap his suit in. Two of the Marines, a Sergeant and a Corporal, followed him in and fell into their couches, slapping their particle beam rifles into the racks provided. The hatch sealed closed, leaving Sean and the two Marines alone.

Kind of silly sending a pair of Marines to guard me, he thought, linking into the ship through the pod's interface. *If we get picked up by an enemy, there isn't a whole lot they can do, except die beside me.* He slapped the pistol holstered by his side, imagining using it if he was picked up by the Cacas, making them kill him so he didn't become some kind of hostage.

The missiles were on the way in, on final approach. Every escort was jamming for all it was worth, doing all they could to mask the heavy cruiser. The *Manila* herself was oriented to put him into space on a path that would hopefully avoid all the debris if multiple ships were shattered.

Twenty light cruisers and fifty destroyers, most of them specialized anti-missile ships, were firing for all they were worth at the incoming missiles. Forty of those ships were interposed between the enemy weapons and the flagship, while the other thirty were further to spinward. They were still targeted by the enemy missiles, but most of the counter fire was directed toward the missiles that could end up targeting the flag. Only the weapons they couldn't bring to bear for the protection of *Manila* were firing in their own defense. Even the carriers were firing everything they had at the missiles coming at the flag squadron, ignoring their own defense.

Sean took a moment to look around the pod, which was much more advanced than the standard model, with three meters of armor and its own electromag field. When he had been told about it, he had insisted that in the future all pods be improved, if not to this standard, then at least enough to significantly improve the chances of his spacers. Then his attention was again taken elsewhere.

And I'm to blame for this, again, thought Sean, watching as the missiles got to the one minute mark, at which time every ship in the force fired a couple volleys of offensive missiles, followed by plasma torps, getting the final defensive fire out. Every one opened up with hundreds of projectile cannon, the rounds set to explode a light second out and fill space with metal.

Sean dismissed the thought, and the blame. He was supposed to be here. He was the rallying point for the Fleet, and everyone had tried their hardest to keep him out of the thick of it. But the enemy had used one of their own tricks against them, and no one was to blame for that. Even if they had thought this was going to happen, space out here was too vast to sweep for ships laying cold.

The missiles the Imperial ships had fired were now detonating, each sending out a hundred one megaton submunitions in a spray that detonated seconds later. Lasers were acquiring missiles, blowing them out of space with a moment's contact. The lack of graviton tracking was affecting the targeting, and they were getting fewer hits than normal. But still hundreds of enemy missiles were dropping off the plot.

Someone was thinking in the fleet that day. Every ship launched scores of countermeasures that sent a signal out to the missiles that mimicked those of the radar striking the vessels. Every ship projected holograms into space that mimicked their shapes to the visual sensors of the missiles. Jamming peaked. In a normal environment this tactic would have had some effect. In an environment without graviton tracking it was devastatingly effective.

Incoming missiles locked on returns that were nothing more than small decoys, or were confused by the visual garbage that filled space. Most of them, the four hundred some odd that made it through the defensive fire, went for proximity kills of objects that were actually much smaller than the target they thought they were going after. One light cruiser and three destroyers still took direct hits, shattering from the impact. Twelve other ships, including *Manila*, took damage from proximity strikes that released heat and radiation into their hulls. And the hyper VII carrier *Zokoku*, the flag of its task group, was left dead in space after five near misses. And then the missile storm was past, a couple of score clear misses sailing off into space.

The klaxons died, and a moment later the hatches leading to the pod opened, revealing a smiling Catherine Mays.

"It's so good to see you again, Senior Agent," said Sean, walking out of the capsule.

"It's good to be seen, your Majesty," said the smiling Agent.

"Kelso. What's going on?" he sent over his com link.

"We backtracked those missiles and located the launching platforms," said the Admiral. "Lenkowski is dispatching some ships to bring them to task."

"Take them out from range, if possible," said Sean, running back into his control room and pulling up the tactical holo. "I don't want to lose any more people than need be."

He looked at the holo as it came back up, breath sucking in as he saw what was going on at the moment. The Elysium/Klashak force was trading missiles with the enemy inner system force. Lenkowski's main force was closing on the primary enemy fleet, trading missiles along the way. And two more of his outer groups were under missile attack from the enemy hidden in the Kuiper belt. "And let those two groups under attack know how to handle that attack. They might do even better than we did in their own defense."

*   *   *

SUPERBATTLESHIP *ANASTASIA ROMANOV*.

Lenkowski was staring at his own tactical holo as his ships moved within beam range of the enemy. The missile exchange had not gone his way, and he had lost many more ships than the simulations had shown he would. The enemy was grievously wounded as well, but still had more beam based firepower than he did.

Just wish I had a couple of the superheavy units, he thought, as *Anastasia Romanov* shook from another particle beam hit. One of his standard battleships exploded, having taken more than her systems could stand. A heavy cruiser, then a couple destroyers followed suit. Moments later a Caca superbattleship blew.

Looking at the figures, Len was not sure how much of a command he would have when he flew through the enemy formation. He was pretty sure they would have more, just as he was sure that the rest of the Imperial ships in the system would put paid to whatever enemy were left alive after he was gone. *Not that it will do any of the crews of this task group any good. I should have come in through hyper and dropped into normal space just outside the barrier, just like the last task group had done*. That group had almost killed its forward velocity in an attempt to come back out and attack again, and was currently exchanging missiles with the Cacas. *And now it's too late to jump, since we'll be crossing the barrier any second now*.

"We're taking a pounding, sir," said the ship's

Captain over the com. "Do you want us to switch over to accelerate through them?"

"No, dammit," growled Len as the ship shuddered again. "Continue decel. We need to extend this engagement out as much as possible, hurt them as much as we can."

"Yes, sir," said the Captain, looking not happy at all about the order, but obeying it.

"Sir," said the Fleet Tactical Officer. "The Margravi ships are accelerating."

"They're what?" blurted Lenkowski, looking at the tactical holo that showed the almost hundred vessels of the allied task force putting on the gees. "Get me their admiral on the com."

A moment later he found himself looking into the spider like face of the alien commander. "What are you doing, Admiral?" asked Lenkowski, realizing that he was actually talking to the entire linked crew of that battleship, represented by this one member.

"We are doing what is necessary, Admiral," said the alien. Its eyes clamped shut for a moment as the bridge behind it shook. Len could see the confusion in the six eyes, a sign that casualties had occurred aboard the ship, and the group mind was having to readjust. "We are not important, except as the defenders of our species, and through them, our allies. So we are striking in the only way that assures success."

They're going to ram, thought Lenkowski. *Dear God, no. They can't do that.* "Admiral. As your commanding officer, I order you to go back into deceleration mode and stick with the fleet."

"And as an allied commander, we must refuse that order, Admiral, and do what we must."

The com went blank, and even though Lenkowski

called for his Com Officer to get them back, he knew it wouldn't happen. The insectoids, who really had little in the way of individual identity, respected the singular minds of their fellow beings. And saw no choice but to sacrifice themselves to save those minds.

Len sat back and watched the tactical holo, as ship after ship from both sides dropped off, while the viewers showed their massive explosions in space. And on his right flank the Margravi ships pulled ahead, aiming for the enemy vessels in a suicide charge. Several of the Margravi vessels exploded under enemy fire, small destroyers, followed by some cruisers. Then they started to strike, a cruiser plowing into a superbattleship, a destroyer into a supercruiser. All hundred of the Margravi ships died. Fifty-three struck targets, in most cases larger than they were, and the Ca'cadasan left flank dissolved into nothing.

*   *   *

"Get us out of here," yelled the Great Admiral, watching as the enemy ships did the unthinkable and took out his entire left flank in a suicide charge. "Order the fleet to retreat." He felt panic running through him. *I was supposed to be the conqueror, and they have thwarted me at every turn.* He couldn't even swear revenge against these creatures. His resources were used up, while there seemed no end to the humans.

"Where would we go, my Lord," asked the Helm Officer, while the Com Officer looked back at him with confusion.

"Away from here. We need to gain space and get into hyper, so we have a chance at running."

The Helm Officer gave a head motion of agreement and started working his board. *There is no chance of running*, thought the Great Admiral. *But it's either that, or stay here and die.*

"Get me the commanders of my task groups on the com," he told the Com Officer, then waited for the well-known visages to appear on com holos surrounding him. "This is what we are going to do, my leaders," he told them, then outlined the plan that would sacrifice most of them, so that his ship and a force of escorts would get away.

*   *   *

"Enemy ships are accelerating, your Majesty," called out Kelso.

Sean nodded his head as he watched the tactical holo that showed the Ca'cadasan ships, what were left of them, vectoring away from Lenkowski's force at their maximum acceleration. *The Margravi panicked them*, he thought, still unable to get the images of the vessels of his allies sacrificing themselves to achieve victory out of his mind.

"Any way we can stop them?" he asked, watching as missile icons continued to move back and forth between the forces.

"I don't see how, your Majesty," said Kelso. "Lenkowski still might be able to kill some of their ships. In fact, I would say it's a sure thing he'll continue killing them. But a lot of them are going to get away."

"I want their flagship stopped. Have we identified it?"

"We think we have, your Majesty. But it's surrounded by other vessels."

"Send out an order to stop it, at all costs," said Sean, clenching his fists. "At all costs, Admiral. I want their leader, alive if possible, but definitely he is not to leave the system."

*   *   *

After hours of running the Caca force was finally away from most of the enemy ships. They had run into the system for about an hour, then started vectoring back out. *We'll be able to jump to hyper in another two hours*, thought the Great Admiral, looking at the viewer which showed the multitude of stars in this Galactic arm. *Then let them try and catch us*. His ships were still capable of faster acceleration than most of the enemy ships, and all had the better shielding that allowed them to transit hyper at higher velocities.   And once they were in hyper.

"We're tracking missiles," came the call from the Tactical Officer.

"Where?" yelled the Great Admiral, wondering if his last plan was about to be crushed.

"Off the starboard stern," said the Tactical Officer, looking back with wide eyes.

"Time to impact, you idiot?" growled the Great Admiral.   As the last word left his mouth the ship shook like it was about to come apart, followed by two more massive strikes. The Great Admiral was standing up at that point, his helmet retracted, nothing to protect his head as he fell back and slammed his crown on the Com Officer's board. Blackness enfolded him, and he knew no more, for the moment.

*   *   *

"We got him," yelled Ngovic, thrusting a fist into the air.

Suttler smiled as he watched the warheads going off on the enemy ship. All were in the two hundred megaton range, not traveling fast enough to add much kinetic energy to their strikes. One missile hit the bow of the ship, taking out a good portion of its grabber ring.   The other two hit the ventral and dorsal hyperdrive projectors respectively, destroying them. That ship would not be going into hyper anytime soon.

Four other of the enemy ships were hit, two going up in plasma globes, the other two sustaining major damage. But the flagship was the primary target, and it had definitely been disabled. And the enemy still didn't know where he was, as he had launched the missiles from positions sitting in space.

"Inform his Majesty that we have his enemy flagship for him," he told the Com Officer. "Awaiting pickup."

*   *   *

CONUNDRUM SPACE. JANUARY 10TH, 1002.

Sean sat on the throne like chair in the large conference room aboard *Augustine I*, which was again serving as his flag for this meeting.   The huge Ca'cadasan male walked across the room toward him, twin sets of arms in restraints, armored Marines marching beside and behind him. The Marines stopped him twenty meters away from the Emperor, then pushed the big being down to his knees.   The Ca'cadasan resisted for a moment, but couldn't prevail against the strength of the suits.

"I believed you thought our positions would be reversed," he told the Caca, standing from his throne and walking toward the creature. He still wore his own battle armor, helmet retracted. While he was sure the creature was under control, he thought it best to not take stupid chances because of bravado. The young man he had been would not have recognized the wisdom he had absorbed in this short vicious war.

"You are the commander of the Ca'cadasan forces that invaded my Empire?"

"I am," growled the male, his hate filled eyes glaring Sean. "And one day you will still bow before us. If not me, then another of our officers. Or our Emperor."

"That day is not coming, creature," growled Sean in return. "You are defeated."

"And we will never give up," shouted the Caca, struggling against the strength of the Marines suits and failing to budge the heavy troopers. "Our people will gather more of our strength, and we will never give up until you are no more."

"I believe you, Creature. Which is why I will destroy your people first. Since you will never give up, and we can't watch our backs forever, I will bring the fight to you. I will destroy you first. Believe that."

Sean looked in the Ca'cadasan's eyes and could see the fear there. *And one day I will see the same in the eyes your Emperor.* He walked back to his impromptu throne and took a seat, watching as the Caca was pulled to his feet and led from the room. *My reign will not be one of progress, but one of war. And when it's over, I'll be damned sure that nothing else in this Galaxy will ever threaten my people again.*

Epilogue

SESTIUS. JANUARY 12TH, 1002.

"I would like some time alone, Sergeant," said Cornelius, looking into SanJames' eyes.

"What is this place?" asked his Platoon Sergeant, standing by the section of fence that had withstood the kinetic strike that had pretty much destroyed everything else.

"Home," said Cornelius, turning and looking at the fields that were now overgrown with native vegetation, mostly scrub, though some of that foliage would eventually grow into the trees that ruled this part of the planet. He turned back to look at his top sergeant, and the men who stood with him. His men. "I want to look around a bit, alone."

"We'll watch out for you then, sir," said the Sergeant, glancing at the forest that bordered one side of the field. They both knew what kind of things lived in those woods. Not anything that would stand up to their weapons, of course, but still dangerous.

Cornelius nodded, then slid through a gap in the fence that had been made by something traveling at high speed. The fence was made of modern materials, and would be standing in this place for a thousand years, even as the forest grew up around it. The robot tractor sitting in the middle of the field was made of similar materials. Some of it might be melted from the strike that had taken out the nearby mobile shore gun. There might be holes in its skin. And what was left would stay intact for as long as the fence. Probably longer.

He walked up to the tractor, pushing his way through the low brush. His feet came down on some bones, one snapping under his boot. Cornelius squatted down and looked them over, recognizing them as the bones of a young cow. *Probably one of the juveniles we were raising, before...* He let the thought trail off, not really wanting to visit there now. But they were not so easily dismissed. He thought of the days he had spent in these fields, sweating under the hot sun, working on this recalcitrant robot, feeding those cattle. *All that work, taken away by monsters from the stars.*

Cornelius stood up and walked over to the place where the house had stood. All that was left were the foundations, and plasticrete slab the actual building had sat on. That, and the heavy door that led to the cellar, the place Katlyn had been sheltering in when he deserted the militia to save her. There was no growth here, the plasticrete was too hard to allow the roots to gain purchase. The door was intact, as was the keypad set beside it. *So, they didn't enter here after all,* he thought, looking at the door, then punching in the code. He started second guessing himself, wondering what would have happened to him and his wife if they had just stayed put.

The door rose, and the smell of death came wafting out. *No. We left this door propped open, so the cats could get at the food in the cellar. And something closed it.*

The lights came on, revealing the square room below, packed with all kinds of goods, rations, tools, and in the center, the skeleton of a cat. *So someone did come here. Most likely the Cacas. And we would both be laying there on that floor, dead. Just like the kitty cat.*

The Lieutenant turned at the soft meow that sounded to his side. He looked over and down to see a skinny cat, a calico, looking up at him expectantly. He recognized the coat pattern. It was one of the kittens they had bought to control the vermin. It had the internal nanites needed to eat the native life, but still must have had a hard time surviving in a place where most of the other animals would have seen it as prey, despite their not being able to sustain themselves on its Terran flesh.

The cat opened its mouth again in a quiet meow. Cornelius squatted down with a smile on his face. "Hello there," he said in a soft voice, putting out a hand as the cat started to shift back from him. She sniffed his hand, then walked in under it, rubbing its back against his palm. "I don't know what we called you," he said in the same soft voice. "Katlyn was into naming you guys. But one thing I can tell you, little lady. You're safe now." *The only link I have to this place.*

Cornelius picked up the cat and held it close, feeling the deep purr flow from the little body into his. He stroked the fur with his hand and looked up at the darkening sky. The sun was low on the horizon, and the first stars were coming out. "I miss you honey," he said in the same soft voice he had used with the cat, a voice he had almost forgotten he possessed. Tears started to roll down his cheeks as he saw the face of his deceased first wife in his mind. *I miss you so much. But I've got another life. A new family, and our son is a part of it.* He looked out at the surrounding fields with a sad smile. *And you thought I would become a Marquis, and country squire. Something I laughed at. And now I'm a knight, and a baron, though I haven't had my barony assigned to me yet.*

He took a breath of the sweet air, as he had often done when this was his home. *Maybe this place will be my barony. Why not?* He shook his head. It would be years before the Empire had the resources to rebuild here. If they ever did. If they survived.

Cornelius looked up at the sky, at the numerous stars of the Perseus arm that were now sparkling in the night. *But first, we have to defeat the damned Cacas. Oh, we pushed them out of the Empire. But they'll be back. It's either them or us, and I'll be goddamned if it's them. I've got a lot of killing to do before this is over, Katlyn. And every one of them I send to hell will have your name stamped on its soul. That I swear.*

Cornelius held the cat tight as he walked away from the house, back toward the men who were waiting for him. This planet was free of Cacas. They were either all dead, or prisoners on the ships above. But there were many, many more where they came from. And the man known as *The Hunter* smiled at that thought.

*   *   *

CAPITULUM, JEWEL. MARCH 16TH, 1002.

"Your Majesty," said the servant, running into the small dining room where Sean was having breakfast with his Empress. Jennifer was in her fourth month, six months away from delivery of his heir. The fleet was in the process of rebuilding, the industrial capacity had expanded by leaps and bounds, and there had been no sign of the Cacas since the counter strike he had led. What they still had in human space had fled, maybe to hiding places outside of the Empire, maybe back to their own realm.

"What is it?" said Sean, looking down at his plate of eggs and bacon, his favorite. *My time is never really my own*, he thought.

"Admiral McCullom is on the priority circuit for you."

"I'll take it here," he said, looking over at Jennifer, who nodded back. As Empress, she had the clearance for all information that reached up to this level.

The holo came alive over the table, showing the head and shoulders of Grand High Admiral Sondra McCullom, the Chief of Naval Operations. Her face looked drawn, and Sean wondered what had happened.

"The Cacas," whispered Jennifer, staring at the holo.

"Your Majesty," said the woman in a quivering voice. "The wormholes we had in transit to Bolthole have arrived."

"That's great news, Admiral," Sean said with a smile. When Sondra didn't smile back, he again wondered what was wrong. "And?"

"They're back, your Majesty. After all this time. And they have probed the defenses of Bolthole."

"The Cacas?" asked Sean in confusion, not sure how their enemy had found Bolthole, much less gotten ships to that space.

"No, your Majesty," said the woman, her shoulders shaking. "The *Machines*, your Majesty. Those murderous robots are back."

*   *   *

CA'CADASAN IMPERIAL CAPITAL. FEBRUARY 20TH, 1003.

The Supreme Emperor of the Ca'cadasan Empire, Jresstratta IV, looked down his long snout at the large male who knelt before him.

"I want the humans crushed Great Admiral

Ljarritta'ran," roared the Supreme Leader of the largest empire in known space. "I want their kingdoms destroyed, and the humans exterminated."

"Your wish is my mission," said he Great Admiral, his eyes averted to the floor. "I swear on my life, and the lives of my sons, and all their prodigy to ten generations." That was the most sacred oath a Cacada warrior could swear, and failure would mean the destruction of his line, completely and forever.

Great Admiral Miierrowanasa M'tinisasitow had failed, much to the shock of the entire Empire. In the entire history of the empire, a conquest fleet had never failed to take the stars it was tasked to bring into the empire. The only time it had even partially failed was the case of the fleet tasked with destroying the humans in their home system. They had destroyed the planet, and most of the humans, but some had escaped.

Great Admiral Miierrowanasa M'tinisasitow had the total of three conquest fleets assigned to his command at the end, over six thousand ships all told, plus periodic reinforcements. And now a mere thousand vessels, probably many less, those who had not been with his main bodies during the human counter strike, still lurked at the edge of the largest human polity and its smaller neighbor. The rest had been destroyed by the humans. The supposedly weak, infuriating humans.

"I accept your oath, Great Admiral, in the spirit and seriousness in which it was offered," said the Emperor, grabbing a delicacy from the plate offered by a crab like slave, bearing food and drink on its back.

A thousand nobles in attendance held their breaths as the Emperor spoke those words. Most had known M'tinisasitow, and his children and grandchildren on down. The Great Admiral had never returned. And his descendants had all been put to death in public executions, so that the society of the Empire would remember the deadly seriousness of such oaths.

"And what is the status of your fleet?" asked the Emperor, gesturing for his chosen commander to stand and face him.

"Thank you, your Majesty," said the Admiral, rising to his feet. "We are still awaiting the arrival of the last of the assigned conquest fleets. Of course, we could leave early, and let them catch up with us in human space."

The Emperor held up his upper right hand. "No. You will wait until that fleet arrives. I want you to be able to hit the humans with overwhelming force. And, since I am not sure how our new ships will perform, it would be best that they were tested in smaller actions, while your other ships bear the brunt of the combat."

The Great Admiral gave a head motion of acceptance, seeing the wisdom of the Emperor's words. He would have ten conquest fleets, over twenty thousand ships, as well as several large task forces from the home fleet, giving him another five thousand ships. Not including the troop transports, freight and stores haulers, antimatter tankers, repair ships, couriers, all the various vessels needed for modern warfare. And he would have one other advantage that the defeated fleet didn't. He would be carrying ten wormholes in his force, the first made at the new experimental production facility the human traitor had established. Not many, as compared to the humans, but they would still let him establish communications between his commands, as well as home, and offered the possibility of opening a ship gate in human space.

"The humans will be ready for you, Admiral," continued the Emperor. "Make no mistake there. They will have been furiously building up their war machine, knowing that we have not given up. You must strike where they don't expect it, and drive into their industrial heartland."

And it was almost nine months to get the news of M'tinisasitow's defeat. Another four months to prepare this fleet, and now another nine months to go from the center of our Empire to the edge of human space. Almost two years, and no telling what they have developed in that time. But we have our own people working on improvements. Some already on our ships, more to come, including those made by the human traitors. The Great Admiral scoffed at that last thought. He couldn't understand a being that would betray its own species just to save its own miserable life. There were many species of slave in the Empire that had done just that, but no Cacada could understand it, except for the few cowards that cropped up in every generation.

"I wish we could send more," said the Emperor, standing up from his throne and walking down the steps to put his hand on the Great Admiral's shoulder, a singular honor among their people. "I would prefer to roll over them so quickly that they had no chance of fighting back. Unfortunately, our war in the Sagittarius arm is consuming too many of our resources."

Meaning we are losing ships and males at an alarming rate, thought the Great Admiral with a head motion of agreement. He had come from war, with an Empire of many species, some of which they still hadn't seen. But they were just as infuriating as the humans had turned out to be. After four years of fighting the Empire was just beginning to make some advances on that front.

"Our hopes go with you, Great Admiral," said the Emperor, clapping his hand down on the big male's shoulder. "We need you to destroy them quickly, then bring those ships back to reinforce our other front."

Neither male thought for a moment that the humans could wait until they won the other war. That was not the way Ca'cadasans thought. The humans were enemy, their location was known, and they needed to be taken down.

The End

Made in the USA
Lexington, KY
11 October 2014